Abendau's Heir
By Jo Zebedee

For Chris, Becky, and Holly.
You are everything to me.

Other Space Opera books by
Tickety Boo Press

Endeavour – A Sleeping Gods Novel by Ralph Kearn

A Prospect of War – An Age of Discord Novel by Ian Sales

The Last War - The Noukari Trilogy by Alex Davis

www.ticketyboopress.co.uk

Copyright © 2015 Jo Zebedee

Published by Tickety Boo Press
www.ticketyboopress.co.uk

Edited by Teresa Edgerton
www.teresaedgertoneditor.com

Copy-edited by Sam Primeau
www.primoediting.com

Cover Art by Gary Compton

Book Design by Big River Press Ltd

ACKNOWLEDGEMENTS

Where to start? Every book had a lot of input, the first more than most. This one has had so much I can't possibly name everyone - for any omissions, my apologies.

First, my long-suffering family. My children, Becky and Holly, who cheer when it's needed, and hug when that's needed. My husband, Chris, for brainstorming, and keeping the house hygienic during writing bouts. One of us has to. My mum for putting up with me being more than a little obsessive. Also, Peter for hosting and building me a website, for interest and support. Linda, for an early beta. The support has been endless, from the wider family too. It is all so appreciated.

And then the writers. I can't mention everyone who has read Abendau although I thank you all. Suffice to say, the entire aspiring writing community at sffchronicles.com get a thank you - without their patience, support and cake, there would be no book. Some, though, need a special thanks: Jim Kane, for teaching me something about military leaders; Em Tett, who cheerled from the beginning and made me believe my characters had enough in them to keep going; Bryan Wigmore for great comments and help with cover musing and sundries. Special thanks go to my long, long suffering writers' group, the Hex-men: John J Brady for awkward, awkward questions that were the right ones to ask; Anna Dickinson for the most pearly sharp teeth; Suzanne Jackson for the eye for detail that makes a novel keep making sense. I am totally in your debt.

And the professionals. Gary Compton, for taking a gamble with a new writer. Sam primeau for her wonderful copy-editing. Last and very not least, Teresa Edgerton, who is more than an editor but a mentor and inspiration, who knew what was needed, when, and what was absolutely not needed, where.

PROLOGUE

ater dripped down the rock behind Ealyn. He strained, trying to turn his head to lick the wall, but his chains prevented him, the magnetic binding on his wrists too strong to be broken. His captors knew him well enough to use subtle things to torment him: the sound of water, so blessed on the hot, dry, Abendau; the prism on its thin chain catching sunlight from a small window and sending rainbows darting; the slow build of pain in muscles held firm, a pain that went deep, full of despair.

To hell with them: he was staying where he was, aware of who he was, even if his jaw ached from gritting his teeth and his hands had blistered from gripping his chains. Whatever she sent his way, whatever temptation, he'd take it and spit in her face. He closed his eyes against the dancing light.

Footsteps sounded, clipped, not the boots of the guards. He tried to move back, but there was nowhere to go; he was already tight against the wall. He tensed at the hiss of the cell opening. The footsteps stopped, right in front of him; he could feel her watching him.

Oh, gods. He waited, head down. *Please let her leave.* He clenched his fists, ears alert, his breathing shallow. She was coming so often now, not giving him time to build his strength.

"Tell me a vision of my future," said the Empress. Her first touch whispered its way past his resolve and he whipped his head to the side, trying to force her away. Once he'd been strong enough, he was sure of it, but after his months held in the cell, this time she held firm. Pain built, deep in his head, a white pain that obscured his thoughts and left only the core of him: the power she wished to use.

"*No.*" His wrists jerked in their manacles, the magnets' hard edges rubbing the broken skin beneath. The clean, sharp pain made his mind a little clearer. "No."

"Tell me." Her voice demanded obedience.

His eyes opened to a slit. He fought, willing them closed, but his eyelids were forced up. The prism's light danced across the walls, inescapable, but he willed his focus away and back to the Empress. Her smile chilled him to the bone; she knew he was close to the end, that she was wearing him down. She knew and she enjoyed it, sadistic bitch that she was.

1

"Give me what I want," she said, "and I'll leave you in peace."

He licked his lips, tongue rasping. She lied: she would come again. He knew better than any that the future was a drug, even for those who only heard it. He shook his head, the effort draining him, and whispered, "No."

"Look at the prism, Ealyn-Seer."

He couldn't stop himself. The light caught his eyes and he fell into the future, moving from the cell, up, up, through the palace to the grand entrance hall. He tried to hold onto the reality of the cell, focus on the pain in his wrists, fill himself with the hatred and anger that had held him to this point, but found himself standing before a stone arch. On a dais to the side a woman and man stood, wearing long acolyte's gowns, like those of the tribal people of the plains. He was forced to his knees before them. Their minds invaded his, their joint powers– greater than the Empress', greater than his had ever been– took his thoughts for their own. Rebel, they said, close to him, echoing each other. He ducked his head, trying to hide. Seer, they said, mocking his attempt: *rebel-seer-father.*

"Look at them." The Empress' voice rang out, and he lifted his head. Their eyes were his green. The woman had the sharp chin and high cheekbones of the Empress, the man dark hair falling over a pale face that could be Ealyn's own. *Rebel-seer-father.* He looked between them and, finally, sickeningly, knew why he'd been taken.

A wave of exultation ran from the Empress, and he could feel life within her, tiny, not even babies yet. She'd got what she wanted: children born of their combined powers, shaped and moulded to further her empire. Who knew how she'd done it, taken what she needed from him– he'd had a whole series of medical tests when he'd first been captured. It didn't matter how, only what it might mean. He watched, helpless in his future, as his children pronounced judgement and sentenced him to the torture chambers of Omendegon.

The vision faded. His head sank forward, drained of all energy. Dimly, he was aware of the Empress leaving and the cell door closing, and could feel only relief. The light danced on the rock ground before him, pin-pricks of promise. It would be easy to focus on it, wander the paths ahead and release himself from the hot, dry cell. It was what the Empress wanted: to trap him, his sanity lost, fit only to give her the knowledge her own psyching couldn't find. To hell with her; he might not be able to stop her, but he was damned if he'd make it easy.

A parrot's screech startled him. The cell became dappled in

warm sunlight. He tried to fight the vision but nothing worked: not pain, not the dripping water. He faded into the future, one where he stood on a jungle-encroached path. Holbec, he decided, near the Banned base. He drew in a sharp breath; if he was back with the Banned, there was a chance he'd get out of the cell. Something buzzed close to his cheek and he lifted his hand to swat it, but the chains of his past self stopped him. The sound of laughter drifted up the path. He turned a corner and two children walked ahead, dark heads together as they talked.

"Hey!" His words were croaked from thirst.

They turned, their green eyes meeting his, the girl's smile wide, the boy's fringe dark over his laughing eyes. Ealyn drew in a sharp breath, and spun out of the vision. *His. They were his.* Just as the cold adults in their acolyte's gowns were. Two futures, not the same. Hope flared, from somewhere he'd been sure was too buried to come alive again.

Around him the rainbows danced. He could take another look to be sure. He closed his eyes, fighting temptation. That path, the Seer's path, led to madness; he'd seen it often in others.
But the children had been happy in the jungle, not sad and used and cruel. Somewhere, there was a path to that future. It didn't matter what it did to him; it didn't matter if it drove him to his death or madness: he had to find it, not let the Empress ruin his lost children. Decided, he lifted his chin and focused on the prism, seeking the path he needed. And when he didn't find it the first time, he looked again. And again, leaving the dry cell to walk the paths of time, hope carrying him where nothing else could have.

CHAPTER ONE

EALYN: EIGHT YEARS LATER

he cruiser came into Ealyn's view. It stayed just beyond his Control range, making him sit forward and take notice. No one should know his ship was being piloted by a Controller: the skill was a rare one, even amongst psychers.

He drummed his fingers on the arm of his pilot's chair. The cruiser was similar to the one in the port two days ago, seen during a supply run pre-arranged with the Banned. That run should have been secure. Even if the Empress knew he'd fled to the rebels after stealing the twins, the chain of communication ran from him to Darwin, and no one else. But he'd lasted this long because of a level of paranoia that ground at his insides, burned acid in his throat, and left his nerves shredded and jumpy. The Empress *was* still looking, covering every planet and sector of the empire. When he'd stolen her children- her heirs- he'd seen to that, and it wasn't as if she could have any more, not after the horrific birth.

He cast out and let the sense of the space fill his senses, the knowledge of how things moved within it, the heat of the stars shaping in his mind. A small fleet of freighters, not far out and closing, moved in tandem with each other. If they were linked to the cruiser, they could easily close off his chance of escape. He took his time, assessing how they flew: nothing more than a Space Roamer convoy, judging by their formation and grace. In which case, they'd avoid him.

He sat straighter. The Roamers no longer flew in their painted ships, the proud planets and stars decals on their finials. They, too, were fugitives from the Empress, trawling space as discreetly as they were able, fighting to remain independent. He looked back at the cruiser, assessing. It had closed on him, its trajectory taking it into his vector. He checked its size and dimensions. It *was* the same ship that had been docked at the port, he was sure of it. He punched in a trajectory away from the cruiser. If it shifted course, he'd know for sure.

A moment later the bigger ship came round. Hell. Ealyn thrust to port. The cruiser was large enough to have a tractor beam and, if they did know it was him, that's what they'd use. Not because they wanted him– he was under no illusions what awaited him in Abendau's palace– but because of the twins. Speaking of which: he swung his seat round and shouted down the access corridor, "Kids! Strap in. It's going to get rocky."

An answering shout was all he needed; the twins were space veterans, they didn't need their hands held like most seven year olds. Hell, they were more able than most adults.

He sent the ship streaking across space, relying not on his instruments but the feel of where he was. His ship banked at an angle no non-Controller would attempt, and he closed the gap between him and the Space Roamers. If there was an entity looking after desperate pilots, he needed the fleet to be Roamers, *and* to ensure they'd recognise his ship as the flotsam of a space fugitive and no threat to them.

The cruiser had picked up its speed, closing the distance easily. Its pilot was good– no Controller, by the pedestrian movement of the ship, but more than competent. He'd be lucky to pull this off. He sped up, twisting, darting, trying to ensure there was no rhythm to his escape, no easy trajectory to predict and cut him off along. He had only a few minutes' lead now: not enough.

He gritted his teeth and increased speed. The engines whined, but he ignored them– where it mattered, in speed and endurance, the ship had more than enough. He thrust hard and something in the back of the ship crashed. He paid no heed, his eyes on the oncoming space fleet. The vector alarm sounded but he flew on. Let the Roamers pick up he was a Controller, let them trust him not to wipe out the fleet. He sent out the thought and picked up the tiniest pulse in return, the sense of the weak Roamer powers that allowed them to know space but nothing else.

He flew straight at the fleet. There was no room for his ship, no hope of anything other than a collision. Despite himself, he braced, muscles bunched, hands clenching. He had full control of the ship now, holding its pattern in his mind; no thruster could move the ship with the deftness he needed.

A bolt passed him. The cruiser, looking to disable him. He squinted, assessing the Roamer fleet, seeking its patterns. He had moments. He held his course, trusting to luck, trusting to anything that might keep him safe.

The fleet shifted at the last moment. He yelled as his ship scraped between two of the Roamers, flinched as another appeared, and banked obscenely hard to avoid it. He passed three more ships, each pilot connected to him, each holding the pure Control of space

5

only a few psychers had, and then he was through the fleet to the other side, into clear space. He let out a whoop, punched the air and sped up, leaving the cruiser with a fleet to navigate through, too far behind to keep track of him.

"Take that, bitch," he muttered. He swung his chair round, ready to tell the kids they could unstrap, but they already knew; they were standing in the doorway, calmer than he was at yet another attempt to take them. A brief spark of fear chased a shiver through him. What if today had been the day they were taken? That thought haunted his nights, his days, fuelled his paranoia: that he hadn't done enough to protect them; that he never would.

"You slaughtered it, Dad," said Kare.

Ealyn's face broke into a smile, and the moment was gone, because they were still with him, still not taken. He went to the twins and embraced them, holding them close. He could feel how thin they were under their flying suits, the fragile bones of their spines. He tightened his arms and they hugged him back. His gaze drifted to the viewing port and space outside. The Empress could look, she could send whatever she had after him; he wasn't going to give his children up, not knowing what she would do to them. He watched, alert, holding his children. Sooner or later, the cruiser would come again, or another one. The price on his head was too high to be passed up. He let the children go. "Go on, both of you, scoot."

He brought up the nav-computer. Not that he needed it. He could feel the proximity of Calixta, the nearest star and system. Space here was remote, its planetary spread barely populated; any ship stood out too easily. He brought up a course for a shipping lane allocated to the Ferran system, imagining the change in space that would come as he neared its star, Ferrus, a bright pull in that sector of the cluster. Straddling the space between the remote outer systems and more populous middle three, its hub would provide easier camouflage. Decided, he punched in his course. He might not need the nav-computer, but the star drive did. The familiar whine as it started up told the kids to brace and, with a nauseating twist in his stomach and a jolt, the ship sped away, stars blurring into something too fast for even a Controller to track.

He leaned back in his seat, stretching. A shower and a shave would make him feel human, and he knew to seize the moment when he could. He made his way along the ship's access corridor, his steps echoing off the metal floor, past his alleged cabin- he couldn't remember the last time he'd slept there- but a thud from the kids' cabin stopped him.

6

"You pushed me!" Karia's voice trickled into the corridor, high and insulted.

"I'm telling Dad!" Kare this time, just as insulted.

"If you do, I'll tell him about the mice."

Mice? What bloody mice? Ealyn pushed the door open. "I'm all ears."

Both twins turned, their faces masks of guilt. Ealyn leaned against the doorjamb and crossed his arms. "On a spaceship? As the pilot, I need to know."

Kare's eyes flicked from side to side. His face cleared. "*Dice.* We lost them."

Karia nodded, too eager, making her hair fall over her eyes. "Yeah, we can't find them anywhere."

Ealyn scowled and looked around the tiny cabin. Even with only one bed pulled down- at seven, the twins could just about fit, sleeping end to end- it was cluttered and messy. How could it be otherwise? The cabin had been everything to the kids for two years- sleeping quarters, school and playroom unless they used the freezing hold. For a moment, he wanted to let them have their mice. Any other child was allowed a pet. But it was too dangerous; this ship was all that kept them safe. "Tell you what, I'll help you look for the *dice.*"

Karia winced. "Dad, it's okay, we'll do it. Won't we, Kare?"

"Very good of you both, but I'd like to help." He opened a locker, ducked a pile of tumbling clothes, and cursed. He tensed at a definite squeak and raised an eyebrow. "Where are they, Karia?" She didn't answer, just looked at her brother who went to say something, but Ealyn cut across him. "*Now.*"

"Over there." Karia pointed at a pile of clothes bundled in the corner. Behind, artfully hidden, was a small cage. Nestled in some fabric, possibly the remains of an old t-shirt, were four- he counted again- no, *five* brown mice. No doubt brought on board during their last maintenance visit to the Banned base and hidden.

He lifted the cage. He had to say something, make sure she knew how important this was: mice could eat through cabling. He looked from one twin to the other, taking in the shared stance. This wasn't just Karia's doing.

She was the one who looked up, though, her face pinched and worried. "Daddy, they were going to die if I left them on the base. Sonly couldn't have made them better, they needed a healer."

"That's right." Kare's head came up. "You said we had to practise psyching. It was hard for Karia, they were so sick." He nodded at the neat cage. "And it took me ages to make the cage. It was hard without soldering."

Ealyn winced at the thought of his son practising metal-work onboard the ship, but his mouth twitched. The practice excuse was about the only one they might get past him. He found his anger melting at the kids' huddled stance, their worry that they were in trouble. It was easy to forget they were only seven, no matter how smart and talented.

One of the mice squeaked, loud in the quiet cabin. It appeared to be looking at him. What was he going to do with it now it was here? He thrust the cage at Karia. "If they get out, I'm putting them in a stew."

"You wouldn't!" Her eyes went round.

"Cool," said her brother. "Mice stew, it'd be better than reconstituted." He touched the cage, his fingers thin and nimble. "Go on, Karia, give us one-"

"No!" She swung the cage to the side.

Ealyn grabbed it. "Enough! They'll escape if you keep flinging it around." He took the cage. The damage was done and, short of killing Karia's pets, he was stuck with them. "We're teasing. But when we're back on base they get handed to Sonly and she can take care of them." He softened his voice; his kids had little enough, it was no wonder she wanted to keep them. "We can't have mice. Not on a space ship. You know that."

She gave a small nod and he patted her shoulder. He wished he could find a way out of this mess to a normal life where she could have a colony of mice and he wouldn't have to care. He turned away, his throat tight. He was lucky to have this small life together. If the price for it was living as he did, constantly on alert, he'd pay it; he couldn't face the alternative, and the loss of them.

***

After breakfast, Ealyn looked at his son. *Today?* He had to do it sometime- he'd been putting it off for months. He rocked back in his seat. "Any more dreams, Kare?"

"Every night." Karia pulled a face of disgust. "He talks in his sleep."

"I don't." But the boy didn't sound his usual cocky self; the dreams, whatever they were, hadn't been the deep ones of forgetful sleep.

"You do. You tell me things when I ask you."

"Don't." The denial was too strong, almost desperate, and he gave Karia a shove.

Every night? Worry gnawed at Ealyn's insides. It couldn't wait any longer; if the dreams were visions they'd start to cascade soon, and the boy had to be taught to control them. His hands had

8

clenched together, and it was an effort to unclasp them. Could he teach the boy and not succumb? Surely after seven years of not Seering he could manage to show the boy once, and then keep an eye from a distance.

"Kare." His voice croaked past his tight throat. "Come with me."

He left, heading down the ship, Kare behind him, and tried to ignore the churning deep in his stomach, the low warning that this was a bad idea.

CHAPTER TWO

Kare followed his dad, trying to keep from showing his excitement, but it was hard. Dad had been teaching Karia Control for ages, but had refused to let Kare learn to Seer, saying they had to be sure what the dreams were first. His dad flung open his cabin and nodded at the bed. "Sit down– I need to get something."

He got down on his knees and rummaged through the contents of an under-floor storage compartment. A few moments later he lifted out a small wooden casket. He handed it to Kare, who ran his hands over the carvings on each side. They were just deep enough for him to track by sliding his fingertips into the runs, and felt like writing. "What is it?"

"It's for you. Open it."

Kare moved the little catch– it fitted his fingers perfectly– and the box sprung open to reveal a prism lying against a dark velvet interior. He lifted the prism, holding it by its silver chain so it twisted and caught the light. "Is it...?" he croaked.

His dad nodded. "It's a Seer's prism. It was given to me, many years ago, by an old Seer." He had an odd smile on his face. "He was a Roamer, he said."

"Can I use it?"

"Yes, I'll show you." His dad reached for the prism, his eyes focused on it, becoming soft and distracted.

"Are you okay?" asked Kare.

"Yeah, I'm fine. Tired." His dad squinted like his eyes were sore, and reached up to a hook in the ceiling. He clipped the silver chain to it, and the prism cast lights all around the cabin. Kare bit his lip. This was it, he was going to step into the future and see what lay ahead for him. He couldn't wait to tell Karia. He took a breath, and it was jerky. The cabin shimmered at the edge of his vision, as if it was fading, but when his dad sat on the bed beside him, making it rock, things came back to how they had always been.

"Okay. First, don't keep the prism up all the time. That's what the Empress did to me, and it leads to the Seer becoming trapped in the future."

"Right." The lights danced, and the room faded again. In the distance, Kare could hear soft singing.

"When you're in the vision, keep focused on me. I don't want you under too long the first time. When I call you, you need to come out."

Kare nodded. His father's voice was coming from far away, and the cabin had almost gone, replaced by somewhere that overlaid it, so that neither was quite real.

"Okay, look at the prism, not the lights. Focus, and you should find yourself moving."

The prism twisted before Kare. The cabin grew warmer, the sound of singing louder. He was standing on soft carpet, the pile warm under his feet.

"Where are you?"

What was the voice? He frowned, straining to remember. *His dad.* He had to remember to listen to his dad....

"I'm in a house. It's very tidy." It was, much more so than the ship ever was.

"Are you yourself?"

Kare looked down. How did he know? It felt like he was too tall and the floor was too far away. "I don't know."

"Describe what you see to me. Take your time."

Kare walked forward, following the singing. He was in some sort of living pod, all white walls and metal. A few holos sat on a shelf and he stopped to look at them. In one, there were two boys. The first looked like him, but with light hair. The other was a giant of a lad, a shock of red hair making him appear angry. Kare looked closer; the first boy *was* him, older and blond but definitely him.

"I think I'm me; there's a holo."

He frowned, looking at the other holos. There were none of Karia or his dad. His stomach jumped, a sick rush of nerves. The singing stopped and a moment later a woman walked into the room. She smiled. "Kare, I thought you were out."

He went to reply but someone called his name, someone he should be able to place, but couldn't. The voice was faint, as if it came from far away.

"Kare!" It was his father. But where was the ship?

"Think about how the cabin feels." The voice was terse, worried. "Concentrate."

He closed his eyes, trying to focus, but when he opened them and the cabin appeared it was hazy, so that it was hard to tell where he stood. A rush of nausea hit him as the air grew colder. The quiet hum of the ship's generators surrounded him, their gentle purring familiar. He blinked and saw his father crouched in front of him, his face worried.

"You okay?" asked his dad.

Kare nodded. He thought so. "I feel a bit sick."

"That'll pass." His dad put his hand on his shoulder, his strong hands massaging the muscles, as if checking Kare was real. "You were away too long; you need to try to come back quicker." He sat on the bed. "Where were you?"

"I dunno. A house. There was a woman."

"What did she look like?" His father's voice was too eager, sharp and questioning.

"Red hair. Blue eyes– really blue. About your age, maybe."

"Gods." His father had paled, a distant look in his eyes.

"I only saw her for a minute," said Kare. Was something wrong with what he'd seen? "But she used my name, so it was definitely me."

"You did good." His father seemed to have composed himself a little. He held up his hand, displaying the signet ring he always wore. "We'll get you a ring so you can tell when it's you."

He stood and reached for the prism. Kare lay on the bed and curled up, all shivery and headachy and tired. His father put one hand on the clip, holding the prism steady with the other. A flash of light reflected in his eyes, and his face changed. He dropped his hand. His throat moved as he swallowed; he looked at Kare with eyes that were dark and hard to read.

"What's wrong?" Kare sat up, ignoring the headache that flared. Everything in him screamed that something wasn't right, something hard to read even with his Empath skills.

"I'll show you how to go in and out of a vision with a bit more control." Dad's words were too slow, confused.

"You're not supposed to have visions." His dad dined out on stories about how he'd Seered so much, finding the way to escape the palace, that he could never Seer again. "You *said*."

"It'll be okay if it's just once, just to show you."

"Daddy, don't..." His dad sat on the bed, and his breathing became slow and relaxed. His eyes glazed over. Kare put a hand on his arm; it was raised in goosebumps all along.

"Daddy?" His dad shivered and pulled his arm away. "Dad?" Kare's voice quavered. Something was wrong, something he didn't understand. Fear gripped him, made him shiver. His dad moaned, and rocked back and forth. "Daddy! Come back."

There was a crash as his dad fell to the floor, back arched. He screamed, a long scream that echoed through the cabin.

12

"Daddy!"

The door banged open and Karia burst in. "What's happening?"

"He went into a vision." Kare dropped to his knees.

Karia knelt on the other side and put her hand on their dad's arm. She looked as shocked as he felt. "He's freezing." She smoothed his hair back. "Dad? Can you talk to me?"

Their father's eyes rolled back. His shoulders heaved with gasped breaths. "It hurts!" Even his voice didn't sound right: blurred and mumbled. "They're coming back. I have to get out."

He was right; they needed to bring him back to the cabin. Now. It was too frightening to see this.

"Dad!" shouted Kare. There was no response. Maybe he'd come back for his name. "Ealyn Varnon, come back!"

His dad's eyes opened, staring at the ceiling. It had worked; everything was going to be okay. Kare started to shake in relief.

Their dad jerked once, twice, and then screamed, a long, pure scream of pain.

"Daddy!" shrieked Karia. She grabbed Kare's arm. "What do we do?"

He had no idea. Another scream ripped the air. "I don't know!"

Her face caught the prism's light, and the cabin wavered in front of Kare, the living pod from earlier overlaying it. He got to his feet, pushing the threatened vision away. "The prism. We need to take it down."

He tried to reach, but fell well short. His father screamed, worse this time, like it was being ripped from his soul. Karia started to cry, pleading with Dad to come back. Kare felt like doing the same, but there was no time; he had to get the prism. He jumped, missed. It was too high. He focused on the chain, letting the power flow from him in a steady line, until it snapped and the prism fell to the floor with a thunk.

The lights stopped flashing. His dad's screams faded. The silence left was louder than his shrieks, Kare was sure of it.

"Daddy?" asked Karia, her voice trembling. "We're here, can you come back?"

Slowly, their father's eyes opened and he sat up, shaking.

"What happened?" asked Kare. He sank to the floor, his legs too weak to hold him, so the three of them were in a line.

"I was..." Their father went pale. He looked between them, and shook his head.

"It was just a bad vision; they happen sometimes." He pushed himself up to the edge of the bed and put his head in his hands. "Go and play. I need a few minutes to myself."

13

Karia exchanged a glance with Kare. "We'll stay until you feel better," she said.

"Leave me!"

Kare jumped; his father never shouted at them like that. *Never.*

"Now!"

Kare grabbed Karia's hand and the two of them fled. The world had changed somehow, moved from the place they'd known, where their dad stood between them and danger, a constant presence who reassured. He needed it to change back; he didn't know what to do if it didn't.

CHAPTER THREE

Screams echoed through the ship. Kare sat in the co-pilot's seat, his eyes burning with tiredness. He felt like someone had twisted him from the inside, so everything was in the wrong place. Beside him, in their father's seat, Karia scanned the panel in front of her. The screams were joined by the vector alarm, and Karia looked over at him. "What do we do?"

He didn't know. Two days ago, waiting until their father got better had seemed like a good idea. Now, the control room was littered with recon packets, and two blankets, dragged from their beds, lay on the floor for the times when the screams had stopped long enough for them to sleep. They had to come up with something better than this. "Move the ship again?"

Karia nodded and inputted new co-ordinates. The vector alarm died away. The screaming didn't.

"Did you try to get the prism off him?" Karia asked.

"Yeah. He wouldn't give me it." His father's hands, clutching it to his chest, the frantic fear in his eyes, fear not of something on the ship, or even a memory but a vision replaying in his mind, over and over. It was all he could do not to give in to his terror and nestle in the seat, shaking. Only knowing that Karia was scared, and needed him to be as brave as he needed her to be, stopped him.

"Did he say anything more?"

Kare shook his head. He couldn't tell her; it was bad enough that he knew.

She glared at him, sensing the lie. "Tell me."

"It was nothing. Just more of the same," he said, but she still glared at him. He'd have to tell her sometime; they could never keep secrets. "He told me he was sorry, that if he'd known our future, he'd never have taken us..."

His words hung in the air. Karia stared at him. "*Our* future?"

Their future. Those screams, the list of injuries, the flinched response when either of them touched him. The shock of the realisation still hadn't sunk in, even though he'd thought of nothing else since. Slowly he nodded. "Yes."

He picked up one of the blankets and climbed into the pilot's seat, so they were curled up together. It felt better, like they were a little safer. He watched out the window, trying to think of any solution. He was supposed to be smart, but he wasn't. He was just like any kid, helpless, needing his parent.

The last volley of screams died away, and it felt like he could think properly for the first time in hours. They had to get help.

"Where are we?" he asked.

"Near Ferran." She touched the control panel, bringing up the details. "About four AU out."

The Ferran system was the closest to Holbec. He sat up. "The Banned. Their base....?"

"We could go back to the base," said Karia at the same time. "We can't stay out here."

He nodded; as ever, they were in tandem, their thoughts mirroring each other. And they were right, there was nothing else for it.

"Can you fly the ship?" he asked. So far, she had, but they were in deep space– even he could manage the plot changes needed. It might be different when there was something to hit. "Through a system, I mean?"

"Yeah." She didn't sound sure. No wonder; seven-year-olds shouldn't fly ships. He bet even Roamer kids didn't. He put his arm around her and pulled her against him. Maybe other kids just weren't desperate enough.

"I could try." He knew what the controls did, after all. In theory, anyway. But the star drive was beyond him - Dad had never let either of them use it, not yet confident of their plotting skills. Without it, the base would be impossibly far away, across the gulf of space between the two systems.

Tears threatened, from tiredness and frustration, from being no use and not being able to think of a way out of this, but he blinked them away. He couldn't just sit in a panic. A moment later he sat up. "The beacon."

"What?"

"The beacon. Darwin made Dad take it, remember, in case the base ever moved?"

Her eyes widened. "Do you know where it is?"

He looked around the control room. Where would his father have stowed it? He pushed back the blanket and got onto his knees, and started to pull open the storage hatches on the floor. Some tools, no beacon. He tried the next, and it was empty. Another, and still nothing. He jerked up the fourth and sitting in it was a plain black box, just about big enough to fill his hand.

"Got it!"

It was heavier than he'd expected, but he managed to get it out and over to the control panel. Now what? He looked at Karia, but she shook her head; this was his department, how things worked.

"Gotta link to the nav-computer," he muttered. He crawled under the panel, looking at the various ports, and finally found one that linked to the external nav-console. He hooked the beacon up, his heart pounding. If he got this wrong, they could end up with no nav-computer and no beacon. Then they'd really be in trouble. He got up, looking at the control panel; the nav-screen was dead.

"You're sure you've done it right?" asked Karia.

No, of course he wasn't. He was still studying basic ship-design, not the details of control rooms. He nodded. "Yup." A red light started to blink and he couldn't hide the smile of relief. "See?"

The ship turned, very slightly. He glanced at Karia. "Was that you?"

"No."

The light stopped blinking and became solid. It had found the signal. A familiar whine started, from the rear of the ship, where the star drive was.

"It's working!" He swung round and hugged Karia, almost lifting her off her feet, ignoring the nausea, ignoring anything except that they'd found a way out of the mess. He was taller than her, he realised for the first time, like he was the big brother. He wasn't sure how that made him feel– they'd always been the same, him and Karia; to be different felt strange. He put her down and smiled; he'd think about that another day, when fear wasn't circling and making it hard to know who he was.

"We're going to be all right," he said, and, looking at the red light, he actually believed it. "We'll get back to the Banned and Darwin will sort things out. It'll be all right."

The thought of Darwin, reliable and solid, almost made him come apart. He wanted to hand the problem over to an adult they could trust. Then it would be over and his dad would get better.

He sat back in the pilot's seat, Karia beside him, and they curled together. The silence from the ship behind seemed worse than the screams.

"Kare?" Karia's voice was low. "Promise me something."

"What?"

"Don't Seer." She looked at him, her eyes earnest and direct. "Please, don't ever Seer."

"I can't promise you that. If I have the power, I have to use it." He kept his voice steady, but the idea of him becoming like his father, trapped in some sort of hellish future, was bigger than he could face. Not here on the ship where his father's screams were all too real. "You know that."

"You could find a way. I know you, you're so smart, you'd find another way of using it. Really, Kare, think about Dad. What if that happened to you?"

A tear tracked down her cheek. He reached out to wipe it away, but she took his hand and held it and they sat like that for a moment. Not use the power? It would get out somehow, it always did, like the way it trickled into his dreams. He looked at her, saw more tears, and nodded.

"Okay, I'll find a way. I promise."

She leaned against him. Her eyes drooped and he waited until he was sure she was asleep and only then allowed himself to think back to his vision and the holo shelf that showed only himself, and he shivered.

CHAPTER FOUR

he beacon flashed insistently, demanding a response. Kare looked between it and Karia's pinched face.

"Well?" He wished he was the Controller and could take the decision, not force Karia to. She was as tired as he was, shattered and stunned by the flight back to the Banned: five days of hellish yells, of forcing some- any- food and water into their father in his increasingly rare lucid moments, of fear growing as more details of the visions emerged. The moment the beacon had taken them out of star drive with no warning, sending both of them crashing. His arm was still throbbing from where he'd hit it off the hard metal doorjamb- at best, he'd be bruised in the morning, at worst in the infirmary getting it set when they reached the base. *If* they reached the base.

"We land." She sounded certain, and that was good, because he wasn't. "Docking in space isn't something I've ever seen Dad do."

"Okay." He silenced the beacon and brought the comms unit online instead, but tensed as a shriek from his father carried through the ship to them. He should be used to it by now, but he wasn't. He never would be.

"Close the door over," suggested Karia.

Guilt leapt in him. All week, they'd put up with the screams, almost as if not sharing it was a betrayal. But now they needed to concentrate. He got up and slid the control room door to, struggling with it. They'd never had to close it since they'd been on the ship; they'd shared everything, the three of them. But when his dad's next scream was muffled, barely audible, the guilt vanished, leaving only relief. He sat in the co-pilot's seat, his shoulders looser, more relaxed. He reached for the comms unit. "Ready?"

"Go." Karia wriggled forwards in the pilot's chair, getting closer to the control panel.

"Banned base, this is Hawk one." He winced at the call signal, remembering the day they'd chosen it, how they'd looked at pictures of birds until they'd found one cool enough for their then-novelty ship-home. "Do you hear us?"

A blast of static split the air, and then a crackled voice. The base had made contact. They would have checked the ship's read-outs, he knew, and confirmed whose ship it was. He requested permission to land and it was given, with no questions as to who was on the comms unit, or why it wasn't his father. Perhaps over the static they couldn't tell. Either that or he sounded more confident than he felt.

A HUD display flashed up on the viewing window, and docking bay five was allocated. Karia paled a little and Kare understood: five was the newest dock, approached awkwardly from the south, over the base. If she came in wrong, she'd endanger everyone on the ground.

"Want me to request they reallocate?" he asked.

"No. Better not to let them know…"

He nodded, understanding. It was bad enough landing the ship: to have people watching in fear, gathered below as she approached, would be worse. Karia stabbed the control panel, activating the landing pattern, and he gulped. The ship felt safe with their dad at the controls; even when they'd left planets in a hurry, sure someone was on to them, or in a chase, it had been exciting rather than scary. This was terrifying.

They dropped through the atmosphere. The lush jungle of Holbec stretched over the planet below. For all his nerves, he'd be glad to get back to base, to decent food, to the outdoors. It had been a couple of months since their last maintenance visit. He'd even enjoy whatever school class they stuck him in this time. Karia, beside him, was quiet, her focus on the ship, not him. When she Controlled she left him behind, going to a place he couldn't follow. It made the long drop to the planet seem endless.

"Base is coming up," he said. Not that she wouldn't know, but it was what a co-pilot was supposed to do: relay data, check trajectories. At least it made him feel included; if she crashed he was going to be just as dead. Already he could make out clearings in the jungle and the long, low main building of the base. He wasn't sure his dad approached so quickly. "Karia…"

"Shh." A smile danced on her lips, her eyes intent on something he couldn't see. He sat back in his seat, so tense his chest and back ached, and tried to be as quiet as possible. Surely, surely she was going too fast.

The ship slowed, almost stalled, and then dropped. He stifled a yell and clutched the seat. He hated this when his dad did it: the drop into the port, the long moments of not knowing when the jolt of landing would come, the hideous turn-over of the grav-reg, the nausea clutching at him. This was worse again, too fast, not safe. He found himself with his eyes closed, and forced himself to open them and focus on the HUD display like a good co-pilot.

"Brace," said Karia. She jumped back in the pilot's seat, and it encircled her, pulling her tight. "We're coming in hard."

He'd known she was going too fast. He ducked his head into his chest, heart racing. They hadn't even warned their dad to brace. Not that it would have made any difference. An alarm sounded, muted, and that wasn't good. Another joined it. His stomach climbed into his mouth and lodged somewhere near the back of it.

The jolt of the ship landing sent his head shooting forwards, then back, even with the braced seat position. Karia let out a yell. The ship rattled, settling into the docking-lock, and then went quiet.

"You okay?" Karia sounded shocked. "I came in too fast."

"Yeah." He wriggled out of the seat. He thought he was, but was too shaky to be sure. He waited a moment, braced for pain to hit, but he was fine. The seat had done its job.

He leaned over the control panel and scanned the docking bay, not quite believing they'd made it down. He wanted to say something, to congratulate her, but the enormity of being back hit him. Once he left this ship, everything would change. It wouldn't just be the three of them, taking decisions for themselves. Suddenly, he wished they hadn't come back, that they'd shut the door over and ignored everything until things were okay again. But that was a useless thought.

"You did good," he said, his voice only barely shaking. "We should get Darwin."

"You do it." She was closing the control panel functions down, calm and in control, and he envied her; she was always better in a crisis, always the more practical. "I need to make sure the ship's ported right. And..." The haunted look of the last days came back into her eyes, all semblance of control gone. "Dad shouldn't be on his own. You know, in case someone comes."

He did know. Their father was scared enough, trapped in a future that terrified him; to be taken out of the ship by people he didn't know, to be brought back to a cold, changed reality alone didn't bear thinking about.

"I'll go." He put his hand on the door, but had to force himself to slide it open. Whether it was because he was worried he'd hear his dad or accusing silence, or the thought of leaving her, he couldn't tell. He walked up the access corridor, taking it in a way he rarely did, as if searing it into his memory, this ship of theirs. The wiring hung loose along the ceiling, the lack of covering making the steady noise of the ship's coolant systems louder than it should be.

21

His dad had talked about boxing it in since they'd first left the base, but never had. His shoes echoed in the metal corridor, the steady beat of his childhood, and the air was dry. When he went into the base his throat would feel clagged the way it always did. He got to the hatch and stared at it before reaching for the controls and putting in the code. It opened slowly, dropping down, the short walkway extending after the hatch had folded against the ship.

The dock was in darkness, silent. In a few moments the dock-hands would arrive, but for now it was just him in the giant bay. It made him feel small, like the child he was supposed to be, the child he'd left behind a week ago. He walked down, feeling the walkway bounce beneath him, and stopped at the bottom.

The spell of unreality broke, and he ran. Through the dock, crashing against the heavy, sealed doorway, spilling into the sparse corridor beyond, which linked the port to the main base. He knew the way- they'd been coming and going from the base for years- and he sprinted. A dock-hand passed him, and then another, but none of them stopped him. They were used to him and Karia coming off the ship; no one knew their world had been turned around and changed.

He pushed through another door, into the accommodation section. Doors stretched along either side of the corridor, all the same grey metal. Once, one of the doors had been theirs, before his dad had decided to take them into space, returning to base only for rare maintenance runs. He couldn't even remember which door it had been.

But he knew Darwin's, at the head of the corridor. He could see it. He was close to getting help, to handing this mess over to someone else. He sprinted, bashing off a woman who said 'hey' but didn't stop him, and reached the door. He fell against it, banging with the flat of his hand. It wasn't until the door opened and Darwin was there, tall as ever, broad, a quizzical smile in place, that something broke and he found himself telling Darwin what had happened, the words spilling out, coming round to the same place, time and again- that his dad was sick, and they didn't know what to do.

Darwin took him into the apartment and sat him down. His three children were there: Eevan, dark and brooding, Sonly asking for Karia, Lichio, the little one, watching with his big eyes. And then Darwin said the only thing that was needed.

"It's okay. You're back. And we'll take care of everything now."

CHAPTER FIVE

K are followed his father and Darwin down the corridor to their ship, waiting where they'd docked it two weeks previously. The last conversations were over, his father's pleas to Darwin and the military leaders of the Banned ended: they had to leave the base. This time, there had been no school, nothing except Darwin's apartment and the hospital block until Dad was released. That and whispered voices making decisions deep into the nights, talking of base security, of options, and what the Empress would unleash against the rebels if she knew he and Karia were back.

He snuck a glance at his twin, walking on the other side of Major Rjala, head of base security. She was looking straight ahead, her eyes fixed on the sealed entrance to the dock. Karia had been forced to say goodbye to a crying Sonly not ten minutes before, a Sonly who'd begged her father to do something, not send them back out into space. And all Darwin had said was that he couldn't, that it wasn't just his decision, that he'd done what he could.

Kare narrowed his eyes, focusing on the Banned leader. He'd lied. He'd taken care of nothing, made nothing all right.

His father walked steadily, but he looked small, lacking the authority he normally carried. His pilot's suit hung on him; his shoulders were tense, his hands shaking a little. Silently, he waited until the sealed door opened, and then stepped through, Darwin following.

Major Berne waited for him and Karia to pass through. Her face showed no emotion, nothing to say she was sorry about the decision she'd taken. He stopped at the bottom of the walkway onto the ship, the same walkway he'd run from two weeks ago, sure he'd reached safety. He didn't want to go onto the ship; there'd be no going back.

"Dad..." he said, and didn't know what he was trying to ask. Stop it happening, he supposed: change their minds.

His dad gave something of a nod, and turned to Darwin. "Please." His voice was strained and husky. "They're only children. Let them stay."

Darwin's face softened, giving hope, but Rjala cleared her throat and he shook his head.

"If it were up to me..." His voice tailed off, and he straightened. "This is the right thing to do. They won't have any life here."

"You know that's a lie." Dad faced Darwin, seeming a little stronger. He pointed at the ship. "They didn't have much of a life there, either. They don't need much."

"We can't." The soft words were more final than the look on Darwin's face.

"Do what you want with me, cast me out, whatever you need," said his dad. "But keep them here. It's the only home they've ever known, apart from the ship." He grabbed Darwin's arm. "Didn't I earn that right for them? When we built the Banned up from the rabble it was? When I trained the flight teams that still defend the base, built your fleet from scratch? Does that mean nothing?"

"Oh, Ealyn." Darwin's eyes flicked from Dad, to Karia, to Kare. "It means everything. It's why we've given you shelter. It's why we're making sure the children have somewhere safe to go." His gaze stopped at Kare. "We can provide two safe houses, you know."

"No." Dad dropped his hand. "We do it as agreed— we choose one each. It's safer."

Karia started and Kare felt her realisation, in tandem with his own. They were going to be separated. That couldn't be. He could face anything, if he had to, as long as she was there.

"You can't." Karia faced Darwin, arms crossed, eyes flashing fire. "You can't do this to us. We've done nothing wrong."

Kare joined her, standing side by side. Solidarity had been the only thing they'd had in life. "I won't leave. Not unless we're staying together."

"Enough." Rjala stepped forwards, away from the door. "We can't keep you safe here. Not with our current defences." She didn't say she was sorry, didn't show any emotion. It was as if she was talking about checks on a tick-flick board, not people. Kare glared at her but she didn't look at him, didn't look at anyone except Dad. "You know that, Ealyn. You led the flight teams during the Empress' last raids. You knew when you left that we had to build up the inner system defences. I'm five years away from them being operational. Until then, I can't guarantee the twins' safety. And they're too important to risk."

He gave a curt nod. He held his hands out, but they were shaking. "Come on, kids. Let's go."

Dad took their hands, closing them in his own. They started up the walkway, side by side. Behind, there was silence. They reached the top, and his dad stopped and turned back.

"Whatever happens— " he said. Kare saw his throat bob as he swallowed. "You did this. You sent us away. Remember that, Rjala. If anything happens, you did it." He looked at Darwin. "And you? You didn't fight for us."

24

"I tried." Darwin's voice raised, but he didn't sound angry, more resigned. He stepped closer, almost onto the walkway. He spread his hands. "It's the best I can do."

It wasn't good enough. Kare dropped his father's hand and took a last, long look at Darwin. He was a nothing to these people who'd said they would help. Sonly had cried when she said goodbye; no one else had.

He took his time, embedding the scene in his memory, the docking bay, dark and empty. Sending them away was being done secretly. They knew it was wrong.

He'd remember Darwin's last sorry; never forget Rjala's cool military stance, hands behind her, back straight. This was how it felt to be cast out– like he was on a tightrope, barely balanced, and might fall at any moment.

He followed his father and Karia onto the ship, but stopped at the top of the hatch, waiting until it thudded shut. There was no way back, no direction to go but towards the future his father had seen. The darkness closed around him, and he'd never felt more alone.

CHAPTER SIX

he ship descended through the atmosphere. Ealyn's hands shook as he laid them on the control panel and commenced the landing cycle. Beside him, entwined in the co-pilot's seat, the twins were quiet, still stunned by events. They weren't the only ones. He shook his head, focusing on the ship; without a port a landing was never straightforward. His hand slipped, sweat smearing the panel, and he'd have pulled out if there was any other way of bypassing planetary security.

Concentrate. He squinted out of the viewing window. The abandoned space yard should be big enough, but any mistake and he'd overshoot. He lowered the ship, and the nose threatened to dip. *Hell.* Alarms blared but he ignored them and reached forward to reverse the thrust, his touch precise. The warnings stopped, the silence in their wake just as unnerving.

"Come on, land, you bitch." He dropped a little more, holding his breath, forcing himself to take his time. The engines sent dust up, obscuring his view, and he swore but kept lowering the ship, relying on instinct.

Now. He touched down with a soft thud and killed the engines, waiting for the dust to clear. When it did, he saw the ship was settled with perfect precision in the middle of the yard. He hadn't lost that little knack, then. On another day the thought would have cheered him; today it only brought relief. He took a deep breath and pushed his chair back, turning to the usual tangle of arms and legs. "Let's go."

"I feel sick." Kare's small voice came from the depths of the seat.

"You always feel sick when we land," said Karia. She uncurled and leaned forward to look out the window. Kare stayed huddled, paler than usual.

"You'll be all right, son, you always are." For a child brought up on a ship, Kare was a terrible traveller- sick at launches and set downs, white through every jump in and out of hyperspace. Ealyn undid his restraints and stood, the muscles in his neck clicking as he stretched. "Come on, we'll get some fresh air. That'll help."

Karia reached for her brother and he pulled himself up using her arm. Once standing, they focused on Ealyn, their green eyes

26

unwavering, the same green eyes through all his visions. He grabbed the back of his seat at a wave of dizziness. The control room swirled and faded, and he found himself in a darkened cell, pain wracking his limbs. *Omendegon*. Again.

He doubled and groaned, bringing a shaking hand up to his face. There was no ring; there hadn't been during any of his recent visions. The cell grated open and he heard the Empress' footsteps. He shook his head; how could she do this? She was their mother.

He had to get back to the ship, where the children needed him, but it was like the last time and he was in too deep–

"Dad!" Karia's panicked voice, her hand tugging his, brought him back to the present.

The cell faded and he took a deep breath. "I'm all right," he said, but the cabin was still blurred and threatened to fade. He gulped, a big breath of air, and it steadied.

"You were in a vision!" Kare's accusation made Ealyn wince, but the boy went on in a high voice, "You're not supposed to. You *promised* Darwin you wouldn't."

That wasn't true. He had promised not to use the prism and had left it at the base. Without it as a trigger, the vision shouldn't have been possible, and Darwin would never have let him leave with the kids if he'd known it could be. What was happening to him? He tried to smile and hide his fear, but it stayed, grinding him down. He had been like this when he'd escaped from the palace and it had taken months to get the visions under control. This time, he didn't have months: if the Empress didn't catch up with him– and she'd been close, many times over the years– his sanity would give out.

Karia slipped her hand into his, and Ealyn squeezed it; he hadn't planned his family, but he'd been blessed to have them. Gods, he would miss them.

"Sorry." He took a deep breath and held his other hand out for Kare. What lay ahead for them, what path would they follow....

"Dad!" the twins chorused. Kare took his hand and *nipped* it, making him jump. The threatened vision faded.

The hatch opened and he stepped onto the gangway, his eyes scanning the yard, alert and ready to retreat. There was no one nearby: the area was full of shipyards– some legal, most not– and his unmarked freighter hadn't merited close attention.

He sucked in a deep breath of the air, metallic and smoky from industry, and the twenty-five years since he had left Dignad fell away, bringing a blast of nostalgia that made the yard shimmer out of focus. He tightened his grip on the twins' hands, wishing he could close the hatch and take them back to space.

The yard started to fade, and he shook his head. How they'd managed to get back to the rebel base last time he had no idea, but he couldn't risk it again. He lifted his right foot and stamped down on his left, so hard his eyes filled with tears. "Come on," he said.

They walked down the gangway. The red sun hung low over the planet, colouring the clouds so the sky looked orange. Around them, stunted vegetation grew in the smoggy heat. Skeletons of abandoned ships, long since stripped of their parts, loomed like sentinels.

Ealyn glanced at the perimeter fence. He wanted to walk out of here and through the streets of Dignad. He would point out places from his childhood, take the children to Shug and make sure his son was safe before he left.

The temptation bit hard, making his breath catch, even though he knew he didn't dare: here he was remembered as a real person, not a holo on a wanted poster. Here, the Empress' army had left his parents lying dead in the street like dogs, and his sister, Marine, running for her life, packed off with one of the apprentices from Shug's yard. He'd fled that day, barely escaping the planet.

The twins let go of his hands, hanging back, their eyes casting around the yard. They moved nearer to each other, staying in the shadow of the ship. It was no wonder: apart from their infrequent visits to the Banned, they were never out in the sunshine.

"It's time," he said.

They looked at him with identical expressions of mutiny. Ealyn beckoned, but neither moved. He sighed, walked over and crouched down beside them.

"You know I have no choice."

They didn't answer, but instead looked at him with their green, green eyes. He looked again around the bleak yard. The boy knew no one on the planet. At least Karia would be with people connected to the Banned, who could call for support if they needed it. But his son would be cast out from everyone.

Decided, he pulled a comms unit and the Banned's beacon from the pocket of his flying suit. He placed both in his son's hands, closing his small fingers around them and holding them shut. The beacon would allow the child some sort of chance, a way off planet if he needed it. Kare's hand felt tiny in his own. A chance? He was seven. He needed more than a beacon– he needed love, a place to grow, someone to train him how to use his powers with the control he'd need. He needed his father.

Somehow, he let go of Kare's hands. He couldn't waver. He'd been over and over this, with Darwin and again alone on the ship, weighing up everything, and there was no other way.

"Remember to call me," Ealyn said. "I'll stay in orbit until I hear from you."

"I'm not going."

"You *are*," he said to his son. "You're going to walk out of the yard, follow the directions on that comms unit and go to Shug; he's expecting you. He'll take you to your Aunt Marine's. When you're there, let me know, and... "

He couldn't say the words and it was Kare who whispered, "And then you're going to leave me."

God help me, I am. Kare's vision had shown the boy with Marine and that only happened if there was a pathway to it. Besides, there was no one he could trust more than Marine. The very fact she'd survived the attack on the family when he'd left the planet, that she'd been strong enough and tough enough to make it through those hellish days, told him what he needed to know: hers was a place of safety. He had to take it; there was *nothing* else open to him, not now. He nodded. "I'm going to leave you where you're safe, and take your sister somewhere where *she's* safe." He tried to smile and hoped it looked reassuring. "Your aunt- she'll look after you."

"Why can't we go together?" asked Karia. The question they'd asked all through the flight, separately, together, pleading. An acrid taste flooded into Ealyn's mouth: to know where they both were, to be able to check.... *No.* He'd chosen one destination, Darwin the other, arranged as a hand-over in a day's time. That way, if either man were taken, both twins wouldn't be given up. He choked out the answer. "It's safer to be apart."

He looked between the children, and wondered which would be harder: knowing and being unable to come back, or the aching blackness of total loss.

"You promise to come if I need you?" whispered Kare, his eyes huge in his pale face. His lip trembled a little and Ealyn guessed he was only just holding back from crying.

"I won't go anywhere until I hear you're safe." He hugged the small, thin body close, trying to ease its trembling. "I love you," he whispered into his son's hair, struggling to keep his voice steady. Kare nodded- a small nod, like he had no fight left in him- against his dad's shoulder.

Karia joined them and Ealyn moved to let her embrace her

twin. Their arms tightened around each other, Karia's head buried against Kare, his head on her shoulder. They were so close it looked like they might become one being. She touched her brother's forehead, pushing his jet-black hair back, revealing his eyes.

"Keep sending your thoughts," she said. "No matter where I am, I'll pick them up."

"We'll come back to each other," said Kare. "As soon as we can." Her shoulders were shaking with silent tears, and he patted her. "It'll be all right. I promise."

Ealyn pulled her away, wrapping his arm around her, and nodded to Kare. "We have to go."

The boy stepped back until he was right up against one of the perimeter fence's launch-shelters.

"Good lad," mouthed Ealyn. He walked up the gangway, his arm around Karia's shoulders. The walkway blurred and he had to blink before his vision cleared. When he looked back, his son's face swam under tears.

He closed the hatch and went to the control room. Karia sat in her seat, silently crying, her eyes focused on the yard and her brother. Her face was so bleak, so lonely, Ealyn could think of nothing to say to comfort her. There was no comfort in any of this. He primed the engines, breathing hard, and stabbed his finger down, taking the ship away from the planet, past the checkpoint and into space beyond.

Dignad seemed to fall away, the yard vanishing into the red background, his son swallowed up with it. He focused on the control panel– he still had to get Karia to safety. He glanced at her: to do this again, leave her as well. And after, he'd–

What?

He'd walk the paths of the future and hope to see evidence– any evidence– that he'd kept them safe. Blow his brains out with Seering, if that's what it took to find out.

"Daddy," Karia said, bringing him out of his thoughts. "There's a ship ahead."

A cruiser waited at the edge of the atmosphere, huge, dwarfing his ship. The same one as before, tracking him? A leak from the Banned as he'd suspected? It didn't matter; nothing did, except he got away from it.

It turned to him. *Gods.* Any other ship he'd face– he had, many times– but a cruiser would easily outpace him. And this time there was no Roamer fleet to hide behind, nowhere to go that wouldn't draw planetary security onto him instead. He glanced at Karia, saw her pinched cheeks, and fought to keep his voice steady. "I see it."

"Daddy, what if they're there for us?"

"They are." He stared at the cruiser, struggling to keep his breathing regular, keeping his ship out of the range of its tractor beam. He thrust to port but the bigger ship turned, graceful against the darkness of space, and tracked him. He squeezed his eyes shut. *Let me be lucky for another day.* After that, they could take him and do what they liked, but please let him get Karia to safety.

"Should we go back?" she asked.

If he did, they'd be caught on the planet and he'd be even more vulnerable there. He hit thrust and the ship streaked forward, firing at the cruiser's starboard cannons. A plasma bolt arced towards him and he ported, barely avoiding it. He cursed; whoever the pilot was, they were good. Better than good; their positioning had cut him off from the safety of space beyond.

The tractor beam surged out from the cruiser and Ealyn reversed thrust, pulling out of range. Its light filled their cockpit, casting over his hands on the control panel, making them look ghost-like and pale. He glanced at Karia, sitting forward in her seat, and remembered his visions of the torture chambers and what their mother would do to them. His hands clenched and unclenched– he *couldn't* give them up to it– he had to get her to safety.

"What will they do?" asked Karia in a small voice.

"They'll try to take us."

The cruiser waited. Ealyn darted from side to side, keeping out of range, but too far back for his lasers to be of use. He moved to starboard, away from the beam. The bigger ship closed the distance, approaching more confidently now. Ealyn's hands clenched, wanting to blast into space, knowing they'd take him if he did. *Wait.* If this was a random pick-up, they might not know what he was capable of. He had a chance, if he could just make it to the spaceward side.

His eyes flicked between the control panel and the cruiser until, at the last moment, just as the tractor began to pull on his ship, he dived. He used the planet's gravity, thrusting to port and twisting. He emerged close to where he'd hoped, and sped up. The first bolt missed, streaking past and exploding in front, making him turn his head from the blinding light. He darted forwards and started to smile; once again he was better, faster and smarter. They'd taken everything from him: his sanity, his friends, his son. But he could still fly–

The ship lurched from a heavy hit on the starboard flank, and his smile faded. He struggled to pull her back but drifted towards the planet, the gravity pulling the ship down. He lifted his hands from the controls. *Think*. His ship drifted, disabled. He reached forward, tried to thrust back into space, but it was sluggish. The cruiser moved and blocked him, its tractor coming round to where his ship was. *Think*.

A restraint clicked open and Karia came over to him. He pulled her onto his knee and kissed her soft hair.

"Can't you fly?" she asked.

He shook his head. "I can't steer, honey..."

She looked out of the window. "You don't need to steer." Her eyes– far too old for her age– met his. "You need to make sure they don't know it's only us," she said. "Then, Kare might get away..."

Ealyn hugged her to him. So brave, it put him to shame. What would she have become, this gentle, clever child of his? He couldn't bear to think about it. He whispered, "Say a prayer for him."

"I did." She rested her head against his chest.

Ealyn put his right hand on the control panel, and Karia nodded against him. He cupped her head, turning her face towards him so she couldn't look forwards, and closed his eyes. He paused for one moment before sending his ship forward into the cruiser and quick, painless oblivion.

CHAPTER SEVEN

PART TWO: KARE - TEN YEARS LATER

Kare paused in the centre of the living room he'd seen in his first- his only- vision. He stared around, committing the house to memory. To say goodbye to this, to walk out and not look back, was harder than he'd ever imagined.

Enough. Brooding wasn't helping. He picked up his backpack and took a last look up the stairs, to where Marine lay sleeping. It felt wrong to leave without saying goodbye, but she wouldn't let him go without a fight and he couldn't bear her tears or pleas for him to stay. He was too scared he'd agree.

He stepped out, into the early morning sun. The heat was already starting to build, and he lifted his face up to the sunlight, relieved to be outdoors, even in air as smoggy and polluted as Dignad's. The door opened and Silom stepped out, already in his mechanic's duds.

"I thought I'd come with you," he said. "Seems the least I can do."

The guilt shone out of him: his girlfriend had been the catalyst for Kare leaving. She'd been friendly, said it was lovely to meet the elusive Kare, but he'd grimaced. All it would have taken was the light to fall the wrong way and she might have linked him to his father. Ealyn Varnon was about the only famous person to come out of Dignad; his face was well known, and Kare was much too like him. To put Silom and Marine at risk was one thing- he'd had no option but to come to them all those years ago. It was a risk already taken. But to endanger Liane and her family was something he wasn't prepared to do.

"It's not your fault. It was going to happen sometime." He settled the backpack across his shoulders. "I'll see Shug, and get away." Shug, who'd told no one Ealyn Varnon's son was on the planet, who'd been as trustworthy as his yard was dodgy. Shug, who knew the sooner Kare was gone, the better- for everyone.

"And then?"

He had no idea. He had a few credits, his father's beacon, brought for nostalgia, and that was it. Oh, and a place at Abendau palace, if he wanted it- his mother still needed an heir. If he went, he'd be welcomed and given his place.

"I'll find somewhere," he said in the end. "Somewhere no one knows me." They left the road, heading for the track that led from the top of the hill to the space-yards. Silom's yard was on the edge of the district, just in sight. It was time to split up. He held out his hand. "I'll miss you."

His cousin took his hand, encasing it in his. "Me, too. Look after yourself, eh? Look me up if you ever decide to inherit the empire. I could take one of your thousand rooms in Abendau."

It was a standing joke; he knew Kare would never inherit. That he'd prefer any future to that one. Not just because of the visions, but because of Karia and what her death meant, for what the Empress had done to his father. They stood in awkward silence for a moment until Kare said, "Your mum. Tell her..."

What? Thanks for risking her life for his? Thanks for being a mother, for giving him some sort of childhood where he was loved? For being the person who'd pulled him out of the loss of his family, who'd helped him find himself? There were no words. He shrugged. "You know- just tell her."

"I will." Silom squinted down the hill. "I better go. Good luck." He left, practical as ever- drawing things out wouldn't make the day easier- and made his way down the cinder-path, through the stunted shrubbery at the edge of the industrial zone, his height and red hair making it easy to follow his progress.

Kare waited until he was out of sight. Now or never. Time to go. He followed the path into the Needles, the narrow streets around the docks. He walked, head down, and couldn't have said if it was because he was afraid to find the yard his father had left him in and have to face it, or frightened he wouldn't recognise it.

He kept off the main thoroughfares, feeling exposed. He never came into the city in daylight. Hell, he never left the house in daylight. He pulled his hood up, hiding his eyes, and kept his thoughts off anything other than getting to Shug's.

The sound of a ship coming in to land pulled him out of his thoughts. It came down low, no doubt plotted for one of the yards, shifting dust in the air, its engines loud enough for him to want to slap his hands over his ears. It landed, and Kare took stock of where he was. Satisfied, he turned the corner and saw the familiar legend, slung over a yard entrance between two comms-masts:

SHUGS YARD- SHIPS BOUGHT- SHIPS SOLD- NO OFFER TOO SMALL

He smiled and crossed over. One quick chat to Shug and he was away. He ducked into the entrance to the yard. Two ships stood in the yard, one a good-sized, but old, corvette, no doubt being wrecked for parts-resale. The other was a small planet-hopper, presumably his transport to the Nova hub, where he'd do what had served his father well for years and bury himself amongst the space waifs, carving out whatever life it gave him.

He crunched over gravel to the small office Shug had taken him into when he'd arrived, all those years ago, shivering and shocked. He remembered Shug's matter-of-factness, his making of hot drinks, sending his son to get Marine, dealing with what needed to be done.

Kare knocked on the door. The yard was quiet, no sound of work being carried out on the ships, no voices cursing. Unease tickled the back of his mind, touching his Empath skills. He tried to tell himself it was paranoia, nothing more, but knew better; if he had a hunch about something, it should be listened to.

"Come on in." Shug sounded normal, his voice relaxed, and Kare put his hand on the handle. He thought about the office – the door opened inwards. Anyone could be behind it. He took another look around the yard. Business was slow, evidently. And his skin was worth a lot of money.

Damn it, if Shug had wanted a quick buck he would have turned him in years ago. He pushed the door open and Shug was behind his desk, smiling, his eyes crinkled. Nothing emanated except a sense of quiet relief that Kare wouldn't be his problem anymore. Kare closed the door after him.

"You're right to go." Shug's eyes were appraising. "You're too like him."

He knew. He'd caught sight himself a month ago in the mirror and had gasped at how much of his father shone out, even with the blond hair. "That's what I thought. Are we ready?"

Shug slipped some documents across the table. "These will get you past hub-security. The papers should get you some work, too, even if it's just as a deck-hand."

A deck-hand was fine. Anything was fine. He took the papers. "I can't ever repay you."

The shipper waved his hand. "I owed your father a life debt." He stopped smiling, leaned closer, eyes glinting. "But it's paid now. Yes? You don't come back."

"No." He'd never see Marine again, or know if Silom did marry Liane like she hoped he would. It was surprising how sad it made him feel, when his life here hadn't consisted of much more than hiding.

"Planet-hopper out on the yard." Shug jerked his head. "Pilot on board, ready to take you. You'll be there in half a day."

"Thanks." Kare turned away, but the niggle was still at the back of his mind, warning that something wasn't right. He opened the door and stepped into the muggy day. The yard was in silence, watchful. He crunched over to the planet-hopper, scanning. If he were a dog his hackles would be raised.

Someone moved, someone in the shadows, and he found himself crouching, ready to run, but it was only Shug's son. His face wasn't friendly. Kare homed in on his thoughts and there was the betrayal. He backed away, heart hammering. Sweat broke between his shoulder blades. The Empress knew about him: Shaun had taken her money.

"You stupid bastard," he said, teeth clenched. Shaun wouldn't gain from this. He'd be stamped out for knowing Kare existed. Anyone who'd known him would be.

A military transport appeared, just behind the planet-hopper, engines roaring. He spun and ran. He ducked out of the yard, into the narrow street, and reached with his psyche. Were Silom and Marine safe, or had they been found? He sought for their familiar minds, but didn't find them.

Shouts came from behind him, the trap springing. His feet beat on the hard streets, his breath was short, growing painful. He dropped the backpack. His clothes, his few books, his holos of Marine and Silom, gone. All he had was the beacon in his pocket, banging against his breast bone.

A beam passed him, touching his arm, which tingled and started to grow numb. Stunners. Hell: all it would take was one to bring him down, and he'd wake in Abendau palace. He sped up at another buzz, and, frantic and panicked, thickened the air behind him, forming some sort of shield.

Kare, go, leave the planet. The thought was as clear as if it had been his own. *They're here.* He caught the sense of his aunt's fear, of Silom's anger. He homed in on them, ducking into the Needles. The alley was narrow and shadowed. He criss-crossed into another, jumping over a shocked toddler, careering off her mother, turned a corner. Let the soldiers try to find him in the maze of streets.

He let his shield fall away; he'd need some power left when he reached Marine and Silom. Following the sense of them, he came out near the main army station and crouched, breathing hard. This was it: the day he'd dreaded all his life, when he'd find out if he was the man he needed to be, if he could do what had to be done to keep his own safe. And if that person was someone he could bear to be.

CHAPTER EIGHT

wo sentries were on duty at the main gate, and there had to be more inside the barracks. Not easy, and made harder by the urgency coming from Silom and Marine, the escalating threat in their thoughts. This was no false alarm. The soldiers knew about Kare, they knew about Shug, they presumably knew where he'd been hiding. It made him cold, to think he'd left Marine sleeping, had watched Silom go to work, and walked them all into a trap.

He crept forward, listening for the pursuing transport. It wouldn't be long before they'd give up the search of the Needles and come back to the barracks. Whatever he was going to do, it had to be now.

He flexed his fingers. He needed to get closer. Decided, he got to his feet. Confidence, his dad had told him. Every psycher had to be confident, to know their power could do the impossible. He straightened up.

You can't see me. I'm just something moving in the corner of your eye, nothing important. He sent the thought to the sentries, putting his whole focus into it, and walked directly to the gate.

He couldn't breathe, sure they would see him, but the soldiers stared ahead, watching the street, paying him no heed. It worked. Bloody hell. He paused at the gate, thinking about the security pad and how to bypass it. A hand scanner. He lifted the nearest soldier's hand. *You can't see me.* He set it on the pad, and the gate opened. He slipped through and scurried across the yard, bypassing four soldiers at the door of the barracks, to a service entry. His heart was beating so hard and fast, he was sure the soldiers should be able to hear it. None of them looked his way.

He crouched in the shadows, grinning. All the practice, kept up over the years after his father had left, the manipulation of objects, the quiet learning of how people in the street were feeling, had paid off.

Don't hurt her. Silom's thought, loud and desperate. Kare's grin fell away. All he'd managed was to get into the yard. He needed to get into the barracks, find Silom and Marine. To do that, he'd need more than a little misdirection of the soldiers- he couldn't afford any coming after him.

His hands broke out in a sweat. He'd always known he might

be faced with this, that one day he might be cornered into killing. But he didn't think he could. Not men standing by a door, their weapons not raised.

Not even for Marine? Or Silom? He sucked in a breath, readying himself. For them, he could. For Marine, he'd do anything. She'd risked so much for him, had brought him up as much her son as Silom was. The whine of a transport sounded, high in the sky. A military-grade searcher, heading for the barracks. In a moment he wouldn't have four soldiers to deal with, but a squad.

Voices reached him. Two soldiers at the barracks palmed the door open, a double security bar. His aunt stumbled forwards. Her hair was wild, her clothes askew. She'd been woken by the soldiers, he guessed. She was pale, a red mark standing out on one cheek, but she caught her footing and straightened, casting a glare at a soldier who'd moved beside her. It would take more than being taken unawares to steal her composure.

Silom took her elbow. He scanned the yard, his eyes seeking, seeking, before he drew in a deep breath, his shoulders relaxing. He must have thought Kare would run, that he'd leave them to face the Empress on his behalf. His fists clenched: did Silom know nothing? Or, in hiding, had Kare seemed weak?

The transport landed and a squad disembarked. Crap. He should have acted quicker. Marine and Silom were pushed towards it, two soldiers alongside each of them. In a moment, they'd be taken off-planet.

Kare stepped out of the shadows. He couldn't take on so many soldiers, but he could make sure they took the right person. Fear coursed through him, raw, making the moment sharp, too real. He swallowed it and managed to keep his voice steady. "I'm here. Let them go– it's me you came for."

"Kare!" Marine tried to wrestle free. "You can't do this!"

He could. He had to. He took a step forward, and it was easier this time. His father had been right: his mother would never give up the search. Not now she knew he was alive. The type of military transports seeking him hadn't been called in quickly; they'd been on-planet, waiting where his dad had died. She'd never given up on someone surviving.

"Get away!" Silom had more luck with his guards, freeing one arm. "I said to run!"

Kare ignored his cousin. He faced the squadron leader. "Let them go."

"Bring the three of them in." The leader had a hard face, his eyes dark pools with no edge of friendliness. "The Empress will want them questioned."

Questioning meant the Empress' interrogators. Was that where his father's screams had come from? Was this the point that led to that history? He thought of Marine, of Silom, thought of them facing that and planted his feet. "Just me. They've done nothing."

"Harbouring a fugitive." The soldier holding Marine tightened his grip on her arm. He pulled her head back. Her mouth opened in a silent gasp, trying to get air, but still she didn't let out a sound. She wouldn't give the soldier the satisfaction, Kare knew. "That's against the law."

"Leave her alone!" Silom launched himself at his mother.

"Don't!" Kare tried to reach him. The soldiers were armed, they were twitchy, they were on a do-not-fail mission. A first shot sounded. Silom yelled, a red line appearing on his throat, and dropped to his knees.

"No!" Kare ran forwards, but another shot fired and Marine fell to the ground. Her red hair spilled across a ground that turned redder. Her eyes were open, stilled. Kare stared at her, stunned. Grief rose in him, a familiar mix of shock and dread, making his legs shake, his stomach clench. It had happened so fast, and he'd let it, damn him. He should have taken charge, dealt with the soldiers. He was supposed to be something special.

Silom crawled to his mother. One of the soldiers was on a comms unit, no doubt asking for backup. He had no more time to delay, no more opportunity to doubt. If he wasn't strong enough, he'd lose everyone.

He focused on the soldiers and pushed them back to the transport. They tried to fight, but he held firm, tumbling them in one after the other, sending his power out in short, sharp pulses. Sweat broke across his brow; to manipulate so many at once, to draw on enough resolve to do that, was harder than he'd known. But no one blocked him; there were no psychers amongst them. At least he had that advantage– they didn't know what he could do. Hell, *he* didn't know what he could do, held in this anger, this moment.

The last soldier slammed into the transport. He closed the door. Sealed it. Thought about what was needed. Oh, hell, he couldn't do this.

He had to. He turned his attention to the fuel cells, imagining heat building around them. Silom was crouched beside Marine, close to the transport: too close. He wanted to find a way to take her away from here– it was obscene to leave her lying here.

"Silom! Get over here!" He had an authority in his voice he'd never heard before, born of desperation, of the sick knowledge he'd fucked up and it wasn't him who'd paid the price. Silom pushed his mother's hair back from her face, murmured something that may have been sorry, and then he ran, joining Kare.

"What do we do?" He looked around the yard. "There'll be more. You can't hold them in there forever."

"I know." Gods, this was hard. He could feel the panic of the men inside, how it was growing– the transport must be getting hot. With each pulse he sent, their thoughts grew stronger. Their fear was through him. It hurt, in hideous waves, part pain, part self-loathing. He found himself grabbing Silom's shoulder to stay upright. He didn't want to do this; he didn't know how he could.

The transport exploded in a single sheet of flame, ending the thoughts of the men. Their pain carried to him, the residue of their fear, and he screamed in the pure knowledge of what he'd done. The transport burned. The air was thick with smoke. Someone pulled him to his feet, someone solid.

"Come on," said Silom, and he had his arm under Kare's shoulder, taking his weight, a weight that was too heavy. "We need to go. Now."

They ran. A transport took off, hounding them through the Needles. Silom was on his comms unit, telling Liane's family to get out now, now, now, and none of his calls were answered. They reached Shug's yard, ducking under the sign. In front of the office, Shug and his son lay, their eyes staring. Already the carrion birds had gathered along the top of the office.

"Keep going!" yelled Silom. The transport wasn't far behind them; it would find them easily, here in the open. Mouthing a sorry, Kare ran past Shug. Another person dead because they knew him. He caught up with Silom and they crossed the bare strip of ground before the yard.

The low whine of a shot reached him, followed by a bolt. He flung a shield up, a searing pain in his head making him yell, but he stretched it so it covered Silom. He was close to the end of his endurance, ready to give up, but no more people were going to die because of him this day. He raced to the two ships. Perhaps the bigger one wasn't stripped yet. But, reaching it, he saw its innards spread out on the ground. Damn it.

"Where do we go?" yelled Silom.

"The planet-hopper!" He was drained, sick, his head thudding. At any moment, the shield would give.

"We can't use a planet-hopper! It might not even have a star drive."

They'd have to. They were out of options. He followed Silom up the gangway. Shouts came from behind. The transport had landed, spilling soldiers after them.

He slammed the hatch behind them, and ran to the control-room. Control-cone, really. The pilot was gone, presumably fled when Shug and Shaun had been taken. Kare dove for the pilot's seat, thanking his father for at least teaching him which end of a ship went up. Silom crashed beside him, starting the control panel, his work at the yard paying off as he checked off the engines, confirmed capacity. Dull thuds sounded– the troops were shooting at the ship.

He took it up, a vertical lift-off at a speed no planet-hopper should be forced to. The sky darkened as they cleared the outer atmosphere, into space beyond. It would take precious moments before the transport followed them, more to alert space-control. He punched in a course, taking them to the dark side of Dignad, away from the hub into deeper space. Let the authorities assume he'd go for the hub; it would be crazy to do anything else in this bucket, after all.

The noise of the engines settled. The adrenaline that had carried him onto the ship left with a crash, leaving him shaking, almost burning with tiredness. He had nowhere to go, he realised. Nothing was safe, and it never would be again.

Grief hit, familiar, borne once, and no easier for it. His shoulders shook as waves came at him, making him double in a silent, bitten off yell. Silom, opposite, looked ahead, his eyes empty. The cost of their freedom had been too high, and who knew how many people had been pulled in, and what would happen to them. All because he'd lived amongst them. It wasn't right. None of it was. With a shaking hand he set the vector-alarm and tried to think what to do next.

41

CHAPTER NINE

teady. That's what Dad used to say: when you were getting close to a planet, you had to keep the ship steady. Kare squinted as Holbec filled the viewing window, a green disc against the darkness of space. He concentrated on the control panel and tried to remember anything else his dad had said about landing a ship.

"Are you sure you can do this?" Silom drummed his fingers on the edge of the co-pilot's seat. His right eye was half closed, and an angry scar stood out where the laser shot had grazed his neck. The mark was almost as red as his hair; another inch, and he'd have been dead.

Kare swallowed at the memory of his aunt, her red hair spread under her, as red as her blood. The image had been coming and going, invading his dreams: her staring eyes, blue as the sea, her stillness. He forced himself to focus on the ship. He had to land this thing. He'd tried not to think about that the whole way through the flight. In fact, he'd been sure there would be no landing, that the basic star drive would burn out, faced with a flight from one side of the stellar cluster to the other. He was lucky the ship even had a drive- not every planet-hopper did. But Dignad was far enough from the twin central stars to merit it in the bigger hoppers, and Shug hadn't cut corners. He'd probably anticipated trouble- it seemed to follow Kare around, after all. He frowned at the memory of Dignad and forced it away. After he landed, there'd be time to think about what had happened, to go over the endless might-have-beens.

"Of course I can land." The ship dropped, quicker than it should, and he adjusted their flight path. "I grew up on a ship."

"It's been ten years. You might be a bit rusty."

"I got us here, didn't I?" Kare glanced at the beacon: *it* had got them here. All he'd done was set it up. Still, if Karia could land a freighter at the base when she was seven, he could manage a planet-hopper at seventeen. Oh, gods, let him manage a planet-hopper.

"Is that the base?" asked Silom, leaning forward. "It's bigger than I expected."

"That's the port." Kare cast his eyes over it until he spotted the docking bays. He selected the landing-programme and sat back, letting the ship take over for now. It was a better pilot than he'd ever hope to be, after all. "The building behind it is the base."

42

He could see it clearly now, the long, low building, set into a jungle clearing, and a flutter of excitement settled in his stomach. Would they remember him? He guessed some might. Darwin le Payne definitely would.

If they did, would they let him stay? His breath caught, remembering the night they'd left. It was entirely possible he'd land the ship only to find himself banished to the outer rim colonies where he'd have to hope his mother didn't find him. Ice fingers ran down his spine at the thought of his father's body, wracked by pain; his screams. There was no hope of his mother not finding him.

"You're sure we're doing the right thing?" There was a slight tremor in his voice and he knew Silom must have noticed, too.

"I'm sure. At least they might give us some credits." Silom looked composed, but he didn't meet Kare's eyes. "Hell, a change of clothes and some unreconstituted food would be good. Besides, this ship won't hold out much longer."

True. "You know, even if they do kick me out, you could probably stay."

"Like that's going to happen." Silom rubbed his neck. "I hope they treat this." He nodded at the planet. "You're wrong. They're going to take one look at you and decide you're their free pass to legitimacy. The heir to the empire, siding with them."

Kare tensed. It was his only card, and one he didn't want to have to play. Still, needs must; he had to get out of his current mess first before he thought about any future trouble. "Maybe...."

"You can't walk in like it doesn't matter. It's *your* name, and your future." Silom glanced forward. "And you need to decide what to do with it in the next few minutes."

"Enough, I know." Kare frowned. Silom made it sound so easy: go with the rebels, or embrace his mother's empire. He hadn't been on the ship when Dad had succumbed, hadn't seen the horror ahead if he made the wrong choice. Kare adjusted the readout settings. "At least they haven't shot at us. That's something."

One of the port's docking bays opened and three fighters came up, taking flanking positions around their ship.

"You were saying?"

"Standard procedure, that," said Kare, not at all sure it was. The port filled the viewing window. It really was huge: five separate docking bay doors, only one of which was open. The ship's control panel flashed, indicating a switch to manual was imminent. He licked his lips and sat with his hands hovering over the panel.

"Lock," he said, his voice amazingly steady. The HUD-display zoomed into the port, letting him focus. He kept his hand on the control panel as the ship cruised in, its speed dropping. He wished Karia was here and he was relegated to the co-pilot's seat again. Silom's breathing became ragged.

"Pilot, identify yourself." The voice was harsh, not friendly.

He glanced at Silom, who shrugged. "They'll have a record of the beacon."

"Right." Kare leaned forward to the voice recorder. "Kare Varnon."

"Your purpose?"

Kare hesitated, sure that saving his skin wasn't the answer they wanted. "I want to join the group."

He looked across at Silom, who nodded.

"Keep flying."

He did, holding a landing trajectory, waiting for the order to pull up and go. The control panel pulsed.

"Permission to land granted. Fighters will remain with your ship; any deviation from your flight path and they will open fire. Come out with any weapons in plain sight."

Relief mingled with dread; he really was going to have to land the ship. He flicked from the HUD to the panel and back again. Planet-hopper or not, this wasn't going to be fun.

"Not especially friendly, are they?" Silom said.

Kare tried to keep his voice bland. "It's a rebel base, what did you expect?"

He flew towards the docking bay. He'd have been more familiar with landing a freighter, the sudden drop into the port; the planet-hopper would land horizontally, and he'd have to time its shutdown just right.

Line the ship up, wait until the nose is in, then reverse thrust– hard, once only– and kill the engines. Don't go at it too slowly. Not too fast, either; just keep it steady. The constant teaching his dad had given Karia on how to fly different types of craft. It had sounded easy then.

"Are you sure you can do this?"

Kare's eyes flicked between the speed data and the bay ahead. *Steady.* "Silom." He squinted in concentration, checking she was lined up, ready to pull out if not.

"What?"

"If you ask me again if I can land, I'm going to throw you out of the airlock."

"Okay," said Silom. He was quiet for a moment, before he said,

"You're very close; shouldn't you be slowing down?"

Probably. The base loomed, dwarfing the ship. The nose of the hopper was swallowed by the docking bay. Kare's hands moved to the thrust command. How far in should he go? He had no idea. He waited another moment, reversed the drive and hit it once, hard. "We're in– "

Alarms shrieked through the ship. Walls flashed past. The hangar engulfed them as the ship streaked forwards.

"We're gonna fucking crash!" shouted Silom. He threw himself forwards in his seat, head down and braced.

Kill the engines! His father's voice echoed as if he was there. *Kill them!*

"Close down!" Kare yelled. He braced and waited for the impact. He was dead, everything was solved. There was a whine as the engines closed down, but the ship was still moving. Something smashed behind them. Silom yelled, wordless and loud. Kare squeezed his eyes closed. *Gods, let it be quick.* There was a crash and he was flung forward, the restraints jolting against his chest. The alarms stopped and he tensed, waiting for pain to hit.

Nothing. He sat up, shaking. Filling the viewing window was a solid wall of metal. He clenched his hands together, tight against his chest, and looked at the white-faced Silom.

"See." His voice sounded like it was going to break. "I told you I could land."

Silom got up and walked down the ship, anger radiating from him. Kare hit the hatch-command and followed, keeping his distance; he might be quicker than his cousin, but Silom could pack a punch. The hatch lowered, letting warm air in, heavy with the smell of oil, carrying Kare straight back to his childhood, and their supply visits to the rebel base, in a way nothing else could. *Gods, he was home.* His eyes blurred and he blinked before Silom noticed. Who was he kidding? This wasn't home. At home, people wanted you.

The docking bay doors thudded closed, and the port stood in darkness for a moment. Then harsh lights came up, illuminating the hangar. A squad of soldiers approached, weapons raised, in their centre a woman dressed in a military uniform, her face stern and unwelcoming. Kare fought back a groan: Rjala. Who else? He stepped onto the gangway, and her eyes swept him up and down.

"Kare." Her voice was cold. Beside him, Silom tensed, the muscles in his arms bunching as he crossed them.

"Rjala," said Kare. A muscle twitched in her cheek, and he nearly kicked himself. She was an army officer; she'd want her title. He looked at her uniform, trying to decide what she was, but didn't recognise the Banned insignia.

"Why have you come back?" she asked.

He stepped forward, one of the soldiers raised his gun. "No further."

"Sure." He stood, trying not to show his nerves. What should he say? The truth seemed as good as anything. "Rj - "- *Ma'am, that's what you called an army officer*- "Ma'am, my mother found me. I had to run."

Her gaze stayed on him and he looked away, but had to bite back a yell: standing behind the soldiers was a little girl, her heart-face thin, her green eyes shining. She held her hand out, and in it there was a mouse. He shook his head. *No Karia; not today.* He blinked and she disappeared, allowing him to turn his attention back to Rjala. "I didn't know where else to go."

Rjala stood for a moment longer, looking him up and down. He tensed, waiting for her to tell him to leave. Finally, she nodded. "We'll get you processed." She turned on heel and took a few steps before she stopped and glanced back. "It's good one of you survived." She gave the ghost of a smile. "Welcome back."

The squad led him and Silom through the hangar, footsteps echoing, to a clearing outside. It was getting dark, just a last line of red in the sky, but it was still warm, a moist heat that made sweat break across his back. The smell of the jungle enveloped him: the high florals of night jasmine; an underlying scent of loam. Something droned close to his face and he swatted it away, but it buzzed back a moment later: a moth as big as his palm, its wings a gentle purple. He remembered this from a child: the jungle as night fell; Karia beside him hunting night-creatures, and the familiarity settled him.

Ahead another building stood, long and low, and from it came the sensations of many minds, all crammed together. He glanced at the soldier next to him. "What's that?"

"The barracks."

Barracks? "Why are we going there?"

The soldier's face was a cross of amusement and pity. "You'll be processed for the army. All new arrivals are."

The army? There had to be a mistake. More to the point, there had to be another option. He'd make a terrible soldier. He thought back to Rjala's cold eyes. She was setting him up, he was sure of it, maybe to make sure he'd leave, or to keep him where she had control over him. Either way, he didn't like it.

"You know," said Kare, "I'm wondering if I can see Darwin le Payne? He knew me when I was a kid."

"Darwin's dead," said the soldier. "About a year ago."

46

Kare's stomach fell, surprising him- he wouldn't have thought it should matter, after the last day on the base. But Darwin had been the only person who'd stuck up for his dad at the end, even if he hadn't stopped them being forced out. Perhaps the passing years had brought things back into focus, had made the memories of the Darwin he'd known as a child, always welcoming them to base, take the place of the bitterness. Hell, maybe he was just growing up.

Kare looked at the barracks. He'd forced himself into a corner in trying to leave Dignad- his mother would know he was alive. There was nowhere else to go to unless he wanted to watch his back every day, knowing all it would take was one slip for the Empress to close in on him.

Right, then. He put his shoulders back and walked into barracks.

How bad could it be, after all?

CHAPTER TEN

Lichio smoothed his jungle fatigues, checking for stains. He'd have liked to get changed into his formal uniform, but when Eevan requested a meeting it was best to move right away, brother or not.

He swallowed his nerves and rapped the door. There was no need to be worried. He'd done nothing wrong. Well, nothing he'd get fingered for. He bounced on the balls of his feet. *Come on, let's get it over with.* At last, a voice, low and authoritative, called for him to enter. He crossed the room until he reached the desk and stood to attention, his eyes fixed on the wall ahead, covered with Eevan's various certificates. Why he felt the need to do so escaped Lichio- surely the major's black panther insignia was enough?

"At ease, Lichio." Eevan nodded to a seat opposite his own. "Sit down."

Lichio sat, fighting the urge to wriggle on the hard seat. Eevan leaned back, crossed his legs, and relaxed into his familiar leather chair.

"You asked to see me, sir?" said Lichio, fighting the urge to call him Eevan. Half-brother or not, Eevan had been adamant that when Lichio joined the army, he'd show proper respect. It was proving more difficult than he'd anticipated, to date.

"We have a pair of new arrivals." Eevan gave a smile, one Lichio knew well, and not in a good way. "I'm placing them in your dorm."

So why not send a memo? "Yes, sir." He waited; let Eevan spell out exactly what he wanted. Lichio wasn't going to make it easy.

"Does the name Kare Varnon mean anything to you?"

"Of course." Lichio fought to keep his voice steady; anything about the Varnons was big news, probably the biggest possible in the Banned. "One of Ealyn's twins. Died a decade ago."

"Apparently not."

He resisted the urge to ask which bit he'd got wrong. "No?"

"He arrived about two hours ago. Nearly wiped out the port." Eevan smirked, and it made him look mean as well as bad- tempered. "Apparently he didn't inherit his dad's piloting skills." He sobered. "How well did you know him?"

"Not very." Lichio picked his words with care. "I was about six when the ship vanished. Sonly knew him better. Do we know how he survived?"

"He wasn't on the ship when it went down. He's been hiding on Dignad until a couple of weeks ago when he tried to leave and attracted the wrong attention. He and his cousin made it off-planet; his aunt died in the escape." Eevan closed his data pad. "A couple of things worth noting. Three weeks ago, an army squad on Dignad were blown up inside a transporter. There were no survivors. Varnon claims he was behind it, that he had no option but to do it." Eevan touched his head. "He claims he did it with his powers, that he's a psycher." His face darkened. "Given what I know of him from the past, I believe it to be true; when he was a child he showed signs of being an Empath. Do you know what that means?"

Lichio nodded. "He senses peoples' emotions."

"He can read minds," said Eevan. "He can crawl around and take your thoughts. Like his mother."

Lichio frowned. That wasn't what an ordinary Empath could do. "Surely not. Besides, aren't there rules for psychers? Their code of conduct?"

Eevan leaned forward. "His father was a maverick. Kare has grown up untrained. He hasn't even attended school." His face reddened, angry. "When we were children he tried to use his powers on me." Lichio managed not to wince; his brother had a long memory and could be downright vicious. "He had no discipline, his father had no rules, he has had no teacher." He rapped his hand on the desk. "Which bit of that sounds good?"

"None." Although most of it was interesting.

"Indeed." Eevan sat back in his seat. "I don't want him using his psyche. Not in my army. In fact, if the decision had been mine, he'd have been kicked off base the minute he arrived."

Oh dear. Eevan over-ruled was never a good thing. "So he stays?" asked Lichio.

"He stays." Eevan's smile widened, making Lichio's skin crawl. "Until we can see if he can live up to the potential of his name. Do you understand?"

"Yes." Since when did he come across as stupid? The heir to the empire, on side and half-way smart, would be an asset; but if he was an idiot or a maverick, he could do more harm than good. "And you want me to do what about it?"

"Work him hard. We want to know what he's made of." Eevan pointed at Lichio. "And make sure he doesn't misuse his powers. I want to know he can be trusted with whatever's in that head of his.

That's why he's in your dorm. You'll report directly to me about it. Understood?" he ordered

Perfectly. "Yes, sir."

Eevan nodded. "Good. You're dismissed."

Lichio stood, saluted, and turned to go.

"Lichio." His brother's voice was quiet, dangerous.

"Yes?"

"Make sure you do this right," said Eevan. "I want him hemmed in, I want it done by someone I can trust, and I don't want any fuck-ups. Keep him in his place."

"Yes, sir," he said. "I understand what you're saying." And he absolutely did.

CHAPTER ELEVEN

Silom glanced at Kare. "What now?" asked Silom. They'd been allocated a bunk, given a brief familiarisation, then left in their bare, utilitarian dorm, with orders to report for duty in the morning.

Kare shrugged, trying for relaxed; there were a lot of people in the building, judging by the mutter of their minds, and it was hard to think. "Food? There's supposed to be a mess."

"Good plan. I'm starving." Silom set off to the right, and Kare followed. If there was food, Silom would find it. Sure enough, the sound of plates clattering reached them, and the first smell of food filtered down the corridor.

They rounded the door into the canteen and Kare stopped, stunned. He'd been here before, with Karia. They'd filled their pockets with supplies to take on the ship. Their dad had caught them, scaring them by grabbing them and announcing he had hamsters instead of kids.

He put a hand on the counter to steady himself, still spooked from seeing her earlier. It had been years since she'd last appeared to him, and he hadn't been prepared for it, even though it made sense- everywhere else they'd shared had been destroyed.

"Did you hear me?" Silom waved a hand in front of his face. "What do you want?"

"Anything." *Nothing.* He turned, leaning against the counter, and scanned the room. It was too bright, the diners' faces in sharp focus, making him nauseous. There were too many people here, their minds pressing on him. He squeezed his eyes shut, trying to find some space for his own thoughts, but still they came at him- snippets of other peoples' lives, threaded personalities, not quite complete.

"Tea, coffee, piss... any chance of an answer?"

Kare focused on Silom, grasping his exasperation; his worry about Liane; grief; new from their flight from Dignad, a sense of growing older.

"Coffee." He reached for some cups but something touched his leg, making him look down. Karia was beside him, stuffing her pockets full of food. Her pocket bulged and he reached for it, sure it was going to overfill. His hand closed on empty air. *She wasn't real.* He jumped back, knocking Silom's arm.

"Watch it!" Plates fell from the tray and bounced on the floor, their contents spilling, seemingly in slow motion. Karia grinned, her smile the same as when they'd been children, and then waved and ran from the room.

"What the *hell* is wrong with you?" Silom snarled.

"Nothing." He staggered to the nearest table and sank onto its bench. He was going mad, he had to be. He hadn't used the power enough over the years, hadn't kept up the right level of intensive- *to hell with that, incessant-* practice his dad had demanded, and it had turned on him, like he'd been warned. Either that, or living as a hermit for a decade meant he just didn't do crowds.

A tray slammed on the table in front of him.

"Try breathing before you pass out," said Silom, his voice pitched low, almost a growl.

He nodded and took a deep, ragged, breath.

"Brilliant. Keep going." Silom took a chip and pushed the plate to the middle of the table, but the smell made Kare gag. He lifted the coffee, inhaling its aroma, and it cut through the onslaught of thoughts, giving him space to think.

"You want to tell me what's happening?" asked Silom.

No. Silom waited and Kare knew he wouldn't break first- he rarely did.

"Too many people," Kare said, eventually. "I can't hold them back..."

"Thought as much. You'll have to find a way, or you'll be known as the resident weirdo." Silom picked up a chip. "What else is wrong? You've been freaking since we landed, and the port was hardly hiving with people."

Kare paused, feeling like an idiot, but it would feel good to tell someone. "I saw Karia. Twice."

"Terrific, now the dead sister's turned up. Fantastic."

"Your sympathy is overwhelming."

Silom leaned across the table. "You need to pull yourself together." His eyes were unflinching. "Either that or admit it's too much, ask for some credits and leave."

"I know." He did, damn it. His father had been the best pilot the Banned had and he'd still been kicked out. He had no illusions; the empire's heir was only useful if he was up to the role. Always assuming he wanted it. He rubbed his temples; if the bloody voices would stop for a minute, he could concentrate. "I know. Give me some time."

"You don't have time." Silom's voice was low. "Either you find a way to deal with this now, or you fall into the liability camp. And when that happens, you can bet your ass we're gone from here." He picked up another chip. "We've got food here and a place to sleep. It's more than we had yesterday." He scraped his chair back. "So either find a way to cope, or throw in the towel. I'll see you back at reception."

He left, his footsteps fading into the murmur of voices and thoughts. Kare put his head back and, instead of forcing the clamour away, listened to it. None of it was threatening and if he just accepted the thoughts, they weren't much more than a buzz. Tinnitus of the mind? He reckoned he could cope with that.

He got up and went after Silom. He didn't have two options; he had one. He'd have to make himself so useful they wouldn't dare cast him out. He put his shoulders back, ready to turn himself into the best damn soldier the Banned had ever had.

CHAPTER TWELVE

General Allen entered the palace's war room, his pace slow, befitting his recent promotion to Head of Intelligence. He took his place at the desk stretching the length of the room, and swept his gaze over the four colonels seated at it. The room fell silent, just as it should, and he swiped his hand over the desk. A screen formed across the centre of the room, visible from all angles, showing the stellar cluster governed by the Pettina Empire. The cluster whose security he was responsible for. He allowed a quiet moment to savour the thought.

The seven central planets belonging to the great families were directly before him, three dimensional and real enough that he had to resist the urge to step out of their path. These first planets, colonised by settlers from the Earth-ship, were the most established, the richest, the centre of the cluster in terms of economy and power as well as positioning. Four, including the giant, desert-covered Belaudii, orbited Ceaton-I; the other three its sister star Ceaton-II.

He adjusted the screen so one of the three mid-zone systems, dependent on and tied to the families for commerce, was enlarged. It was the most remote of the middle systems, close to Ceaton-II with a small space hub providing port facilities to the Candelan system, the furthest out of the nine. That space hub explained the system's expertise in space repairs, servicing the inner, richer planets who didn't want their air polluted by the industry. It was said, if you wanted to scrap a ship, or buy one reputedly already crushed, Dignad and its sister planets were the place to go.

The four outer systems, Candelan and three others separated from it by the twin star systems, disappeared off the screen, which pretty much summed up their significance to the empire.

The general zoomed in on Dignad. He paused, letting his annoyance show, and cast his gaze around the room. Several of the faces already looked guilty; news had obviously travelled.

"With reference to the recent breach of security– "

The door opened and a squad entered, wearing the gold and red livery of the Empress' personal guard.

"General, our Lady commands your presence," said the captain.

The words chilled him to his core. He placed his hands behind his back, gripping them together. "I have a briefing...." He nodded, indicating the colonels, each of whom was studying the desk and avoiding his eyes. They knew, as he did, that if the Empress required his presence, he would go. They must also know what it was regarding. He gave a curt nod. "We'll continue when I return."

The captain and his squad fell into place around Allen, who kept his head up, remaining composed. As he marched through the palace from the sterile military quarters to the opulence of the central chambers, his heartbeat quickened, pounding in his ears. His hands slipped, threatened to tremble, and he grasped them even tighter.

He turned a corner and ahead stood the gilded doors of the Empress' anteroom. He slowed a little, but the guards kept marching and he was forced to keep step with them. His mouth was as dry as the desert. The captain opened the doors and stepped forward.

"My Lady, the general, as you commanded."

"Thank you, Captain. Leave us."

The soldiers melted away and Allen stepped into the room. The doors closed with a thud, so loud he almost started, but held himself in check, staying at attention, back straight. From behind her desk, the Empress' looked directly at him with soft, grey eyes, her mouth tight and unsmiling.

"You may kneel."

He fell to his knees and bowed his head as she reached to the centre of him, tendrils of her touch oozing through him. He fought to stay calm, but his breath was coming in wheezed gasps. A spike of ice made him screw his face into a grimace. Still she went deeper, remorseless and sharp, punishing him for his failure. She increased her hold, making his head thud in sick waves. He let out a strangled sob and ceded to her and for a moment they stayed like that, mistress and servant, all promotion forgotten, his position in her army irrelevant. Soon she would release him, and he wouldn't carry the fear of this moment forward, but a determination to serve better in the future.

"The matter of my son," she said. "Explain yourself."

Head down, he struggled to think past her presence. "M - my Lad - " he said.

She pulled out of his mind, a leech slithering through him.

"Explain yourself," she said again.

"My Lady, he- "

"Look at me."

His heart thudded- one, two, three times, each louder than the last- and he lifted his head. Her eyes, soft like liquid lead, regarded him and for a moment he felt at peace. A new blast of power hit, taking the breath from him.

"You have one minute, General."

The throne room swam around him, and he gritted his teeth; he had to concentrate.

"My Lady, we know where he is." Thank her presence, he had something positive to tell her. Her eyes softened and her anger turned to pleasure, washing over him in waves, making it hard to speak. "I have the means to bring him to you."

"Excellent, General. Come, sit before me."

He stood, light headed, and sat at her desk, his eyes fixed on her seductive gaze. Already the pain had ebbed, the satisfaction of being allowed so close to her, in her inner circle, replacing any doubts.

"I want a full update, Allen. Take your time, leave nothing out."

He took a moment to bring everything he knew about Kare Varnon to the fore of his mind. "He's fled to the Banned, my Lady."

"His psyche?"

"He showed no indication of powers at any stage on Dignad. We interviewed everyone who had contact with him and there's little to go on."

"Where were they interviewed?"

"On Dignad, by the local forces. My Lady, very few had any knowledge of him. Those who knew him– some neighbours, the cousin's girlfriend– were brought to Abendau."

"The Great Master oversaw their interrogation?"

He fought a shiver at the thought of the Great Master, his lady's tribal brother who ruled the dark chambers buried deep in the palace: chambers so secret that, even with his general's rank, he'd never seen them, only heard whispered rumours of what they held. The Great Master's family had given the Empress shelter when her parents' transport had crashed in the desert, not knowing they harboured Lord Pettina's daughter, inheritor of the powers she'd used to bind the tribes to her. He was the closest to her, the nearest thing to a brother she had.

"Yes. Taluthna was most ... diligent, I believe."

"The outcome?"

"Taluthna's report outlines that none of them had any indication your son was a psycher." He paused, licked his lips and dared to say, "My Lady, we still don't know he is."

"*I* know," she said. "He was bred to have powers. Why else did I throw away half a fleet to capture Ealyn Varnon? Do you think I liked the man? He had the old powers and they were merged with mine. I felt the children's power from the womb." He quailed under her anger, and waited until she went on in a quieter tone, "The boy is disciplined, then, more than his father ever was."

"It would appear so, my Empress." He trawled his mind. He had to find something to placate her before she decided to encourage him further. "We have found some evidence that he has an ability to know peoples' feelings."

"An Empath, then."

"Perhaps. Also, he has a very high level of skill with computers. One of his neighbours shared that with us."

"The neighbour lives?"

"No, my Lady," said Allen. A frown crossed her face and he continued, hurriedly. "The Great Master, he took care to ensure all information had been gleaned. He- the neighbour, I mean- knew the boy better than most; he had some work done on his security system by Varnon."

He paused, not admitting how little that neighbour had known: a conversation with Marine Dester and two brief meetings with Varnon hardly constituted informed knowledge. Since then- four years ago- the neighbour hadn't seen Varnon. It was a depressingly familiar litany. Only Dester's girlfriend had met him recently, and even then it had been fleeting, revealing only that Varnon was quiet and polite and usually avoided her. He'd shown absolutely no sign of psychic powers, except in a single conversation when she'd fallen out with Dester, where he may have known her thoughts. It was subtle, if he had, and could have been nothing; by the whispered account he'd heard, the girl would have said anything to stop Taluthna.

"I don't want to know about computers, Allen, I want to know about his psyche."

Allen snapped his attention back to the Empress. "My Lady, we don't know that he has any." He gulped. "Forgive me, my Lady, I meant there is no evidence."

"Yet, this apparently powerless boy managed to overcome a platoon of soldiers and escape Dignad."

He inclined his head. This was indisputable: the transporter's doors had jammed, their security overridden, before it had blown up. "My Empress, we don't know what happened. None of the soldiers survived." He took a deep breath. "I do know where he is and how to find him. I will bring him to you. I have a means to track him, my Lady

I'm arranging its placement. I will- "

"Be silent."

He licked his lips, his whole body rigid. She made him wait, her eyes disdainful. The room seemed to close in, and he needed to breathe but when he did, it made a snorting noise. At last, the Empress nodded, and his shoulders relaxed, just a little.

"He must not be harmed," she said. "It's a pity he is with the rebels– alone, he would be easier to take."

She clicked her fingers and a hologram of Kare, taken as he'd escaped Dignad, appeared over the desk. She zoomed in, and Allen noted how like Ealyn Varnon he was. The same hologram had been issued to each army and fleet in her empire.

"Take a full fleet and five squadrons, and use them only for the pursuit of him. I want him before any of the great families discover his existence."

Firepower wasn't the answer. The rebel base was buried in a hostile star system, surrounded by sentinel planets. To get close enough for an attack would require not only the huge resources offered, but someone within the rebels to undermine the approach sensors. Without that, any fleet would be destroyed. To have the additional requirement of keeping one person alive– out of thousands– meant only a full ground assault would complete the mission.

"My Empress," he said. "May I counsel patience? I will have him tracked. If he is taken off-base we will have a better chance of taking him."

Her eyes narrowed, but she knew the base as well as he did. They'd discussed the parameters for an attack many times, had attempted it twice, and had been repelled by the rebels before they entered the system.

"Arrange to track him then," she said. "And be ready to take him at the first opportunity. You may go."

He stood, bowing to her. "My Lady, I will find him for you. I have a security team following up on any documentation found in the house. Some are giving useful leads." He paused, wanting to get away, knowing he must be seen to withhold nothing. "My Lady, they include adoption records for Ealyn and his sister. They may be worth following up, in case the boy runs again."

She stared at the holo of her son. "Colonel Phelps reports to you?"
"Yes."

She nodded. "He has a background in intelligence."
"Indeed."

"Instruct Phelps to track Ealyn's background."
"Yes, my Empress."

"You are dismissed."

Allen walked from the room, closing the door behind him, and took, finally, the deep breath he needed.

**

Averrine looked at the hologram of her son, turning it to see him from every angle. She'd never known him; he'd been taken before she came round from the birth. She focused on his eyes. Ealyn's eyes. She clenched her fist. It was *his* fault: he'd poisoned the boy against her. Did her son know his father had condemned him to a childhood hiding in attics, when he could have been here, heir to Abendau?

She crossed to the window, her cape shifting in the slight breeze, and looked down at the palace gardens, the surrounding city and the red desert beyond. *This* was what he'd been born for. Her father had failed to hold his empire, but she had. Now it was her son's to take and carry forward. Without him, the Pettinas would cease; there was no other heir, and no means to acquire one. The great families were united in that matter– they knew only by holding firm could they ever reduce her empire. He must be made to understand this was his destiny. She hadn't survived the Bendau uprising for her empire to fall because of a seventeen-year-old boy–

She turned back to the hologram. There was nothing of her in the boy. He should be her legacy; she'd *made* him for that purpose. Instead, he had accepted Ealyn's heritage. Her fists clenched. He must be brought to her and forced to obedience. Only when bound could he inherit. All he had to do was come, or be brought.

CHAPTER THIRTEEN

Silom's snoring woke Kare, familiar enough that it took a moment to realise there were other, less known, sounds: running water, someone turning over in their bed, a bird screeching. *What the hell?* Kare opened his eyes and took in the austere room, very different from the cluttered room he'd shared with Silom for years. Sleep dropped away, and the memory of the day before came back. He fought not to groan: the *army?*

Better get on with it. He got up, lifting the fatigues he'd been issued, and walked to the shower room. It was cold, really cold, and he turned the water as hot as it would go before jumping in. A quick wash and hand rubbed across his chin to decide if he needed to shave- it'd do another day, he reckoned- and he got dressed. The trousers- jungle greens, as far as he could tell- were too big for his thin waist, and he had to clinch the belt as tight as it would go, but the t-shirt was a good fit, and the jacket, when he put it on, had a satisfying weight across his shoulders. He caught sight of himself in the mirror and paused for a moment. Actually, he looked the part; maybe soldiering wouldn't be that bad.

The dorm was stirring, some soldiers taking showers, some pulling on their fatigues. He followed Silom to the mess, and swallowed a jolt of envy as Silom turned to another recruit and started to chat. Silom was more practiced, that was all; he wasn't the one who'd had to keep people away for years. He smiled, knowing he was feeling sorry for himself, and took his food to one of the tables, ignoring the shadow of a little girl at the door. He hoped that stopped soon.

Silom sat opposite him. "Chang's been telling me all about Major le Payne. Tight on discipline, apparently."

"Eevan le Payne?" Things were just getting better by the moment.

Silom gave his cousin a long stare. "Something I should know about? Before we start in his army."

"Not really. I wouldn't have said there was a lot of love lost between us, though."

"Meaning?"

Oh, hell, it had to come out some time. Kare put his spoon down. "We had a fight once, and I knocked him over."

"*You* knocked him over?"

"I used my psyche." Kare looked down, trying to remember the details of what had happened, but it was hidden under years of more vivid childhood memories. "I scared him, I think. I was five and pretty angry, and wanted to teach him a lesson- he'd told me my dad was crazy."

"He had a point."

"Maybe. Anyway, Dad came in, told me he could feel me from one end of the base to the other. He dragged me away by my ear-literally, by my ear- and that was the last time I saw Eevan le Payne."

Silom shook his head, looking resigned. "Not the best start, then."

"No. But I'm sure he's over it by now." Kare finished his coffee and set the cup down. The rest of the recruits had started to leave. "Let's go, find out what's ahead."

They got to the barracks and waited on their beds as the other recruits left for the practice ground. A few minutes later, just as the quiet had started to grow uncomfortable, they heard the sound of footsteps approaching. A tall lad, younger than them, came into the room, his steps jaunty. Emanating from him was a sense of mischief, a belief he was smarter than anyone.

"Bugger me," he said, his face a mask of amazement. "It is you." He held his hand out to Kare. "But when did you go blond?"

Kare frowned, trying to place the youth, but nothing occurred. He shook the hand proffered. "And you're...?"

"Lichio." The lad smirked. "Le Payne."

The penny dropped. The little brother of the le Payne family, the pain who'd followed his sister Sonly everywhere and constantly asked if he could play with her and Karia.

"Nice to meet you again," said Kare. He nudged Silom. "This is my cousin. Silom."

"I know." Lichio shook hands with Silom, too, managing not to look too discomfited when his hand was enclosed in Silom's. "Nice to meet you, too." He held his hand up, open-palmed, as if a tour guide. "And this is my dorm. I'm your mentor during your basic training."

"Which means?" asked Silom. His face was hard to read, his emotions less so; he wasn't impressed by their new friend.

"Well, now, what does it mean?" Suddenly Lichio looked serious, like he had some substance behind him. His eyes were sharp. "It means I'm the only person in this barracks on your side. You'd do best to remember that."

The sound of more footsteps approached, these ones heavier, slower.

"Stand," said Lichio, and his voice carried a crisp command, surprising Kare; the Banned started its people early, it would seem. He got to his feet, as did Silom. Lichio shook his head. "To attention. My brother wants to meet and greet you himself. And you don't want to give him a reason to dislike you. Not right away."

A tall man, almost as tall as Silom, dressed in a formal military uniform, stepped into the room. Kare found himself straightening, his hands clasped behind his back, and he tried to hide his surprise; he hadn't expected Eevan to look so like Darwin. A colder Darwin, with darker eyes, but there was no mistaking the resemblance.

"It's been a long time, Kare." Eevan's words were flat, unfriendly. It seemed twelve years hadn't taken away the memory of their fight. Damn.

"It has. Everything's changed."

"I don't normally take time to allocate new recruits myself, but given your... history, I thought I would afford you the courtesy."

"Thank you, Eevan," Kare said.

"Thank you, *sir*." Eevan's dark eyes challenged Kare to oppose him.

"Thank you, sir."

Eevan jerked his head at his brother. "You're dismissed, Lichio. Take Dester with you."

"Sir." With a quick, hooded, look to Kare, the younger man saluted and left. Silom followed, his narrowed eyes carrying a warning. Kare gave the smallest of nods; don't piss Eevan off. He knew.

Their footsteps died away and Eevan's face changed, became nastier somehow. He guarded his emotions well, though- he'd had some training in dealing with Empaths, evidently.

"Varnon," he said. "I remember you from the past. Any special talents you have must not be used on active duty unless ordered by your commander. Clear?"

Abundantly so. Kare stayed at attention, feeling strangely exposed before the older man's glare. "Yes, sir."

"Dismissed."

Kare left, back straight, and fought the urge to look back. Not use his psyche? Eevan may as well have asked him to stop breathing.

CHAPTER FOURTEEN

ours later- he had no idea how many, the day had become one long, exhausting ordeal- Kare leaned forward, his hands on his knees, breathing hard. He swallowed against a wave of nausea, determined not to throw up again, and glanced at the obstacle course ahead.

Silom, beside him, laughed. "There's no way you can do that. I'm just about keeping up, and I've been working at the yard for three years."

Kare straightened, the muscles across his back and legs cramping. Briefly, he wondered what Stitt would say if he lay down and refused to get up again. He glanced at the drill captain and she gave him a mocking smile. She looked as immaculate as when she'd started the day, with her uniform still in place and her hair coiled into a tight bun.

"I'll do it," he said.

The whistle blew and the first pair of soldiers set off. A couple of minutes later the next followed. Kare stepped forward, and waited for Captain Stitt to give the okay to go. All credit to her; anyone who made him work this hard deserved respect. Lichio le Payne stood beside her, his arms crossed and a small, unreadable smile on his face. At the next whistle Kare and Silom set off.

Kare ran, overtaking Silom, his slighter build making him quicker over the flat. Reaching the first low hurdle he jumped, but his legs had doubled in weight over the day, and he clipped the final one. *Bollocks.* He put his hands out, sure he was going down, but managed to get one foot planted. Somehow, he stayed upright.

Ahead, Silom swarmed up the tall wooden wall, using one of two ropes. Taking a deep breath, Kare ran to the wall, took hold of the rope and leant back, looping it round his foot like he'd been shown. He hadn't got it right, and slipped back, yelling as the rope pulled through his hands.

"Get on with it! You're not on holiday!"

Stitt's voice seared through him. He straightened, glaring at the wall. He could do this. He had to. He ran at the wall, this time locking his foot, and hoisted himself up until his arms could pull him up the last bit. He shook with exertion as he struggled to get over the lip of the wall.

"Come on, your ass is hanging out, it's not pretty!"

It wasn't funny; he was trying as hard as he could. Anger washed over him and he pulled himself onto the top of the wall. He paused, taking a deep breath, blowing it out so hard that it lifted his fringe from his eyes– he could see why the army guys all had crops– and jumped down. He landed, hard, the impact jarring the breath from him. Still, he'd got this far; now for the rest.

He stopped. The row of bars in front of him was easily seven feet from the ground. Silom was nearly across, his hands moving in a rhythm, making it look easy. Kare's breath burned his chest. He didn't know how he would even manage the jump onto them.

"Varnon, we want to get to the mess today. Move!" shouted Stitt. He glanced at her, and decided he didn't respect her: he hated her. "Move, or I'll keep you here all night!"

He ran, jumped, and grabbed the first bar, already struggling. His left hand slipped off, making him gasp at the jolt and he had to grit his teeth to bring it back up. Below, he heard muted laughter. He *couldn't* give up and face them. His hands started to slip, sweaty from the run, and he kicked his legs, desperate not to fall off.

"Come on, you can do it!" shouted a different voice– le Payne, he guessed.

He swung his legs, trying to get enough momentum to shift one hand onto the next bar. He let go with his right, missed, and knew he was going to fall. Instinctively, he snapped the air beneath into something more solid, so he could hold on. Hell, if he wanted to, he could have walked on it. He grasped the next bar and remembered Eevan le Payne's order. He hesitated, his arms still burning. *Fuck it, they have to catch me.*

He moved along, keeping the air beneath him a little denser than it should be. He dropped off the end and saw Silom climbing out of the waist deep water ahead. He jumped into the water, pushing it to the side, splashing through it, instead of wading. He got out, making sure he'd brought the level up, so that he sloshed as Silom had, and ran to the climbing wall. He scaled it easily, his psyche supporting him, and for a moment thought he might overtake Silom. He didn't, quite, and had to wait at the top for Silom to go down the zip wire.

Kare put his hands in the supporting loops. "Go!" said the soldier beside him, and he jumped into empty space, hurtling down, grinning as he did. He landed in a small pool of water at the bottom.

He took his hands from the sling and straightened up, his muscles protesting. He'd done it. He looked back over the course, smiling. He'd sleep like the dead tonight, he reckoned. Captain Stitt walked across, slapped Silom on the shoulder and said something that made him smile and nod. She walked to Kare, and her eyes narrowed. Her smile fell away. She touched her head and then his temple, and he sensed just the tiniest bit of power, insignificant in comparison to his own. But enough to have sensed his. He closed his eyes as realisation clicked into place: a captain in charge of a basic training squad?

"My office," she said. "I'll deal with your cheating there."

Her voice was loud, designed to carry. Kare opened his eyes, and fought not to wince at her disdainful stare. "Yes, ma'am."

"Come on," said Lichio. His face twisted into some sort of sympathy. "I'll show you where to go."

As they walked away, the other recruits watched in silence. Kare's face burned with shame and he limped from a cramp in his leg. They crossed the field, passed a group of recruits running circuits, and went into the barracks.

"Cheating won't have helped your popularity," said Lichio. "Neither will ignoring the major's orders." He paused just slightly too long. "You might want to be more careful."

He opened the door to Stitt's office, and Kare went in and waited. He stood with his hands clenched behind him, and every muscle and joint in his body ached. His hands slipped and he wiped them on his trousers. At the sound of footsteps he replaced them, drew his shoulders back and stood to attention. Stitt swept past and sat at her desk.

"Major le Payne issued you one order," she said.

"Yes, ma'am."

"Remind me, so I can rule out stupidity?"

"I wasn't to use my powers, ma'am."

"Which means not only did you cheat, you also disobeyed orders. Was it because you didn't care or you thought you were too smart?"

Kare hesitated, not sure what to say.

"Answer me, Private."

"I made a mistake, ma'am," Kare said, his teeth gritted.

She glared at him. "You didn't answer my question." He shook his head slightly, and she raised her voice, just a little. "Now."

"I thought I was too clever," he said, closing his eyes against her disdain. He opened them a moment later, and she stared at him until sweat broke out across his forehead. She knew what he was thinking, he was sure of it. Was this how he made others feel, when he picked up on their thoughts? If so, he couldn't entirely blame them for finding it odd. The silence stretched until he had to speak to break it.

"I- "

"Be quiet." He closed his mouth and Stitt went on, "I have a whole squad of recruits who are working hard to complete their training without resorting to shortcuts."

"I'm sorry, ma'am."

"I'm glad you are- you can remind yourself of that while you take care of my shit work, and I have a lot of shit work. Consider yourself on that duty for the next two weeks. And I don't want to see you here again. Clear?"

"Yes, ma'am."

"Dismissed."

Kare saluted and walked out of the room, his head held as high as he was able. Outside, Lichio stood with a bucket and a rag. Kare looked at him, stupidly. Lichio handed them to Kare.

"Come on," said Lichio. He led Kare to the gymnasium, and pointed at the floor. It wasn't just big- it was filthy. How had it got so dirty? A platoon of soldiers, just back from the practice field, crossed it.

"It's to be cleaned until it shines. When it's done, come and get me."

Kare looked at the rag in his hand, and took in the size of the floor. He walked to the furthest corner, his steps echoing, got down on his hands and knees and started cleaning. He heard more footsteps and looked up to see his squad walking through.

"Enjoying yourself, Varnon?" shouted one of them, and there was a general rumble of laughter. Stitt entered the room behind them and he put his head down. He looked around briefly as they left and saw Silom staring back at him.

"Asshole," Silom mouthed.

I know.

He had no idea how late it was when he finally rocked back and threw his cloth into the dirty water beside him. He'd never been so tired in his life. All he wanted to do was sleep. He heard voices behind him, but didn't turn, couldn't turn, his muscles were so sore. Stitt and Eevan passed him and walked across the wide floor, leaving muddy footprints on it. He waited until they'd left, and blinked, his eyes dry and grainy.

He got up and walked to the utility room, where he emptied the dirty water and refilled the bucket. He returned to the gym, knelt, and silently washed away the dirty footprints. His eyes closed at least twice, but he kept going until he'd finished. He straightened.

If he had to wash it again, they'd find him asleep there in the morning. He heard footsteps and waited, resigned.

"How are you doing?" Silom knelt beside him.

"If you put one foot on that floor, I think I might kill you," said Kare, his words slow and sluggish.

Silom looked over the wide expanse. "Did you eat?"

"Lichio sent something." He couldn't remember what it had been, only that he'd eaten it.

"Come on, then," said Silom, but Kare shook his head.

"I have to get Lichio to check it. You go up."

"I'll wait. You look like you might collapse."

Kare got up, emptied the water and went to the office. He knocked on the door and waited until Lichio responded. He didn't dare lean against the doorframe in case he fell asleep.

"Done?"

"Yes."

Lichio walked to the gym and looked at the floor. Kare waited, hoping he would say it was okay and wouldn't make him do it again. Lichio took his time, rubbing his chin, ratcheting up Kare's tension, before he turned to Kare and nodded. "Dismissed."

Silom jerked his head at the stairs and Kare climbed ahead of him. When he reached the dorm, he walked to his bed and lay down, his feet still in their boots, hanging off the side. He didn't have any memories that night. Instead, he slept.

CHAPTER FIFTEEN

Sonly sat on a patch of cleared grass just outside the base. Behind her the perimeter wall marked the edge of the dense jungle that, as ever, threatened to encroach. Her eyes scanned past the grey, utilitarian base and medical wing until she picked out the barracks and its practice ground. From here, the soldiers looked tiny, like ants.

One of them would be Kare Varnon, doing his basic training. She hadn't met him yet, but she wanted to. She wanted to know how much he'd changed. His arrival had brought back memories of Karia and had made the grief she'd felt at the time real again.

Everyone else, when they talked about his arrival, thought only about how they could use it to further the Banned's cause. None of them seemed to remember that a little girl had been forced from the Banned to her death. Instead, the focus was on how unreliable Ealyn had been, how he'd brought the Empress' attention onto the base, and whether they should keep Kare in the Banned now.

Rjala had even gone so far as to describe Kare as "an inconvenience" in a cold voice that had made Sonly shudder: every great family who hoped to challenge for the empire, should the Empress die, would think so too. As for the Empress.... The last time the Empress had known where her children were, she'd attacked the base so many times, she'd almost brought the Banned to their knees.

She closed her eyes, remembering the terror of the base evacuations of her youth, the alarms blaring as her mother ran to the port, Sonly's hand clasped in hers, Lichio carried in her arms. How they'd been bundled onto transporters and made to wait, lights dimmed, never sure if they'd be forced into space, or if the Banned fighters would fight the attack off.

Please let it not come to that again. She hugged her legs to her chest. Because, one way or another, Kare *was* staying with the Banned- Michael had said that he was better with them than his mother, and as head of the board his decision was binding. At least here, the damage could be limited. An heir floating around the Outer Zone systems, waiting to be picked up, would be worse. And then Michael had spent yesterday making notes on how to use Kare's presence to align the Tortdeniel family with the Banned. He'd even talked about letting her come to the meeting with their ambassador, giving her the additional experience she needed to run for election to the board.

The door to the base opened and Lichio emerged, taking off his jacket and slinging it over his shoulder. He walked over, limber and graceful like a cat, spread his jacket out, and dropped easily onto it.

"Are you feeling okay?" he asked. "You're not working?"

"I'm taking ten minutes off to see you. Did you see Rjala?"

"Ten minutes; I'm honoured. Yes, I've just left her."

"And...?" She knew, of course- she'd put through the requisition for his lieutenant's insignia- but he deserved his moment of attention. He had little enough, following Eevan who'd made captain by the time he was eighteen and major at twenty-six. The Banned brought people on early, of course: school lessons were interspersed with the playing of war games and training for base evacuations. The knowledge of their rebel status was a source of pride, many joining the army on the day of their thirteenth birthday. But Eevan had come through quicker than most, leaving Lichio looking second-best, even though his own career was hardly lacking.

He smiled, his eyes shining. "I'm getting my first field post and a promotion. It's a small campaign, but even so..." He sobered a little. "Although I'll have to tell our dear brother he'll need to get another mentor to do his dirty work for him."

She found herself smiling, despite herself. Putting Lichio onto watching Kare had been a typical Eevan move- dirty, but at a distance, so his hands were clean.

"That's brilliant, Lich," she said. A group of kids wearing identical baseball hats walked past them and down the jungle path. Their teacher yelled for them to stay on the path. Jungle skills, she guessed, or just a bug hunt. "What about Angela- won't she miss you?"

His face screwed up. "It's possibly not bad timing on that front, either." He paused. "There was the small matter of her finding out about Gina..."

She swatted a hornet away, its red stripes a warning of danger, and it droned off, towards the denser jungle. "You never learn."

Lichio propped himself on one arm. "They'll get over it. I'm surprised at the promotion; I'm not sure what I did to deserve it- "

"You probably didn't do anything." She laughed. That was another reason he hadn't matched Eevan's progress; he understood the army wasn't all there was to life. "They can't put you in the field as less than an officer, given your heritage. You'd have been chucked in as a private otherwise."

"Urgh, don't."

"So where is the posting?"

"Ah, that's the only downside. It's on Corun, in the Tauric system, the back end of nowhere...."

"Stop it," she said. "It can't be that bad." But the Tauric system had never been fully invested in, leaving planets not fully terraformed, or habitable but without access to the technology the better populated systems had. Any post there would be hard-earned field duty stripes.

"Trust me, it is."

She pulled a strand of creeper-flower, tight in to the grass, so that it unravelled and ripped. If Lichio was going off-base, she wouldn't get a chance to pick his brains again and it would be useful knowing more about Kare, given the politics building around him.

"Lichio," she said, trying to keep her voice casual. "What's our new arrival like?"

He wasn't fooled, but then Lichio never was, and he sent her a sly smile. "Why?"

She should have known he'd make her say what she wanted, so she couldn't deny it. "Just... it would be good to know what way he thinks. If he's going to stay with the Banned, we need to understand him."

Lichio tutted. "Bad, Sonly- he's a person, not a toy." He grinned. "But, yeah, okay. He's a bit of an asshole, if you have to know. Got caught using his powers on the training ground. But I've met worse."

To hell with it. Lichio could dance around hinted questions all day. She faced him: better just to ask openly. "Is he Emperor material?"

"Hard to know. He hasn't been here long. He fled his previous planet, leaving a hell of a mess and half the security in the middle-zone looking for him. I doubt if anyone would look like a future Emperor given all that."

"You don't go for a few weeks, do you?" she asked.

He glanced at her, a slight smile on his face. He knew what she was up to. "No. Why?"

"It would be good to know more," she said. Everyone else on the board had access to the information she needed- how was she supposed to run a campaign, being the only candidate who didn't have it? "Please, Lich. You know how much I want to get in." She paused, priming him for the killer blow. "And if I do, think how much it will annoy Eevan."

70

"Playing dirty, eh?" He grinned, though. "You got me. What do you want to know?"

"Everything. His powers, what he can do, what he thinks about things, what he wants from us- "

"The colour of his underwear?" Lichio raised his eyebrows at her. She blushed, cursing herself for it, and he laughed. "Black."

"What?"

He grinned. "His underwear: it's black."

"You looked!"

He rolled his eyes. "Of course I didn't look- what do you take me for? I have some standards. The guy turned up without a change of clothes..."

"Of course, it's all army requisitions." It was hard to imagine the heir to the empire turning up as so many did at the Banned, owning nothing to his name. "Clever Lichio."

He got up and lifted his jacket. "I better go, then, start my mission." He wiggled his fingers as if he was a magician. "See if he's actually managed to complete training for today. In fact, there's your first bit of intel." He smirked. "Whatever powers he might have, he's a truly crap soldier."

She got up too, brushing herself off. It was getting hotter. She glanced at the practice ground, remembering her own basic in the blistering heat, and it was hard not to feel sorry for the recruits.

"Be careful," said Lichio, his voice low and serious. "When I'm away- Eevan is still here; watch yourself."

She drew her shoulders back, acting braver than she felt. "I can deal with Eevan, you know that. He might think he's Dad's equal and should lead the group; I don't. I need to get back to work, Lich."

"That's two of us." He grinned. "Agent one, at your service."

CHAPTER SIXTEEN

Stitt put her hands on her hips. "Dismissed!" said Stitt.

Kare sat on the grass, the sunshine pounding on his back, and drank some water. He passed the bottle to Silom, who took a long drink and passed it back for Kare to tip the remainder over his head. It ran through his crew cut and down his face and gave some relief, but he knew from experience it would be temporary.

"I'm knackered," said Silom.

Kare looked up at the sky; it was getting late and the heat should fall soon. It still astonished him, how quickly it changed from day to night here. "At least you haven't had extra duties. I never knew I could be so tired and still move." Not just move- run, take obstacle courses, do weaponry drills.

"Spare me- you brought it on yourself."

Kare looked over and saw Captain Stitt watching him. "More of Stitt's shit coming up," he said, and stood before she had the pleasure of summoning him. At least it was the last day of his two weeks. "Save me some food."

He started to pick up the equipment the squad had left out. He wasn't aching the way he had every other day. Perhaps he was getting used to the work.

"Varnon," said Stitt.

"Ma'am." He straightened.

"Put your backpack on," she said. He did and it settled across his shoulders, comfortable for now. She nodded at the trail round the base. "Twice."

He opened his mouth, wanting to protest. Twice was a six mile run, and he'd been on the training ground since early morning. Stitt stared at him, and he knew she was waiting for him to admit he was too tired.

"Yes, ma'am."

He set off, knowing the rest of the recruits were watching him, and ducked under a branch to join the trail, his boots hitting the ground, steady and sure. He hated this, absolutely hated it. The jungle was dense around him, the path beaten though it, and there were occasional flashes of bold reds and yellows as he disturbed the ever-present parakeets. They squawked as he passed, warning each other. He kept going and only realised he'd reached the practice ground when the foliage opened out. The other squaddies were gone. He stopped and lifted a bottle of water, taking a drink, and saw Stitt watching him from the edge of the jungle path. The shadows had lengthened as the day fell towards evening.

"Sooner you get on with it, sooner you're done. Or are you too crap to finish?" she said.

Kare shook his head, panting. He shrugged, shifting the backpack- it seemed to have doubled in weight- and crossed to the jungle path. It was darker under the canopy, the daylight fading, and his feet were less sure, stumbling with tiredness, every step draining him further.

He stopped for a moment to get his breath. Glancing back, he knew Stitt was too far away to sense if he used his psyche to make his legs less tired. Take the weight of the backpack. The jungle was quiet around him, the birds roosting, any emerging night animals waiting for him to move on. No one would know. He paused, on the verge of using it–

He would know. Worse, he'd never know if he could have completed the run without resorting to his power. It had never seemed important before now- his powers were a part of him the way his eyes were, or the birthmark on the back of his ankle. But over the past weeks, as he'd got used to not relying on them as often, he'd found himself wondering how much of who he was lay with them, and how much came from somewhere deeper, somewhere close to the centre of him. Somewhere more honest.

He started to jog again. Dim lights from the road running between the base and barracks punctured the shadows from time to time. He was utterly drained, hungry and thirsty, his shoulders aching, but he concentrated on each step, each single step, one after the other, on and on through the jungle.

The path evened out as he reached the practice ground. He shrugged the pack off and leaned forward, hands on his knees. The ground swam under him, and for a moment he was sure he'd either pass out or throw up, but his vision cleared. He took a deep breath and straightened. Stitt stepped out of the darkness and handed him a bottle of water which he took and drank deeply from.

"I don't want a repeat of your cheating," she told him.

Kare nodded and wiped his mouth. "Ma'am." His voice was small, but he didn't care. Frankly, it was a miracle he had the strength to speak.

"Put away your pack. Consider yourself dismissed."

"Yes, ma'am."

He saluted and she left him to take his pack to the shelter and set it with the others before making his way to the empty dorm. He smiled when he saw a sandwich sitting on his bunk. He'd have to thank Silom later.

He sank onto the bed and picked up the sandwich. A note sat on his pillow- IN REC-ROOM- but he was too tired to get up again. Instead, he finished the sandwich and lay back. He had no idea how long he slept, but when he woke, the room was dark. At the sound of the other recruits returning, he turned onto his side. Someone kicked the end of his bunk and hands grabbed him, pulling him from his bed, ripping sleep away.

He tried to get away, but whoever it was held him firmly. He twisted, but it made no difference. He went to flex his power, but remembered Eevan's warning- using it against a person was bound to mean more than a couple of weeks washing floors. His head was pulled back. He tried not to show how scared he was, but could hear his harsh breaths and knew his attackers would, too.

A fist hit his stomach, forcing the breath from him. Someone else backhanded his face, cracking his nose, and he cried out at the pain. The hands holding him let go and he crashed to the ground. He tried to crawl to the corridor, but a kick sent him sprawling. The shadow of another boot came at him, and when it impacted with his chest there was another crack and a spear of pain. He screamed, hoping someone- anyone- was in the barracks and could hear him. He rolled into a ball, protecting his head. More kicks came, on the small of his back and across his shoulders. Blood ran down his throat, choking him. "Stop," he pleaded, the word muffled. Another kick. Another. Each thud was just a spark of pain, distant now.

"Enough," said a new voice. "Leave him alone."

The boots stopped kicking.

"Fuck off, Dester," said one of the voices.

"You fuck off, Ashe. You've made your point. Now leave him alone." There was a pause. "Unless you want to take me on, instead. I'm up for it, come on ahead."

Kare lay, not sure he'd be able to move, and wondered what was broken. His nose, definitely, and his ribs.

"Not tonight, Dester."

Silom laughed. "You haven't the balls to face someone your own size. Piss off, then."

The boots left and arms under Kare's shoulders pulled him to a sitting position, and leaned him against the wall. Silom's face blurred in and out. From him came joint waves of concern and anger. Anger, not just at the attackers but at Kare, for bringing more trouble onto himself.

"We need to get you to the doc," said Silom.

"Wait," croaked Kare.

"For what? Them to get a few mates and finish the job?" Silom reached up and turned on the light over Kare's bed. He crossed his arms, appraising. "You're in a right mess."

"I can fix it," Kare said. Silom's unspoken thoughts were right. This would bring more trouble, either from the recruits, or the Banned thinking he was divisive, that even in barracks he was a trouble-maker. He couldn't afford to give a reason to get rid of him. Sweat broke out across his brow as he focused on his ribs, fusing them. The pain worsened as they shifted, but he forced himself to keep going, taking his time; if he didn't get it right, they'd stay out of shape. A long groan left him as they straightened. He swallowed against a wave of nausea.

"You need a doctor," said Silom. Kare couldn't answer him, but he shook his head. The pain in his chest eased, and he was able to breathe.

He took a deep breath and thought about how his nose should look, dreading what he had to do. He started to straighten the bones. They crunched and ground against each other, bringing tears to his eyes.

"That's gruesome," Silom said. His voice sounded like it was far away.

"It's fucking agony," Kare gasped. If Karia had been here she'd have fixed it in seconds. He half expected her to appear, but she didn't- that part of returning to base seemed to have stopped. He braced himself for one last effort, clenching his fists and, teeth gritted, forced his nose straighter until the pain ended.

"It's not straight," Silom said.

"How bad is it?"

"It's okay. Makes you look tough."

"Tough's good." He couldn't face any more, not tonight. "Can you help me up?"

Silom held a hand out and Kare pulled himself up with it, onto his bunk. He started to shudder, and even when he wrapped his arms around himself, the shaking didn't slow. His teeth chattered as he said, "T-thanks, Silom."

"I noticed one of them checking me out before they left." His anger seemed to have abated- he sounded more resigned than anything. "I figured I'd see what they were up to."

"W - Who was it?"

"Ashe, Raj, Tommy and Chang."

"Why?" asked Kare. Nothing was making any sense to him. "I haven't said two w-words to them."

Silom got off his bed, leaned down and touched a blood spot on the floor. He held his finger up. Kare looked at it. That was his blood, and it was all over the floor in huge droplets. He swallowed against the returning nausea.

"I suspect it's their way of telling you they don't like you." Silom stood up. "I'm going to get a cloth."

Kare sat, looking at the bloodstains, his body aching. He closed his eyes and remembered the hard boots coming for him. At the soft noise of movement, he looked up, expecting to see Silom. Instead, Lichio entered. He looked around the dorm, and then at Kare.

"You're okay?" he asked.

Kare nodded. *Okay?* He guessed so. "Yes."

Lichio came over to where Kare was sitting and looked at the blood on the floor. "I was told you weren't."

"You were told wrong," said Kare, but he was shaking again.

Lichio sat down on Silom's bed. "Do you want to tell me who it was?"

Kare shook his head. "Nothing happened."

"I heard you had a couple of broken bones and a medic would be needed." Lichio looked Kare up and down. "Now, you've obviously dealt with that– and I'm not going to take that further. To be honest, given the chance, I'd do the same. But I need to know who it was."

Kare looked directly at him. "I don't know what you're talking about. Nothing happened, and if it did, it happened in the dark and I couldn't see anyone. I'm fine."

Lichio stood. "Your choice," he said. "I can't force you." He rubbed his face, fingers tracing the line of his jaw. "But, look... if you need someone to talk to, you know where I am."

Kare stood too, relieved his legs were able to hold him. "I appreciate it. But really, nothing happened."

Silom came in and Lichio moved towards the door. "I'll leave you to it."

Kare watched him go as Silom started to wipe the blood from the floor. He sank onto the bed and put his head back; three more weeks and he was through basic training and would be assigned a proper squad. It had to be better than this.

CHAPTER SEVENTEEN

ichio rapped on the door of his brother's office, waiting until the low voice told him to enter. He stepped in and stood to attention.

"At ease." Eevan leaned back in his soft chair. "I believe congratulations are in order. A lieutenant, no less. Sit down, why don't you?"

Lichio sat and tried to ignore his heart jumping at the compliment, annoyed that his brother's regard meant anything to him. Still, he smiled, not able to stop himself. "Thanks."

"You wanted to see me?"

Lichio stretched his legs out- the pleasantries had been shorter than usual today. "Yes, thanks, sir. There was an incident in the barracks last night."

"An incident?" Eevan picked up his data pad and opened it, his movements relaxed. "What sort of incident?"

"One of the new recruits got hurt."

"Really? Which one?"

"Varnon." Lichio paused, remembering the blood, the bed kicked out of place. "It wasn't as severe as it first looked, but I thought you should know."

A frown crossed Eevan's face. "That's lucky. Has he got steel skin, do you think, or did the boots miss?"

Lichio frowned, sure he hadn't said how Kare had been injured.

"They got interrupted," he said. He kept his focus on his brother, but Eevan's face was impossible to read. "Varnon's big mate stopped them. He was lucky."

"Very. Do you know who they were, the attackers?"

Lichio shook his head. "No, I don't." He smiled, very slightly. "Do you?"

Eevan pointed his finger across the desk. "Your smart mouth's going to get you into trouble, Lich." He closed his data pad. "I don't think there's anything to report here. He cheated and these things cause a response sometimes. I trust this will go no further."

Lichio sat a moment longer, remembering how shook up Kare had been, and then nodded. "No, I can see that it shouldn't."

"You're welcome. Did I hear something about you going to Corun?"

He smirked and Lichio struggled to keep his voice steady. "Yes, that's right."

"It's a hellish place. Let's hope it's a short placement."

Lichio stood, wondering who had chosen Corun. Actually, *knowing* who had. Sometimes his brother was a hard person to like. "Let's hope so. May I leave, sir?"

"Go right ahead."

He let himself out and stopped in the corridor. If Eevan had it in for Varnon, it wouldn't stop here. And even if he wasn't close to Varnon- hard to see how anyone could be when the bloke had a wall around him that screamed keep away- he didn't envy anyone in the firing line of Eevan.

He wasn't close to his brother, either- there were too many years between them- but he knew the dark anger behind the vicious attack, done from afar with the touch of a real bully.

He turned to leave. It was none of his business. In a couple of days he'd have left for Corun, and Kare Varnon would be someone else's to look after. Except... Sonly had asked if he was Emperor material and, in truth, the answer was no. Not at all.

And yet, there was something about Varnon, a way of dealing with what came his way and getting on with it. He'd dealt with Stitt's shit as well as anyone Lichio had seen and, whilst he'd been shaken up last night, he'd held himself together. He could be important to the Banned if they could bring that out of him: too important for Eevan to go too far with, and he damn nearly had last night.

He walked down the corridor and knocked on Colonel Rjala's door. He must be mad, doing this. But he hated bullies. More than that, he couldn't *stand* being told what to do, especially by Eevan.

"Come in!" The crisp voice made him automatically straighten and check his uniform.

He went into the familiar, sparse office. No plaudits on the wall here, to soften the sense of a desk in a barracks that could be moved at any time. The only personal touch was a single holo, in a small enough setting to be grabbed in a moment and shoved in a pocket. Behind the desk Colonel Rjala sat, her greying hair cropped close to her face, her blue eyes steady.

"Lichio," she said. "Can I help you?"

Lichio walked over and she indicated for him to sit. "Ma'am," he said. "May I speak off the record...?"

***

78

At the practice ground, Kare faced Ashe, and enjoyed a sense of satisfaction at his confused face. If he could complete the course, his day would go a long way to making up for the night before. Eevan might have been behind the beating– he was sure he had to be– but Ashe had no doubt been the ringleader of the attackers.

The whistle blew and he ran, clearing the hurdles easily. Grabbing the rope, locking his foot in it, he climbed the wall. He jumped down, slipped a little in the mud, and ran to the monkey bars, leaping and missing them. He stepped back, took a breath to settle himself, and tried again, this time catching the bar. Moving across, he still struggled, but the rhythm came a little easier. At the end he jumped into the water and gasped at the cold as he waded through.

When he stepped out, his boots were slippery and he took a moment to plan his climb. He started, planting every step before he took another, and was close to the top when his right foot slipped from its support. His left hand loosened, two fingers pulled back by the force, but he managed to hold on. He scrabbled with his foot, but there was only empty air. His right hand started to pull off the wall, and he tried again to find the support. This time his foot caught the edge of it, and he was able to steady himself. He curled his injured fingers back onto the handhold– *gods, that hurt*– and pulled himself to the top. His hands slipped into the sling, and he waited for the okay before launching into the long swoop to earth. Hell, it mightn't have been graceful, or fast, but at least he'd finished.

He landed to the sound of clapping and looked up to see Lichio giving a slow round of applause. Kare walked over, cradling his injured fingers, and Lichio fell into step beside him.

"Well done, Karl."

Kare raised an eyebrow. Lichio handed him a bunch of papers and Kare took them with his good hand; they were identification documents in the name of Karl Bell. He smiled. *An invisible man, just like I was an invisible boy.* "When do I go?"

"Transport's ready. Silom - who's now Simon - is already on board. If we have to hide you both, it's safer having you in one platoon. The less who know, the less chance there is of a leak."

"What about basic?"

Lichio shrugged. "The powers that be say you can finish in the field."

He wasn't being kicked out, then; he'd convinced them of that, at least. And he wasn't going to be left to be Eevan's punchbag, either, which was good. "Who knows my identity?"

"Colonel Rjala, the chair of the board and the major. That's it."

"And you," said Kare. "I'm not being rude, but what relevance is it to you?"

"I'm going, too. The colonel wants a link man for you. I'm it." Lichio made a face. "And it's sir."

"Sir?"

"You don't think I'm going in as a private, do you?" Lichio looked mildly horrified. He tapped the insignia on his shoulder, a crouched Lynx, teeth bared. Somehow it suited him. "It's Lieutenant le Payne, and that's Sir to you. Private."

Kare waited a moment, not sure what to make of that comment. In fact, not entirely sure what to make of Lichio le Payne. Silom had warmed to him over the last few weeks, and that was a good sign, but he kept himself too guarded for Kare to be sure of him. Slowly, he felt his face break into a smile. He liked him, he decided, surprised.

Later, after a shower, he sat on one of the window seats of a transporter as it started its long, slow launch. The seats reclined, but that appeared to be the only bit of comfort; cargo space obviously had priority over the passengers.

He braced for the first moment he dreaded, when the inertia regulator took effect. His stomach churned, partly through habit, he was sure, until the initial launch was completed and he could lean forwards and look out the viewing window.

The Banned base had disappeared into the jungle, the lush green fading as they rose through the clouds and reached the high blue sky of the final atmosphere. There was a jerk as the ship switched to its star drive, the usual rush of sickness, and space blurred around them.

CHAPTER EIGHTEEN

Six months later

Michael snapped his data pad off. "The inertia-reg will switch over in a moment," said Michael.

Sonly made a face– she hated landings– and closed her data pad. She put her head back as her stomach lurched, then settled. It was over so quickly, it was silly to get tense about it.

"Okay?" Michael put his hand on her arm.

"Yes, thanks." It was worth a space flight to get the chance to meet ambassadors from the Great Families. That it was being held at the busy Ferran hub, with the added element of discovery and danger, made her excitement swell and hands tingle; she *had* to do well. She turned her thoughts to the meeting ahead, and the thing that had been niggling her through the flight. "Why are both the ambassadors meeting us now? Isn't it sudden?"

Michael pulled at his greying beard, taking his time. "With us negotiating traffic allowances with the hub, we're close to holding the outer rim. Tortdeniel want to get into the communities, improve their education and tie extra planets to them. Balandt get to extend their banking interests. The outer rim gets the type of development we can't fund."

Sonly shook her head. "That's all very plausible. But both of them? We've had the upper hand in Ferran since last year, and it's now they want to deal?" Her eyes narrowed. "They know about Kare, don't they?"

"Yes. What of our young heir? Any progress?"

She took her time: Michael knew she'd been getting word from Lichio and that it had included snippets about Kare. But she didn't want to reveal just how much. She was a little surprised, herself– next time the Banned decided they needed a super spy, she'd nominate Lichio.

"He says he has no interest in becoming Emperor," she said. Her seat shifted a little as the ship touched down. "He wants to replace it with something else."

Michael cursed, and her eyes widened. Usually he was

circumspect around her, treating her like one of his granddaughters.

"That," he said, "will never be supported by the families."

"I know. But, you know, the Banned were formed to oppose her, and there's a part of me that thinks Kare has it right and we *should* remove everything that bitch has built."

"Quite the rebel."

"Maybe," she said, shrugging. "And I know what you're thinking: aspirations aren't going to win the war."

"Exactly. Which means we need to work on Kare. When is he due back from Corun?"

"They leave tomorrow."

Michael undid his seat fastenings and pulled his long jacket over his shoulders, not bothering with its sleeves. With its silver trim, it gave him a gravitas she had no hope of emulating. "He's eighteen and has never had tutelage in politics. When he gets back, he'll have learned the basics of the military- "

"The very basics, he needs more- "

"Granted. Rjala can work on that; we'll work on the political side." He paused. "I think I might arrange for you to do that- he'll be more comfortable with someone his age, it's less likely to put his back up at the start."

Another sign of trust. She resisted the urge to smile, getting up and stretching instead. "That means he's staying on the base. Isn't that risky?"

"With a new identity."

Sonly shook her head. "It's no good. Lichio says anyone who knew Ealyn will recognise him. A new identity hides nothing."

"Surgery? It's expensive, but ..."

And painful. "There might come a time when we're glad he looks like one of his parents," she said. "We should reignite the old tales about Ealyn and the twins, so that when he meets the families there will be no denying whose son he is. That builds the link back to the Banned."

They moved to the hatch, and Michael turned to her as it opened. "Good. You know, if you *do* want to follow your father's legacy, you need to be able to take decisions- rational, planned decisions, not emotional ones- *and* know you're doing it for the right reasons. Aspirations, like you say, won't win the war."

"I know." Even so, she was glad today was about trading agreements and not Kare, because she didn't know how she felt. They were using his name everywhere, and he hadn't said they could. It didn't seem right. But if they didn't....

Michael stepped onto the ramp and she followed, focusing on the two people waiting at the bottom. The private docking bay they had been allocated was empty, but the Ferran insignia reminded her to be careful. The wrong eyes, the wrong person hearing her name could be lethal. It was, she suspected, one of the reasons Michael had brought her: being so young and not yet on the board, her face would be relatively unknown.

"Louis," Michael said. He shook the first ambassador's hand, and Sonly decided– he was so tall and thin– that he must be the Balandti. Michael turned to her. "This is my associate, Sonly le Payne." He nodded to the other psycher, a woman. "And this is Margueritte Tortdeniel."

Sonly stepped forward, holding out her hand. "It's lovely to meet you."

Margueritte nodded. "Darwin's daughter?"

"Yes." Sonly looked at her traditional Tortdeniel dress, high collared, its rich blue material shimmering in the light, and wished she could have something so lovely.

"It's nice to meet you, Sonly," said Louis. He contrasted against Margueritte's colour, in the traditional Balandt black from head to toe. Even his boots, polished beyond what seemed possible, were jet in colour. She supposed it was the banker-genes running through the Balandt family– she'd never come across one who was anything but painfully sober. "I met your father, once, when he was still with the Empress' army."

"That must have been a long time ago."

"Nearly thirty years." He gestured down the corridor. "This way."

Sonly followed, moving a little closer to Margueritte. "Your dress– it's beautiful," she said. "I just had to tell you."

The Tortdeniel's face broke into a smile, and Sonly relaxed a little. She'd been worried it was the wrong thing to say.

"Thank you. Very few people mention it. Especially the men; clothes are wasted on them."

Sonly's eyes opened slightly, and she paused, not sure how to respond. The other woman's eyes challenged her but a smile remained in place. Finally, Sonly shrugged slightly, and said, "Well, what can you say about black?"

They walked into a small boardroom and Sonly pulled out her data pad, bringing up the figures she had prepared for the meeting. If they could pull this off, there was a nice income stream for the Banned; a five percent levy for access to the Banned-controlled outer zone was more than reasonable.

Michael paused at the door. "The facilities? May I?"

"Second on the right," said Louis.

Both ambassadors sat opposite Sonly, and there was an awkward silence. The Balandti smiled, his eyes meeting hers, and he seemed friendly enough for all his long face and thinning hair. "We hear your group has had an interesting... arrival."

She fought to keep her face straight, and not look around for Michael. "Arrival?"

"We heard," said Margueritte, "that the Empress' son is alive and with the Banned."

What should she say? If they were voicing it so openly, they knew, and she needed them to trust her. "Yes, that's true."

"And does he support the Banned? Is he standing with you against the Empress?" Balandt's voice was casual, but his posture was on edge, alert, and she warned herself to be careful.

She gave a smile she hoped was relaxed. "Yes, of course. He came to us, not Abendau."

"And he is in the position to take the Emperorship, should his mother... pass on?" Margueritte asked. She, too, was alert but there something in her eyes, something just a little less calculating, that made Sonly sure she understood more of the nuances of the situation. Had she grasped why Kare was with the Banned, and how he felt about the empire? If so, caution had to come first: none of the great families could get any hint of Kare's feelings about the empire. Change could be a threat to any of the families, supported and enriched by the status quo as they were. Even remaining under the Empress, paying her tariffs and abiding by her rule, might be preferable. It was impossible to know for sure- the game was too finely played between the families; nothing was ever as it seemed on the surface. It was why she loved politics.

She picked up the glass in front of her, took a sip of water and set it down. *Come on, Michael.* The two ambassadors watched her. Michael had said she had to be prepared to take hard decisions and stand over them. She sent a mental apology, smiled, and said, "Absolutely. He is committed to overthrowing the Empress and continuing her empire in a peaceful manner."

The door closed behind her and Michael slipped into the seat opposite her. Their eyes met for a short moment, and he gave her the slightest of nods. Her smile widened, and then she looked down at her hands and it faded. She'd promised something she might not be able to deliver.

"But that's for the future," Michael said to the ambassadors.

"He's currently undergoing tutelage in the military and politics. When it's time, you'll meet him and have a chance to discuss it further. Now, we're proposing a ten percent levy."

There was a harsh laugh from the Balandti. "We pay the Empress four." Margueritte may be the ambassador who grasped the nuances of the people she dealt with, but when it came to numbers, no one sneaked anything past a Balandt. It was why they had the richest planet, with its huge financial district under a glittering dome that had cost millions of credits and provided a means of reducing the gravity so non-worlders could utilise the financial hub.

Sonly broke in. "That's for legal trading routes, and you pay taxes on top of that. This is illegal; the Banned planets carry the risk of attack and protect you from it. Ten is fair. You'll have to come up."

"And you down."

Sonly met his eyes, the typical pale blue of his people, and held his gaze. It was going to be a long day. Which was fine: she had all day. She pulled her shoulders back, pasted a smile on, and said, "Eight. That's our lowest; any further and we aren't gaining anything from this."

CHAPTER NINETEEN

Kare crawled under the table, cursing the wall's disrepair- if he managed not to electrocute himself on the exposed cabling, he'd be lucky. He worked his way through the wires, matching colours, until he completed the last connection and backed out, the smell from the old flooring making him gag. A shower, that was the first thing he'd do at barracks. Then he remembered he wasn't going back to barracks; it would have to wait until his transporter was established in hyperspace.

He stood and looked around the group in front of him, taking in their mismatched uniforms and inconsistent weaponry. They ranged from a girl of about thirteen up to a man who looked well into his eighties.

"Okay, then." Kare pointed at the computer system he'd taken apart and rebuilt over the last week, pleased to see lights pulsing on its control panel- at least it still worked. "This direct-links the Corun comms to the Banned fleet. It will be much, much quicker. That's the weaponry tied in, too."

"Karl!" called a familiar voice. "Time to go."

Kare joined Silom, answering a flurry of questions as quickly as he could. As they stepped outside they were surrounded by children.

"Do the magic," one of children said, a boy of about seven, with a grubby face and eyes that were too big for the rest of him.

"I can't," Kare said, "I have to go."

"Please," asked another child.

There was a clamour of voices and Kare raised an eyebrow in question. Since Silom's promotion to lance-corporal, he outranked Kare. For now; he was doing okay in the tech squad. Better than okay, now he'd learned the systems.

"Five minutes." Silom's voice was stern, but Kare could tell he was struggling not to smile.

The children gave a small cheer as Kare reached into one of his pockets and took out a sweet. The lad who'd been brave enough to ask first focused on the sweet, and his eyes widened even more. Kare paused, angry- what they really needed was a decent meal, but he couldn't give them that. Instead, he'd raided most of the sweets in the barracks, exchanging whatever tokens he had for them. There was nothing to buy here, anyway; pretty much everything was embargoed- the system's alignment with the Banned had cost them what little support they'd had from the Al-Halad family. He hoped the rebels were making things better and not worse. He wished he could make the planet better. He wished he could provide a newer dome, one that let enough sun in for crops to establish. Each wish was as useless as the last- all he could do was his job: train them; establish reliable comms to military support; entertain their kids. It felt like very little. He tossed the sweet from hand to hand. "Whose ear is sore?"

The children laughed, and pointed to a little girl in the first row who flushed at the attention. Kare took the sweet and moved it quicker than they could see, then drew it out from behind the girl's ear. He gave her the sweet, and she grinned at him. He flicked his wrist and more sweets flew out, landing in the hands of the children, his aim exact. He let one float down, over their heads, like a butterfly, and delivered it precisely into the last empty hand.

"That's me, I'm cleaned out," he told them, and turned away.

"If you ever jack in the army, we could use you as a kid's entertainer," Silom said.

"Their childhood makes mine look idyllic- it's nice to give a bit of happiness," said Kare. They started along the path leading from the city to the barracks. "At least Lichio is more open minded than his brother about psyching. You heard him: so long as I was careful, and it was outside barracks, he was okay with it."

"Only 'cos you scared the living hell out of him, telling him it'd build up if he didn't. I think he thought you might blow up the barracks."

Kare grinned at the memory of his meeting with Lichio. "It's true, though, I do need to use it. I saw what that did to my dad; I don't intend for it to happen to me. So, it's practice all the way, making sure I keep up with it."

He crossed the street, avoiding Silom's eyes. Keeping up with it was getting no easier as he got older: each time he thought he'd mastered the power, it grew again. Sometimes it felt like it was going to explode out from his ears, that he couldn't hold it any longer. He sped up, glad to use up the energy in him- he'd *have* to control the power; who knew what would happen if he didn't. On a good day, he'd probably only take a few buildings with him...

"You worry too much," said Silom, catching up. "Tell you what, I'll be bloody glad to get back to the base. I'm fed up with grey."

Kare nodded. Before he'd arrived, he hadn't believed Lichio when he'd said Corun was as grim as anywhere in the outer zone.

Now he knew better: the grass, the buildings, even the people looked grey. He glanced up at the dome covering the city, reinforced to the point where most natural light had been filtered out. On the central planets it'd be a smart-dome, maintained by a force-field, but here an old-fashioned, self-sustaining dome was all the planet– or the Banned– could afford. The greyness might be a small price to pay for protection against the toxic air beyond, but he yearned for real air and warm sunlight.

"That's two of us." Kare checked his comms unit. "We're going to be late."

They started to jog towards the barracks and space dock, taking the road rather than going through the park. When he'd first arrived, the heavy gravity had made it impossible to run; now, after months of training– it turned out Lichio could give Sergeant Stitt a run for her money– he easily ran past the mix of families on their way to the park and workers on lunch. He and Silom reached the space dock with a few minutes to spare. They pulled into formation.

"About time," said the corporal in front.

"Sorry."

The light changed and the airlock leading from the dock, through the dome to the space-side, opened. They followed the squad through the short connecting tunnel onto the transport.

Kare sat beside Silom and strapped himself in, pulling out his data pad. A thud from below indicated the last of the equipment had been stowed, and the launch engines started up. He kept his head down, preferring to focus on the figures– the comms on Corun had been challenging to get right, and now he knew the configurations he didn't want to lose them. Even so, he had to steel himself for the familiar stomach lurch. It settled a moment later, and he relaxed. At another lurch, he glanced at Silom. "We've changed course."

Silom swore. He nodded to the front of the transport. "They're getting the masks out."

"Shit." Kare focused on the commanders, bunched at the front of the transport, and listened in, knowing he shouldn't.

Rawle had leaned close to Lichio, his jaw tight and tense. His words were too low for the soldiers to make out. "We're the nearest unit." He took a quick look along the ship, as if doing a head count. "We have to go back."

Corun grew larger in the view port. They *were* returning, and at speed. Word spread through the platoon. Charl unstrapped and took his place at the inventory, lifting weapons out, checking each for its charge before allocating it to his sergeant to hand out. Kare took his, checked it a second time and saw Silom pull an extra charge pack out of his equipment bag. He wished he'd thought to do that.

"Get the masks prepared." Lichio's voice was crisp, its usual laconic edge gone.

Silom exchanged a sharp glance with Kare. Rawle moved between the aisles of the ship, handing out breathing masks and deflecting any questions. Sharp fear came off him in waves, making Kare's breathing tight. Something had happened, something big. If it came to combat, let him be up to it. Let him not freeze or panic. He tried to tell himself he hadn't on Dignad, but that had been different.

People were in danger here, people he'd been living amongst for months. He'd focus on them, make it personal if that's what it took. He pulled his mask on, the musty smell off-putting at first, but easing after a couple of breaths. The voices from the rest of the platoon became muted and anonymous, their ranking designators the only means of identification.

As the ship re-entered the atmosphere, Kare joined his designated squad at the rear exit. Silom stood beside him, weapon cradled, radiating calm. Lichio braced at the hatch.

"We're covering the east." Lichio's voice was steady, but his eyes skittered over the squad. It would be his first time leading a platoon, Kare guessed; at seventeen, even with a lifetime at the Banned behind him and four years in their army, it was a heck of a responsibility. "As soon as we land, deploy, and move into the city. This is a pick-up; any survivors, we get them out. There are ships en route from Phoenix base for the other settlements."

"Sir, will there be hostiles?" asked Silom.

"No, it was a series of air strikes against the domes. There were no reports of hostile fire."

Lichio pulled his mask on as the ship set down and the hatch opened. The squad exited in formation, with Lichio last to leave. The ship's engines whipped up the sparse grass, and they moved forward, weapons cradled, over the flat landscape.

Lichio pointed to his left. "Karl, Simon, keep to the middle. Charl and Rawle, move ten feet further out. Keep in contact with me."

Kare stepped forward with Silom, his eyes squinting against the light. Light? He put his head back and saw the dome wasn't cracked, but shattered, letting sunlight stream into the city. Bodies lay all around them, some on the grass, others in their transports. They looked like they were asleep. He knelt beside one– the garage owner who supplied the base– and put his hand on his throat.

"No pulse," he told Silom, who nodded and walked on.

Kare followed, his eyes sweeping across the outskirts of the city, focusing on the minutiae; it was easier that way. He saw a small family, just ahead, and went over to them. The mother lay, hugging a child close to her, his head turned to her. Beside them was another child of about seven. He guessed they'd been trying to get to one of the breathing stations. He pushed the child's hair from her forehead, and his breath hitched.

"Silom," he croaked, his voice carrying over their closed comms band. "Is it?"

Silom nodded. It was the girl whose ear Kare had taken the sweet from. He wiped a smudge of dirt off her face. She reminded him of Karia. That thought took the breath from him, and his eyes moistened. He blinked and looked towards the town's park, where he'd taken a jog around the lake and past the playground most mornings. Were bodies littering it, too?

His fists clenched. They'd known when they attacked the dome the children would die just as quickly as the rebels. Some might have been close enough to get to a breathing station, but very few, not with such an impact. He looked up at the dome; it seemed a lot of trouble for a planet with as little going for it as Corun. A task force would have come from the middle zone systems, spent weeks in hyperspace, and risked Banned-controlled space. All for a remote planet that couldn't defend itself, let alone present a danger to the empire. It didn't even have any minerals worth mining.

"Why does the Empress want somewhere like here?" A chill rose through him. "Surely her empire is big enough."

"I think it'll never be big enough," Silom said. "She's greedy."

She was, too. She'd killed the people here for greed, just because she could. Kare pulled his mask off. Toxic air assailed his throat. It stank, a high, acrid smell that hit the back of his nose, making him snort against it. This was how the child had died: she must have been terrified. He coughed as his throat closed. This was how a whole city had died.

Hands grabbed him, spinning him round.

"Put the mask back on!" Silom tried to reach it, but Kare tugged it on, protecting himself from the death surrounding them. An hour earlier, and he'd have been dead with the Corunians. He choked for another minute or so and then it eased.

"I had to know how she felt," he said, his eyes streaming.

"You're an asshole," said Silom.

Kare ignored him. An hour earlier, he'd have been under a table in a ramshackle building with no hope of getting out in time.

Cold realisation soaked though him, chilling him. Oh, gods...

"Mike on." The dull sound of the communicator filled his mask. "Cat 1."

He waited a moment. Come on, come on, he needed this dealt with. A voice echoed through the mask. "Le Payne here."

"Lieutenant, it's Karl."

"Go ahead, what have you found?"

Kare's eyes met Silom's. "We need to pull the platoon out, sir. They're here for us."

"Private, what have you found?"

Kare swallowed, his throat still burning. "Sir, Corun isn't the target. I think they're here for me. Why attack Corun– what's here for them? And we'd just left, sir. They knew we'd come back and be easy to locate."

There was a pause at the other end and then a quiet curse. Be smart, Kare urged; be as smart as I think you are. The volume in the comms unit increased as it was switched to platoon-wide.

"This is Lieutenant le Payne. Pull back to the transport. I say again, pull back to the transport."

Kare closed his eyes for a moment, sending a silent prayer of thanks, and pointed at Silom. "Let's go."

They started to run to the descending transport, Rawle and Charl converging from the right, just ahead of them. As they neared the ship, a thin needle of laser passed them and Rawle fell to the ground, clutching his leg. A second beam passed and Charl fell, too, his screams louder. Kare hesitated, but Silom pushed him forward and they hit to the ground, near the rear hatch. A moment later Lichio joined them, weaving across to the transport.

Kare looked up and saw, coming in formation, at least two platoons, maybe more, of the Empress' army. Lichio crawled forward and lay flat on his stomach, taking aim, surprising Kare with his professionalism. Beside him, Silom fired, too, their shots keeping up a continuous rhythm.

"Where's the rest of the platoon?" yelled Kare. He brought his own weapon round, all his training making it a smooth movement, one done without thinking. He opened fire. Lichio jerked his head at the transport.

"Get on."

"We can't leave them!" Kare started to get up but Lichio pulled him down.

"If you go back, you're dead." He nodded to the transport. "Go!"

Kare paused. "Sir, I can get me and Silom over to them and back. I can use my power to make a shield."

"You're sure?"

"Yes." He could be back on Dignad, desperate and scared. Nothing had changed. "I've done it before."

Lichio looked at where the two injured soldiers lay. "Okay, go."

Kare nodded and scrambled over to Silom, refusing to pay attention to his throat narrowing in fear and the blood coursing so quickly that he could hear it booming in his ears. "Stay close."

He stood, Silom beside him, and brought the shield up around them. Silom tensed.

"Calm down," Kare said. "I can't hold it if you fight me."

Silom nodded and relaxed a little, letting him strengthen the shield. He took as much time as he dared, smoothing it, making sure it was strong. Satisfied, he took a deep breath. "Run!"

Kare stayed as close to Silom as he could. They sprinted the fifty yards to Rawle and Charl.

"You take Charl," said Silom. He pulled the bigger corporal to his feet, supporting him under his shoulders. Kare did the same with Charl, and half-dragged him towards the transporter. As they reached the front of the ship, the shield weakened. Kare's head thudded and he put his free hand on Silom's back, focusing on keeping him within the decreasing shield wall. Charl seemed to grow heavier with each step.

"Quicker," he gasped. Silom sped up, running along the side of the ship. Rawle used his good leg to support him, making it look like they were running a drunken three-legged race.

A laser, aimed at either Rawle or Silom, hit the shield and Kare was sure he couldn't hold the shape any longer. He released some of the protection around him and focused on where it had hit, repelling it. Silom reached the back hatch, and Kare trailed Charl forward and stood in front of Silom and Rawle. He released the shield off them, backing up, staying close enough to block them with his shielded body, instead. The throbbing in his head eased and he strengthened the shield a little. He'd pay for this later.

Hands reached out, taking Charl from him, and Kare tried to control the shield so that it shrank but didn't fail. It didn't work. His power drained, and the whole thing collapsed. He tried to bring it back, but was too tired. He reached the hatch, but had to stop, dizzy. He put his hand out, bracing against the ship, and looked back at the blurred line of black soldiers, indistinct through his tiredness. They had a clear shot.

92

"Get in!" shouted Silom, and Kare stumbled backwards, into the ship. "Close the hatch!"

The ship lifted off and he turned his face away from the swirling dust. He heaved the heavy hatch to, struggling with it, and was relieved when Silom reached out and secured it. Kare waited for the light at the door to turn green and pulled his mask off. He coughed a little, the air not quite cleared but breathable.

"Karl!" At Lichio's shout he turned and hurried down the ship. He took a moment, assessing the wounded. Rawle's injury looked superficial, but Charl lay still, a laser burn across his whole lower back, through to the muscle and oozing in the middle. Kare put his hand on it, hoping he had enough power left in him.

"Hold him down," he said. "It'll hurt."

He wished he had Karia's ability to heal quickly and effortlessly. He put his hand on the wound and Charl screamed, trying to writhe away, held down by Lichio and Dane. His pain reached across to Kare, filling his head, making his own back ache. Kare tried to ignore it, but the pangs thudded through him; sometimes it was no fun being an Empath. He gritted his teeth and kept going until the pain eased, and he felt peace fall over the man, the peace of a body sinking into its recovery. He took his hand off, drained, and turned to tell Rawle he could do no more, but the wounded man caught his arm and stopped him.

"Don't. It'll heal."

Relief washed through Kare- he didn't know if he could face doing it again. It had brought back the memories of the escape from Dignad, when it hadn't been just one person's burning pain that had brought him to his knees, but a whole platoon's. Bile rose in him at the memory.

A hand clapped his shoulder and he turned to see Lichio. "You've done enough. Well done."

Kare looked at the silent faces of the squad. They hadn't known who he was, or what he could do. He could feel their shock, the residual distrust of a psycher tinging into something unpleasant. He wanted to tell them he hadn't changed, that he was still the same cack-handed private they'd been working with for months. The image of the dead girl on Corun flashed in front of him. He was the cack-handed private she'd been murdered for. He pushed past the watching soldiers and ran to the toilet.

He stood at the sink and fought the urge to retch the way he had in the shipyard on Dignad ten years before. That day, the last of the debris had burned up and fallen around him, like fireflies in the dying light, and he'd thought it was pretty. It hadn't been until he realised it was his ship: his home, his sister, his father, that he'd emptied his stomach- his whole self- onto the dry earth. Tonight it was the dead face of the girl that flashed in front of him, cramping him. He splashed water on his face until the cramps eased. Someone came in, but he didn't turn.

"Are you okay?" Silom's voice was calm, and he, at least, wasn't disgusted.

Kare nodded, but doubled over again. He swallowed and got his breath back. "They didn't shoot at me."

"You probably didn't notice. You were focused on the shield, and we were running."

Kare rubbed his mouth with the back of his hand. He stood and pushed through to the main section of the ship, and dropped into a seat. Lichio sat beside him.

"What about the other settlements?" Kare asked.

Lichio shook his head. "The same. I suppose if they came so far, it made sense to finish the job."

They looked at each other for a long moment, and Kare knew the other man had worked it out.

"They didn't shoot at me," he mumbled. "They had a clear shot when I was on the gangway, but they didn't shoot."

"I know," said Lichio. "I saw."

A *whole planet?* Kare went to say something to Lichio, and then clamped his mouth shut. He lifted his head enough to see Lichio's shocked, white face. *He knew, too. A whole planet.*

CHAPTER TWENTY

A hard shake woke Kare. The transport was quiet, almost empty, and it took a moment to work out where he was.

"We've landed," Lichio said.

Kare sat up and wiped his eyes, surprised he'd slept through a space landing. "Do you have any water?"

Lichio handed him a bottle from his backpack; with a drink, Kare's headache eased a little.

"You okay?" asked Lichio.

"I'm fine." Better than fine: he had two arms, two legs, and a set of lungs that worked– it was more than the people of Corun.

"Rawle and Charl are on their way to the medical centre. You're booked in, too."

"Why? I'm okay."

"I'm your officer, and I want you checked over."

Kare was too tired to argue. "Okay, sir."

He got up and followed Lichio from the ship. As they walked to the medical centre, the bright greens of the jungle, contrasting with splashes of red and orange, almost overwhelmed him, blurred one moment, glassine-like the next. A bird shrieked, making his head thud again. He glanced over– why was Lichio with him, and not Charl and Rawle? Even on Corun he'd stayed close. He stopped. "You weren't just there to lead the platoon."

"I told you I was there to link back. It also gave me some field experience," Lichio said.

Kare looked at Lichio for a moment longer, but couldn't pick up a lie. Lots of other sensations, yes: mild concern, caution, but no lie. His eyes narrowed: Lichio evidently had some knowledge of psychers.

"I'm surprised you wanted the experience, given where it was," Kare said.

Lichio shrugged. "I might not have been so keen if they'd told me about Corun before I accepted." He spread his hands. "I was offered the post before you were in the squad. Make of that what you will."

Kare cocked his head to the side, thinking what he knew of the other man: the brat of the family, his older brother the military star, his sister the rising political leader. How do you keep up with that?

By befriending a possible future Emperor, even one who didn't want the role? He started to laugh. "Do you think I'm a prize?"

If Lichio was in any way embarrassed, he hid it well. "I don't know. But I like to keep my options open."

Kare wanted to warn Lichio it was dangerous to come too close to him. To do that, he'd have to tell him about his dad's visions. He shook his head: the visions had died with Ealyn; he'd made his own future, and chosen his own path.

"I might not be the prize you want," he said, and left it at that.

"We'll see." They reached the hospital, and Lichio nodded to the doctor waiting. "A full scan, please. Top to bottom. I'll come, too."

Kare looked between the doctor and Lichio, realising what was being checked for.

"You're wrong," he said. "There was no opportunity to plant anything– it has to have been a security leak."

"I hope so. It'll be one of the few times I'm happy for someone to say I told you so."

The doctor handed Kare a robe. "Get dressed in that, and come through."

An hour later Kare sat beside Lichio on the edge of a hospital bed, cradling a coffee. In front of them, a screen showed a close up of Kare's stomach lining and the tracker attached to it. He went to take a sip of coffee but stopped, wondering what they'd planted the tracker in. He set the cup down.

"What do we do?" he asked.

"First, we get it out. After that, it'll have to go to Colonel Rjala," said Lichio.

A sinking feeling came, part dread, part resignation. He had to face her sometime, he'd known that from the moment he'd elected to stay in her army. He just wished it wasn't today, that he'd had more time to think about what he might say to her. "Why not the major?"

"She has the remit for security."

There was no point arguing; he had no chance of winning. "Fine."

Lichio looked at Kare. "You have a problem with that?"

"No." Kare was careful to keep his face impassive. Thankfully, the doctor came back a moment later.

"If you lie back, we'll get this done now," he said.

Kare lay down and something cold touched his navel. He stared at the ceiling, trying not to think about what was inside him, his skin tingling, becoming numb.

"It'll only take a few minutes," said the doctor. He nodded at Lichio. "You can wait outside, Lieutenant; I don't need an audience."

Lichio left, and the doctor turned on the spotlights, making Kare's eyes smart. He closed them and took a deep breath. His thoughts drifted to Colonel Rjala, bringing a bitter taste into his mouth as he remembered the day his father had been forced from the base. Logically, he knew it had been for the group, but...

They'd had so little, he and Karia. He remembered how jealous he'd been of the le Paynes, with their toys and space to play. The time he'd fought with Eevan it wasn't because he disliked the other boy, exactly. It was more that he wanted to *be* him, to have his own room and bed. Anything but their cramped ship, with its freezing cargo bay for a playroom.

A sharp tug in his stomach pulled him out of his thoughts, and he opened his eyes, gasping a little. The surgeon appeared in front of the light. "That's the offender," he said.

Kare looked up, not able to see the tracker, it was so small. "When?"

"No way of knowing. I'll have to report this, you know."

"I think Lieutenant le Payne has that in hand," he said. "Can I sit up?"

"Yes."

There was a sharp pain in his stomach when he did. He put his hand on it, healing it, the skin knitting smoothly together.

"Nice talent to have," said the doctor.

Kare smiled and held out his hand, letting the doctor drop the metal tracker into it. He clenched his fist: it was so small he was scared he'd lose it. "Is it still transmitting?"

"Probably not- they're programmed to stop once removed."

"Makes sense. No point chasing my shit around the outer zone..."

There was a discreet knock on the door and a nurse came in, carrying a uniform. Kare looked at it and raised an eyebrow.

"Lieutenant le Payne sent it."

"Thanks." Kare waited until the doctor and nurse left, and got dressed. It was the first time he'd worn his full uniform rather than field fatigues, and it was stiff and uncomfortable. He opened the door to find Lichio standing in the corridor, buttoning up his own formal jacket.

"There's a reason for this?" asked Kare.

"The colonel likes her soldiers to look professional."

They left the hospital, Kare holding the door for a nurse to pass through, and walked through the base to the military zone. They stopped when a voice called Lichio's name. Both men turned to see a blonde woman coming towards them: Sonly le Payne.

"You're back!" she said, and gave her brother a hug. Kare smiled at the change in Lichio. With everyone else he was slightly smug, a bit of a know-it-all, but the hug he gave his sister was genuine. Lichio saw Kare watching them, and pushed Sonly away.

"Just back," Lichio said. "We're on our way to see the colonel. There's been a bit of a security breach."

"I heard; it's more than a bit." She turned to Kare. "I'm sorry, I'm being rude. You're Kare, aren't you? I remember you from when you were a child."

"Sonly. It's nice to meet you again." She'd been the only person sorry to see them go, he remembered. She'd faced her father, barely to his waist height, and tried to insist he change his mind.

She nodded, and her eyes darkened. "I'm so sorry about Karia," she said. "I think about her a lot. We used to hunt for mice together."

A shard went through him at the casual way she said it. He remembered her coming back with Karia, both of them carrying mice. That had been during their last normal visit to the Banned, before his dad became ill. They'd been holding the mice against them, sure they were going to die. He remembered how their blonde and brown heads had been close together as they'd whispered about how to get the mice on board. His twin had met his eyes and he'd known he was going to be asked to help. He took a deep breath. "You made me smuggle them in and I got holy hell for it in the end. You know, you're the first person I've met who remembers her." Or the only one who was prepared to admit to it. His voice was hoarse. "It's nice; it makes her real."

She put her hand out, touching his, and her feelings connected with his mind, pushing everything away: Lichio, the base, the meeting with Rjala. Nothing mattered except her. The intensity made him dizzy and he had to pull his arm away. *Where had that come from?*

She looked confused, but managed a smile. "I'm sorry about Corun." She looked between him and Lichio. "All those people. You must have known some of them."

The memory of the little girl flashed in front of Kare. "Yes."

She reached out, touching him again, and it was like she was burning him, it was so intense. He swallowed, the words he was about to say forgotten, but couldn't bring himself to look away from her steady eyes. They stood for a moment like that and her eyes were so blue he could drown in them–

He jerked his arm away, breaking the connection. She wanted him for what he could bring the group, nothing else. Even now he could feel, under the concern, coolness like she was assessing

98

everything. She looked down at her hand and then back to him, her eyes full of confusion. Her conflicting emotions of concern and calm consideration thudded through him.

"We should go," he said. His voice sounded strangled and strange.

Lichio nodded. "We better, Sonly; the colonel is waiting. I'll drop round later."

"Fine," said Sonly, her eyes still fixed on Kare. "*Are* you okay, it must have been a shock that she'd traced you?"

She seemed so genuine, her eyes meeting his, no guile evident, and he started to wonder if he was wrong- it was almost impossible to fake that sort of emotion. His heart was beating loud and fast and hard-

Something hit his knee, and he looked down to see a ball at his feet.

"Sorry, mister!" said a boy of about seven from down the corridor.

Kare kicked the ball back to him. "No problem." He turned to Sonly, making sure he didn't touch her. "I'll see you again." He walked away.

"What the hell was that about?" Lichio said, as he caught up.

Kare didn't answer. *A prize.* What sort of crap thing was that to be? In his case, the worst sort. One who could suck them all into his dad's dark dreams, pull them down into the maelstrom ahead. He clenched his fists, wanting to hit out in frustration; he wasn't even normal enough to spend time sinking into a girl's eyes.

Lichio caught his arm. "Well?"

"Nothing," he said. *Everything.* "Are we nearly there?"

"Another couple of corridors."

They walked in silence, Kare's hand clasping the tracker. This was what his mother was capable of: finding him, hunting him, removing anything that stood in the way of getting him.

Lichio stopped and knocked on a door. He stood back and fiddled with his sleeve, and Kare's stomach jumped. When a calm voice told them to come in, he hung back, letting Lichio go first.

He followed, stopping in front of Colonel Rjala's desk. What was she was thinking when she looked at him? Did she see the boy she knew, or his dad? He hardly knew what his own thoughts were, flitting from the hideous day she'd forced him from the base to the day he'd returned, when she'd given him a chance. She was glad someone had survived, she'd said, but did she mean it? He could read nothing from her.

"At ease," she told them and nodded to the seats opposite. "Did you bring the tracker?"

Kare set it on her desk. She picked it up, looked closely at it, and then turned to Lichio. "Lieutenant, what do you make of this?"

"It had to be planted at the base," Lichio said. "There's no way they could have tracked Kare, otherwise. The platoon was isolated and I saw no evidence, at any time, of his identity becoming known."

"The attack, are you sure it was targeted?"

Lichio paused. "I don't see how else to view it, ma'am."

She nodded and turned her attention to Kare. "You agree?"

"Yes." He could barely meet her eyes, ashamed at having cost so many lives.

"What do we do with you?" she asked, and he lifted his head. "You warned us she would try to find you; perhaps it's time for you to suggest what happens next."

"I think you should keep me on the base," he croaked. Her eyes remained steady and he blurted out, his voice bitter, "Either that, or hand me over and get what you can for me."

Lichio looked at Kare, his mouth open, but Rjala didn't show any surprise. He kept his gaze on her, telling himself it wasn't a betrayal of Ealyn and Karia to be sitting with her. Except...she'd sent them to their deaths and he wanted her to know that. He clenched his fists, digging the nails into his hand, and told himself to calm down.

"The Empress might want you, but that won't make us give you to her. Quite the opposite, actually- we'll do what we can to keep you from her," Rjala said.

They hadn't when he was a child. The Empress had *always* wanted them. It was just now he was old enough to be useful to the Banned. His anger faded away, replaced by a dull ache. He was an outsider here, just as much as he had been on Dignad. The last months with the platoon, he had believed he fitted in, that going to the gym and the games room, even out to the bar to drink the local piss that passed for beer, made him normal.

"Keep me here," he said. "Have me scanned every week- I didn't expect a tracker, not in the short time she had. Be ready. I think she'll try to take me, rather than the base- she won't risk losing me. I'll be the shield you need to keep your people safe."

His voice was dull, his thoughts equally so- it was as if he was talking about a stranger.

"You expect her to try again, then?"

"Yes, sometime. She'll be patient, though. She'll wait for an opportunity, not rush it. She knew I was on Corun, must have known the whole time, but waited until I made a move. Just like on Dignad- she didn't assume I was dead, she waited. I can assure you that in the ten years I was there she did not know of me: I barely stepped out of the house; I was on no databases; I was invisible."

"I believe you."

"She'll know the tracker's been found, and she'll expect security to be increased. It won't be now she attacks; it'll be when you- and I- least expect it."

He fell silent. It was all so bloody unfair; he hadn't asked for this and didn't want it. If he could, he'd hand his power back and walk away, useless to anyone. Except- he turned his hands over and looked at the thin ribbon of blue on his wrist- they'd have to take his blood, too.

"A security detail?" Rjala asked.

Anything but that. He shook his head. "No. A security detail can be infiltrated, or swayed."

"We can assign good people- they'd be vetted."

They'd be dead. "No."

Even after Corun, they didn't get how remorseless she was. He thought about trying to tell Rjala again, and stopped. What was the point?

"Ma'am, what she offers will be enough to sway anyone," he said.

She tapped her fingers on the desk and finally nodded. "I'll put you in the tech division; your sergeant says you have an aptitude for it," she said. "They're a small team; it's easy to increase its general security."

He sat forward; this was his chance to prove he had more to offer than his blood and his powers. That he could be valuable for himself, not his heritage.

"Ma'am, you know I was helping to improve the comms systems on Corun? Some of what I did could extend out, make a difference to our inter-space time delay. I'd really love to take that further- "

"You misunderstand me," she said, her voice cutting across his words. "I don't intend for you to tell me what you're going to work at."

Disappointment filled him but he tried to bite it back. "Yes, ma'am."

She must have noticed because she smiled, a slightly warmer smile. "I'm not dismissing your ideas, but if it's good it'll be good in a year's time- better, in fact, more thought out."

It was good now. "Yes, ma'am."

She nodded. "As well as the tech team, we'll be introducing you to some of the work Michael does."

He tensed. "No, I'm not doing that."

She frowned. "It's not your choice."

"Ma'am, I'm happy to do whatever you like in the army, anything at all, but I will *not* be trained up to be a political tool.... I've had all my life to think about this." Years, cooped in the house, studying the great families, their liege planets, devouring every filche and book Marine brought home to him. "I'm not prepared to fill that role. With respect, ma'am."

Rjala leaned forward, across the desk. "Then you're a fool." He pushed his chair back, and her voice whipped across to him. "Sit there; you haven't been dismissed." She looked at Lichio, who'd been so quiet Kare had almost forgotten he was there.

"You are dismissed, Lieutenant- you did well on Corun," said Rjala.

Lichio stood, his eyes wide, surprised at either the dismissal or the compliment. "Thank you, ma'am."

There was silence until he left the room and then she turned her attention back to Kare. He tried to read her, but couldn't. He blinked: it was rare for someone to stay so hidden from him.

"Do you think it's just the Empress who wants you?" she asked.

"Of course not; most of the great families do as well. Do you want me to list them, tell you which will want to keep me alive and which will want to kill me? I *know* all this, Colonel."

She paused for a moment. "I think you've decided that if you say no, and say it loudly enough, that's it. That if you keep refusing, no one can force you to it."

"Yes, ma'am." He kept his voice bland, uncomfortable at how close she was coming to his thoughts.

"I suspect you're feeling sorry for yourself, wishing it wasn't like this."

He swallowed and ducked his eyes from her scrutiny.

"All you're doing is making yourself the weakest person in the game," she said. "With only one card to play. And if that card gets taken from you, you have *nowhere* to go." She paused. "If you choose to stay here, there will come a time when your mother may change her ambitions for you. She needs a blood heir- you don't have to be it."

"I'm her only- "

"She captured your father, tortured him and destroyed his mind. She took his sperm and made you. It was, I think we'd agree, a calculating way to go about it."

"Yes." Their father hadn't quite put it as bluntly as that, but he'd known his mother had created them for their power; that they weren't born from love. It didn't matter, though, it never had- his dad had his faults, but lack of love hadn't been one of them. He leaned back in his chair, trying to find a way to ease the tightness in his chest that made it hard to breathe properly, but nothing had felt as raw as this for years, not since he'd first reached Marine and told her what had happened.

"Then you understand you as her heir is only one option.

Draining what you have and killing you is another." He winced. "You have a choice, Kare, you can sit here like a lamb and wait for someone to use you, or you can learn how to do the using."

"I don't want it," he muttered. He couldn't face the idea that they might have died for nothing. If he played his mother's game and stepped up to being a true heir to the empire, he may as well have been raised in the palace, Karia with him. Her death, his dad's death, would have been for nothing.

"I didn't want to lose my home planet and be taken in by the Banned," said Rjala, and he sensed her anger, quickly smothered. "I didn't especially want the Empress' heir turning up in my army. I got it; I'll use it. You have your name, your blood, your psyche- you need to learn what you can do with them, and stop behaving like a child." She smiled, and it was the smile of a cat about to pounce. "Darwin le Payne was an excellent political operator- he took this group from nothing to a credible opposition. Sonly learned from him- he spent years teaching her, wanting her to follow him- and you could learn a lot from her. Michael is prepared to release her for a few hours a week to give you a share of that knowledge."

"Why should I?"

"Because I'd hate to see your father's death wasted." He drew in a sharp breath and she must have noticed, because she nodded and went on, "Ealyn and I, we didn't like each other; I guess you know that."

"Yes." It was, he reckoned, the understatement of the year.

"He thought I was obsessed with protocol; I felt he didn't put the group first." She waited until Kare nodded. "But I respected him. When Ferran Five- that's where I'm from, the fire-forests- was liberated, he led the squadron that broke past the Empress' fleet. He brought down their last cruiser but took a bad hit, defending the transporter. When they lifted him from his ship, he was half dead."

Kare leaned forward, fascinated. His dad had never told them much about his past, only the future.

"There were only three hundred of us left by then. Out of half a million. Another day- perhaps a week- and we'd have been wiped out. The fire sprites stole heat from the people in the forests, sucked them dry in the night. We were being picked off one by one, taken from the stockades to feed their need. The army didn't bother to chase us; they just left us in the forest to die. And we would have, except for the squadron your dad led. So, I respected your dad as a pilot. I have never met a better one, or a braver one."

That, at least, was true. "Yes."

"He took you so you'd have a choice, not have your mother's will

103

imposed on you, and you're *wasting* that opportunity. You're alive because of the Banned support– we provided the only safety your father had for years. But the base wasn't secure then. We were being evacuated all the time. All it would have taken was one agent getting lucky and finding out you were there, the wrong word back, and you'd have been targeted. That you are here vindicates our sending you away."

"Dad wasn't well when he left, and you knew it. He should have been supported."

"Your father refused to take anyone on that flight with him. Darwin himself offered to go but your father said if anyone was going to abandon his kids, it would be him." It sounded like his dad, all right. Her eyes softened, just a fraction. "I am sorry about what happened, just as I was then. But faced with the same choice again, I'd take it. It was the only way to ensure your safety. Anyone else on the base could have been replaced– but not you and Karia. That blood you hate is important." She leaned forward. "Being passive won't win you anything, and it's not what he'd have wanted. Ealyn Varnon was never passive in his life."

Also true. There was a silence and Kare realised she was waiting for his response. "And if I don't want to be Emperor? Do I get to refuse?"

"That's a much smarter question," she said. "If you don't want to be Emperor, then you need to find a way to be something else. And you *won't* do that by refusing to discuss it."

Could she be right? He'd studied what he could– self-taught, in the attic of his aunt's house, while Silom went about his normal life– and knew at least some of what she was saying was true.

"So," he said, looking up at her, meeting her eyes. Try being the user, that's what she'd said. "My idea– I'd like to explore it, ma'am. If I agreed to meet up with Sonly..."

He stopped at that thought, remembering the waves of emotions Sonly sent, the connection they made with him, like they were a dart targeted at the very centre of him. Part of him wanted that connection to another so badly, he'd risk anything. Another part of him knew it was a terrible idea, that he needed to stay distant. But, still, the memory of her touching him, her blue eyes...

"No," Rjala said, mercifully taking his attention. "Your meeting with Sonly is for your benefit, not the group's. Take your idea to your officer when you get to the tech squad."

He paused, knowing– as she must– that no officer was going to look at it, not from a private who had so little experience.

"Ma'am, if I agree to meet Sonly, please let me outline it to you."

"No, Private. It goes through the official channels." Her voice was firm, leaving no room for further protests.

"Yes, ma'am." Her pale eyes still watched him and he found himself nodding. "I'll meet with her. If you think it will help."

"I think it will. We'll take it slow," she said. "I'll release you for an hour a day."

An *hour* a day. He gulped. "Yes, ma'am."

CHAPTER TWENTY-ONE

aran Phelps watched out of the window of the war room, scanning over Abendau city far below. The desert air dragged at his throat, making him cough. He doubted he'd ever get used to it. He'd been based on Belaudii for five years, yet still yearned to escape the incessant heat.

He frowned. If he wasn't based here he'd have to leave his Empress. Her presence ran through the palace- it seemed to flow through the very walls themselves- and out, past the lush palace gardens into the city beyond. When he closed his eyes, he was comforted by it. More than that, it sustained him. Enough that he'd been prepared to leave Hiactol behind and ask for a transfer from their home army to the Empress'. One meeting with her at an official reception, and she had bound him to her, so much that he'd followed her, sure of his vocation. And she'd rewarded him amply since.

He opened his eyes and his chest contracted, mostly in excitement but with an under-layer of fear. She had built her empire from the ruins of her father's, forcing obedience from the Great Families with the power of her mind. The blood of the other families lay on Pettina hands- her father's coup had removed any family heads with the stature to threaten him- and yet they submitted to her and recognised her absolute command. He smiled, a tight smile. They were compelled to: once her mind was known, it was impossible to pull away. The very thought of displeasing her made his shoulders itch, right in the middle of his back.

Ealyn Varnon. He shivered, despite the heat. He'd been given a mission, to find the source of the Varnon powers, and hadn't completed it. His breath froze, turning him immobile for a moment, and then he relaxed. He was getting close, but although he'd traced the birth parents of Ealyn and his sister, he still hadn't found the origin of Varnon's powers. The sister had none, nor had her son ever demonstrated any. The birth family were being tracked down, one by one, but so far there had been nothing. A throwback? It seemed an easy option. He stroked his chin: not one of the family had green eyes. It was possible his progress to date might be found wanting.

He touched the glassine screen in front of him, running his

106

finger down its smooth surface. He may not have fulfilled her mission, but it was Allen who had lost her son– *again*– and would face her anger. Besides, he was deep in her favour.

He turned at the sound of footsteps to see a white-faced Allen enter the room. Their eyes met, and for a moment he had some sympathy for the other man. The general nodded but didn't speak, his eyes hard, and Phelps knew he would deflect any blame he could. Let him; Phelps was confident it couldn't be laid on him. More than that, this must be close to the last opportunity for the general.

The door opened again and both men straightened to attention as the Empress entered the room. She was breathtaking in a deep purple robe over a military style suit. Her soft grey eyes contrasted with the rich colour; her hair fell lightly around her face and onto its collar. His blood quickened at the sight of her, and she must have picked it up because she gave him a knowing smile and a slight nod. Whatever he had been called for today, it was not for failing her.

Both officers bowed to their mistress, low and deep, prepared to sink to their knees if ordered. Her presence washed over them, filling Phelps' mind and body. It was like a drug– he understood that– but one he had no means, or desire, to combat.

"You may sit."

The Empress walked to the head of the table and cast her eyes around the group as they took their seats opposite her. Phelps heard the general's inhaled breath and watched as he raised his eyes to her. She responded with a flare of power. Allen paled, but kept his head up. He had mettle in him, still.

The Empress turned her gaze to Phelps and he fought to keep his eyes forward, impassive. He had no reason to be afraid. He had advised against the attack on Corun: Varnon was an Empath who'd feel a trap; they had no idea what powers he had or how to counter them. In this case, finesse was needed, not force. He had been vindicated. He glanced at the pale and sweating Allen– if it was him, he'd be scared too. Very scared.

"I have been informed they found the tracker."

Allen opened his mouth and licked his lips. The Empress' power blasted across the table, hanging in the air, compelling an answer.

"Yes, my Empress, it was found after he left Corun," said Allen, impressing Phelps with the steadiness of his voice.

"Your men failed to take him on Corun," said the Empress. "Why?"

"It is hard, to take someone without harming them. We did have him, my Empress, but the platoon pulled out. We missed closing him down by moments."

The general's voice was less controlled, the words running together. Phelps raised an eyebrow, the inflection perfectly understated, but the Empress turned to him. He forced himself not to quail, but a muscle twitched in his cheek.

"If you were in charge?" she asked, confirming he was here as a possible successor. That made sense- she would never dispose of Allen until she had a successor firmly in place. He took a deep breath.

"I have a squad trained to infiltrate the rebel base. I would be seeking to corrupt the young le Payne boy- or someone close to the central structure- to get near enough to attack the base while my men lift Varnon." He paused. "I can place the squad at General Allen's command, if you wish."

It was a risk, but a calculated one. If Allen used them well, Phelps would remain in his shadow. If he squandered them, Phelps might gain position.

"Do so," she told Phelps.

"Yes, my Empress."

The Empress' eyes swivelled to Allen, who was breathing loudly now. Like a horse. Phelps was careful not to react.

"See you get this right," she told him. "He will be ready, now, expecting an attack. Let him relax, develop a routine." She turned her eyes to Phelps. "You have placed some of your specialists in the group?"

"Yes, my Lady."

She smiled, filling him with her pleasure. He inhaled deeply, striving to hold on to the sensation as long as he could.

"Good. When the moment has come, inform Allen. I want him taken and brought to me."

Phelps inclined his head.

"Allen," she said. His eyes fixed on hers, and he looked terrified. "There must be no more failures."

The general licked his lips; he'd pay a high cost for failure. For a moment- just a moment- Phelps questioned why he'd ever joined the army.

She reached out, touching his mind: caressing him, encouraging him, giving him belief and confidence. He relaxed, the room expanding around him as he breathed so deeply it felt endless. He grew hard, pleasure spreading beyond what he'd known with even the best whores in the Old Quarter.

She pulled her psyche from him and he fell forward, his pleasure fading. He opened his mouth to ask forgiveness for his disloyal thoughts. She shook her head and he felt her understanding that it was fear which had driven him. That, like anyone else, in her presence he could be weak. He bowed his head. She must know he was bound to her, so tightly he could never betray her. The very thought made him nauseous.

"Work with Phelps on this. Ensure you know how the team works. Learn my son's pattern. Bring him to me."

"Yes, Empress," said Allen.

"My Empress," agreed Phelps. She met his eyes, smiled, and he knew what she promised. His hardness came back, growing so that it was painful, straining against his uniform trousers, and still she smiled, knowing.

CHAPTER TWENTY-TWO

S only put down her data pad and glanced at the time, a flutter of nerves building. She took a deep breath to compose herself; Lichio had been teasing her about Kare since they'd met and, whilst she'd laughed it off, it wasn't funny. Michael wouldn't let her work with Kare if he had any concerns. There was a rap at the door, light and quick, and her stomach jumped.

"Come in!" she said, hooking a strand of hair behind one ear as the door opened. Kare mirrored her, running a hand through his hair. It was good to see he had let it grow a bit- it suited him better than the military crop... *stop it!* She smiled her best professional smile and nodded at the seat opposite. "You got away, then. Sit down."

He did, and she noticed he had something in his hand, but it was too small to tell what it was. There was an uncomfortable silence. She lifted her data pad.

"I pulled together some information about the great families, the empire, some of its income," she said. "I thought we'd start there."

He cleared his throat. "I don't think that sort of thing is going to help me much- I probably already know it."

The arrogant sod. She flushed. "We'll see. I might be able to add *something* to your extensive knowledge."

"I didn't mean it that way," he said. He looked embarrassed and she calmed down a little as he went on, "Sorry. I wondered, though, if we could talk about an idea I had, when you're finished?"

She bristled again. He wasn't doing her a favour by being here- he'd been ordered to it by his commanding officer. She took a breath and remembered she was supposed to be winning him over. "Fine." She smiled.

She brought up the first screen: a list of the families and their associated spheres of influence. She zoomed in on the star system of Ceaton-1. "The most populous system, and the most politically powerful," she said. She tapped Belaudii. "Planet of the Pettinas. You and your mother."

"Not me." He sounded faintly horrified. "I will never take her name. She is the Pettina family. I am a Varnon."

She didn't argue. One day, it would be brought up more

110

formally, no doubt. For now, it wasn't a fight worth having.

She pointed around the rest of the system. "The other two most powerful families are in the nearest planets. Clorinda and the Peirets. Both govern a lot of planets in the middle zone, both have a big family and substantial wealth. But they don't pull together, and your mother takes advantage of that."

"Well that, and the mind manipulation," he said, and pointed to his forehead. "She'll have them both under her dominance. She'll know to keep them close."

"Quite." Suddenly, she was uncomfortable. The mind manipulation he might have inherited– no one knew the full extent of his powers, and so far he hadn't seen fit to share them. Hurriedly, feeling exposed, she turned back to the safety of politics and pointed to the last of the four planets, far out from the star, half iced over. "And Taurine–"

"Home to the Al-halads." He ticked off one finger. "Specialists in terraforming since their own planet had to be carved out of an icefield."

So he did have some knowledge. She brought up the Ceaton-II system, but he ticked off another finger. "Balandt, bankers." Another tick. "Hiactol, military specialists." And another. "Tortdeniel, the humanitarian face of the families. As much as any of them are." He ran his hand through his hair. "I'm sorry, but I understand how things are set up now. What I need to find out is how to change it."

She resisted the urge to groan. Rjala had warned her this would be raised– and Lichio's reports had told her, too. "You can't change it– you don't have the influence."

He leaned forward, drawing her eyes to his. How on earth did they get so green? They weren't flecked, or hazel, just the purest green she could imagine, their darker rim only emphasising their depth. She pulled her gaze away– she wasn't interested in the colour of his eyes....

Actually, she was, but only because they proved who he was.

"Let me lay out my cards." He paused, and seemed less sure of himself. "My card: apparently I only have one. I will not be Emperor. Not for you, not for anyone. I know most people think they want it: the palace, the money, the power. Not me."

She took her time to choose her words. "It's going to be difficult for us, then. If you support the Banned– if you want our objectives to succeed– that's what you need to consider."

"I think you're wrong."

111

"Why am I wrong? Enlighten me."

He stood and started to pace. "Look, you think the empire is the only model that can exist, therefore you have to go for it."

Of course it wasn't the only model. Did he think she hadn't studied politics to get where she was? That she had no understanding?

"We get more support if we go for it." She said it slowly; if he wanted to treat her like an idiot, she could repay the favour. "The great families don't want change, and they are the ones we need to convince. They own the armies- their planets supply the troops, their funds pay the wages. We can't hold the empire with an army the size of the Banned's- the Empress' is ten times our size- we *need* the families. Which means we need to put forward a model they'll support, one that safeguards their economies, ensuring whatever change happens is relatively peaceful."

He leaned over the back of his chair. "You could devolve the empire, put someone- not necessarily me; in fact, preferably not- in as president. Keep the overall structure, the links between the planets in a confederacy, but remove her empire. It *could* be done."

She paused, wanting to tell him no, it was impossible. His eyes met hers and she didn't think he was trying to be stubborn. If pushed, she'd say he was more scared than anything.

"Can I ask why you won't consider the other?" she said, but she kept her voice soft, non-confrontational. "It would let me bring in the smaller families. Individually they can't challenge the Peirets and Clorindas, but collectively they'd make an impact."

"Sure." He moved his seat back and dropped into it. "She killed my dad and sister. That's one reason. She's chased me since the day I was born. That's another. She wiped out the entire planet of Corun just to capture me- "

"Those are the reasons you don't like her, not why you won't consider putting yourself forward."

"I'm getting to it. The ones I've listed are the reasons why I will *not* carry her name. She *created* me to be her legacy. She left my father so badly damaged he went crazy." He paused. "She engineered me to have powers no one fully understands. She didn't care it might destroy me, or Karia, provided we were able to do what she required. For all those reasons, I won't be what she wants, which means I *can't* be Emperor."

He waited while she took in his words, but still looked at her with a quiet intensity. His dad had that same intensity, she remembered, a way of radiating confidence. Maybe it was to do with being a psycher. But Ealyn had only ever had the faint touch of nervousness, the desperation to be listened to, at the end.

"It must be hard," she said. What must he have heard, on the ship with his father? What did he know that was driving him to clash with everyone? "Having people tell you what you should do."

"I'm coping." He glanced down, and she realised none of it- the smugness, the arrogance- was anything other than a way of keeping himself safe. He leaned forward to her and set a memory filche on the desk.

"What's that?" she asked.

"I'm prepared to deal," he said. "I know I'm no use to the Banned- in fact, I'm a drain on the group- if I don't reach an agreement with you. This is an outline for a project I'd like to manage. It will create close to real-time comms throughout the group, reducing the current space-delay- you'll thank me for it, one day."

Real-time comms in a space army. It was the nirvana they'd been seeking for years, what technical director after technical director had tried for. Her father had thrown resources at it, sure it was the one thing that could give the Banned an edge. Their fleet was small enough, in comparison the Empress', to utilise it.

"How?" she asked, careful not to show the interest he'd sparked. But if it was true, he was right- she'd bargain for it. *If* it was true.

"An interface. It'll link via the fleet and use their boosters to carry the signal. Provided we get the configurations right- the ships' capacity and alignment- it will speed up comms. Not to real time but much, much quicker than now. Certainly enough that the Banned could command remote battles from the base, pull the campaigns onto one strategic platform."

Not to real-time, then. Her shoulders dropped in disappointment. "It's been tried."

He smiled, a slow smile that made her stomach turn over. "Not by me. I've looked at your systems and I can get it closer than anyone else."

The arrogance was back. She found her fist clenching. His eyes looked down at it and she unclenched it.

"Why are you annoyed?" he asked. "You've tried to use me since the minute I arrived here- you've probably sold me to half the outer rim, already." She dropped her head so he couldn't see her redden. Not just the outer zone, but the Ferrans, and the families. "There's no point being coy- I can *feel* how true it is. You did it even though no one asked me."

She raised her head. "I did it because I had to."

"It's not your name," he said, his voice soft, perhaps a little hurt. "But I'm not surprised– everyone else wants a part of me, why wouldn't you?"

She shifted, uncomfortable. If she had the choice again– today– would she do what she had and promise him to the families? She wasn't sure, not anymore. She lifted the filche, changing the subject. "You said you'd deal."

"I'll let you use my name as a possible president and sell me to the outer rim, to any families you can.... I'll turn up when you need me to, and look as shockingly like my father as I suspect you'd like me to." He touched his hair. "I'm growing this back– he always wore his a little longer than me." He paused. "I want my own project group– my chance to prove I'm not just here for my name, that I have other things to offer. But I'll warn you– the colonel has already turned me down for getting ideas above my station."

"You'll meet anyone we need you to?" she asked. "And you'll back the Banned in public?" It would be the least that Michael would seek.

He leaned back in his chair, stretching his legs out. "Yes. I'm no orator, though."

"We can address that. You'll allow us to use your name?"

"Yes, provided you do *not* sell me as a future Emperor."

He reached forward and put his hand over hers. A warmth spread through her, the same warmth as in the corridor earlier. She didn't know what lay behind it, whether it was that she liked him, or the opportunity he offered, and she hated herself for not knowing, for being as much a politician as friend.

"I mean it, Sonly. I have to know I can trust you on this."

She met his eyes, and swallowed. Michael had told her to bring him into the group and force his commitment, no matter how she did it. But he wanted commitment to the empire, not a presidency. Still, a presidency was a start; they could work on the rest once he'd come to accept that. She wriggled her hand free and closed the other around the filche. Rjala would hate her for this. "I'll see what I can do."

"Thank you."

She paused: she knew so little about him, and if she was wrong to back him.... "There is one other thing I'll want."

He smiled. "Shoot."

"My brother– I missed him. He'll be on the project team."

"Lichio?"

She nodded.

114

"That's okay, he's okay, but I have my own condition." He paused. "No more reports on me- if you want to know something, just ask."

"I don't know what you mean," she said, disappointed; she'd believed he wouldn't read minds. She supposed this must be how he'd felt when she'd used his name.

"Of course you do- your brother's smart, I like him a lot, and he's reasonably competent around computers. But there is no security system I can't bypass if I want to, and after I realised he was on Corun for me, I *really* wanted to."

"You shouldn't have looked; I'm sure they were listed as private." She kept her voice steady, but she was pleased, nonetheless. Snooping in someone's files wasn't, perhaps, a particularly edifying act, but it was better than reading their mind.

He pulled a face. "I believe they might have been.... Look, if you can get the agreement for me, I'll work with you. If you don't, I'll get a skinhead and deny all knowledge of my parents."

Her mouth started to curl and she hastily hid the smile.

"And, perhaps, we could be a bit more open," he said. "I'm not out to get the Banned, I'm here partly because I had nowhere else, and partly because I wanted to come back. All the way through my childhood, I wanted to come back...." Wanted to, but couldn't. No wonder he didn't trust her or the Banned. "I'm on your side- I just don't want to be Emperor. Deal?"

She nodded. "Deal."

He stood to go, and she had an image of him trying to deny his father- even bald it'd be impossible. She broke into a smile.

"What is it?" The confidence he'd shown was gone, replaced by something- an edge of embarrassment, a little ducking of the head.

A warmth spread through her, and she had to look away. She absolutely had to learn to control that. "You'd look ridiculous with a skinhead."

"I know," he said, and he smiled too. "I really do. So, please, see what you can do, save me from it. Please..." He left, closing the door behind him, and she slumped back in her seat. Lord, this was getting complicated, and she didn't need it, not now. An hour, every day... she might have to reduce that; give him some books to read instead, or get Michael to do some of it. But first things first: she pulled her comms unit to her. "Rjala," she said. "We need to talk..."

CHAPTER TWENTY-THREE

Silom looked across the desk at Lichio. "So, where *am* I being posted to?"

"You're staying with the 42nd. Planet called Merrandron, in the Calixta system, naturally habitable, not terraformed. We have a base on Nero."

Neither name was familiar to Silom. "Nero?"

"Their satellite."

"A naturally habitable satellite too?"

Lichio's face twisted, as if in apology. "Sorry, no, the base is the only thing on it, and it's got an artificial atmosphere. But the planet is better, if you get the chance to go over. A little on the cold side... take some thermals."

Bastard. "Sir, I'd like it on record that I've requested a transfer to the Holbec base."

"It's on record." Lichio leaned forward. "It's not going to happen, though."

"Why not? Because I'm space debris, first to die for the Banned?"

"No, not at all." Lichio looked shocked, and Silom's lip curled- this boy had no idea that half the people who arrived at the Banned were fodder for a war that had already taken their homes and families.

"No, really," said Lichio. "You're a good soldier, you'll do well. In fact, that's why your transfer isn't going to go ahead." He sighed. "I think your career will be better served by being split from Kare." Silom's fists bunched, and Lichio put his hands up, as if in surrender. "It's common practice to disperse those who arrive together. If it hadn't been for the security implications, we'd have done it earlier."

"I want to appeal against your decision."

"Feel free." Lichio paused. "Look, don't take this the wrong way, but- has he got some sort of hold on you? Something you're not telling us?"

Silom took a moment and then started to laugh. "You're wondering has he been Influencing me? Wriggling his fingers and making me jump?"

"The thought crossed my mind."

"No. I learned how to keep him out of my head a long time ago."

"You seem very sure."

"I am."

Lichio drummed his fingers on the table. "If I'm right, you were forced to leave your home because of him. Your mother was killed because of him. Your girlfriend... "

Silom's coffee from earlier threatened to come up. "Do you know what happened to Liane?" He could barely get her name out, the fear was so great. He'd hardly managed to think about her since he got to the Banned, knowing what could have happened. Knowing that his last call to her father had been to a dead comms unit, and that his warning to get out might have been too late.

"No, we just know she's not on Dignad anymore."

Silom rubbed his hand on his chin, taking deep breaths. "The Empress?" he said.

"Maybe. Or the local boys."

It wouldn't have mattered which- the same thing would have happened. It was horribly, sickeningly wrong. And his fault- he'd known about Kare when he'd met her. He should have kept his distance and never got involved with anyone. Kare had never moaned about the sacrifices he'd made, had never commented on the nights Silom had gone out with his friends, when he'd lived between four walls. Anger bubbled up, and he didn't know who it was directed towards- Kare, for being a fucking saint and getting on with things, or himself for not being able to. Or the empire, for Liane. For the whole damn mess. He just knew he wanted to hit out, to hurt: to make things right.

"Are you all okay?" asked Lichio. "I'm sorry, I should have been more careful in how I said that."

"It wasn't Kare's fault," blurted Silom, and almost kicked himself for doing so. Lichio had been nosing around for months now, and he hadn't risen to it.

"I didn't say it was his fault. I said it happened because of him," said Lichio, and his manner, his offhand way of dealing with it, made Silom respond.

"He was leaving *because* of Liane, to keep her- us- safe."

"He could have left before."

"You don't know what it was like."

"So, tell me."

Tell him what? The fear of someone finding out, of coming home and finding troops waiting for him? The worry that a knock at the door would be the army? The knowledge that he had a life and a job and his mate couldn't even leave the house? The secret part of him that resented

Kare turning up on their doorstep and changing everything? It wasn't fair, to feel like that. Kare hadn't had any choice. He'd been a kid, on the run. But what had happened wasn't fair, either. The image of his mother, lying cold on the ground, came to him. It had been months since he'd allowed himself to think about her, and Liane, and the whole mess on Dignad. Lichio waited, silent, and he knew he wasn't getting out of this office until he gave him something to quash the thought he was under Kare's power and didn't have a mind of his own.

"We had to move all the time, we couldn't bring anyone back," he said, picking his words. He could tell them what they wanted to hear, but not the secret in the heart of him. "From the moment he arrived, we had to be careful– more than careful."

Lichio cocked his head. "Must have been a pain, for all of you."

"We got used to it."

"Even so, you must have found it hard. A saint would have– glory boy turning up and your life changing. Come on, you were– what– eight?"

"Nine," said Silom. He looked at Lichio, saw his eyes were sympathetic, not judgmental, and the words spilled out of him. "My dad died when I was five, and it had just been me and my mother. So, yeah, it was hard, and no one told me anything about why we had to move, only that I had a cousin and I wasn't to say. My mother was really strict about it and you didn't go against her when she really dug in." He paused. "But it was harder for Kare."

"So when did you find out who he was?"

Silom took a moment to count it back. "When I was sixteen. I caught him practising his powers and it all came out."

"Exciting, was it?"

Anything but. "Not especially."

"Really? It's just, it must have been something– finding out you're living with the Empress' son."

"It was... different," Silom said. It was hard to explain his relief at finally knowing, and the fear at understanding the stakes involved. "But I'd always known there was some big secret, so it didn't change much."

"Something did, though," said Lichio. "Otherwise, presumably, you'd both still be on Dignad."

Silom took a breath. "I met Liane, and it became serious."

Lichio nodded, his eyes understanding. "Bad enough keeping a secret in just one house..."

"Yes," said Silom. "When I brought her round to meet my mother, Kare stayed out of the way. Then one night we had a fight, and she stormed out. She bumped into Kare, skulking round the back, waiting for her to go." He looked down at his hands. "So, I had to tell her this was my cousin, and he was sitting there, looking terrified. She must have known something was wrong. Anyway, a couple of days later, Kare told me he was going." He paused. It was good to talk about it and be honest; it felt like something he'd carried inside, something that had pulled him down, was lifting. He met Lichio's eyes and refused to look away. "If I'm honest, I was relieved. Glad it was over. Even though I knew it was a hell of a thing to do- walk out at seventeen with a backpack, no ID, relying on a Dignadian shipyard owner for your life. But I was glad- I was getting my life back. You understand?"

"Yes, I can completely understand. But it went wrong."

"Yes. When I knew, I tried to contact Liane, but she wasn't there. Later, I reached her dad and told him to get her out, that they'd be looking for her, and it was serious, and he said he would. He *promised* he would..."

"Maybe he did. All we know is she's not on Dignad."

"Gods, I hope so." He glanced up, and saw nothing in the other man's eyes to say he'd done the wrong thing. "I wouldn't have got off the planet but for Kare. But Mum didn't, and Liane didn't. He saved the wrong one."

Lichio met his eyes. "So why hang your life around him?"

Was this man stupid? "He came back for me when he didn't have to." And that made up for some of the anger. He'd been worth someone risking their life for. But it went further than that, deeper, into the bond formed as boys, a brotherhood moulded by his mother. "Besides, I have Mum to repay the Empress for, maybe Liane too, and Kare is the best chance of doing that." He paused; he'd said enough. More than enough. "Sir, may I be excused? I need to pack."

Lichio nodded. "Yes, of course."

Silom stood up, saluted, and walked to the door.

"Silom."

"Yes, sir." He turned back.

Lichio's face twisted with something dangerously close to pity. "I'll keep your transfer request active."

Finally. "Thank you, sir. Just for the record, I hate the cold. You could list that as another reason."

***

Lichio waited for Silom to leave before getting up to go to the project room. He stepped outside, wiped his forehead, and ducked onto the jungle path. A group of recruits passed him, their packs slamming against

119

them as they ran. Poor buggers: the heat was murderous.

He stopped and took a slug of water. Something rustled to the side of him. He lowered the bottle and watched the jungle, his training coming back, but there was nothing there. He started to walk, a little quicker, and heard it again– following him, close by. His hand snaked towards his blaster. Still nothing. He could see where the path opened out, and sped up a little more.

Hands grabbed him. He twisted, trying to reach his weapon, but they held him too firmly. They pulled him back, into the dense jungle.

"Shit..."

Something covered his mouth, and his throat was pushed back, making him breathe in against it. The jungle above him blurred, the greens fading into one great wall of colour, and his legs went from under him....

The sound of birdsong, high and repetitive, woke him. He opened his eyes and found himself in a jungle clearing, propped against a tree. The heat had fallen and he didn't know if he'd been unconscious for a long time, or if it was just cooler under the canopy. He tried to stand, and found he was able to, although his legs were weak and shaky.

He looked around; there was no one there. Had he dreamt it? Passed out in the heat? His mouth curled: passed out in the heat, crawled somewhere and propped himself up? He doubted it.... He turned, saw something hanging from a leiandi-palm nearby and pulled it down: a message filche, one of the projector-type. He activated it, and the message streamed in front of him, its details displayed against the clearing's floor. He gulped and looked around. A *fortune*. He checked the figures again and did a mental calculation in his head. He could buy his own pleasure planet for that, or leave the army, not have to fight because he was in the Banned and it was what he was brought up to do. With this sort of money, he could get work as an ambassador. No one would know he wasn't from the higher echelons with this, and he could change things from within and fight clever.

He gulped, as the final temptation hit. If he was free from the Banned, he could be honest about who he was and not care what Eevan thought. The idea of that freedom was dizzying, and he had to wait for a moment, in the still clearing, interrupted only by bird calls, before he could read the filche again, this time to the last line.

He clicked the message off. He'd known who they wanted, of course he had, but not what they might offer.... Anything he wanted– that's what it said. It didn't have to be money.

He stood in the quiet of the jungle, and knew the meaning of temptation.

CHAPTER TWENTY-FOUR

ichio closed the screen he was working on. "I'm finished." He glanced over at Kare. "So should you."

"It's astounding you haven't gone already."

"That's not the right way to do it."

"Do what?" Kare stifled a yawn.

"You should say, 'thank you, sir, for staying and helping me with my not inconsiderable backlog.' "

"Thank you," said Kare. He paused, before adding, "Sir."

Lichio smiled, as Kare had known he would, at the standing joke; he hated calling Lichio sir when he was technically over the project. That Lichio was the nearest thing to a friend here at the base, now Silom was gone, didn't make it any easier.

"Anyway, you've seen my bunk," said Kare. "There isn't a worse one, or a shittier barracks, in the whole group. Remind me that, next time I go over the colonel's head."

"Hard luck." Lichio gave the smug smile of a man who had his own bedroom. "Do you want to come for a drink? I'm meeting Sonly."

Kare rolled his eyes: no amount of explaining that pushing him and Sonly together was a bad idea had made a difference. "No, I'll finish the last stuff and go back to the barracks later," he lied. He wasn't sure if Lichio knew he spent every night in the project room. If he did, he'd never commented, and Kare hadn't had to admit he was too frightened to sleep where he should be, in case he woke to find himself being taken from his bunk. At least here he could lock the door.

"Of course you will." Lichio's face was expressionless, his feelings bland, hard to read. Kare could, if he wanted, have delved a little deeper. He didn't.

"I'll see you tomorrow," Kare said. "Early, please. Or at least on time."

"Naturally."

Kare bit back his response; the day Lichio was early, he might faint. Yesterday, he'd sent a lame message about having a message to do at the barracks, and hadn't shown up for the afternoon.

Lichio left, locking the door behind him, and Kare leaned back in his seat. At least it was comfortable; he'd insisted on that. He looked at the calculations spread across the screen in front of him, and closed it down. He'd learned, from experience, he couldn't do the computations needed when he was tired, and a single mistake could mean the system failed.

He got up and lifted a bundled-up blanket from the corner. Wrapping it round his shoulders, he snuggled back into his seat, his feet propped up on another, and closed his eyes. He'd just started to doze off, a dream about figures– sums, sums, and more bloody sums– taking over his mind, when a soft sound woke him.

He sat up and looked around. The room was quiet, the only light coming from the banks of suspended screens. Plenty of places to hide. He cast out with his powers, but could feel nothing. He settled back and heard the noise again. This time, he realised it was a rap on the door. He got up; if it was an attacker, they were unlikely to be knocking.

He went to the door, saw Sonly through the glass, and paused. Why was she here? He thought about slinking back to his seat, but her eyes met his, making his stomach turn over in the lazy way it did every time he saw her. He opened the door a little and stepped back. She smiled and he smiled back, before reminding himself this was going nowhere. Whatever Sonly wanted, it wasn't what he had to offer.

"I'm sorry," she said. "I was looking for Lichio."

"He's gone."

She pushed the door fully open and came into the room. "When?"

Kare looked at the screen next to him and checked the time. "About half an hour ago."

Sonly touched the screen, which filled with figures. "It's like another language," she said. "And yet Lichio told me you're close to doing what you said you would." She gave a small smile. "I'm glad. I would hate to have gone over the colonel's head for no reason."

Kare didn't answer, and the silence lengthened. He was too warm, and not just because of the stuffy room. He'd been on the project team for six months now, and had met Sonly most days during it: in their sessions– ended now, and he suspected she was just as relieved as him– or with Lichio, or... *or because you went looking for her.* He pushed the thought away, angry with himself.

She walked around the room, and he tried to think of a reason to refuse her, but couldn't. This was her organisation, she was practically on their board, and their funds were paying for his project. *Rjala's project.* It still rankled with him, that they hadn't let him keep the credit of it being his creation. They'd left him as a private– outranked by everyone else in the team- and called him a specialist advisor. He wondered if they were trying to set him up to fail, or if he was being paranoid. Most likely, the colonel was still pissed off at him.

Sonly reached his chair and lifted the blanket. "You *sleep* here?"

He wanted to deny it, but her eyes were sharp, missing nothing. "Sometimes." He took the blanket off her. "It's better than barracks. A lot better than my bunk. That's all."

"You can't run this without sleep," she said. "I will speak to the colonel."

Kare nearly groaned at the probable outcome of that. "Don't; it's fine. The chair is very comfy, and I sleep well."

She reached out, surprising him by cupping his chin and turning his head so it was lit by the nearest screen. His breath stopped as she leaned in and looked at him. He wrenched his head away.

"I don't think you sleep well," she said. "To be honest, you look like you sleep like shit."

"Thanks. You know how to make someone feel good."

She giggled, her mouth tipped upwards, her eyes glittering as they reflected the light and she was... lovely. That was all, just lovely. He stepped back and leaned against a desk, his hands tightening on the edge of it.

"I sleep badly no matter where I am." He looked down, annoyed at telling her that. The silence in the room expanded until he raised his eyes to her. She'd stopped giggling and was watching him instead. He wanted to look away, but didn't; instead, he clenched his hands even tighter.

"Why don't you sleep?" she asked.

He waited a moment, and then, amazingly, found himself saying, "I have nightmares."

"What sort?" Her words were soft, full of concern. It had been so long since someone had spoken to him with real concern, not since Marine had gone, and it moved him in a way he hadn't expected. He didn't know if it was because of Sonly and how she made him feel, or his loneliness. He tried to joke. "At the moment, sums."

She waited, silent, and he swallowed. When he opened his mouth again the words flowed out, tripping over each other.

"About what lies ahead: being chased into a corner, my psyche failing, and not being able to help myself." He clutched the desk so tightly it became painful. "About ending up crazy like my dad."

She took his left hand from the side of the desk. He looked down at their entwined hands and tried to pull away but she moved closer, so that the heat of her body warmed him.

"They're only dreams," she said. "They can't hurt you."

"You're right." He took his hand away, and tried to put a little distance between them. "Lichio stayed late, but he went-"

"He said he'd call me when he was done, and when he didn't, I thought I'd come and get him..."

Kare's eyes narrowed, and he made a mental note to have a long, pointed talk with Lichio in the morning about minding his own business and not Kare's. She was still standing close to him, and he put out his hands to move her. He touched her shoulders and before he could think about it, before he knew he'd moved, his lips were on hers. She pulled him closer and kissed him back, her mouth open, hungry. He put his arms around her, melting into the kiss, and for a moment there was nothing other than her hands on the small of his back, her body tight against him, and her kiss, lips soft, opening under his and- *you can't.*

He pulled away. "We can't do this..."

"I know, I agree, I've tried not to." Her voice was small in the darkness.

"I'm sorry, I shouldn't have- " The confusion was coming off her in waves, filling his mind. Sadness, too. He shook his head, and it was one of the hardest things he'd ever done in his life. "It's just not possible. I'm sorry."

She turned from him, and he thought it was to hide her upset. She couldn't, not from him. He followed her to the door, closed it behind her and locked it again.

"Goodnight," he said into the darkness. He went back to his seat and pulled the blanket round, knowing he'd been right and couldn't let her come any closer. Except... another part of him needed someone to be close to. He shut his eyes, squeezing them tight, wanting to know he was doing the right thing, that he was following the right path, and wishing he had someone to ask.

CHAPTER TWENTY-FIVE

Kare sat up, gasping for breath, the blanket clutched to him. The nightmare had been so real- it always was- and he struggled to remind himself it was a dream. It wasn't even his dream: the pit, Beck, the torture all came from his dad's visions. Even so, in the dead of night, it was hard to be convinced.

A noise stopped his thoughts, a whisper in the dark, and the chair was kicked back from under his feet. Someone dropped into the seat opposite, silhouetted against the soft light of the monitors. Kare cast out, ready, and stopped when he picked up who it was.

"I've just spent tonight with my upset sister," said Lichio, at last.

Relief spilled through Kare. That was it? He took a deep breath. "I'm sorry I upset her. What time is it, Lich?"

"It's about two o'clock in the morning. She just left."

Kare sat up straighter and put his blanket to one side. It was heavy, soaked with sweat. "What do you want me to do? Tell her I'll go out with her because her little brother says I have to?"

"I want to know why not. Not just with Sonly- I know it's complicated- but with everyone. Why not come for a drink? For no reason other than we're mates. You went out with the platoon on Corun, you had a good time, so why not here?"

On Corun, it had been safe- there had been a crowd of them. Silom had been there. Here, to get close to one person- he couldn't imagine it. He paused for a moment, before saying, "I don't know what you mean. I'm friendly, we have a laugh, what more do you want from me?"

"Your trust."

Kare's breath drew in sharply. *Oh, that.*

"Lichio," he said, glad of the darkness and the chance to hide his face. "It's not that I don't trust you; I do. And it's not that I don't like Sonly, because I do. I think she knows that."

"Damn right, she knows it," said Lichio, and Kare winced.

What do I say? He wanted to deflect it, as he always did, but stopped. Lichio had turned up in the middle of the night, because it mattered to him. He was offering something that Kare knew he needed, and it was getting harder and harder to stay distant.

"My dad," said Kare, "had some visions before he died." And how little did that describe the hellish weeks on the ship? "I won't tell you what they were- even Silom doesn't know the details- but letting anyone get close to me is dangerous for them. The sort of things he told me, it's not what you'd want your friends to face. That's all."

"That's all?" said Lichio, and he amazed Kare by starting to laugh. "Your dad's visions? Your dad was mad. You're basing your life, your friendships, on the visions of a madman? You're crazier than he was."

Kare took a deep breath in. He hoped not. The memory of the dream came back to him. The nightmares had been there as long as he remembered, but as he'd got older they'd become more frequent. Now they came most nights. What would happen if one night he couldn't get out of it? Being stuck in them had driven his dad mad- he didn't think he'd fare much better.

"What if he's right?"

"What if it turns out I'm going to destroy your life, and don't know it?" said Lichio. "What if? What if not? Live for today, you asshole."

Kare didn't reply. Live for today and forget about what lay ahead was what he'd tried to do all his life. It had never worked.

"You asked what I want," said Lichio. "I want you not to cross your arms every time I say something that isn't about work. Not to refuse to go for a drink."

"Right." Kare took a deep breath. *Live for today.* Lichio had stayed late tonight and not because he had to. It was Kare's workload- his formidable workload, admittedly- that was behind, not Lichio's. He'd been a friend to him since they'd come back from Corun, good fun to be around, sympathetic about the project team, doing small things to make the disparity in their ranks easier.

"Okay," said Kare. "I will stop crossing my arms. I will go for a drink, sometimes, when I have time. I'll try."

"Good. One other thing- tomorrow, when my sister comes to meet me for lunch, I'd like you to take her out instead," said Lichio. Kare took a deep breath in and Lichio laughed softly. "That's right: ask her, and tell her what you just told me, see what she says to it. You're driving each other mad- at least talk about it." He stood up, and kicked the seat he was on away from Kare. "And stop hiding down here. Your bunk's not that bad, and no one is going to creep in during the night and steal you away. It's an army base; there are guards. Go, get a decent night's sleep and sort your head out." He reached the door. "I'll let myself out."

Kare watched him. *Trust.* He paused. Did he trust Sonly and

Michael? Rjala? He looked around the room- they'd given him this, at least. He thought of Sonly and how he'd been able to tell her his fears and let her hold his hand. How he'd kissed her, and hadn't wanted to stop.

He reached into his pocket and lifted out a message tab. He turned it over and over in his hand, knowing the contents- he'd memorised them as soon as he'd received it six weeks ago. Even so, he activated it, and a life-size hologram came up in front of him. His mother took shape, composed and regal, sitting at a desk in, he assumed, the palace of Abendau. She smiled and it softened her face, just a little. She looked like Karia.

"Kare," she said, her voice low and inviting, her eyes looking directly at him. She seemed so real and close that he should be able to touch her. "I invite you to come to Abendau and work with me. You are my heir and if you come to me, of your own volition, you will be recognised as such. My empire will be yours to inherit. You will be treated as royalty, welcomed and embraced." She paused, as if knowing he would have to gulp against the temptation of knowing her. "Come to me, talk with me. You are my son; you should be with me." Another pause. Her eyes grew narrow, harder. "Should you fail to do so, it will be considered an open rebellion against my rule, and you *will* bear the consequences."

The message ended and he lifted the filche. Karia had been her daughter, and she was dead. She hadn't wanted either of them- his father had told him so many, many times- she'd hoped to turn them into robots who did only her will. He wanted to shred the filche, destroy it like it never existed. Instead, he slipped it back in his pocket. He couldn't remove the one connection he had to her, but he could stop carrying it around. Stick it at the bottom of his backpack and stop thinking about the temptation it held. Or the terrifying prospect of turning from being wanted by her to being considered her enemy.

Slowly, he got up, put the blanket back in the corner, and walked to the barracks. As he slipped into the dorm and undressed before climbing into bed, he thought either he had to trust the Banned, or leave. And he had only one other place he could go. He pulled the covers around him, tried to work out when he'd last slept here, and reminded himself there were guards to keep him safe. He closed his eyes. *Trust.* It sounded so easy.

CHAPTER TWENTY-SIX

Silom stood, waiting for his eyes to adjust to the darkness.
<GAME START>
He brought his laser gun up, taking care to keep his breath quiet.
<SCOPER SELECT>
He paused, deciding what was best in the dark cave.

"Spider," he mouthed, and there was a soft buzz of confirmation from his gun. He stepped forward using the stim pad at his feet, keeping in the shadows. Nothing. He took another step and saw the scoper in front of him. He brought the gun up and fired, but missed the activation point on the spider's back and the spider disappeared, making him swear under his breath.

Cobwebs clung to his face as he pushed into a side cavern. Nothing there, but he took the opportunity to scan the main cave from the darkness. Quiet. He stepped out, took the path to his left. Still no sign of Charl, but he kept his gun up. He didn't want to use it- a scoper attack was the quickest way to win the game- but it didn't pay to be complacent.

Movement. Ahead. He crouched, waiting until he was sure it was a scoper, and took his time, making sure of his aim. This time he hit the target on its back. It set off, scuttling across the cave. He followed, and watched the spider jump his opponent's wrist, making his gun clatter to the floor. The cave lit up and Silom grinned. *Done.* Three spiders, and he'd only needed two. He checked the display details: two minutes. *Beat that.*

<GAME END>

He pulled his visor off and looked over at the other cubicle, where Charl was holding his arm against his chest. "Fuck you, Dester."

Silom laughed and faced the small crowd of soldiers watching. "Who's next?" No one stepped forward, and he couldn't blame them: six months' practice combined with the personal security training had paid off; it had been at least three weeks since anyone had taken him. Even that had been lucky- they'd nabbed a scoper as soon as they'd logged on. "Bring it on!"

Still no one, and he stepped out, holstering the gun in its bracket. "You're all chickenshit."

The small crowd parted, and Kym stepped through, slim in her cargo trousers, her vest top showing tightly muscled arms. "I'm up for it."

There were cheers from the crowd, and Silom smiled, a slow smile. At last, someone worth playing with. He swept into an exaggerated bow. "Be my guest."

Charl handed her his gun and helmet, clasping her hand with his good one for luck. She tightened her other around his for a moment, and then stepped into the cubicle. Silom lifted his gun and pulled the visor down. The games room vanished.

<GAME START>

It wasn't a cave this time, but a forest, filled with the sound of birds and the smell of pine. He walked forwards, his gun up and ready. No Kym. Hell, she was like a wraith. He cursed, stopped, checked again. Nothing. What scoper would she have selected? Hoverfly, bat?

A movement to the side, and he turned, loud and clumsy. He pulled up his gun, but didn't shoot- he'd already done enough to pinpoint his position. He took a step, stumbled, and looked down to see a rat at his feet. *Crap.* He kicked at it, waiting for the bite, but it wasn't a scoper. Silom pulled into the shadows, barely breathing. Where the *hell* was she? He cast his mind back, trying to remember how she'd played it last time. He smiled and turned. A snake, a scoper this time, reared up and he stepped back, but was too slow. Its bite- an electric pulse, but by the *gods* it hurt- made him yell and stumble back, his knee threatening to crumple under him.

<GAME END>

"Yes!" yelled Kym. "Now who's champion!"

He ripped his helmet off, heard laughter, and took a moment before he turned to face the crowd, making sure he had a smile plastered on his face.

"Need a seat, Dester?"

Rawle pulled one out, indicated it with a nod. Silom stepped out, careful not to limp. "Piss off, the lot of you." There were a few more catcalls and he grinned- he probably deserved it.

He turned to Kym, who was smiling from the cubicle. "Another?" she said.

No way. His leg had stiffened, and it would be at least an hour before it wore off.

"Not now. Where'd you go?" he asked, jerking his head back to the cubicle.

"I stayed behind you. You always follow the same check pattern; I just moved with it."

He nodded. "Good to know. I need to vary it."

She jumped down and came over to him, nudging under his arm. He didn't stop her, but there was a familiar sharp pang of guilt. He pushed it away; he couldn't do anything about Liane. Even if she was alive, she was in a different star system. Besides, the only thing he could offer was a place with the rebels, and fuck her life up even more.

He pulled Kym closer. Le Payne had been right: getting away had given him space to deal with what had happened on Dignad. That Kym had been patient enough to let him had been a big thing. She pushed him up against the counter of the bar, his attempt to stop her less than valiant.

"I win," she said, shifting against him.

Always. He kissed her, one hand running through her hair, and her lips tasted sweet, like toffee. There were whistles from Charl and his crowd. He raised one finger behind her back, and they got louder, until he pulled away. He wanted her: now. "Come on, let's get out of here."

CHAPTER TWENTY-SEVEN

only clenched her fists and barely resisted the urge to hit her brother; at six-foot-three to her five-four, she'd come off worse. Instead, she smiled: there were other ways to fight, and she was whipping his ass politically. The board elections were next month and this time she'd get in, she was sure of it.

"I'm not saying you're wrong." Eevan folded his arms. "I'm saying you should think about the position it puts you in. *If* you're wrong, and you tout him, you're the one who'll look like an idiot."

She stood up, her hands clenched against the table. "It's my risk, Eevan, and whilst I appreciate your... concern, I'd remind you I don't spend my time advising you about army personnel."

He stood too, and for a moment she thought he was going to leave, but he came over to her. He brushed the hair back from her ear, and she didn't stop him. Instead, her breath halted. He leaned so close his breath on her neck was a whisper.

"I've heard rumours," he said. "You're getting friendly with him. It's bad enough that Lichio is his mate; it doesn't look good if you get close as well."

She whirled to face him, angry. "Who I'm friendly with isn't your concern."

"Only trying to advise."

As ever, he made it feel like it was her fault, that she was overreacting; he hadn't hurt her, or done anything other than talk to her, after all. He never had.

"I don't appreciate being told what to do, Eevan."

He backed away, his hands held out in contrition. "Sorry. It's only because I worry about you. I'll go." He paused. "But just ask yourself whether it's best for the group, or for him."

She watched until he left, but his words stayed with her. Lichio was adamant he'd been behind an absolutely vicious beating on Kare, one that could have done a lot more damage than it had. One he was fairly sure *had* done more damage. She sat down, a little shaky. She liked Kare: the way they'd been in the project room last night had been new to her, like they had a connection, an understanding. She pushed her hair back. It was lonely, being responsible, having to always watch what she said. The idea of having someone outside of that, a friend, was tempting. Last night, she'd thought Kare might be one.

But if it caused more trouble with Eevan than she already had... she picked up her comms unit, planning to tell Lichio she'd meet him at the mess. She slammed it down on the table. To hell with that, what right did Eevan have to tell her who she could or couldn't be friends with? She grabbed her data pad, knowing not to leave it unattended when Lichio was on the base. Not because he'd do anything with the information, or use it against her, but because he was perennially nosy, and it didn't pay to encourage it. She closed down her office. To hell with Eevan.

A few minutes later, she stopped at the door of the project room and took a deep breath. She had to face Kare sometime. But she'd been so forward, taking his hand, getting him to talk about his dreams. In the darkness and the quiet, it had seemed right. And when he'd kissed her, she'd known he liked her- no one kissed like that if they didn't- but he'd still sent her away.

She pushed open the door, forcing herself to walk straight in and not hide. Today was different from the quiet of the previous evening: busy, with technicians gathered at their workstations and detailed configurations written on panels around the walls, mostly in the same neat writing. The relaxed atmosphere was nothing like other project teams she'd visited, where talk of deadlines and requirements took precedence over the work.

She stepped further into the room and spotted Lichio walking towards her, deep in conversation with Kare. Lichio saw her and nudged Kare, who looked up. He blushed, and the knowledge he was embarrassed too made her a little less nervous. Something Lichio said made him smile, and her stomach filled with bubbles of excitement.

Lichio stopped at a work desk. Kare walked up to her, but didn't seem to know what to say, and she wondered if she should speak first.

"I'm sorry," he said at the same time as her, and they both laughed.

"You first," she said.

"I'm sorry about last night," he said. "I wasn't expecting it."

"It was my fault; I shouldn't have disturbed you." Sonly looked at Lichio; he'd better hurry up and save her from this.

Kare cleared his throat. "I wondered if you'd go for lunch with me. I'll try to explain it to you."

Sonly glared at her brother, who smiled, his face as innocent as an angel's. Someone called for Kare across the room, and he turned to go.

"I'll get it," said Lichio, waving him back. Sonly decided when she got him on his own she'd kill him.

"I'd be lost without that brother of yours, you know," said Kare. He leaned against the desk, his ankles crossed, relaxed and casual in fatigue bottoms and a standard-issue black t-shirt.

"You're joking. He's only in the project because I asked you."

Kare smiled and his eyes danced, just like his dad's had when she was a child, but he wasn't as like his father as she'd first thought. Ealyn had been fey: thin as a whippet, bursting with life and temperament. She'd been a little afraid of him, he'd been so intense. Kare wasn't as thin, and he seemed softer than his father- more in tune with the rest of the world.

"You didn't ask- you told me," he said. "He's brilliant, actually. He just hadn't been challenged enough. Watch your back; when Lichio finds his feet, he'll be the equal of any le Payne."

"Are you mad? He lives to have fun." She knew it wasn't true, though- that Lichio's relaxed manner was a front. She was just surprised someone else had noticed.

"Yes, but very intelligent fun. Unlike your other brother, who has very intelligent non-fun." He glanced at her slyly. "What about you, Sonly? I think you'd be in the fun camp if you took a bit more time off."

Uncomfortable, she changed the subject. "It's really relaxed here. Most project teams I've visited aren't."

"They should be- it's how you get the best work. Poor Colonel Rjala, it tormented her at first. If I wasn't ahead of plan, she'd have stopped me. The colonel judges by results, so that's what I give her. It's awkward that your little brother's more senior than me- that everyone is- but we've worked around it."

Sonly kept her face bland, hoping she wouldn't give away that he was about to be promoted for his work here. Rjala had been very persuasive in proposing it, pointing out he'd be training officers in the use of the system. He couldn't do that and still hold the rank of private. It was one of the more surprising things Rjala had done, and she had wondered how Kare had won her over. Now, looking around, she could understand.

"So, are you going for lunch with him?" Lichio asked. He looked at Kare. "You did ask her?"

Kare rolled his eyes. "What I forgot to say: he lacks subtlety."

"He was born that way," she said, pleased to see the rapport between Kare and Lichio. She couldn't resist teasing Lichio after he'd so blatantly set her up. "Mother used to say he got a double charm gene to make up for it."

133

Lichio shrugged, not remotely embarrassed. "It's overrated."

Sonly waited, wondering if the offer was genuine or if he was only trying to please Lichio. She bit her lip.

"Really, I'd like to," he said. "I'm due a break."

It would be good not to have this awkwardness hanging between them. She nodded. "Yes, then. That would be nice."

As they left the room, his comms unit buzzed. He glanced at it quickly, and laughed.

"What is it?"

"Silom. Sounds like he's found a way of keeping warm. Good."

"How?" She didn't really know Silom, only through stories from Lichio, but he hadn't sounded like someone who'd struggle to find company. They reached the servery and picked a tray each.

"Not how: who. Some soldier." He put a cup on the tray. "What do you want?"

"Oh, tea, please."

They picked up their food and she glanced around. Two young women were in one corner, drinking coffee, a toddler beside them in a high chair, squeezing chips in his hand. She led the way to a table in the opposite corner and took a seat overlooking the jungle. The room was so bland and plain, much like the rest of the base, the long window dominated. A hummingbird hovered just outside, facing her like it was looking at her, the red feathers on its throat ruffling as it sang. Kare set his tray down, and it flew away.

"The mess is quiet, at least," Sonly said. She lifted her fork, feeling self-conscious. A bit of life around the place would have given her something else to concentrate on.

"Give it half an hour."

Sonly's comms unit buzzed this time– she really should turn it off over break-periods– and she went to answer it but hesitated. Kare smiled innocently, pulling it off nearly as well as Lichio.

"I need to know you won't listen in," she said.

"I won't. I don't do that."

He started to eat his food, ignoring her. She looked at him for a moment longer. If she couldn't trust him, she was a poor judge of character. She got up and moved to the window, leaning against it. Here, the base was close to the jungle and she could see birds flitting, seeking the rich blue flowers of the jungle-stock. She took the call from Michael, arranged a meeting date– relieved it wasn't anything more– and ended it.

"Thank you," she said, returning to the table.

Kare looked up, shrugged lazily and smiled. "You don't need to

134

thank me- I have no interest in snooping in others' conversations. I have enough difficulty keeping up with my own. But I still get to close doors from across the room. I have to have some perks." They ate for a few moments in silence, and then he put down his fork, clearing his throat. "About last night."

Suddenly, Sonly had no appetite. Now he'd brought it up, she was embarrassed all over again. "You were right- we shouldn't get involved. I'm sorry."

"That's just the excuse." He took a breath. "I have a problem letting people get close to me."

"Why?" She nearly kicked herself. Of course he had a problem with it- practically anyone he'd been close to was dead.

"I worry they'll end up getting sucked into what's going on around me," he said.

"Surely that's their choice, not yours."

"What if I know more than they do?" He pushed his food round his plate, not meeting her eyes.

She put her fork down. This was the sort of thing the Banned needed to know- what his father had confided in him. Ealyn had been held in the palace for months before he'd escaped and no one knew what he'd learned. "Do you?"

"No. Well, yes, maybe."

She waited, hoping he'd start to make sense soon. A quick movement took her attention: the hummingbird was back.

"You know the Empress has tried to take me," he said. "Well, my dad thought she might succeed, and if she did, it would be bad."

"Sorry, but again: why is that your choice?" He took a drink of his coffee, waiting for her to continue. "You've warned me, you've presumably mentioned it to Silom, maybe Lichio, too. Now it's up to me to say sod off, or sod it."

He spluttered his coffee, choking with laughter.

"What's so funny?"

"You; you're like a force of nature. I feel like I'm being hit by a hurricane."

She ducked her head; it wasn't the first time such a thing had been suggested. Normally it was in the office and put rather more politely, but even so.

"Sorry, I've embarrassed you," he said.

"Not really." Sonly took a mouthful of her food and set her fork down again. "I think, if I'm honest, it *might* be awkward. We have to work together, and that will increase if- when- you take on a more public profile." She got up to lift her plate across, feeling very proud of herself. Her voice hadn't wavered, not once.

"Sonly?" Kare's voice was quiet.

"What?" She didn't look at him, not wanting to acknowledge what she was turning down.

"Apparently, I like forces of nature," he said. "I can't stop thinking about you. I keep asking Lichio about you, trying to think of ways I can."

She hadn't expected him to say that. Her cheeks went hot, and she felt butterflies starting in her, small darts of excitement. "You do?"

"Yes. Look, how do you relax?"

Was he mad? "Relax? Kare, I'm running a division of the organisation. I have a brother who is constantly, and I do mean constantly, plotting against me. I get up in the morning and I work, and I go to bed at night, having worked. I don't have time to relax."

"You should. It's important."

"According to my little brother, this is like the pot and kettle. He says you never stop working."

Kare had the grace to look away. "You're right, we both should. When did you last sit down and just have a chat with someone? I have a late meeting tonight, but it'd be nice to drop round after, about ten. If you'd like me to."

She hesitated, and he got up, facing her. He was close enough to smell his faint cologne, almost buried by the spiced coffee. Close enough to see his chest rising and falling with shallow breaths. She wasn't the only one who was nervous.

"I'm not offering anything other than friendship," he said, and he sounded sincere. "Like I said, I find it difficult to get close to people. But I'd like to be your friend, get to know you better."

It felt like he was standing too close, almost crowding her, but she didn't want to step back and break the moment.

"Can I trust *you*?" she asked, remembering Rjala's warning that they didn't know his agenda, or why he'd come back.

"Yes," he told her, his voice a whisper, his eyes looking directly at her. "You can trust me, Sonly le Payne. I won't let you down."

She believed him. She broke her gaze away first. "Come round," she said. "After your meeting. I'd like that."

He nodded and walked away, and Sonly watched him go. She sighed; could she have have found anyone more complicated?

Later, sitting in her apartment, she ordered herself not to look at the clock again. It was only five past ten, and Rjala was planning to tell him about his promotion, so the meeting might have run on. Even so, when she heard the rap on the door, she jumped. It was already familiar, how he knocked, a quick rap, and it was nice to have something she knew about him. She smoothed down her top and walked to the door. She lifted her hand to open it and stopped. *Be cool.* She waited for a second knock and this time she let him in.

"Hi," she said. Now he was here she was shy, almost tongue-tied. "Do you want a drink?"

"Yes, thanks." He looked around the apartment. "This is very nice."

"It was Dad's," she said. She forgot, sometimes, how unlike the rest of the base it was, filled with her books, a few holos, even a couple of pictures on the wall. The rest of the base was so sparse, it was impossible to escape the sense of being on a military base, even in the more public areas. She'd tried to create something different. Somewhere to relax. "The idea was he'd have somewhere to go where he wouldn't be disturbed all the time. It's self-contained; there's a bedroom and a bathroom, a small study. I'm not sure why they put the kitchen in, though; he couldn't cook and neither can I. Michael didn't want it- he has family accommodation and is happy there, so he offered it to me."

"You don't cook?" He picked up a holo of her father and looked at it, his face hard to read. She wondered what he thought of them all, what memories he'd carried of the last visit to the Banned, before Karia died. She'd never fogotten the horrid finality of her father closing the apartment door against her pleas for the twins to stay. If she couldn't forget it, how could he? She'd ask, but now wasn't the time to bring the past up, not when the future, and what she wanted for it, hung before her.

"No," she said. "Why would I when there's a mess?"

She handed him a glass of wine, and he took it over to the small sofa and sat down.

"I love cooking," he said. "I used to have something ready when Silom and Marine got home. It passed the day."

"I thought you lived in the attic."

He laughed. "No, they let me out from time to time. I wasn't a prisoner; I just had to be discreet."

She sat beside him and yawned, the late night with Lichio catching up with her. She moved a book onto the table beside her.

"So you read," he said. "That's something. What else do you do other than work?"

She blushed. Was she really so bad? "Lots of things. I go swimming at the barracks pool when I can."

"You can teach me."

"You can't swim?" She took a sip of wine to hide her surprise.

"No; there aren't many swimming pools in attics..."

"Of course, I didn't think." She yawned. "I'm sorry, I've been busy."

"Can't you offload some of it? Get yourself a Lichio? Although you're not stealing mine; he's far too useful."

She smiled; if she could get the sort of work out of Lichio that Kare did, she might consider it. "He would drive me mad. He'd always be late, and he'd snoop through everything."

He laughed. "He does that on me, too." He leaned in, conspiratorially, as if Lichio might be listening. "What I do is I leave some fairly non-essential stuff where he snoops and keep the rest with me. All the time."

"You're about the only person he hasn't out-manoeuvred," she said.

"I wouldn't say that."

They fell silent, but it was comfortable, unforced. It was like the night before, when something had built between them. He was watching her, openly, his eyes focused on her, but it didn't feel uncomfortable.

"How did the meeting go?" she asked, breaking the silence.

"Very well. I guess you heard?"

She nodded. "Yes, I've known for a couple of days. Congratulations, Lieutenant. I couldn't tell you- it was confidential."

"It's fine. It was nice to be surprised," he said, his eyes locked on hers, as if he could see her very soul.

She set her glass down. "It's just, whatever happens- " *don't force it, you don't know anything will* "- that won't change- the confidentiality."

"Really, it's fine. I don't snoop, I told you that. You know, what you said today, about me making your choices for you?"

"Yes?"

"I thought about it." He ran a hand through his hair. "All day. I got nothing done- Lichio thought it was hilarious. I'm going to be a bit mysterious and say there *are* some things I can't tell you. Not because I don't want to, but because I promised Karia I wouldn't tell anyone about some things that happened on the ship, near the end. It was one of the last things I promised her."

"Okay," she said. She had asked the same from him, after all.

"I will tell you my father predicted that if I stood against my mother, others around me might be hurt, too. In building the system, fighting for the Banned on Corun, I've stood against her, and she *will* see it that way. I'm certain of that. Dad was, as Lichio pointed out, close to insane but he was still a Seer, and it's hard to discount him."

"Aren't you scared?" she asked. He didn't look away, but she saw a muscle twitch in his cheek.

"Sometimes." He took her hand and entwined his fingers through hers, rubbing the palm of her hand with his thumb, making her light-

138

headed. "I'm telling you so you can make your mind up. I've tried pushing you away, and it's not working. So I thought I would just tell you, and let you decide. What was it you said– see if you wanted to say sod off or sod it?"

She paused, thinking about his words, and the atmosphere built around them, filling the apartment.

"Sod it," she said. He kissed her. She could feel the heat of his body, the strength in his arm as held her against him, the tension in him easing. She tilted her head back, eyes closed, savouring the warmth of him, the closeness, how his lips were on hers, insistent, how his hands tightened on her waist, bringing her even closer. There was no way she could deny this. When he broke off, she made a soft noise of disappointment.

"I really, really like you," he said, his voice shaking. "If I stay any longer, I'll not be able to say no to you, and I want you to take another bit of time, and just think about what I said."

"I know what I want," she told him.

He stood up, and she did too. She took his arm and pulled him towards her but the soft fabric of his shirt slipped through her fingers. He put his finger on her lips, gently, and shook his head.

"Just take some time, even a little time, and be sure. I know I must come across as a bit paranoid– not sleeping in barracks, not leaving the base– but I'm not. I know what my mother is capable of. Think about it, before we let this go further. Please."

She kissed his finger and he groaned, telling her what she already knew– if she wanted, she could make him stay.

"I'm going," he said. "I have to, but I swear I'll see you tomorrow. Just sleep on it for tonight, okay? I'm going to go to my own bed, in the barracks, to do the same."

She thought about keeping him here, and then decided against it. Not if he didn't want to.

"You know it's not because I don't like you?" he said. "You know it's because I do like you that I'm going?"

She nodded, not trusting herself to speak, and let him open the door and go.

For a moment, she stood in the quiet apartment. Perhaps he was right. It had been so urgent between them, so overwhelming, that she had barely breathed properly all evening.

She got up, taking their glasses to the kitchen, and poured some water, turning off lights as she did. A few minutes later she snuggled down in bed and then groaned. *Lichio.* If she didn't call, he would; he was far too nosy not to.

He answered his comms unit quickly. "Hi, did you change your mind?" he said, his voice low and intimate. She wondered, briefly, which girl he'd been with, but decided it was best not to know.

"Hi, Lich," she giggled, "that probably tells me what sort of evening you had. Bad luck."

"Your sympathy's touching," he said, in his normal voice. "Where's Kare? You should be entertaining him, not calling me."

"He's away."

"Hard luck. That's both of us blown out. It went well, though?"

"Yes, and that's all I'm telling you, so stop digging. I'm only calling because I'm going to bed, and I didn't want you waking me."

Her brother's voice softened. "I'm glad it went well. I'll talk to you in the morning."

Sonly put down her comms unit and turned out the light. She was just starting to drift off when the unit went again. She cursed and turned the light back on.

"Yes?" she asked, tersely. She was always nervous of calls at night. When she'd been growing up, it was often a call that had got her dad up, followed by the sirens ordering an evacuation of the base.

"Sonly, when did you say Kare had left?" asked Lichio.

"About half an hour ago."

"He's not in the barracks, nor the project room. I sort of thought I'd catch up with him, but I can't find him."

You sort of thought you might snoop. "Call his comms unit."

"I did- he's not answering."

Sonly sat up. A cold finger of fear ran down her spine. He'd told her he was still a target.

"Lichio, get down to the port. Tell them to stop all flights. I'll meet you there."

Lichio didn't respond and she knew he probably thought she was overreacting, but she didn't think she was. Kare had left to go to the barracks.

"Sonly, he'll be around somewhere, don't panic."

"Now!" she said. Her voice *was* panicked and her heart was beating too quickly, making her breathless. She got out of bed and started to dress. "Lichio, go! I'd rather be wrong and have flights delayed than..."

He must have caught the desperation in her voice, because this time he said, "I'm on my way."

Her comms unit went dead and she finished dressing. Running, she left the apartment and went to the port. Something was wrong; she knew it.

CHAPTER TWENTY-EIGHT

hermals. Next time Silom saw Lichio le Payne, he'd shove a pair of them somewhere he wouldn't forget. He shivered, his hands- in thin, thermal gloves- gripping his bolt-caster. He flexed his fingers, knowing to keep them supple, and glanced up at Merrandron's sky. Grey, heavy clouds rolled in; it was going to snow again.

"There."

He followed the line of Charl's finger and saw the small group of soldiers emerge from the barracks.

"Wait."

This was what he liked about being a corporal: taking on a mission, being involved in the planning and trusted to carry it out. He brought his caster up, waiting for the last man to pass the transport. The scope zoomed in on the man, feeling oddly off-target with its calibration for the lighter gravity. Silom checked his features against what he'd been shown and confirmed he wore the livery of a general. Silom's mouth tightened- a general who'd ordered the massacre two weeks ago on Callazon. There was a low buzz as the target was confirmed, and he pulled the trigger, a bolt pulsing above the snow field. The general let out a cry, the bolt lodging in his neck, burrowing.

"...two, one," counted Charl, and the general's carotid exploded in a gush of blood, spraying across the snow. His knees buckled.

"Go!"

Charl and Silom skidded down the hill, steps off-kilter, too light and fast, to where Davos and Kym were waiting, scoots primed. Silom climbed behind Kym, his hand around her waist. "Go!"

They crossed the snow to the waiting Banned transporter. The scoots cleared the wide gangway, their treads adjusting easily, and before the soldiers had dismounted, the gangway was closed and the transport lifted off, ready to join the Banned squadron above. Silom pulled down his hood and took off the balaclava underneath. "Well done, everyone. Good job."

The squad moved into the main cabin and Silom sank onto one of the seats, tired but proud. Space battles might be what newcomers wanted to be part of- he guessed there was an Ealyn Varnon in everyone- but this type of mission was pretty bloody satisfying, too.

Kym sat beside him, pulling off her thin gloves. Her hair, too, was mussed, but it suited her.

"They'll have to close down the Nero base," she said.

"I expect so. They wouldn't have attacked so close, otherwise." He paused, took a deep breath- he had to tell her; he'd been putting it off for a week. "I've been offered a transfer."

Her eyes widened a little. "Where to?"

"Back on base."

"Why the hell would you go to the base? It's boring- you'll end up stuck in a training role or something."

He rubbed his hand over his chin. She was right, it was in the training corps. "I haven't accepted it yet. I wanted to tell you first."

"I don't want you to go," she said, softly. "I like working with you."

"Really? That's the only reason you don't want me to go?"

She smiled, her eyes shining. "Well, one of them..."

He was quiet for a moment, not sure what to tell her: that his friend was at the base, and he was choosing him over her? He'd be lucky if she didn't shoot him, and with her aim, he'd be singing soprano. He put his head back on the seat rest. "It's complicated."

"Why?"

He could try the truth: sorry, I have this cousin, and his father said he's going to bring down the Empress, and I'm pretty sure I'm involved somewhere, that I met him for a reason. Oh, and by the way I'm crazy about you, and the last girl I was crazy about got- what? ...killed, questioned, escaped... her life turned upside down in some way because of it all.

"It just is. Look, if I did go back- we'd see each other, right? On leave and what not."

"It wouldn't be the same."

True. "I'll think about it."

A door opened and one of the pilots came towards him.

"Corporal Dester?"

"That's right."

"There's been a change of plan," the pilot said, not quite meeting Silom's eyes. "We're to go directly to Holbec."

"Why?"

The pilot looked away for a moment, and then back. "They didn't say why. Just that you were to be brought in."

Silom's heart started to beat too quickly. It had to be Kare, there was no one else they'd recall him for. What had happened? Had he been taken? Or thrown his head up and left- and he might, if he thought he was becoming too much of a danger. He nodded

142

his thanks and tried to stay calm; he'd find nothing more out until they landed and even at top speed, that was six hours off.

"What was that about?" asked Kym.

He paused for a moment, before reaching out and taking her hand. "That, I think, was the shit just hitting the fan."

***

In the port- at least she'd called it right, wherever Kare was, he hadn't been found- Sonly gripped Lichio's hand so tightly it must be hurting him, but he didn't complain.

Eevan paced opposite, casting dark glances across at them. "Ma'am, if they have him..." his words trailed off as he looked at Rjala.

Sonly swallowed, determined to face the truth. "They'll question him."

"They will." Lichio put his free arm around her shoulders and hugged her. "I'm sorry."

She gulped and nodded; questioning in Abendau meant only one place. She wondered what exactly they did in Omendegon, and pushed the thought away. It might not come to that. Oh, lord, please let it not come to that.

"Surely his information is limited to the project only?" asked Eevan.

Sonly looked at him, hating him. Kare was a person- more than that, a person who'd been holding her and kissing her a couple of hours ago. Tears pricked her eyes; why the hell hadn't she made him stay?

Rjala crossed her arms. "If they have him, it's serious." She glanced at Sonly. "Serious enough we'd have to consider relocating. The project overarches our offensive and security programmes; the base would be compromised. How are we fixed for that, with Michael off base?"

Her words cut through Sonly's fear, making her focus. "If we have to, we can: it's prepared. I'd have to see Glen; he needs to mobilise the emergency base team." Rjala nodded, and Sonly went on, "But that's only if they have him, and he talks..."

Eevan snorted. "When he talks- he'll not last two minutes in Omendegon. He may be some genius programmer, but physically he's a sack of shit." He spat in disgust. "Let's hope we can find him. We've got ships tracking anyone who left tonight, but they have to board each- there'll be some we don't get to."

Rjala took the decision. "Focus on what's here. If he's gone, we can't do anything except prepare."

"How sure are you he hasn't decided to go himself? That he wasn't here to get the information you've kindly given him?" Eevan asked.

143

"I'm sure," Sonly said. "He wouldn't do that; he wouldn't betray us."

Rjala paused, and then said firmly, "I'm sure. I trust him implicitly."

There was movement at the entrance to the port and a sergeant came towards them. Sonly's heart jumped, sure they'd found him. The sergeant stopped in front of Rjala and saluted. "Colonel, we searched his quarters, and found this."

He handed something to Rjala. Lichio's arm tightened on Sonly's shoulder, and she bit her lip.

Rjala looked at the object. "Thank you." She waited until the sergeant went away. "It's a message tab."

She set the tab down and projected the image in front of them. Sonly gasped at the familiar features of the Empress. They listened to her words, and when the image faded there was silence.

"He's known all this time she could get to him," said Sonly, eventually. Tears started to form in her eyes, mostly from anger. *Why the hell didn't he tell us?*

Eevan slammed his hand against the wall, making her jump. "The stupid bastard."

Lichio shook his head. "It's not that. He'd worried you'd put a security detail on him. Silom *begged* me to let him stay at base so he could be with him. He knew Kare wouldn't risk anyone else- that he thought too many people had already died around him. *Damn* him."

"Calm down, Lichio," Rjala said. "This isn't your fault, or Silom's. A security detail isn't what we should be focusing on. How the hell have they got into the base? He shouldn't need security here- it *is* secure."

Sonly shivered with shock. "Kare's the one who decided to take the risk, Lich."

Rjala interrupted. "And if... *when*... he gets back, he'll face me about it. Eevan, this doesn't change anything; continue the search of the port."

Sonly sat- she didn't know how long- and watched the search in silence, tears pricking her. She grew numb, the word Omendegon circling her thoughts.

Someone knelt in front of her and she turned her eyes to them, but it took a moment to realise it was Eevan. She slumped against Lichio, his arm encircling her shoulders. Eevan looked at Lichio and gave a small shake of his head before turning his attention to Sonly.

"We've searched every ship," he said, gently. "He's not on any of them. We have to guess they got him out as soon as they took him. I think you have to assume he's gone, Sonly."

He's gone. The words ricocheted. She turned her head to Lichio, looking up at his face. It was so blurred that, but for the blond hair, he could have been anyone.

"What next?" asked Lichio.

"We'll alert the spy network at Abendau, and hope they can tell us if he turns up." Eevan turned to Sonly. "You'll have to get in touch with Michael; he's the only one with access to them."

"Okay." She took a deep, shuddering breath. "If he does get taken to Abendau, we move. We'll have to."

Eevan patted her knee, awkwardly. "It'll be hard for you if he is taken. I'm sorry." He sounded almost human.

"Does Silom know?" she asked. "Someone should tell him."

"His ship is due to land," said Lichio. "I've asked him to report to me."

"Thank you. I'm going to my room," she said. If the base was to be moved, she had preparations to carry out. It was the last thing she wanted to do, but staying here, waiting for news that could never be good, would be even worse.

"Do you want me to come?" asked Lichio.

"No, wait for Silom; he shouldn't hear it from a stranger."

"At least let me send someone with you," he said.

She was too tired to fight about it. Plus, the thought of returning to the apartment on her own made her shiver again. The last time she'd been there, Kare had been with her, vibrant and alive and kissing her, and she knew the moment she walked in, the memory would hit her. She nodded, and Lichio waved a soldier over to them.

"Will! Go with Sonly," said Lichio.

Sonly followed the soldier out, stepping round the search teams without thinking. They reached the apartment and Will led her to the sofa.

"Sit there– I'll get the lights on."

Sonly nodded her thanks and closed her eyes. She didn't open them when she heard a soft noise behind her. "Thanks, Will," she said. There was no response and she looked round. He wasn't there, and the apartment was still in darkness. "Will!"

There was no reply. She got up and recoiled in horror as a hole appeared where she'd been sitting, the padding from the sofa expelled into the air in a soft puff. She dived to the floor and pulled out her firearm. She lay, trying to quieten her breath, not sure where the shot had come from. The apartment was silent. She got up, keeping low and quiet, and moved towards the alarm point. A shot grazed her leg, making her slip and cry out.

She rolled onto her side as her attacker stepped out of the bedroom. He was dressed in a dark uniform, his face masked. She raised her gun, but he had already taken aim. Her breath froze as he

145

fired. The bullet came at her and she tried to roll but it was too fast. It touched her chest, and stalled, as if stopped–

She looked up to see a new figure, framed in the door to the corridor. Her attacker's focus moved to the newcomer and she took her chance, crawling to the panic button and hitting it. Its shrill alarm filled the small chamber.

There was a yell and the framed figure in the doorway reeled back, shot. She knew who it had to be.

"No!" She got to her feet, planting them as she'd been taught at basic.

Taking aim at her attacker, she clicked off the safety, ready to fire. Before she could, the man fell to the floor, blood spraying from his neck. Something touched her foot, and she shrieked when she looked down and saw the dull shine of his lifeless eyes. She bit the scream back, and kicked the head away.

"You okay?" asked a rasping voice, barely audible over the alarm.

"Kare?" She knew it was him, that it had to be him, but still couldn't quite believe it. She could see where her attacker's head had rolled to– he'd *killed* him.

"'s– me." He slumped to the floor, making her forget about the dead man. She ran and knelt beside him, horrified at the amount of blood spreading out and out. His shirt was soaked. She pulled it up, supporting his weight, and saw the huge exit wound in his back. He cried out at the pain.

"It's okay, I have you." She put her hand against the wound, trying to stanch the blood, but it flooded into her palm and down her arm, soaking into the thin material of her cardigan. The sound of footsteps running made her look up to see Silom and Lichio and a small squad of soldiers.

"It won't stop bleeding! Help me: it's everywhere."

Silom pulled his shirt off and pressed it against the wound.

"Get the medics!" he told Lichio. Quickly, Silom's shirt soaked through and he glanced desperately at Sonly. "This isn't good. He can heal the wound, but he can't make blood."

He slapped Kare, and got a small murmur in response.

"Kare, you need to close the wound quicker. You're losing blood." He slapped Kare a little harder. "Now, Kare." He glanced round. "Someone get some towels from the bathroom. And get the alarm off!"

Silom lifted his shirt away and looked at the wound.

"Good lad," Silom said. "Keep going, get it closed, then we'll get you sorted."

Sonly, with Kare still slumped against her, looked at Silom, and he nodded slightly. "It's closing. Keep going, another bit and you're there."

146

Someone handed Sonly a towel and Silom took his shirt away, throwing it to the side. She pressed the towel to the wound. Silom was right, the bleeding had slowed. Kare's eyes flickered slightly. His face was very pale, and sweat beaded across his forehead. The alarms stopped, but the silence seemed just as loud.

"What's wrong with his hand?" asked Silom.

Sonly glanced down; she had been so focused on the gun wound, she hadn't noticed more blood running down his hand.

"Oh, lord," she said, "his finger."

She could see, now, that his little finger had been excised, a thin thread of blood running from the wound. The knucklebone was visible, white through the blood crusted around the joint. She was still looking at it and trying to think what it meant when the medics pushed her aside. They lifted Kare onto a stretcher bed and began to work with him. Silom moved to the side to let them work, his mouth drawn down, his hands clenched.

"Silom, I'm sorry," she said. "This should never have happened. Not on the base." And she'd be damned sure someone found out how and why, and made sure it couldn't happen again.

He shook his head. "Sounds like my cousin had plenty of warning."

The paramedics lifted the stretcher, their faces impassive.

"I should have insisted I stay and watch his back," Silom said.

Lichio came up to them, his face shocked. He looked around the apartment, at the blood covering the wall and carpet, and the headless corpse on the floor.

"What happened?" he asked, but Sonly didn't respond. She clutched her arms, trying to stop shivering.

Silom stepped forward and looked at the body. "I assume Kare happened," he said. "That's new: he's never done that before." He sounded off-hand, but he was pale and shocked. Kare, it seemed, had talents he'd never shown anyone.

"Kare? Kare can decapitate people?" Lichio's voice was high, and his eyes flitted between Sonly and Silom.

"Apparently," Silom said.

"He beheaded someone," protested Lichio, his voice rising.

"I know. You might want to think about that the next time you roll in late or hungover."

In another circumstance, Sonly might have laughed, but not tonight, with danger touching them all, even in her calm apartment in the centre of the Banned base, where it should be safe.

"Hell," Lichio said, sombre and shocked. "We'll get someone in to clear up." He tapped Sonly's shoulder. "Don't go into the bathroom- Will's in there."

147

"Is he...?" asked Sonly. Lichio shook his head, and she started to shiver again.

Silom walked to the door of the apartment. "I'm going to the hospital." He looked down at Sonly's leg. "You should come too, get that looked at."

Lichio stepped forward. "You two go on. I'll liaise with Rjala and Eevan- they need to find out who our headless friend is and if he's on his own."

Sonly walked beside Silom. His bare chest and arms were smeared with blood, and he looked as shocked as she felt.

"How does he do it?" It would better to keep Silom talking and busy. "The healing?"

"I don't know," Silom said. "I'm not even sure he knows. He'll tell us, if we ask, that he just moved a part of his mind. It's one thing he's never worked out- where his power came from. Ealyn didn't know anything about his background, nor did my mum." He paused for a moment. "Kare's tried everything to find out- he said it was important to know, that his worked differently from anyone else's, but he couldn't."

"There are other psychers," she said. "He's not unique."

Silom glanced sideways at her. "Know any others who can take the head off an attacker?" She shook her head. "Thought not."

He opened a door and Sonly stepped outside. The jungle was starting to come alive, the caw of a parrot breaking the silence, a streak of light visible in the sky. The lights from the hospital block shone out against the darkness.

"Why is it so important he finds out? I mean, he knows his mother blended two powerful psychers- isn't that enough?"

Silom paused before saying. "He's frightened he won't always be able to control his powers. That they'll get too strong, take him over."

The image of the headless body flashed before her. Kare did that- it was hard to believe. She'd been kissing him earlier, had wanted him to stay, and it turned out he could have killed her as easily as kiss her. The thought made her stomach turn over, like she was ill. She took a sly, sideways glance at Silom. He was able to handle it, so why couldn't she?

"Silom, I like him," she said. It felt odd, admitting to it. Normally she kept feelings to herself, too well trained by her father to allow anything that could be used against her be known openly.

"That's good. He's a nice guy."

"But, how do I handle it?" They reached the hospital and Sonly palmed the door pad, waiting for it to recognise her and admit them. "How do you?"

148

Silom pushed the door open and looked at her sideways. "Are you serious about him?"

"I'd like to be," she said. "But I need to know I can deal with what he can do."

Silom looked her up and down, before he nodded. "Okay, the first thing you have to know is he will always have a sense of how you're feeling. He calls it his buzz, and can't turn it off. So if you're sad, he'll know it; if you're in a good mood, he'll pick it up. I tell myself it's not knowing my thoughts, it's just like being with someone who's very tuned in."

"How do I hide anything from him?" She couldn't imagine how it would feel, to be with someone who had no regard for the privacy she'd worked so hard to cultivate in the midst of a teeming base. Something of her uncertainty must have shown, because Silom gave a vigorous shake of his head.

"Not like that. He won't read your mind. I've never, ever known him to. Well, once when he was about eight, he tried to change Mum's mind about something. She sensed him, gave him the dressing down from hell– she had a bit of a temper– and he's never done it since."

The base entrance opened and the trolley pushed past them. Kare was pale, almost the colour of the sheet, and unmoving. A mask was over his mouth, but even so, his chest rose and fell with the shallowest of breaths. Everything they were talking about, what Kare could or couldn't do, might not matter. She'd spent months pussyfooting around him, following protocol and keeping her distance. She'd been an idiot. She trembled and Silom's hand reached out and took her elbow, giving her support. They fell into place behind the medics and followed them to the ward. Silom pushed forward and spoke to the doctors, but Sonly hung back; there was no point in crowding the doctors. She brought her hand to her throat as she watched, knowing it was an excuse. She wasn't going forward because she didn't want to claim him as hers.

Silom walked back. "Do you want a coffee? They're going to give him a transfusion, and it'll take a while."

"A transfusion? So he'll be all right?"

Silom paused. "He's stable. They had to stop on the way over, and...."

"And what?" she asked, her heart beating too fast, making her dizzy and sick.

"They had to resuscitate him."

Her heart skipped a beat, fluttering in her chest, making her gulp against the eerie feeling. "I thought it was nearly impossible to kill a psycher." But she knew the truth. The bullet had ripped through his skin; his blood had run into Silom's shirt, covered her cardigan. That wasn't someone who was immortal.

"They killed his dad. Being blown up does that to any man. If Kare loses too much blood, he'll die. If they take a head shot at him, they'll kill him. It's a little harder, that's true, but he's flesh and blood, the same as you or me." He nodded down at her wound. "I told the doctor you were injured; someone's going to come and have a look."

She sat on a bench as he selected two coffee pods from a supply on the windowsill. He snapped them open and handed her one. She cradled it in her hands, taking comfort from the warmth. Silom sat beside her, bare-chested, and she wondered if he was cold. His hand was shaking as he brought the coffee to his lips, and she was glad neither of them was sitting alone.

"You know, he *will* be all right," Silom said. "Once he gets his powers back, you'll be amazed what he can do. The first time I found out he was a psycher, he was hovering a couple of foot in the air, drinking a glass of water. With no hands." He looked at her and grinned. "When he saw me, he forgot what he was doing, fell and dumped the water on his head. He's not exaggerating what he can do, and while he says he's crap at healing– I think it's because Karia was so good– to you and me it'll look like a miracle."

"The finger?" *The trails of blood running from it, the shine of bone.*

"I doubt if he can do anything with that; growing one back goes beyond healing. I think."

"Do we know who the attackers were?" These were all questions she should have asked before she'd come to the hospital. Her leg could have waited.

"Looked like Star ops to me. If it was a squad, there'd have been six of them. One was probably a psycher, given who the target was."

"Are they all dead?" she asked, still finding it hard to believe Kare had carried this out and proved to be so deadly. She wondered what Eevan was making of it all.

"I don't think he'll have left them in the position to come back for him."

Sonly shivered. Did she want to know Kare better? Or should she say this is close enough, and she couldn't go any further. She looked down the corridor, at the door they'd taken him through. She thought of him in the apartment, kissing her, how it had been so right, and glanced back at Silom.

"What we were talking about earlier? Coping strategies." He

nodded. "Keep going, as many as you can tell me, please."

Later, after they'd treated her leg, they let her visit Kare. She'd thought he would be asleep, or so drugged he'd make no sense. Instead, he was sitting up and his colour was coming back. He had a drip in his arm, though, and looked exhausted.

"You seem a lot better," she said.

"I'll be fine. How's your leg? You're limping."

"It's a graze," she said. "It's been treated."

"Do you want me to fix it?"

"No," she said, sharply. "It's okay."

Silom came in and walked up to Kare, his fists bunched. "You're an asshole," he said.

"Call it as it is, Silom," replied Kare. He faced Silom, not backing down, and it was Silom who looked away first, throwing himself into the chair beside the bed.

"What the hell were you doing? Hadn't you scanned?" Silom asked.

"No, I hadn't. I was in a very unusual place for me: a relaxed mood. This'll teach me, but I'd had a good night, a promotion, a..." he glanced at Sonly and gave a small, private smile. "Anyway, I fucked up, I wasn't careful enough."

"And the tab? When were you planning to tell us?"

Kare looked between Silom and Sonly. "It was found, then. I hadn't planned to tell anyone, anytime. I guess you know that."

"The colonel intends to talk to you about it," said Silom. Kare winced. "One thing that's going into place is a security team."

"A security team can be infil- "

Silom cut across his words. "Shut up. For once, Kare, shut up and listen. You nearly died. Okay?" Slowly, Kare nodded. "The infiltration argument is just an excuse, one that people buy. I know that you'd prefer to ignore this and hope it'll go away. But, it won't. Okay?"

"Go on," said Kare. His voice was clipped, but he didn't look away from Silom.

"I'm going to head up the team for you. I did some extra training on personal security. And, before you make some smart comment, no, I didn't do it for a fucking hobby. The one person you can trust- the *only* person you can- is me."

"You can't," said Kare. "What about Kym?"

"I talked to her on the way in. We'll see each other when she's on base leave; maybe at some stage she'll ask for a transfer. It's fine." He swallowed, and looked away, just for a moment. "Besides, I don't know how close I want to get. You know, after..."

"Liane. That was a long time ago, Silom. You have to let it

go sometime."

"Like you let things go?" Silom made a cutting gesture with his hand. "Leave it. It's enough for you to know I will be staying here, on the team."

Kare's mouth tightened into a thin line. "No. I'll refuse it."

Silom glared at him. "It's not up for discussion. You're targeted. Star ops don't expose themselves to this level of risk for nothing." He paused. "Plus, I get a promotion, and it's better than a training role."

"They were Star ops?"

"You didn't know?" asked Silom.

"I wasn't sure. They knocked me out, and when I came round they were taking my finger off. They had been planning to take me, but couldn't once the port closed. So they changed tack and decided to give me some encouragement to bring myself in later. They said it would be a reminder for me, that I wouldn't forget I was wanted in Abendau."

"They did a clean job," Silom said, and Kare looked at him, his mouth open.

"Glad it meets your professional approval. It still hurt. A lot."

"What happened then?"

"They said they'd take something else, something precious, so I would never forget what my actions had cost. I asked what, and they said I should have asked who." He looked at Sonly and gave a sad smile. "I knew who it would have to be. I broke their psycher's neck, shielded myself, and dealt with the others."

"You took out six Star ops," Silom said, and Sonly could hear the respect in his voice.

"Only if you count their psycher. I was pretty desperate– it's a good motivator. You're right, though, I was lucky not to be taken. Whoever realised I was missing did a good job; if the port hadn't closed I'd be halfway to Abendau by now."

"It was Lichio," said Sonly.

Kare groaned. "I hoped you wouldn't say that."

She managed a half smile at that, but Silom remained grim-faced.

"Why the hell weren't you shielded at the end?" Silom asked.

Kare looked away.

"He had shielded me instead," admitted Sonly. "Why, Kare?"

"Do you need to ask? Or can we just leave it that it seemed right at the time."

Silom made a disgusted noise and Kare turned back to him, a flash of annoyance in his eyes.

"You know why." Kare ducked his head a little, and then lifted it again, facing his cousin squarely. "I'm not having others being taken for me. Besides, I didn't think he'd try to kill me; the Empress doesn't want that."

"I don't think he knew it was you," said Sonly. "You were silhouetted."

"That makes sense," Kare said, and put his hand on his chest. "He certainly didn't shoot to miss."

Silom stood up. "I'm going to go, and let you think about things. You need to decide how you're going to deal with this, and that doesn't include ignoring it anymore."

"It's one incident," Kare protested.

"You've had a tracker placed, and a tab. Now a Star ops team. And Corun. That's not one incident."

Kare put his head down and ran his hands through his hair, massaging his temples with the balls of his hands. When he looked up, his eyes were scared, almost haunted.

"You can't have a base this size without some leaks," he said.

Silom's hands clenched into fists, and for a moment Sonly wondered if he would actually hit Kare. He unclenched them.

"They got a Star ops team in," said Silom. "That takes more than a spy. They sent them in for one person. And do you know what?"

Kare shook his head.

"It's for someone I don't want them to get. Please, at least try to think of a different future, do what you can to stop it. Please."

Kare glanced at Sonly and then back at Silom.

"Enough," he said, his voice tight. "I'll cooperate."

"I'll hold you to it," said Silom, nodding towards Sonly. "I even have a witness. I'll see you later."

Sonly sat where Silom had been. "He's not happy," she said.

"I noticed," Kare replied, dryly. "Silom's over-protective, that's all. I'll talk to him about this security thing, though, see if he'll back down if I agree to take a team. He shouldn't have to stay here just because of me."

"He knows you're in danger." But what sort of danger? What wouldn't he talk about? "I've never known them to come into the base before. We're worried, to be honest."

"Please," he said, "I really have had enough. How are you? You've had a shock: not your average first date."

"I'm okay, I think." She could tell her voice was sharp, and he glanced over, his eyes narrowing slightly.

"Are you?"

She paused. He'd taken a man's head off and killed five others. What did he expect her to say?

"It was self-defence," she said. "What you did."

153

"You didn't answer. See, I told you it was complicated and to think about it. If you've changed your mind, it's fine, I'll back off. With no recriminations, just the offer of a complicated friendship. I can handle it, I'm a big boy."

He didn't quite meet her eyes as he said it, and she knew he didn't mean it, that he wanted her to say she could deal with it. *He shielded me instead of himself.*

"I can do complicated," she told him. "Although you might want to have a chat to Lichio. Silom's scared the life out of him about your disciplinary approach."

He raised the ghost of a smile at that. "Silom's right about one thing. We nearly died. If that bullet had hit you, if I'd lost a bit more blood or healed any slower, we would have. It's just, this is a dangerous business, and I'm feeling very lucky to be alive."

"Me, too."

"Then, let's not waste it," he pleaded. "She'll get me sometime. Silom doesn't want to accept that— that's why he asked me to think of a different future— but she has more resources, and wants me very, very badly."

"She might not."

Kare shook his head. "One day, I'll have to face her, but I'll go when I'm ready, not when she calls me like a dog. For now, I want to be with you. I have never felt this way before about anyone."

"I know," she said. "I feel the same. I like being with you."

"What I want is to spend as much time with you as I can. I shouldn't; I should keep you safe, but being apart last night didn't keep you safe, did it?"

She waited, and the silence lengthened as she thought about its implications. How long did she have until they caught up with him, or her? Or the base? Did she have time to waste, when it felt this right?

"I feel the same way," she said. She leaned down to kiss him and he pulled her to him, kissing her with the same passion as the previous night. As he put his arms around her and she pressed against his chest, she could feel no weakness in him, no sign that he had been close to death so recently. Now, he was alive and strong.

"Bugger," he said, as she broke away. "Can't you take me back tonight?"

She pushed him away, gently. "Get some more rest— you'll be all the readier," she teased.

He broke into a broad smile at that. "It feels good, today," he said.

He was almost dead earlier. He'd just found out his mother was so determined to take him, she'd risk an ops team, and it felt good?

She didn't understand him, and yet she did. Why waste a life in fear? It was what being in the Banned had meant, all her life: the need to live for the moment, not think what could lie ahead.

He nodded, no doubt picking up her mood. "I'm free. Let my mother plot as much as she wants; she can't take today from me. She'll never take today from me."

CHAPTER TWENTY-NINE

Averrine walked through the gardens of Abendau palace, towards the formal maze. She stopped- from here the palace looked exactly as she'd planned it, the red stone of her father's castle in Bendau replaced by imported white stone evidencing her wealth. She cast out, letting the sense of her filter into the city's streets and the minds of its people. They responded, and the city seemed to expand under her power, becoming more connected to her.

She took a moment, breathing the lush air, so different from the rest of Belaudii. She'd promised herself, when she'd been in the desert, that one day she'd have somewhere reclaimed from it. Somewhere where water wasn't treated as a commodity to be savoured, but instead used to feed and provide growth. The moat running around the garden constantly needed replenished, ice couriered across half the system, from Taurine, to do so, but it was worth it for this, the one place she could take time to savour what her work had delivered.

Discreetly, her captain of guards stepped forward, bowing. "My Lady, they're ready for you."

They could wait. She crossed the gardens, stopping at a red rock path, and frowned at a few weeds poking through. She saw one of the gardeners and brought his attention to her. He paled, but walked over with the sort of decorum half her generals failed to achieve. His face had a sun-kissed swarthiness, his eyes were the brown of the tribes. That explained his decorum- the tribes knew her as Lady Averrine and revered her as their own. It was what she offered others, if they could but see it. If they would find within themselves, as the tribes had, proper reverence for her, there would be no need of armies and generals.

"Have the path cleared," she said.

"Yes, my Lady."

He turned, taut muscles rippling across his back. Should she order him to attend her? *No.* The tribes would not approve of a boy so young. A pity. She continued through the gardens, into the palace, and to the boardroom, where her generals and colonels waited.

She focused on General Allen, standing to attention, his fear filling the air. She turned the full weight of her power on him- he had to know he had failed her- and he whitened. She touched his mind, his body, let her power spread through him. He was drowning in the feel of her, his head back, mouth open, mixed waves of fear and pleasure, each the stronger for the other.

He'd pass out in a moment. She pulled her psyche from him, removing it completely. He gasped, and she knew it was starting, the gnawing emptiness. She cast her gaze around the room. They need not think only Allen contributed to this. Their heads went down as she touched them. Except one–

Phelps kept his head up, breathing deeply under her anger. She stared at his thin, aquiline face and flat grey eyes. He raised his chin, embracing her power as the others failed to, luxuriating in her presence. Already, they'd known each other once– soon, she would own him as she did no other.

She walked to the front of the room and sat behind the desk. They knew why they were here– they had attended court martials in the past. She would see to it that an example was made, one that would reverberate through her officers. An example that was needed; it was a *boy* they were seeking– a psycher, yes, but still a boy– failure could not be accepted.

"Kneel," she said.

Allen fell to his knees, his breath rasping. She didn't even need to compel him– years of serving under her was all the compulsion he needed. His fear turned to terror, emanating in sick waves. Any minute now and he would start begging: to stay, to be allowed his place.

"The matter of my son," she said.

"My Lady, they were Phelps' men," Allen said, and licked his lips.

Indeed they were. She looked at Phelps– perhaps it was time to see how *he* responded to pressure. She focused on him, increasing her hold on him, but he faced her, not wilting beneath her displeasure, but drinking it in.

"Your team?" she demanded.

"My team did their job." His voice was steady, cold almost. "They got in and lifted Varnon. Allen moved earlier than I advised. If we had waited, we could have finished the job. Destroyed the rebels as well as taking Varnon." He took a deep breath. "My Lady, the base itself is not an obstacle. Reaching it is. Once we remove the first defences and warning systems, the base is ours."

She nodded– he had put his objections on record, and that had been a risk. If Allen had completed the task, Phelps would have been discredited. "And your investigations into Ealyn Varnon?"

At that, he paled a little. "They remain... active." She waited,

157

until he licked his lips and went on, "Ealyn Varnon did not come from where he purported to. The family have all been checked and there are no psychic powers evidenced, my Lady. I haven't discovered where he is from, but I can tell you who he is not. If we get the boy and access to the genetic base, I have a range of possibilities to match him against."

She pushed into him, telling him he had failed, and at that he did react, closing his eyes, his face twisting into a grimace. Satisfied, she turned back to Allen.

"Your excuse?"

"My Lady, I... please, you need to understand..." His words fell over themselves, becoming incomprehensible. He was of no use to her, broken as he was.

"Exile," she said. She let the word ring out and carry. "Permanent exile." They- the generals, the guards- would know that as the lie it was. Once removed from Abendau, Allen would lose the sense of himself, the strength she had given him over the years. He'd be lucky to survive a year: most didn't, even those she hadn't held so closely.

"You can't. Please, not that," he begged, his voice shaking with the realisation of what was ahead: the loneliness; the unfillable need within him. "My Empress, mercy."

Two of her guard took his arms, drew him to his feet. His gaze circled the room, clouded. She'd seen it before, the loss of focus, the confusion of a mind abandoned. She waited until he had been taken from the room and his pleas had faded from her hearing, before turning to the others.

"To attention," she commanded.

They got to their feet and looked ahead, their backs straight. Her eyes cast around the group, and when she reached Phelps his eyes met hers.

"Come to me," she told him. "The rest, you are dismissed."

A collective sense of relief filled the room, and she smiled at the speed with which they emptied it. Today's lesson would not be forgotten. Phelps crossed to her and knelt.

"Stand," she told him, after some moments. He did, meeting her eyes, unbowed, and she said, "You know what I want."

"I know what you say you want."

"Go on."

He paused, and she forced into his mind. He gasped as she burrowed, reminding him he was her tool and *would* answer when commanded.

"You say you want your son," he said, each word squeezed from his throat. Still, his eyes met hers. "You don't," he continued.

"Tell me why."

"Ten years ago, when he was a child, you wanted your son. Even two years ago, when he left Dignad, you wanted him. But what you wanted was a boy to mould, not a man."

At last, someone understood. "He is still a boy," she said. Would he have enough within him to tell the truth, even if it was not what she wanted to hear? She continued, "He is barely twenty, he can be moulded."

"A boy does not do what he did on Dignad. He's an Empath; he must have felt the soldiers' pain as they burned in their transport. It must have been overwhelming, yet he still did it. A boy does not destroy a Star ops team. A man does. A man poisoned against you by Ealyn. He is no heir to your empire, and never will be." He paused. "My Lady, I can't tell you where Ealyn came from. I can tell you his powers were not like any I have studied. You combined them with yours, my Lady. We don't know how powerful the boy is, but to take out an entire Star ops team, he must not be underestimated. We must consider how we take him, and how we hold him."

Averrine indicated for him to sit opposite. He was the first to understand it wasn't about the person. She had created the boy, had carried him herself rather than use a surrogate, had felt him move in her belly, him and his sister. He was hers and had refused to come and fulfil what she had created...

"What do you suggest?" she asked.

"His notoriety is growing within the Banned; he is devising a system to enhance their capability. I suggest you use him as an example. He has a legitimate claim to your empire, yet he has turned against you. It must be shown such a one cannot hope to stand against you."

"And do you propose to take him for me?"

Phelps lifted his chin, calm and proud. "I do."

"How?"

He leaned forward and she could see his hard eyes, intelligent and demanding. "I will hunt him. I will bring those who know him to me and corrupt them: I would ask you to bind them fully to us and our cause." He paused. "I will find a way to hold his powers in abeyance. When I take him for you, he will be a lamb at your mercy." She inclined her head in acceptance as he continued, "If you permit me, I will learn everything about the *man* who has rejected you, my Lady, and seek him for you. It may take time– "

"I want him now."

"Then you will ruin the job. When I bring him in, it will be done in one movement that he cannot escape. It might take years to do what I need to do, to chase him and harry him, but when I am ready, I will take him, my Empress. If that is your command."

The Empress looked at him a moment longer, and then nodded. "Bring him to me, Phelps, and I will see you are rewarded." She sent a blast of power his way, let him feel it and know his reward. Already, he was addicted, his eyes glittering.

He bowed deeply. "My Empress."

A hint of his pride crossed to her, a belief in his destiny. She let him feel her pleasure, saw how his eyes closed, the way they hadn't under her wrath. He breathed deeply, his chest rising, and she sent more of her power to him, filling him. He opened his eyes, and they met hers, not hard now, but adoring, the way they had been after he'd taken her two nights ago.

"Phelps," she said.

"My Lady."

"Fail, and you follow Allen." She smiled; let him understand this lesson. "And you will feel the loss of me more than any."

A muscle in his cheek twitched, but he managed a faint smile. His chin came up as if he relished the challenge. "My Empress, I will not fail."

CHAPTER THIRTY

PART THREE: KARE – FIVE YEARS LATER

Kare woke and stretched. Somewhere under the covers lay Sonly, her blonde hair the only part visible. She slept like a hedgehog, like she shut down and hibernated. He'd told her that once, and her response had been almost as prickly, too.

He pushed back the covers, got up and pulled on his uniform trousers, tightening the belt. It rode over the top of the waistband and he swore softly; the Banned uniforms must have been designed by a sadist. Either that, or Sonly had bought them on the cheap. Since she didn't wear them, she showed little sympathy. He smoothed them down and wished he could wear his field fatigues, but with his promotion to major, Rjala had made it clear he was expected to wear his full uniform when on duty.

When am I not? He'd spent half the night in the project room, commanding a battle waged on a different planet, light years away: that was the trouble with a systems-wide war, someone was always awake, somewhere. It was peculiar to take leadership over soldiers he'd never met and didn't know. Even stranger that they obeyed him, treated him as their commander. He frowned– the time delay, particularly now they were battling in the middle zone systems– was more significant than he liked. He wondered if he could beg a few days off battle command to review the configurations.

He padded barefoot to the small kitchen area and pressed the selection screen and waited– he'd never seen Sonly do even this much in the kitchen. Her default was to call the mess and see what arrived.

Two cups emerged, and a plate of toasted bread. He carried them back to the bedroom and set Sonly's coffee, strategically, on the table beside her and then sat on top of the bedcovers and ate his toast. After a moment, the blonde hair moved.

"Toast?" There was a groan and he grinned, finishing his. A hand emerged and he put the other slice into it. "Get up," he said.

There was a shuffle, and she emerged from the covers, her face flushed and hair sticking up. He leaned over and gave her a quick kiss: he loved her best in the early morning, when it was just them, and she could be Sonly, not Miss le Payne, the cool, organised rebel leader.

"What time is it?" she asked.

"Seven. I have to go in a minute."

Sonly took a bite of her toast, and reached for her coffee. "You think you'll do it today?"

"We should; our position's good."

"You said that last time."

"I was wrong."

She made a disgusted noise. "It's no good telling me you were wrong. I need you to be right. Without Nevagus..."

He got up and pulled on his shirt, zoning out her words. He understood: Peiret, the first of the influential lead families, would open negotiations, but only if the Banned proved they could take and hold a planet in the middle zone. *Tell it to your bloody brother.* He managed, showing great restraint, not to actually say it- he hadn't found any way of proving it was Eevan who was sabotaging the campaign.

He lifted his jacket and boots, leaned down and gave her a kiss. "I'll do my best, okay?"

Two hours later, as the last ship confirmed its status, Kare nodded to Lichio. "Tell your brother we're ready to attack."

"Colonel," Lichio said into the comms unit, "aerial defence systems are destroyed. Major Varnon confirms ground assault is viable."

Kare watched the screen which dominated the small room. "If he doesn't do it this time, Lich, I'm taking it to Colonel Rjala."

"He won't like that."

"I don't care what he likes. I've been playing this game since I got the system in place. You're more used to him than me; am I wrong?"

Lichio shook his head, emphatically. "No, he's doing it to piss you off. He knows it's incredibly hard to prove retrospectively."

"I could invite Colonel Rjala along next time. She can see for herself."

"I think we can do better than that." Lichio smirked. "I did some overtime last night. You owe me for it."

"Have you grasped the concept of who's in charge here, Lich? It's up to me if I owe you," Kare said, but smiled as he did. It hadn't been an easy transition for either of them, as Kare had passed Lichio in seniority, but now they'd settled on an easy familiarity when working alone. It probably helped that Lichio had always had an older brother and sister on the fast-track to emulate- he'd long since learned his value didn't lie in promotion after promotion, but in being good at what he did, at being reliable and smart. In fact, staying under the radar might be preferable for him- who knew what he might get landed with if anyone caught on to how capable he was.

Lichio put on an innocent face. "Have you heard of managing

up? I took a crash course when you got promoted. If I told you I'm capturing the real-time, undiluted ops data from this battle- from both yours and Eevan's command consoles- would you change your mind? No technical jargon, no interruptions, just a line by line account of this attack. And not one which can be manipulated later, no matter how senior the manipulation is." Lichio handed over a sheet of paper. "It only takes a couple of minutes to produce."

Kare read it through, smiling as he did. Working with Lichio drove him mad with frustration half the time, and then he came up with something like this. "Thank you; I should have thought of it. A day off: no more." Kare saw Lichio's smile. "Who is it this time?"

Lichio made a hurt face. "That's not fair- I've been with Janis for three weeks now."

"A record?"

"Maybe." Lichio nodded at the screen. "He's not going to attack."

Kare slammed his hand on the desk. "I need to be the one who makes that call."

"You can't. He's in command."

The comms unit flashed. Kare watched it for a moment, and then said, "You better talk to him, Lich. Lord knows what I'll say to the bastard."

Lichio nodded and activated the unit. "Sir," he said smoothly to Eevan.

"Inform the major: attack is not viable, I say again, not viable."

Lichio waved Kare away. As Kare stepped back, he glanced at the report and picked up his comms unit. He pressed a familiar connection and waited.

"Colonel Rjala?" he said after she answered. "Ma'am, may I request an urgent review meeting into Nevagus? The final attack just failed."

Rjala sighed. "That's disappointing. I'll arrange a meeting with yourself and Colonel le Payne."

"Thank you, ma'am." He set the unit down.

"You're going to confront him with it directly?" asked Lichio.

Kare turned to face him. "Yes. I want to see the bastard's face when he realises I've sunk him."

"Be careful. You really don't need any more enemies."

"He's not a new one."

"True," said Lichio. He paused, drumming his fingers on the control panel. "You said I know him better than you."

Kare opened the programme Lichio had created and quickly worked through it, seeing how the data had been blended. Satisfied, he requested a copy.

"He's a terrible enemy," Lichio said. "And he'll hate being

shown up to Colonel Rjala. Tread carefully, that's all."

Kare straightened. "You know how important this campaign was. I can't let him ruin what Sonly's worked so hard for, just to get one over on me." He paused. "Plus, he's not the one living with her– I'd take his anger over hers any day of the week."

"I wouldn't. He'll hold a grudge– Sonly just blasts it out, there and then."

"Let him. The kicking I took in barracks– I've always thought he was behind it. Maybe he's not the only one with a long memory. I need to stop him now, show him I'm not going to hide from him."

But it went further, into territory he didn't want to explore, but had to. If Eevan was prepared to go against his board, to undermine a campaign to score points, what else was he capable of? Without evidence, there would be no way to push the Banned into controlling Eevan a little closer. He was the commander of their ground forces, the lynchpin of the military, with half the senior echelon firmly in his pocket. It was too much of a power base to go unchallenged– that way lay something much more ominous than a single campaign falling through.

"I understand. Hell, I *agree* with you," said Lichio. "But look at it from Eevan's perspective. He thinks you came back and got your own way with everything. He's smarting. If you humiliate him to Colonel Rjala, it'll go deep. If you take any advice from me, keep your temper, present the facts and go."

"I won't lose my temper," said Kare. "I'll present this to Rjala and be civil and polite when I do so. I'll even kiss his ass if I'm told to."

***

Rjala sat at her desk. In front of her, Eevan– tall, broad shouldered and imposing– had his arms crossed and a smirk on his face. Kare faced him, his eyes flashing. She'd never known him to be so angry and she wondered if she should intervene, but decided against it. This confrontation had been building for some time. It was better here, with her, than anywhere more public.

"Why the hell didn't you attack, Eevan?" demanded Kare.

"I think you meant, 'Why the hell didn't you attack, *sir?*' " Eevan said.

"Okay. Why didn't you attack, sir?"

"Because, *Major*, the planet's defence systems were still in place," Eevan said. His emphasis on Kare's rank seemed to work, as the younger man visibly calmed himself. Rjala relaxed a little.

"The ground units only. You outnumbered the enemy two to one, and I had aerial support for you. Sir," said Kare, his voice steady.

"It was my call, and your system told you something different than mine. The planet couldn't be taken."

Eevan smirked a little more. Rjala saw Kare's jaw tighten, a flush come up on his cheeks. He hadn't calmed down. In fact, he was angrier than she'd ever seen him. He reminded her, for the first time, of his father; when she'd first joined the Banned, Ealyn Varnon had commanded the aerial forces with a restrained passion- and a readiness to confront anyone who didn't match that passion- she hadn't seen since.

"You didn't want to take it, you mean. You're a petty bastard, Eevan." Kare planted his feet, glaring at the older man.

"Enough, Major," Rjala said. Time to stop this, before one or both ended up disciplined. "I won't allow such disrespect to your senior officer. Either back up your claim or back down."

Kare ran his hand through his hair, before handing her the report he'd brought.

"Yes, ma'am. You want proof. This is the operational data for the Nevagus campaign: troop sizes, planetary defences, space capacity. Also, the detail on the status when our esteemed colonel called off his attack."

Eevan reached for the report, but Rjala held her hand up, stopping him. She began to look at the clearly laid out figures, her experience making them easy to understand. She took care not to let her face betray her thoughts.

"And this came from where?" Rjala asked.

"My very able number two," Kare said. "It's amazing what he'll do for a day off."

If Lichio was prepared to build evidence against his brother, he must feel it merited the trouble it would bring him. And Eevan must know what the report contained- his face, red, holding back barely controlled anger, told her that. *Damn* Kare- he should have brought this to her privately. She looked at Kare, saw his tight jaw, and hoped he knew what he'd done.

"Leave me," she said, her words clipped. "I'll call you when I want to see you again."

She waited for the door to close after them, and read the report through from beginning to end. Twice. There was no room for doubt, nor could this be dealt with by her alone. Kare was right- he *was* a bastard.

Rjala opened her comms link. "Michael," she said. "I need an emergency committee meeting."

"Why?"

"I don't want to talk over the comms. Some people in this base are too technically able."

He sighed. "Do you want Sonly or will it be a conflict of interest?"

Rjala did a quick calculation. "We need her for quorum. Glen's off base."

"We have Eevan."

"Eevan can't come: conflict of interest."

"I see. I'll round up Sonly, and you can tell us what our two military geniuses have been up to."

As she waited, Rjala read the report again, made another call, and had just finished when Sonly and Michael entered.

"I hope this is good, Rjala," Sonly said. "I had a budget meeting. The Peiret fiasco has left a hole in it."

"Would the Peirets reconsider if I guarantee we'll take Nevagus in three days?" It was, Rjala knew, grasping at straws.

"No, it's too late, now." Sonly looked drained. "It took everything I had to get them to agree this extension. Their ambassador made it clear they would go no further." She rubbed a hand over her eyes. "In fact, he left just after the attack was aborted. He's probably halfway across the system by now."

"We can do nothing about it now." Michael nodded to Rjala. "Perhaps you'll tell us why you called us."

"I had an interesting meeting earlier, where Kare called Eevan a petty bastard."

"The reason?" asked Michael. His face was impassive, but his eyes watched her, missing nothing.

"The reason Eevan's a bastard, or the reason Kare called him it?" asked Rjala, struggling to keep her voice calm.

"Start with the first: why's Eevan a bastard?" Sonly asked. "I could name a couple of reasons, but let's hear the current one."

Rjala slapped Lichio's information on the table. "That. Eevan had the chance to take Nevagus, and chose not to."

"After the last board meeting?" said Michael, his words sharp.

Rjala nodded and waited for the information to sink in. "I spoke to your other brother, Sonly, who compiled this information."

"And what did Lichio say?" Sonly asked, her eyes glittering with anger.

"He said he and Kare spent the last month staying late to get aerial support to Nevagus; that they worked very hard to take this planet. He also informs me Kare had the defences down on three occasions, each viable. Lichio said, and I quote, if he had Kare's talents, Eevan would be a frog by now."

Sonly gave a short laugh. "I'm sorry, the image, you know." She sobered up. "Lichio's right. I've almost got to the point where I've forgotten I have a partner, he's been working so much. I'll have to apologise; I wasn't very nice this morning."

"I'd have done more than call Eevan a bastard," Rjala said. She wondered, briefly, if it *was* possible to turn someone into a frog. "There's no doubt about it: the planet should have been taken."

Michael drummed his fingers. "What do you want to do, Rjala?"

She nodded her thanks for him not imposing a solution on her. "I'll speak to Kare about his attitude. He can't call his officer a bastard, and he should have come to me in private. With Eevan- it's more complicated. He has an impeccable record up to this, and he would have lost men taking the planet. He has some grounds to argue caution but, given the nature of the campaign and its importance, I had made it clear a robust strategy was to be followed. He failed to carry that order through." She pursed her lips. Eevan le Payne was a strategist. He'd lost more men in battle than Nevagus would have cost. That would not have stopped him. "It's a personal attack, I think- a way to make Kare look bad."

"We can't let it go, Rjala. He ignored an agreed objective," said Sonly.

Michael nodded. "It has to be a formal warning, on record. And, whilst his motivations may be personal, he didn't put the Banned first."

"I genuinely don't believe this is in character for him," said Rjala. "He lives and breathes the Banned; I've never known him to do anything like this before."

"It's a serious incident. Rein him in. Keep him close. And ensure the warning carries the possibility of demotion should any other incident come to our attention."

Rjala winced. "It's very hard- we have parity..."

"You have authority."

She shook her head. "Dotted line, only. The board sits over us."

Michael nodded. "Perhaps a better structure, one that *will* enable you to keep him under supervision. Promote Kare; he can take over the flight teams."

Interesting; to do so would mean accepting Kare was able to stand up to Eevan and had enough kudos of his own. He had the support of the flight teams, she knew- he'd been working with them for three years, now. No one had better knowledge of the Banned systems. Still, she hesitated, thinking of the brooding Eevan and how he'd respond to Kare being equal to him, especially if he was given a warning, too. *He broke an agreed objective, one I issued him. I can't let it pass.*

"I think Michael's right," Sonly said. "It also frees more of your time for the security remit."

"If they have parity, who'll referee?" asked Rjala.

Michael stood up and extended his hand to her. "You, General Rjala; if you'll accept. Proposed by me."

"Seconded by me," Sonly said. She recorded it on the minutes and waited for Rjala's response.

"It might work," she said. "Accepted by me."

***

Sonly walked, as quietly as she could, into the small office in her apartment. She sneaked up behind Kare, who was engrossed in his work, and put her arms around his shoulders.

"I knew you were there," he said and squeezed her hand.

"You're no fun." She kissed the back of his neck, just below his still-cropped hair, before sitting on the table, blocking his view of the screen. She waited until he sighed and pushed his chair back.

"How come you're here?" he asked. "I thought you had a day with the budgeting committee ahead."

"I got called away. I heard someone was very rude to their senior officer."

He rolled his eyes. "There's nothing private in this base. How did you hear?"

"Your boss called a board meeting. She wants to see you in an hour."

Kare's face paled slightly. "Oh, shit," he said. "I shouldn't have said it. But he has been blocking me at every opportunity. I couldn't have let this one go. Even Lichio's frustrated, and he doesn't have to work directly with the bastard. Honestly, a saint would have said what I did."

"You shouldn't have risen to it," she told him. But she wasn't sure she wouldn't have. Although Kare had to realise there were better, more political, ways of dealing with things. "Or you could have seen Rjala privately."

"I know. How much shit am I in? Come on, tell me."

"You know I can't." Sonly ignored his pleading eyes– let him learn something from this. Next time he might play the game better, if he

168

had to sweat things a little. "She was annoyed; that's all I'll say."

Kare waited and she smiled, knowing he was trying to read her mood. It had taken months to learn how to stop him, but now she was adept at it. Tell the truth and keep it general had been one of Silom's best pieces of advice. Fill your mind with so much crap he can't get to the core was another.

"You're getting good," he admitted. He reached past her and dumped the work he'd been doing onto a filche. "I'm going to get a shower; I don't want to give the colonel another reason to get annoyed."

He stood but Sonly stopped him, pulling him to her. They kissed for a moment, the usual frustration of a snatched moment away from the demands of the group making it more urgent than it should be, his hands moving on her back. She arched towards him but he broke away and put a finger to her lips.

"I have to get ready," he said, his voice hoarse. She ran her finger down his jacket and he swallowed, hard. "Be good; this is serious."

He walked away. Sonly smiled and counted inwardly to herself. She'd reached five before he turned and walked back to her.

"One day, I'm going to find a way to say no to you and mean it," he said. He kissed her, this time longer and slower. He stopped, the desire clear in his eyes, so intense she felt her stomach lighten, excited. "I have an hour, you said?"

***

Stepping out of Rjala's office, all Kare could feel from Eevan was anger and hatred, stronger than ever tonight. For a moment, just one, Kare wondered if he had made a mistake, handling this the way he had. *No.* He'd had no option– it had to be dealt with. Even so, it wouldn't do any harm to give Eevan his place now.

"Eevan," he said, "perhaps this is a good time to start afresh." Eevan sneered, but Kare continued anyway. "I'm friends with your brother, I love your sister, and I'd like to work on a more professional level; mutual respect, if you like."

"You know the way you're fucking my sister?" Eevan's face twisted, removing the resemblance to his father, making him look older and meaner. "The best thing you could do is go fuck yourself instead."

Don't lose my temper; Lichio's right about that. "Forget I said anything."

"I'd take you in a moment," said Eevan. "That's if you have the balls to face me without using your powers. Or without the general to hide behind, you conniving shit."

"You know what?" Kare said, his temper building. "I don't know what hole you crawled out of, Eevan, but you can piss off back into it."

It wasn't eloquent, he knew, but at least it summed up his feelings. He turned and walked away, before he could say something worse. Silom strolled over. "I'd have floored him."

"And give him the pleasure of seeing me disciplined?" Kare tried not to show how close he'd been to doing just that.

"Good point. Can't you do something else? Ants in his bed, trousers mysteriously loosened?"

Kare grinned, and his anger receded a little. It was good to have Silom back on the base; he didn't take things as seriously as everyone else, didn't treat the Banned and its business as untouchable. "Have you been talking to Lichio? Trust Eevan to make it personal, he's one dislikable sod."

Silom shrugged. "It's because he doesn't have a life outside the army, and you just made him look bad in it. Let him throw his toys around for a day or two."

"True, but I could do without things like that being flung at me." Eevan's words came back to him, the dismissiveness of his and Sonly's relationship. "You know, I might do something about that." They reached the apartment and Kare went in to find Sonly grinning at him. "You're a witch; I thought I was getting demoted."

"Congratulations." She sobered, a small frown in place. "How did Eevan react?"

"Oh, you know, poisonous. I did try to say we should find a way to work together. I'll not repeat what he said. But it made me think there's something I should ask you." His throat tightened, the words sticking in it. This was something he should have rehearsed, not decided on at the spur of the moment.

"Go on then."

He thought about backing out but instead took a deep breath, swallowing his nerves. "Will you marry me?" he asked, the words falling out in a rush. "Eevan said something about you and me, something crass. I just thought, I'm proud of what we have."

"Marry?"

She was going to say no- he hadn't thought of that. This had been a mistake. He should have set something up, ordered some dinner in, made it romantic. Too late to think of that now. Instead, he went down on one knee and looked up at her. She blushed, and warmth spread through him, a tingling in his arms and legs. This was the right thing to do, something he should have thought of long ago.

"I love you. Please, Sonly, marry me. Be my wife." He waited

170

just a moment, and decided he couldn't resist saying it. "Piss your big brother off."

She smiled, her eyes full of mischief, dancing in the soft light. "Well, if you put it like that: yes, I'd be delighted to."

"You will?" He forced himself to take a deep breath and got up. He moved to kiss her, but she stopped him, a look of horror on her face.

"What is it?"

"What will I wear?"

"You'd look lovely whatever you wore," he told her, pushing her hair back from her face. "But it doesn't have to happen overnight. Take your time, make sure it's the way you want it- you'll only do it once." He paused, not wanting to push his luck. "Well, hopefully, anyway."

CHAPTER THIRTY-ONE

Sonly smoothed her dress down, a little embarrassed by how special it made her feel. The traditional deep blue suited her fair hair well, and the long, sleek cut emphasised her slim figure. "Does it suit me?"

Lichio stopped fiddling with the sleeve of his formal uniform, tucking an end of red braid out of sight, and looked her up and down. "You'll do."

Brothers. Just once, it might have been nice to have a sister. "No, really."

Lichio grinned. "You look lovely. Dad would have been really proud. So would Mum. And they would have been pleased with your choice, I think."

"I hope so. He liked Ealyn, despite everything that happened, and Kare has a way about him- an intensity- that reminds me of Ealyn." She checked the time. "Will Eevan come?"

"He should." Lichio pushed her hair behind her ears. "It doesn't matter anyway."

"You know I asked him to stand for me," admitted Sonly. She pulled her hair forward. "Don't do that- I don't want to look like I'm working."

"Of course you did. You know better than to ignore him. It's a good thing he didn't, though; he'd have spent the day glaring at the groom."

She laughed and then sobered. "The groom's response might have been a problem. I've warned him he's to do nothing to Eevan today, no matter how much he's provoked."

"Spoilsport, think how it could have livened things up." Lichio held out his arm. "Ready?" She took it and they started to walk through the base. "I'm glad it's me, Sonly."

They reached the door of the Banned's small chapel, and when it opened she was amazed to see how many people were squeezed in. The Banned always enjoyed a wedding- there was little enough to celebrate- but this was more than she'd ever expected. Her team had softened the look of the room with jungle flowers in jars around the room, their blues and violets matching the off-cuts of her dress tied in bows around them.

There was a murmur as some of the guests noticed her, and then the room went silent. Her stomach jumped with nerves and she tightened her grip on Lichio's arm.

"Leave it attached," he whispered. She relaxed her grip.

They walked slowly to the front of the room to a collective intake of breath. Even Eevan, sitting near the back with a crowd of his army colleagues, nodded at her and seemed to approve. At the front Kare and Silom waited, their backs to her. As she joined them Kare turned to her, his face stunned.

"You're beautiful," he mouthed. She smiled and the world shrank to this one moment in time, where he was the only one who mattered.

Rjala entered from the anteroom to the left, her footsteps steady, and the hush deepened. Sonly gulped– this was it, she was going to commit to Kare and promise to face the future with him. Nerves welled up and she felt sick.

"Ready?" asked Rjala.

Was she? Kare looked terrified, as if expecting her to refuse, and she lifted her chin, knowing what she was doing was right, that there was no one else she'd rather share her life with. Lichio left her side as Kare took her hands.

"As persons of faith," said Rjala, her voice carrying through the room, "we are here today to give our blessing, and ask the blessing of the eternal force which governs our lives, for this marriage between Kare and Sonly. We ask that they be bound together by your eternal love, to face what may lie ahead. It is our prayer that they stay loyal to one another and faithful." She looked up to the crowd. "If anyone has a reason this pairing should not take place, they may speak now."

There was silence in the chapel and Sonly held her breath. If Eevan said anything– if *anyone* said anything– she would kill them. Rjala held her gaze, smiling a little, as if to say don't worry. Kare made a small grimace, and she almost giggled.

"Sonly le Payne," said Rjala. "Will you accept this man as your partner, pledge to stand with him and face the future together?"

"Yes."

Rjala turned to Kare, repeating the words. He looked at Sonly throughout it, and at the end his voice rang out through the chapel. "I do."

Silom stepped forward, and she took the ring he gave her and slipped it onto Kare's finger, noticing his missing finger as she did. Lord, what was she doing committing to him; where would it bring her? He gave a tiny frown, and she knew he'd picked up something of her thoughts. He slipped her ring on, squeezing her hand very slightly, as if to say it would be okay.

173

"You have made these pledges before the eternal force, and before us, your witnesses. Together we will celebrate your union."

Sonly smiled- he was right, this was right- and heard the cheers as Rjala told him he could kiss her. She closed her eyes as he leaned in, cupped her chin gently, and- like she was something precious and special- kissed her in front of the room.

Later, Sonly wiped the tears from her eyes. She really was going to be sick with laughter. Beside her Kare's face was serious as he tried not to rise to Silom's merciless speech about him, but she knew it was an act and he was struggling not to laugh.

"He assured me he could fly the bloody thing," said Silom. "And then he nearly took the port out. That landing was more terrifying than anything I've faced in the field... which brings me to the last gift."

There were cheers in the crowd as he pulled out a comically large, obviously homemade medal. He searched the crowd until he found the person he wanted and nodded to them. "Captain Stitt; for going over and above the call of duty in training what was *undoubtedly* the worst foot soldier I've ever served alongside."

Kare started to laugh at that, properly laugh, even as he glared at Silom. As Stitt passed her little one- Sophie, if Sonly remembered right- to her husband and came up to take the medal, Kare leaned over and confided, "I'm going to kill him later."

Sonly giggled. "You shouldn't have asked him; you knew what would happen. No one else had as much ammunition on you. Oh, my sides are sore."

Kare glanced around the room and saw Eevan. "Which is more than can be said for your big brother. The only thing sore is his face."

Eevan did indeed look like he had toothache. "Ignore him." She intended to. Let his quiet menace dominate other days and places, but not this one.

Silom wrapped up with a last joke and sat down to huge applause. Sonly nudged Kare. "You're up next; follow that."

"Mine's easy." He gave her a smile more intimate than any before, as if they were alone, making her breath catch in her throat. "You're beautiful and I'm the luckiest man alive."

She watched him stand up and say exactly that, and wanted to keep this moment forever: put it in a bottle so that she could pull it out when she wanted to. She closed her eyes, mentally taking the picture: Kare, serious and earnest, telling her he loved her; Silom, musing loudly about what she'd ever seen in his cousin; Lichio, clapping along, meeting her eyes and smiling.

174

Later, much later, she lay beside Kare in their bed, her fingers tracing a pattern across his chest. He smiled at her, lazily, half-asleep.

"Did you really think I looked nice?" she asked. She snuggled against him, her head on his shoulder, luxuriating in their closeness.

"I told you. Lots. You were beautiful."

"You didn't think I looked at all fat?"

He started to laugh. "If I say yes, this could be the quickest marriage in the history of the Banned. No, you didn't look fat, you looked perfect." He trailed a finger across her breasts, making her shiver. "Anyway, you aren't fat, you know that..."

"Good," she said, but her hand moved down to her stomach, and she rubbed it, imagining she could feel a swelling. He watched for a moment, before putting his hand over hers. It was warm against her, cupping her. Too late, she realised she hadn't guarded her thoughts.

"Sonly?" he asked, and raised an eyebrow.

Suddenly shy, she nodded.

"When? How?"

"I think you should know how."

He didn't smile. "When?"

"I'm nearly four months," she said. She'd held off telling him during the wedding preparations. It had helped that he'd been working so hard: it had been easy to hide her tiredness, and how little she'd been able to eat through the nausea. She wondered why they called it morning sickness, since it was there all day long. "I didn't mean to tell you tonight– I'd planned it for tomorrow. I had a meal booked."

"I thought you were taking precautions," he said. There was an edge to his voice that was hard to place and, for a moment, she thought about lying.

She faced him instead, meeting his eyes. She'd thought long and hard about the decision– she'd stand by it. "I stopped."

"You stopped?" He pulled away from her and sat up.

"Yes."

"Why?" he asked. "Didn't you think to talk about it?"

She sat up too, draping the covers around her shoulders. "I thought about it, and decided you'd say no." Knew he'd say no, that he wouldn't understand her need to do this, a need that had dominated her thoughts for months, growing more urgent, as if time was running out for them. She couldn't tell him any of that; it would bring the demons he fought, every night, to the fore and give them strength.

"I would have." He got up, pulling his trousers on, his movements jerky and angry. "This can't be, Sonly. It's bad enough I'm here, but another Varnon... what the hell is that going to do?"

His reaction was what she had expected, but she was still disappointed. A small part of her had hoped he'd be pleased.

"It's going to give us a baby, one that I want." But it went deeper than that, the reasons for her decision. It went beyond her need, the hungriness of wanting a part of him, into the politics she was immersed in. He only saw himself, not how things could be changed if they took control. "And it gives us the legacy. Here, at the Banned, the future…"

He turned to her, his face angry, like she'd never seen him before. "That's complete crap. You must know if- when- this news gets out, the target switches."

"We can keep the baby safe on the base," she said. "Do you think I did this without thinking?"

"No- you don't do anything without thinking about it," he said, his voice cold. "What *were* you thinking? I won't take the empire- could the child?"

"No," she gasped. This was a Kare she'd rarely seen, a Kare without trust. He'd been like that when he'd first returned to the Banned, but it had dissipated over the years. She'd thought it was gone. "I told you- we're working to change things, not sustain them." Tears welled in her eyes. Couldn't he sense the need in her? Couldn't he tell how deep this went in her? "Kare, it's going to be a baby. Our baby. Not some sort of political thing- otherwise I wouldn't have done it." She put her hand on his shoulder, but he shrugged it off. "And we will do it- we're breaking through more and more."

"I know that," he croaked, and now she could see in his eyes what was driving him. Not wariness, but fear. A fear of something worse than she knew, something that chilled her. "But you won't mind if I surround you with security and tell you not to leave the base until he- or she- is born? And when the baby is here, I'll surround it with more guards than you can count."

"It's not that bad," she said. It couldn't be. She knew what it was to be a fugitive- she'd been brought up in the Banned, she was worth her own considerable bounty.

He shook his head. "It is. You've created *exactly* what the Empress wants."

She grew hot and angry at his words. The Empress, his invisible mother, was more important than their future. She was like a carrion crow on his shoulder, the definition of his fear. Ealyn had done that- reinforced a belief that she was too great an evil to be faced, that she was more than just a poisonous woman, bent on

176

taking people and using them as she wanted. Surely, Kare must see her for what she was– an opponent, one the Banned were facing up to. "*If* I have, I've created it because it's yours and mine to create. Not hers. What bloody right does she have, dictating to me whether it's safe to have a baby? What bloody right does she have to you?"

She stopped, knowing her voice was too high and emotional. They sat in silence for a moment and then he groaned.

"Oh shit, Sonly, I know. And I'm not surprised you've done it, not really. But you should have talked about it first."

"Maybe I should have, but I knew you'd talk me out of it. And I want one. And now I have one, and I intend to keep it." She looked around the room. "Here, at the Banned. Where it's safe. She can't take the base, Kare. She can't get near it."

Kare watched her for a moment, shadows crossing his thin face. "She could; nowhere is so secure it can't be taken. It would be a huge undertaking, it would take a massive attack force, but she could take it. So, security, all the way." He smiled, his face softening slightly, and she found herself relaxing. He knew now; the worst was over.

"Because she isn't getting you," he said. "And she isn't getting what you have."

A chill settled on her. *So, what is she getting?* She reached out to him. "Kare- you won't leave us, will you? You'll stay and keep the baby safe?" It was the worst ploy in the world, a card she'd never planned to play, but the darkness in his eyes, the tightness in his shoulders, in the corded muscles of his arms, were scaring her more than any prospect of facing the Empress ever could.

He leaned over and kissed her. "Of course I won't leave. I want to see who's in there, first."

"First?"

"Stop worrying." He took his trousers off and crawled into bed. She lay beside him, the closeness of earlier gone, a space between them.

"It'll be fine," he said. "Go to sleep; you must be tired."

***

Kare lay in the dark and waited until he was sure Sonly was asleep before getting up and walking to the sitting room. He sat on the sofa, the only sound the quiet hum of the food preparation unit. A computer screen shone from the office, giving him enough light to see. He rested his head on the back of the sofa. *Fuck.*

What the hell was he to do now? He closed his eyes, imagining

Sonly as she had been earlier, laughing at Silom, happy. He made her happy, just like she made him. He felt like screaming. She was wrong on so many levels: that the base was secure enough to hold a baby- they'd sent a Star ops team in for him, a baby was an easy snatch; that he'd sit and wait for his mother to come for the child. Oh, *gods*, what had Sonly done?

What he would never have dared to: taken his life back from the Empress.

Part of him admired her and wished he was half as brave. Another part wanted to shake her and ask if she was mad.

Is she mad? He didn't know. She might be right, that the child was the future if they were kept safe, allowed to grow up. To do that, the focus had to be switched from them.

Am I brave enough? He didn't have an answer. He got up, walked to bathroom, and locked the door. He looked at himself in the mirror and saw he was white, like a ghost. It made him think of Karia and he looked round for her, but she wasn't there- she hadn't been there since the earliest days at the base. Perhaps he was a ghost, too, sent from his father's visions, part of a distant world and only a visitor here. He lifted his hand and it was shaking- he was all too real. *I can't do it.* He sat on the edge of the bath, in the bright bathroom, and willed himself not to throw up. He tried to convince his body it would be okay. That he would be okay.

Liar. He dived across to the toilet, reaching it just in time, and, as he'd known he would since the moment Sonly had told him she was pregnant, threw up. He emptied his stomach, put his head on his arms, and waited for the inevitable retching, the attempt by his body to reject what it knew and find a different future. He started to shudder, and realised he was crying. He wasn't brave enough- he never would be

My father screamed for days. He pushed the thought from his mind. He couldn't think of his dad, not now. *Beck. The pit. Omendegon.* Again, he pushed it away- it was a dream, a nightmare, not real. He tried not to think of anything except that he had to find courage and hold it in his heart until he did what was needed. He retched again. And again, long into the quiet night.

CHAPTER THIRTY-TWO

Sonly woke to a bright room, the auto-lights raised to replicate morning. She pushed back the bedclothes, unease settling in her. Kare would normally have brought her breakfast by now. The unease deepened into something close to fear. How annoyed was he about the pregnancy? Protectively, she put a hand over her stomach and reminded herself she was right; he just hadn't seen the implications of it. She was the politician, not him, and she had to trust her instincts.

The living area was quiet, but a sound of tapping came from the office. She pushed the door open and leant against the jamb. Kare was sitting at the desk, surrounded by notes, working between three data pads. He finished what he was inputting and looked up, making her draw in a breath. He looked terrible: his skin pale, and his eyes dark shadowed.

"How long have you been up?" she asked. And what had he been doing, in those dead hours?

"All night."

She took in his pallor. "And when did you stop throwing up?"

He glanced at his comms unit. "About three hours ago."

She pointed at the work surrounding him. "May I?"

"Go ahead. I'll make some breakfast."

She sat and read through the papers, taking her time. Plans for the city of Abendau, details of the dynasties of the great families, the structure of the empire. A military planning document. She stopped reading when he set a plate down and went round the other side of the table with his own.

"Well?" he asked, indicating the table. "What do you think?"

"Are you serious about it?" He had never shown any indication of this before and yet, laid out in front of her was months of work.

"I am." He rubbed his temples. "You can tell that this isn't about the baby. I've been planning it for the past year, and thinking about it for much longer."

"How long?"

He sat, quiet for a moment, before meeting her eyes. "Since I was seven, and knew it had to be me."

Sonly looked again at the papers spread out in front of her. "Talk me through it. You can't operate in a vacuum– you're part of the Banned and our wider strategy. You should have discussed this long ago."

"Why?" He looked desperately sad. "She only wants me."

But that wasn't true. She wanted to stamp out any opposition. She'd taken planet after planet, and she'd keep doing so.

"Hear me out." He picked up one data pad and handed it to her. "That's yours. The political stuff I want you and Michael to feed into. What we'll offer the central planets: autonomy to rule themselves. It's what the great families want, and it starts to remove the empire. For the middle sector, repeal of martial law, with support and resources to build up their own armies again and the chance to self-govern. Any alliances they want to maintain with the families, that's up to them. For the outer rim, freedom to rule with the Banned supporting their infrastructures; removal of the embargo and free trading conditions, allowing them to take control of any resources they have."

She read through it, taking her time, amazed at the amount of detail he'd put into it. She remembered her thought from earlier, about her being the politician, not him, and almost laughed.

He handed her the next data pad. "That's the proposed governance of the new confederacy."

Michael would never agree to a confederacy. The fallout from a change of ruler would be enough without changing structures. She opened her mouth to argue, but her gaze fell on the last data pad, lying on the desk between them. She pointed at it. "That one?"

"That's for the general," he said. His hands were tight into fists, his neck corded and tense. He met her eyes, and took a deep, deep breath. "It's a task force to take Abendau port and palace and get me near enough to the Empress to confront."

He meant it. He, who'd always said he wouldn't go to Abendau, would never take her place. She looked down at the table, not able to meet his eyes. Not able to agree any of this, not if it risked him so much.

"Why now?" she asked. Why in secret, why not brought up at the many board room talks over the years? "If it's not the baby, what has brought it on?"

He drummed his fingers on the table, a slight smile on his face. "Because you're right," he said. "We have the dynasty, and she'll want to topple it. I suppose to say it's nothing to do with the baby is a lie– you've given me the push I need. But this has been coming, you know that. The Banned has grown so much, we have to be bold sometime. This is it; our time to move. And to do that, we have to go for the top- we have to take out the Empress." He reached across the table and took her hand. "Will you back me, to the board?"

She let him hold her hand, caressing it. Should she? She'd told Michael, years ago, that he might be right, that they should aim for a change. Again, she looked around the desk, and back at him. His eyes met hers, tired but direct, and she nodded. Let him have the future he could face, not one forced on him by his mother, the Banned, or even her.

"I'll back you," she said. She looked down at her coffee and pushed it away, nauseous. "You know I will."

He yawned and pulled his hand away.

"Get some sleep," she said. "I'll wake you in an hour or two."

She waited until he left, making sure he'd closed the door, and looked around the table again. She picked up a sheet of paper, but the words were impossible to read, swimming under her eyes. A teardrop fell on the paper, and spread out, blossoming like her fear. She'd set this in motion and if she was wrong, Kare would be the one to pay. *Please, please, don't let me be wrong.* She closed her eyes and wondered where to send such a thought to; she'd never been religious. Anyone who'd listen. *Please, look after him. If there's anyone there, look after us all, and let me have done the right thing.*

***

"Get in."

He crawled, one leg dragging behind him, his chest punctured by sharp pain with every breath. He stopped at the edge of the shallow pit and pulled himself in, screaming as his leg thudded down. Hard hands turned him over and strapped him down. The lid closed and he lay, naked, in darkness, barely breathing. He tried to clench his fists but they wouldn't tighten. His hands weren't broken, but shattered.

A soft whispering. A movement on his leg. He tried to move, but was strapped too tightly. Another movement, more- something climbed his bare legs, nipping- each barely noticeable, blossoming into a collective agony.

"Stop," he whispered. Still they moved up: insects, climbing on each other.

They reached his face, and he clamped his mouth shut. He forced his hands to claw, using the pain to keep him conscious. To faint, to submit to this... they'd be everywhere if he did. They were climbing up his nose; into his ears, and he tried to shake his head and dislodge them. More came, the bites everywhere, sharp pins.

Another bite, this one sharper, close to his balls, and he jerked and

181

yelled. The insects invaded his mouth and throat, choking him, and panic rose. He thrashed against his restraints, choking, keeping his eyes closed against the skittering...

The lid opened and the insects dispersed to the blackness. He gasped, gulping the air.

"Well, Dog?" The mocking face of Beck stared at him, his eyes impassive.

"Please; mercy." He was aware of nothing other than this man. "Mercy."

His tormentor's face hardened, and he shook his head. "You begged."

Fear ran through him, like it was alive, and he tried to shake his head but couldn't. The lid came down, the darkness surrounded him. A whisper. Something cold touched his foot. Water. It rose around him and he knew they'd drown him and he couldn't go past this point– he'd endured so much, but he couldn't remember who he was or how he'd got here, or what to do to save himself...

Kare sat up in bed, the covers twisted around him. The nightmare had been gruesome, worse than most. He pushed his hair back and took a moment before getting up and padding to the living area, where Sonly was curled up on the sofa. He sat beside her and leaned his head on the back of the sofa.

"So, what now?" she asked.

"I have to talk to General Rjala. And Silom and Lichio. Then, the board."

"When will you go?"

"Not until the baby's here," he said. "I told you that."

"Kare? It'll be all right, won't it?"

She wanted him to say yes, and it would be easy to. But it would be a lie, and she'd know it.

"I can't tell you that," he said. "If I win, it'll be all right. If I lose, it won't."

"What happens if you lose?" she asked. "I know your dad told you some things, but I don't know what they were."

How much should he tell her? He'd stood with her, in front of everyone who mattered, and promised to share his life with her. She had to know, it was her place to know. Still, he hesitated. What would Karia say– would she understand why he'd broken their promise and told someone? Yes, he decided, she would; she wouldn't want him to be on his own.

"The time we left the Banned," he said, "the time before we were split up, Dad had some visions."

"What were they?"

He swallowed. "Omendegon." Even the word sounded evil. "He kept going back to the vision, time and time again. He asked us to kill him, the pain was so bad, and he kept saying the same name, over and over and over again: Beck. It was..." What word could do it justice? Those weeks on the ship, the growing realisation of the detail, whose future it was. He had to say something- she was waiting for him to. "Awful," he managed. "Worse than I can say."

Sonly cocked her head on one side. "But he didn't go to Omendegon, he died."

"I know." He waited for her to work it out, dreading the moment she did.

She pulled her hand away and brought it up to her mouth. "You."

Me. He nodded, his eyes never leaving hers. "Yes." Her face crumpled, and he reached for her hand. "He said it was one of us. He said that there was a path to glory, that we could bring down the empire. And there was a path to Omendegon. He didn't know which we'd follow. That's why he went mad: he was trying to find the way forward that would save us from it."

"You can't go to Abendau," she said. "We can find another way to do this. Approach the great families directly, like we said we would. Start to take her power base. Reduce their support of her, and their revenue."

"I can, and I will." He wondered if he could find the words to convince her. "Sonly, I've spent my life terrified of this." He swallowed, and took Sonly's hand. "Waiting for it. I have a better chance if I go in myself. If I wait for her to take me, I don't. I stayed here, knowing what he'd seen, and chose to stand against her. Now, I need to find out which path I chose."

She went to interrupt, but he held his hand up.

"It's not just that I don't sleep. I work all the time and you know why, don't you? Because when I'm working, I'm not thinking about it. He told us we'd lose everything dear to us: our friends, our family, everything we valued. When I was seven that didn't seem as scary- I'd already lost it all- but now I have so much more than I ever dreamed of. I have you, my friends, my role, a baby soon. To be asked to- made to- give all that up is frightening. But it's also why I have to go."

He tipped her chin so she was looking at him, her blue eyes round and scared.

"I can't be the person who causes that pain in you. I can't be the one who harms our baby, or gets Silom killed, or Lichio, because I didn't have the courage to face it. But I can't tell you it'll be all right, because I don't know. I could try to Seer it but it might frighten me so much I never do it."

"Are your dreams visions?" she asked, and he closed his eyes against his fear that they were. That, even though he'd chosen not to look, the future was still in his mind.

"I hope not," he said. "I think they're replaying what Dad told us, and aren't real." He smiled and she tried to smile back, but her lip wobbled. He pulled her close to him and whispered into her hair. "I promise you one thing, I'll do my best. That's all: I'll do my best."

"I know you will," she told him. "It'll be enough, I'm sure of it."

Gods, he hoped so. But at least it would be over and he'd know. Later, as the day drew to a close, Sonly hugged a mug of tea to her but shivered so badly she had to set it down before it spilt. Beside her, Kare was quiet.

"What now?" she asked.

He took a drink of his coffee, wincing, and it was no wonder, given its strength. She'd often thought if she opened his veins she'd find caffeine flowing through them.

"I'm going to tell Silom and Lichio. I suspect Lichio already has an idea, and Silom knows a bit about Dad's visions, so I can't see it shocking him. In the morning, I have a meeting with the general and if I convince her, then it's to the board."

"Eevan and Glen will vote against it," she said. "There's no way Eevan's going to let you have the glory. You have me and hopefully Rjala."

"I'll have to abstain, won't I?"

"Yes. That leaves Michael." She paused for a moment. "He's important. Eevan may be able to force a conflict of interest with me, too. If so, and it's deadlocked, the chairman's will be the carrying vote."

"You know him better– how do I convince him? What does he want?"

Sonly thought for a moment. "He's for the Banned, through and through. So, you need to convince him it's for the group, not personal gain. If I were you, I wouldn't fight for a confederacy yet. That would be enough for him to veto you. Depose your mother first, and have any discussions after. Once you're in place, he will have less room to manoeuvre."

"Win the battle and not the war?" He took another drink and stared ahead of him. "I'll think about that." He picked up his comms unit. "We may as well get the next bit over with, yes?"

Later, as Kare outlined his plans to Lichio and Silom, she thought how odd it was that he'd managed to make this sound matter-of-fact so quickly. He was going to attack Abendau, but was talking about it as if it was a planetary campaign in the outer rim. Silom listened, his face impassive– resigned, really. Lichio, on one of the small kitchen chairs, didn't look surprised in the least.

"What do you think?" asked Kare, when he'd finished. He leaned against the food unit and folded his arms.

"If you can get the right team in place, it's viable," Lichio said. "Risky, but you know that."

Kare nodded, and his attention moved to Silom. Despite the casualness of Kare's posture, she could see the tension in him: a tightness around his shoulders, a wariness in his eyes.

"You know what I think," said Silom. "What I always think: you risk too much of yourself." Kare went to interrupt, but Silom cut him off. "It's never stopped you, though, and so far you've been right. I didn't believe your system would make the difference it did; I would never have believed you could wipe out a Star team single-handedly. If you're telling me, honestly, that you think this has a chance, I'll support you. Will I be on the team?"

"Who else is going to watch my back?" said Kare. "If you want on the team, you'll be on it. You know that."

Lichio stretched. "You've made your mind up. Let me know what you need me to do, and I'll start working on it." He looked over at Silom. "Drink?"

"Have a drink here," said Kare. "If this gets okayed, we'll be busy. Who knows when we'll get another chance to relax? And I can't go to the bar without half the protection squads of the Banned following."

Kare poured some drinks and moved over to the sitting room, dropping onto the sofa. The others joined him, Sonly beside him on the sofa, Silom and Lichio on chairs. He was right, they didn't do this often enough.

She watched, sober and aware, and fixed the thought of this night, and the memories of the three men, in her head: Lichio, telling an absolutely filthy story, his angelic face at odds with the language used; Kare's eerily accurate, if slightly slurred, impersonation of Eevan; and Silom, roaring with laughter at it, his face turning puce as he choked on his drink.

"We've had a good run, haven't we?" Silom said after he'd stopped laughing.

"The best," agreed Kare. "The absolute best." He stood and swayed slightly. "I'm knackered."

The jokes were a little risqué, but Sonly laughed them off as she went to the door with Silom and Lichio. When she came back into the room, she found Kare stretched out on the sofa, snoring slightly. She kissed his cheek and pulled a blanket over him.

"Some messiah," she laughed as she turned out the light and went to bed. Later, in the deepness of the night, he crawled in beside her and put his arm around her. His breathing deepened as he sank back towards sleep.

"Kare."

"Hmmm?"

"I don't want Eevan to be part of the raid," she said. Kare nodded against her. "Can you stop him?"

"I'll sort it," he told her. "Gotta sleep."

"You're going to suffer in the morning," she said, and when he didn't answer she realised he was already asleep. She'd remind him in the morning. Eevan couldn't be involved in this, not when Kare was risking so much already.

CHAPTER THIRTY-THREE

At the rap on the door, Rjala looked at Glen. "I have another meeting, I'm afraid." She checked through the troop allocation figures one more time, compared it to his budget allowance and nodded. "It looks fine."

He stood, taking time to put his papers back in his folio in the right order, a typical accountant. Once finished, he pushed his chair in and opened the door.

"Kare," he said, his voice neutral, making Rjala smile to herself. He may not share Eevan's open hostility, but he had made no secret of his distrust of the psycher over the years.

"Glen, good to see you," Kare said, showing a commendable ability to rise above it. He glanced at Rjala. "I can come back, General."

"No, it's fine. Sit down." She waited for the door to close. "You asked to see me."

"Ma'am, I wanted to talk to you about the possibility of a task force."

"A task force?" Rjala looked at the data pad, as if for inspiration, and then back at Kare. He looked like shit. "Remind me when I asked for a task force?"

"You didn't, ma'am."

She sat back in her seat. "That's right. I didn't. What is your task force for?"

"For attacking the palace of Abendau."

"Why?"

He passed a report across the desk to her. "I've talked to Sonly, and she agrees that, politically, we could be in the position to challenge the Empress. To do that, I need to get to Abendau and confront her. I have the stronger powers, ma'am, I'm sure of it."

"I never thought you were so ambitious," she said. "Why now?"

"Sonly's pregnant." Rjala drew in a sharp breath, and he nodded. "Ma'am, if my mother gets the bloodline, the Banned loses viability."

"And if you lose? What then for the Banned?"

"Then you still have the baby."

She noted how tightly his hands were clasped together. Let him spill out whatever was in his mind, and she'd see where it went. "Go on."

"Ma'am, psyching at my level takes years of practice. When we were kids, Dad made us work at it every day- he was relentless. I've been working hard and I think I'm better than I ever was. It makes me believe we have to move now, before she gets a chance to take the child."

"We can keep the baby safe."

He laughed, harshly, humourlessly. "Like you kept me and Karia safe? One of us is dead, the other can't move without a security detail. I'd like an opportunity to ensure my child isn't just safe, but has some kind of normal life."

"I'm not inclined to base my operational decisions on your personal feelings, Kare."

"Ma'am, I know that, and I'm sorry if that's what it sounded like."

His timing was good. She tightened her grip on the report he'd given her. The plan was good, too, almost identical to her own.

"Continue," she told him.

"Thank you, ma'am. I'm prepared to be presented as an alternative to my mother. Sonly believes she can bring some of the families on board, and the middle sector, too. We already hold the outer systems. But that's not enough, not as long as my mother is in power. I need to confront her, remove her from Abendau. For that, I was hoping you would consider a small task force."

Time to challenge him on his thinking. She leant forward. "How good are you? Don't lie, don't exaggerate, just tell me. Can you defeat your mother? If we get you to the position where you can confront her, can you win?"

"I believe I can, yes. She uses mental dominance, primarily; so can I."

"I've never seen any proof of that." Her eyes narrowed: he'd say whatever he needed to get her agreement.

"I said I can, not that I did. I can certainly safeguard myself against it."

"Safeguarding yourself is not the same as winning," she said. "I need evidence."

"You want evidence?" There was a whisper behind her. She turned, but the room was empty. When she looked back, her eyes met his, drawn to them.

Look away, she urged herself, but she wasn't able to turn from him. She tried to close her eyes, but couldn't. His eyes held hers, hard like emeralds, unflinching, unmoving. His face was impassive, displaying no effort, yet still the hold on her mind increased.

"Say yes," he whispered, the words echoing through her mind: compelling.

"Yes." It came automatically. The pressure relieved, just a little, and she gasped in relief. It built again.

"Right now, you'd do anything I asked. Isn't that right?"

"Yes," she said, the word wrenched from her. Her head hurt, bringing tears to her eyes.

Again, his hold increased. And again, dulling her thoughts and putting his will in their place. She put her hands to either side of her head but he held her even firmer, his eyes hard and impassive. She tried to shout for him to stop, that he was hurting, but couldn't.

As quickly as it had started, his dominance ended. She slumped forward in relief.

"Are you all right?" he asked. "It's not very pleasant, I believe, especially in a mind as strong as yours, ma'am."

"Have you done this to anyone else?" she asked, shaken.

"No." He spread his hands. "I can't prove a negative, but I hope you know me well enough to believe me."

Did she? She saw nothing sinister in his eyes now. Instead, he looked like a very tired and, she suspected, hungover young man.

And yet, he'd held her mind, completely. She'd have done anything he asked to get him to stop. And he'd had the balls to wield it on her. That's what was needed if the Banned was going to do what it was created for and overthrow the bitch in Abendau. Her eyes moved to the photo frame beside her and the dark-eyed, smiling girl within. *I promised I'd make her pay for what she did to you, to everyone on Ferran Five.*

Rjala touched the screen inlaid in the desk and projected its information between them. A detailed plan of the palace of Abendau was highlighted on it.

"I think you'll find my plans are far in advance of yours, Kare," she said.

He took his time looking over the screen, reading the information displayed, and slowly a smile spread over his face. "Ma'am, this is incredible. The port is definitely the weak point. If we get into it, we can take the palace."

"There is one thing I haven't worked out how to overcome, and that's their voice recognition. We could use an agent."

"Maybe," said Kare. "Can we find out about the system used? There could be a way to bypass it, if I can get the details."

"I'll get someone onto it." Rjala leaned back in her seat. "One thing, Kare."

"Yes?"

"I will only agree if it's operationally sound. This isn't a crusade for you and your family, this is about the Banned. If it looks viable, I'll support your decision. But if it isn't, I'll refuse you. Is that clear?"

189

"Perfectly, ma'am."

"You can go."

He didn't stand, but instead said, "Ma'am, may I speak informally?"

"Go on."

"My childhood was more difficult than you can ever know," he said, "and it wasn't fair. Dad was ill, he'd lost himself, and he was still expelled. When things went wrong it was as much the group's fault as his."

Kare ran his hand through his hair, the way he did when he was agitated. He dropped his hand, and the directness, the accusation, in his eyes went through her like a knife. She'd always wondered if he would bring it up and how she'd feel when he did. The answer was ashamed, like she was looking into the accusing eyes of Ealyn warning her that whatever happened would be her fault. It had felt like it, too, when the news of the crash had come through. And it had felt even sharper since Kare had returned, the survivor of a part of her life she'd hoped would be buried forever, the action she was most ashamed of.

"I remember," she said. "What happened on the ship? Neither of you would tell us."

Kare shook his head. "What happened on the ship died with them; there's no need to go back to it now. My child isn't to be treated that way, no matter how much pressure is put on the Banned. I want your promise that if I'm not here, this little Varnon will know that it wasn't just Darwin who built the Banned, but Dad, too. I had to fight to get recognition while the le Paynes were treated like royalty, and it was wrong. Terribly wrong."

"I'm sorry," she said, surprised to find her eyes stinging; it had been years since she'd let anything affect her like this. "You're right. When your dad arrived back from Abendau, he carried you as if you were his greatest prize. And do you know what, Kare? You are. I'm proud to have you as my colonel, I'm proud to say you're the best in my army. I'll see your child is given their place. That if you're not here, they'll know they're not just a le Payne, but a Varnon, too. You have my word." She picked up the photo beside her. "I've hardly thought of Lena for years, you know. I'd look at her photo from time to time, without thinking of the person in it, if that makes sense."

"Who was she?"

"My lover. My life. She died for me, and I swore I'd live for both of us. I tried to."

He reached across the desk and put his hand over hers,

clenched tight. "No one could have lived it better, Rjala," he said. "I'm glad you told me."

"Thank you." She pulled her hand away, and got her emotions under control. It wasn't easy. "I'll support you in the boardroom."

"Thank you," he said. "Ma'am, there is one other thing. I need you to agree to an operational matter, and allow me access to Captain Stitt."

***

One more, thought Kare, as he walked away from Rjala's office. He'd given Sonly his trust, promised Rjala his powers– now he had to give Michael what he needed: his honour.

His head thudded, partly from the effect of the drink last night– he'd known at the time he'd suffer, but had promised himself he wouldn't regret it– and partly from the effort of holding Rjala's mind. He'd expected her to be hard to dominate, but had been taken aback by just how difficult. And that was a non-psycher. His mother did it to people every day. She was the strongest mind-dominant in the galaxy, and he was going up against her. He must be mad. Mad or desperate.

He mulled over that. Desperate, he decided, and desperation might give him the strength he needed. Again, his head throbbed, and he shook it to clear it a little; gods, she was tough.

He reached Michael's door and rapped on it. *This is the hardest one.* Michael, as chairman, knew the antipathy between him and Eevan, and wouldn't want to be seen taking sides.

A low, measured voice asked him to come in, and he did, sitting in the seat offered. Michael looked at him over thin glasses, his grey beard neatly trimmed, white against his dark skin.

"You asked to see me, Kare?"

"Did Sonly give you the data pad?" asked Kare. He hoped so; his head was pounding so much he didn't want to start going into the details again.

"It was very interesting."

"Michael, I need your support to take it forward. At the moment, I think the board will be deadlocked."

Michael opened the data pad. "Everything in it is possible, given time and support. Resources. All the things the Banned lacks."

"If we take the empire, we have the resources. We have an army, income from the planets– that's in there, in the terms– and

191

the legacy. It will work, provided we take out the Empress, and the general believes we have a viable chance of that."

"And if you don't? If you get taken, where does that leave us?"

Kare paused. He'd known this would be Michael's concern. *My honour*, he reminded himself.

"If I'm taken, I won't betray the Banned."

Michael snorted. "Do you know what they do in Omendegon?"

Oh yes, better than you. He'd watched someone tortured in it; held their hand while they were. Omendegon wasn't some dark secret to him, a place where people disappeared to and never came back from. "Yes."

"Then you know you'll tell them what they want. Psycher or not, they can hurt you quicker than you can stop them. They'll lock you in a cell with no one to manipulate, and torture you until you break."

All true. Kare forced himself to keep breathing in deep, measured breaths. Even so, his heart felt like it was beating too fast and the pounding in his head grew worse.

"You know too much for us to send you in," said Michael. "If you were just proposing a task force, I'd say yes. What can an individual soldier tell them? But you're a colonel, you know how our military works, all our systems. You've helped place spies."

"Do you know what I did with the spies?" Kare asked, seizing on the opening. He'd thought he'd have to bring the conversation round to them himself.

"Something about blocking their real memories and placing a false identity."

Kare nearly smiled, he was sure Michael knew the details of what had been done.

"Yes, a block that's programmed to safeguard them if they're mind-swept. It took a lot of time to perfect, but now they're in, we know it works." He leaned forward to Michael. "I've put one in my own mind, one that will come into effect should I be captured. It will not lift, no matter what duress I am under, and it will block me from telling them anything about the Banned. I have one problem, though."

Actually, he had several- not least, telling his wife about this.

"Which is?" asked Michael.

"I placed it, which means I can remove it. You asked me if I know what happens in Omendegon. Yes, I do. I'm not a stupid man."

Michael touched the data pad. "I can see that."

"I'm assuming they can get me to talk. I am, after all, just as susceptible to pain as the next person."

"What do you propose?"

Kare took his comms unit from his pocket. "Do you mind if I make a call?"

"Go right ahead," said Michael. His eyes watched Kare, revealing nothing, and the waves of emotions coming from him were slight. Either that or Kare was too drained to pick them up.

The comms unit was quickly answered.

"Now, if you will," said Kare. He put the unit down, and a few moments later Captain Stitt entered the room.

"Sarah, thanks for coming," said Kare. He turned to Michael. "I want you to witness this, so that when it comes up in the board meeting you can confirm I have done it." He looked back at Stitt. "Did the general speak to you?" She nodded. "Then you know what to do."

Stitt reached her hand out, and Kare felt realisation stir in Michael. "You can't," he said.

"I already have," said Kare. "This is just the precaution, nothing more. Sarah, if you put your hand on me, I'll do the rest."

He took her power, small though it was, and moved it to the compulsion he'd placed in himself and sealed it. He waited a moment, made sure it was complete, and then moved his head away.

"Thank you, Sarah," he said. "Can you confirm that your power is now holding my compulsion. That, without you, I won't be able to lift the block."

"Yes," she said.

Her eyes met Kare's, and he gave her a smile. "Thank you. Dismissed," he said.

Stitt left and Kare waited, facing Michael, feeling oddly calm now he'd done it.

"You're as mad as your father," said Michael.

"If I was, the general wouldn't have agreed to it. She understands it's an operational decision, that I'm one man amongst many. I don't know how many times I have to say this before I'm believed: this is my fight. Not the spies I might give up, or the troops I'd betray, or the group whose secrets I'd reveal. Or my family's. It's mine. And I was going to do what I just did, however I did it. I could have compelled Stitt, but I didn't: I was honest, with the general and now you. If you send me in, I won't betray the group."

"You're brave then, if you're not mad."

There was a lump in Kare's throat. He didn't know if he was, just that he didn't have any choice. "Will you back me?"

Michael looked at the plans. "I think I'll have to. This is the best chance we've ever had, and you know it. Yes, bring it to the boardroom, and I'll back you."

Kare stood, his legs shaking. It was tempting to blame the hangover, but he knew better. Brave? He almost laughed. He wasn't brave, he was terrified.

My trust, my power, my honour.

Now, he just had to deliver.

CHAPTER THIRTY-FOUR

Six months later.

Kare stretched. "I had no idea it would be so bloody," he said. Silom yawned, and Kare wondered if he was boring him. But he'd had no idea he would feel like this, like he'd watched a miracle happening. After the birth, he'd sat and held his daughter while Sonly was checked over. He'd even cooed, and he had been sure people didn't really do that.

"You know, it took hours. I kept seeing the head and thinking this is it, and then it vanished again."

"Enough," Silom said, his face horrified. "Can we go in?"

"I'll check," Kare told him. He bounced over and opened the door opposite.

"Are you okay with Silom coming in?" he asked. Sonly nodded, her eyes tired but bright, and he called Silom in.

"You look a lot better than I expected," Silom said. "In fact, you look a hell of a lot better than Kare."

Kare barely registered the insult. He leaned over and looked at the baby in Sonly's arms. Whatever it took to keep her safe....

"Do you want to hold her?" Sonly offered Silom, who took a step back, eyes darting, making Kare smile. Lichio had been much better, holding the baby and talking to her like she understood him.

"You must be joking," Silom said. "I'd drop her." He smiled, and took a closer look, not making any move to hold her. "Although I might need the practice– Kym keeps saying she wants one. Better not let her within ten feet of this; it'd finish the argument off. Anyway, what colour eyes? I have a lot riding on green."

"Blue," she told him, and his face fell. She paused for a moment, making Kare smile. She knew all about the bet Lichio and Silom had made. "But they might change; we won't be sure until she's about six months old."

"Make sure you tell your brother that," Silom said. He reached out and stroked the baby's head, surprising Kare with his gentleness. "She's very cute."

Kare took the baby, unable to resist any longer. She fit into his arms, a comfortable weight. He looked down at her half-closed eyes, her mouth pursed like a bud. "She's more than cute. She's lovely."

"What's her name?"

"Kerra," Sonly said. "I chose it; she's my little bit of Kare to keep while he's away."

Kare grimaced. When Sonly stopped telling everyone that, it would good. Anytime soon.

"That's nice." Silom's words were deadpan, but Kare was sure there was a laugh hidden in them. He looked around the ward, taking his time, scanning. "How long will you stay here?"

"I'm going to go back to the apartment today," she said. "Then we have a couple of weeks before you and Kare go."

"Let's not talk about it," Kare said. "You know, Silom, I reckon you're right with green." He touched the baby's mind, very gently. There was a small response, a light finger of sensation in his own. "She certainly has some powers."

The door opened and a nurse came in. Silom jerked his head at the door, desperately rolling his eyes, and Kare handed the baby back to Sonly. Time to put Silom out of his misery. "We'll wait outside."

The two men walked to the door of the hospital wing and stood in the sunshine. Kare tipped his head up to the sun, enjoying its warmth, wishing he could stay and not go to Belaudii with its desert winds and its city waiting to reclaim him. He'd been planned, conceived and born in Abendau and had always known it lay ahead for him. He didn't want it. A shiver ran through him, and he forced his mind away from the doubts, focusing instead on a crowd of teenage girls sitting on a bench nearby, laughing over something on a comms unit.

"I should try to get outside every day," he said. "This is nice."

"Don't even think about it," Silom said. "You're hard enough to protect without taking up rambling."

Kare grinned; it was exactly what he'd expected Silom to say. A sharp sting on his neck made him draw his breath in a hiss.

"What is it?" asked Silom, alert, eyes casting around.

"Nothing, an insect." He put his hand up, feeling for the sting, and turned at the sound of footsteps.

"Poor baby." Sonly had changed into cargo trousers and a tunic top, her hair neatly styled. He looked down at the crumpled t-shirt he'd pulled on when she'd woken him. He guessed his hair was probably sticking up, and he needed a shave. Silom was right; he was more freaked out than she was.

"I'm glad you agree. I thought you might say something predictable about labour pains. Do you want me to carry her?" He took the baby, keeping her head up, the way the nurse had shown him. He nearly cooed, remembered Silom was there, and stopped himself.

Silom nudged him and he looked up to see Eevan approaching. He pointedly ignored Kare and looked at the baby instead, before turning to Sonly. "Congratulations."

"Thanks," Sonly said. "We're *both* very pleased."

"I suppose you are," Eevan said. Sonly ducked into the transport, and as Silom closed her door, Eevan turned to Kare. "That's another thing for you to worry about: a new Varnon."

Kare couldn't decide if there was anything more than the usual nastiness behind his statement. "Don't worry, Eevan: a couple of weeks and you'll be rid of me." He passed the baby to Sonly and got into the transport.

"I wish he didn't know about the attack," admitted Sonly.

"We had to tell him sometime. It'll be fine, Sonly, don't worry. Only Rjala and I know the details."

Even so, as they were transported back to the main base, his thoughts kept going back to the dark, brooding eyes. Absently rubbing at the sting on his neck, Kare glanced at the baby beside him and tried to dispel the lingering doubt that there was something very, very wrong here.

***

Kare opened his eyes. The room was dark around him. The baby was quiet and Sonly asleep. He sat up, careful not to disturb them. *The buzz of minds was gone.* He tried to reach out and turn on the soft light in the living area– nothing happened, and his throat tightened with fear. He started to pull on his clothes.

"You all right?" asked Sonly, her voice sleepy.

"Something's wrong," he said, and heard an edge of panic in his voice.

"It's quiet, go to sleep."

"My powers are gone."

Before Sonly could respond there was a knock on the door; when Kare opened it he found Lichio and Silom. He should have known who it was.

"The general sent me; she needs you in the control room," Lichio said.

"A drill?" He knew it wasn't– he'd have been told if there was one planned. The first alarms sounded, blaring through the base.

The bedroom light came on, and a moment later Sonly appeared, her clothes from earlier on her, Kerra in her arms.

"An attack!" Lichio shouted, just audible over the alarm. "Huge, well planned."

"Take Sonly and the baby- get them away," Kare said to Silom. His cousin shook his head, not able to hear, and Kare pulled him into the quieter apartment. "Get them out for me!"

"I'm not going anywhere," Sonly told him.

"I'm staying with you," Silom said, simultaneously.

"I don't have time!" Kare told them. "Sonly, you're needed if there's anything to salvage." He pointed at Silom. "You being here won't make a difference to me, but you might to them." Silom paused for a moment. "Now, Sergeant," Kare said, firmly.

"Yes, sir." Silom seemed to find it easier now he had been given an order.

Kare turned to Sonly and kissed her, quickly. "If I can, I'll come back to you," he told her.

"If you can," she said. "That's it?"

"That's it." He paused, meeting her eyes: this *was* it; whatever lay ahead had to be faced now. He pulled her close, kissed her head, and then the baby's soft skin. She smelt of milk, of washed new skin. He barely knew her; he didn't know how he could leave her.

"Look after her," he said, his words croaked. He met Sonly's eyes. "Keep her with you, and safe."

"Kare- "

He shook his head; he couldn't face what she had to say. "Please, go: I need you to..."

She nodded, her eyes shining with tears. "I love you."

"I love you, too." He swallowed, and his throat was hard and hot. This wasn't what he'd wanted, a rushed goodbye, the sickening knowledge there was nowhere to go except into battle. "You know that."

She turned, Silom's arm on her elbow, guiding her. Kare watched them leave, saw Sonly look back once, and then looked at Lichio. "Let's go."

Lichio nodded, and Kare saw his own emotions mirrored in Lichio's face: the fear of staying behind, the brief, bitter desire to run instead.

"If I thought I could do my job tonight without you, I'd have sent you with them."

"I know, but I wouldn't have gone, sir."

They set off at a run to the control room, hearing a series of explosions rip through the base. They ducked through the people

198

emerging from their rooms, some going to the evacuation points, some to their stations. As they arrived at the command room, Kare flexed his mind to reach into the room, to get a sense of what was happening and–

– *nothing.*

He cursed softly. What if he was nothing without his psyche: a coward? Swallowing his fear, he opened the door and turned to the two nearest soldiers. "Seal the door; we don't need to be distracted by that."

As the soldiers moved forward, Kare realised one was Captain Stitt. He put a hand on her shoulder, and she nodded to him. "Sir."

He sat beside Rjala and put an earpiece in, while Lichio scrolled through screens. Kare swore. The enemies were everywhere, the Banned fighters pushed back.

"You're in charge of the air defences, Colonel," Rjala said. "I'm going to have to run the ground forces."

"Why?"

"Eevan hasn't turned in for duty."

Kare noted the thin line of her mouth. *The bastard.* "How did they get so close?" he asked.

"No comms," she said. "They came in silently. Also, the initial defence systems didn't work. By the time we picked them up they were practically at the base."

"Fault?"

"No. It was taken out– from our level." Their eyes met. "I've been busy all day, and I hear you have been too."

The whole base? His men; his family?

"I called him right," Kare said, with no satisfaction. On any other day, he would have known if the system was tampered with; it was alarmed and linked to his personal computer. Today, he'd been too busy to even think about it. He paused, sick at the idea he could have stopped this, but pushed the thought away. There would be time in the future to go over the endless might-have-beens.

He leaned forward, spoke into his communicator. "Sector four engage: safeguard the approach to the base."

Ships converged where he'd ordered. Rjala was pulling together the disparate platoons who'd been defending with no leadership, isolated from each other. It seemed she was getting somewhere, there was talk of pushing back the attackers, and his air forces were holding all but one approach. They were taking huge losses, though, more every minute as the Empress' fleet came in massive numbers, wave after wave. He heard a soft curse beside him.

"They've got the blast cannons in," Lichio said.

"How many?"

"A lot."

There was the sound of a blast, distant and muffled. The base rocked, the impact designed to shatter the walls that stood against their enemy shaking the base to its foundations. The lights flickered in the room around them. It was, Kare knew, the beginning of the end.

"How many transports away, Captain?"

"Twenty-two so far, sir."

Another huge blast rocked the base, and Lichio looked at him, his eyes wide. He hadn't betrayed him, Kare realised, more relieved than he should be. He'd wondered over the years, knowing they'd try to get to him through those around him, if he'd been wrong to trust Lichio.

Lichio swallowed and said, "We're not getting away with this one, sir."

"Doesn't seem like it. And there'll be no miracles from me tonight. They've taken my powers away."

Lichio's face was stunned. Kare shrugged; it was so simple. Take out the mind– however they'd done it– and you take out the psycher.

"There goes plan B," Rjala said, behind them. "I'm sorry, Colonel. Get the last transports away now. At best, you have minutes."

He leaned forward and gave the order. On the screen, the last three transport ships lifted off, a squad of fighters with them, and he knew they weren't full. He watched the line of people left behind, their only hope of escape gone, and saw the Empress' troops enter the hangar. His people fell at their laser fire, the small amount of returning fire making no impact. Was Sonly with them, lined up for death, or had she made it to one of the transports? Even if she had, she'd have to get across space, to the relative safety of a new, less secure, base.

At the sound of screams he turned and saw the door had been breached. A shot took Stitt on the chest, and she fell, lying across the doorway. The first of the invading soldiers stamped on her as he walked in. Her hand clenched, and Kare listened to her last, agonised breaths. If he'd had his psyche, he'd have ended it for her.

"Which is the leader?" their captain asked, and Kare saw, with no surprise, Eevan enter the room.

"That one," he stated, as he pointed to Rjala. "And that's Varnon." He faced Kare, exultant in victory, and Kare squared up to him. The bigger man stepped back slightly, but as Kare moved forward, hands took his arms and started to pull them behind him.

"You treacherous fucker. Your sister's in a transport running a space blockade, or dead in the base." And his baby. Fear choked him. "Your little brother's on his way to Omendegon with me."

With enormous pride he saw Lichio step forward. "Your soldiers were slaughtered, without an officer to command them. To get me? Am I really worth that much to you? Why?"

Eevan kept his eyes focused on Kare. "Because my Empress commands me," he said.

"You poor bastard," Kare said, with a harsh laugh. He struggled against the hands on him, his anger giving him strength, and threw the soldiers off. He had never had so much hate. It filled him, distorted him, making him feel like a different person. "She got to you, did she? Or did you offer her me? Did you deal with her, Eevan, and think you might win? Well you didn't; no one wins except her."

"Kare!" Rjala stood, her blaster drawn, the same firebrand his father had known. He moved to give her a clear shot, and a pinpoint of laser passed him, missing by centimetres, and hit Eevan, centred between his eyes.

"Drop your weapon!"

She smiled and raised her blaster. He tried to break free, to stop her, but shots rang out and she fell.

"General, no!" shouted Lichio.

Kare tried to reach her. Hands grabbed him, firmly this time, and pulled him back. She didn't move. He pulled forward a little, and then stopped. She'd had no block, no way to keep her secrets safe. Even at the last, it had been about the Banned; a life to be proud of, indeed. Something cold pressed against his temple.

"Don't move," said a voice. "We came for you."

A muscle moved in Kare's cheek. "Fine, kill me."

"Not you." The gun moved to Lichio instead, and Kare met his eyes. He couldn't be his killer. The soldiers surrounded Kare, and his arms were pulled behind into cold cuffs. At his feet, Eevan lay dead.

There was movement at the door and two men entered: the first tall, lean, with flat grey eyes, his insignia showing him as a general. He smiled as he looked around the room. Kare looked from him to the other.

"No!" He pulled at his manacles, trying to free himself, but it made no difference. He twisted, trying not to face the man who'd been in his nightmares since he was a child.

The general nodded to the man beside him. "He's all yours, Captain Beck."

The huge soldier reached for Kare and pulled him forwards. Kare closed his eyes. The future was here, the path his father had known; whatever was ahead, let him at least show courage.

CHAPTER THIRTY-FIVE

The darkness, that was the first thing. The cold and fear. They were all distractions from the pain spasming down his back. His legs were cramped; his chest burned each time he tried to take a breath.

Kare wrenched his thoughts away. The attack: the base was gone and the death toll must have been huge. Had Sonly made it to the reserve base? His breath hitched– he knew where it was. How long until she'd move, knowing he held the information? He didn't know, but he silently thanked himself for placing the block.

The block. With Stitt dead there was nothing he could do to remove it; there was no way out for him. Fear came rushing, attacking him, and he had to think of something, anything else. *Beck.* The darkness filled with pinpoints of light. Beck, whom his father had screamed for mercy from. Karia had pressed against Kare and they'd promised each other if they met him, they'd run. He pulled against his restraints, but there was no give in them. He groaned, low in his throat.

How long had he been here? He reckoned somewhere between half and a full day. His piss was cold underneath him, so it must have been hours since he'd given in and crossed the first line from free to owned.

The door opened, light spilling in from the corridor, and he squinted against it. The person who entered was huge– bigger than Silom, even– sending fear spiralling into every corner of his mind. He squeezed his eyes shut, took a deep breath, and opened them again: not seeing was worse.

"Hurts?" said Beck. His footsteps echoed as he crossed to Kare, and there was the pinprick of another injection. How many had they given him now?

He kept his mouth closed, afraid that if he said anything, the dam protecting his mind might fail, and he'd keep going until he betrayed everyone he loved.

Beck put his hand on Kare's head; it was warm against the newly shaved skin. Kare tried to move from under it, but Beck forced his head forward and down. Pain arced across Kare's shoulders, radiating through his arms and chest. He tensed, and the knots in his legs tightened. Another sharp push and he shrieked.

"I asked- did it hurt?" Beck's voice was low, menacing.

"Yes!" Kare's arms strained against the back of the seat. He sucked in a breath. "It hurts."

Beck let go, and his arm pulled back. Kare tried to move, but the blow knocked him to the side, sending pain shooting through him.

"It hurts, *Master*," said Beck.

Kare shook his head, dizzy, and clenched his mouth closed. Beck laughed, low and rumbling. He walked to the door and Kare sucked in a deep breath of relief- he'd done it, held out against his demands. His torturer turned back with something in his hands.

"I came to give you some food."

Food. His arms would have to be released to eat. He waited as the guard went behind him, ready for the relief. Instead, hands clasped under his chin and pulled his head back. Something was put against his mouth and he clenched his jaw against it.

"Open."

He tried to wrench his head away, but Beck held him firmly, forcing a thick tube into his mouth, so far that he gagged. Thick liquid, sour, burning his throat, poured in. He choked, but still more came, spilling out and down his neck and chest. Panicking, he fought, but his shackles were too tight, and the liquid only stopped when Beck took the tube away. Kare lifted his head and swallowed the last of it, hard. Beck moved in front and waited, a smile on his face.

"Water." Beck lifted a jug and the panic came back, worse now, so basic and primeval Kare lost any sense of where he was, or what was happening to him, focused only on the need to get away. The chair rocked, pulling at his back and shoulders, and then settled. Effortlessly, Beck pushed his head back.

"No!" Kare fought, wrenching his head from side to side, adrenaline masking his pain, but another tube, this one narrowed, poured water into his mouth and down his throat. He pushed against Beck but was held down and still it came. He swallowed and swallowed, great gulps of water, retching it back up and then gulping again until black dots danced in front of his eyes. He was drowning. No breath came, just water, gushing down, unstopped and unstoppable. Beck pulled him upright and waited as he retched, gasped air, and retched again.

"If you throw up, I'll feed that to you, too."

Kare swallowed the threatened bile and started to get the

choking under control. He struggled against his chains; it was as effective as his last attempt.

Beck's soft voice stopped him. "I know you, I know your thoughts."

He stopped struggling and listened. It was important to listen.

"I've lived and breathed you for years," Beck continued. "I've listened to the spies tell me about you. I've watched your captured soldiers break, in Omendegon, and sob out everything they knew about you. I interviewed Eevan le Payne for two days, and he told me you like to be in control, all the time. Well, you no longer have a choice about anything. Your life will be governed by me and if I want you to eat, you'll eat. If I want you to sleep, you'll sleep. If I want you to sit on a seat in agony, then that's what you'll do."

He left, and the room plunged back into darkness. A wall of pain hit Kare, coming from everywhere– his muscles, his throat, his mouth– accompanied by his father's pleas for mercy, as vivid now as when he was seven. *I can't face it; I can't.*

***

Lichio sat, propped against the wall, his hands loosely shackled. The atmosphere in the main hold was muted. Guards carrying whips were interspersed amongst the prisoners, and armed guards were stationed at each of the doors. A walkway ran across the top of the room, overlooking the prisoners.

"I reckon we're nearly in," Lichio said. He had no clear idea how long he'd been held in this room, the lights never dimmed, his shackles only loosened for food and toilet breaks. At least a week, judging by Silom's beard. Probably more. Given the size of the ship, and presumably its hyperspace capability, they could easily be near the Ceaton systems. "They changed drives."

"Maybe we'll get lucky and crash." Silom, beside him, seemed composed but Lichio couldn't decide if the big man really was less frightened or just better at hiding it. Whichever it was, he was right. A space crash would be quick; whatever lay ahead on Abendau wouldn't be.

"How many of us do you reckon there are?" he said, wrenching his thoughts back to the present.

Silom looked around the hold. "A thousand?"

"Something like that, maybe a little less."

Silence fell between them as a nearby Banned soldier squared up to a guard, who pulled out his whip and lashed the soldier, corralling him until more guards convened and shackled him tightly to the wall.

"That was pointless," Lichio said. "I wonder if Sonly made it?"

"I don't know." Silom sounded frustrated; Lichio had asked more than once, as if it was a scab that had to be picked and picked at, until it went away. "I got her as far as the transports. Kym isn't here, either. She'd have been fighting on the base."

"I know. Maybe she made it, Silom." Lichio paused. Something still wasn't right. "Are you sure about the baby? It doesn't make sense to kill her- surely she was what the Empress wanted."

Silom scowled. "I'm sure: I heard the shot. I don't think they realised who I was, or the baby."

"Will you tell Kare?"

"If I can. He should know." Silom's eyes were bleak. His hands clenched. "Where the hell is he?"

There was no answer to that; Kare hadn't been seen since Lichio had been taken onto the ship, and the giant guard with Kare had peeled away from the main group with him.

"Solitary?" How much worse would that be? Without Silom to talk to, he'd have gone mad with fear days ago. He glanced at the big man. "You know they tried to bring me in against him?"

Silom's mouth dropped open. "When?"

"Just after Corun. What they offered me, Silom..." He looked up at the ceiling, not wanting to meet his eyes. "...I was tempted. Anyone would have been."

"Not me."

Lichio, remembering the day in the jungle, the sharp taste of desire in his mouth, shook his head. "Don't be too sure. I went straight to Eevan and told him- I had to tell someone, so I couldn't take it. Does that make sense?"

"I suppose." Still, Silom scowled. "Were you really tempted?"

"Briefly. I wouldn't be now." He moved his hands, the chains clinking. "The thing is, if I'd despised him, I'd have been very tempted." He bit his lip. "What if it was me who put Eevan onto it? What if this is my fault?"

Silom shook his head. "They'd have tried him at some stage, anyway. They'd have kept going until they found someone to sell Kare out." He spat. "You're sure about his powers?"

"Yes."

"That's hard to imagine." Silom nudged Lichio and nodded to the door opposite them. "There he is."

Lichio looked over and saw the guard first, before noticing

Kare behind him, his arms tightly shackled behind his back, his head shaved. Silom started to get up.

"Sit down," Lichio said, "and think. At least he doesn't look hurt."

Silom snorted his derision. "Look again, Lich; it isn't always obvious."

Lichio looked a little closer and he could see, now, the tight set of Kare's jaw, the red marks on his neck and the darkening bruise on his jaw line. Kare cast exhausted eyes around the room, as if searching for someone, and stopped when he saw Silom. He paled even further.

"I'm going over," Silom said. "He should know. If they want to beat me for telling him, then so be it."

"It might not be you they punish. This isn't the moment, Silom."

Silom settled back, grudgingly, and the guard led Kare to the front of the room dominated by a pair of huge cargo doors. As they walked away, Lichio could see how tightly his arms were shackled, and the strain on his shoulders. The Banned men fell back as Kare passed, forming an unplanned honour guard for him.

"Why isn't he fighting?" asked Silom. "They'd have to kill me before I'd submit."

"And that's going to help us, how? He knows this is about him, and he's not going to fight; not your way, anyway."

"So what will he do?" His eyes were focused on Kare, all his earlier composure gone. He looked the way he'd been when he first realised Kym wasn't on board, like he was ready to crack. Lichio touched his arm, clumsy in his shackles. Silom nodded.

Lichio dropped his hands. "He'll do his best, Silom."

The guards unshackled the restrained prisoners and called the others forward. The cargo doors opened, dwarfing Kare, who stood at their mouth, swaying. Lichio nodded at Silom and together they walked forward and stood either side of their colonel. What was left of the Banned army formed up. His brother had done this. He still couldn't quite believe it.

When the cargo doors opened fully, Lichio stepped onto a raised walkway which stretched across to the palace of Abendau. He glanced over its low parapet, at a crowd gathered in the gardens below. Another crowd waited where the walkway opened out at the palace. *Quite the event.* The guards pushed him forward but he held back for a moment, not wanting to face the shouts and goading. A firmer push made him walk forwards.

Lichio didn't look at the crowd, but focused on the entrance ahead, noticing how it was formed from a blend of old and new stone. It seemed to him a sign, telling them her empire was ageless. She was right: without Kare, there was no one else who could face her.

They reached the end of the walkway, and he shrank back from the crowd, glad of the guards' protection. The crowd's spit still reached him, stinging his face. He reached to wipe it away, but stopped. *Kare can't.* He looked again at his friend, saw how he faced the crowd, his face unmoving, his eyes looking ahead. *I'm a le Payne and need to be proud of it.* His dad would want him to be. Still, he trembled as he passed, and cast his eyes down against their hatred.

He stepped into the entrance hall and his breath quickened when he saw the archway opposite, knowing it held the ancient castle of Abendau, around which she'd built her palace, and the path to Omendegon. He imagined himself being taken into its dark portal, and had an urge to run or fight. He glanced first at Silom, standing with his fists clenched, and then at Kare, who must be more frightened than anyone. Briefly, their eyes met and Kare visibly took a deep breath. With a nod, Lichio turned to face the archway, ready to be pushed into it. Instead, his focus was taken by the soft noise of the crowd sinking to their knees as if an invisible wave had swept over them. Kare's guard forced a hiss of pain as he pulled on his arms and brought him to his knees.

"Give the order," said the guard, "or I'll lengthen the list of your people visiting Omendegon."

"Kneel." Kare's voice was hoarse, but loud enough to carry through the hall. Lichio hesitated, everything in him wanting to resist, until Kare glared at him and he sank to his knees.

As he did, a weight smothered his thoughts. Sweat trickled between his shoulder blades and he struggled to draw breath. He lifted his eyes to the balcony and saw, regal and imperious, the Empress, her face hard, untouchable. His fear turned to terror. Beside him, Kare gave a low moan and the Empress smiled as she swept her son's mind. How bad must it feel: to know how to fight her, to have had the power to, but be unable.

Kare slumped forwards and the room waited in silence as they watched her dominance. His head stayed down, and Lichio held his breath, willing Kare to find his power and face her with it. A moment later, Kare pulled himself up and focused on her again, but he was pale and sweating, drawing on every strand of strength within him. Lichio switched his attention to the Empress, and his terror returned. He'd been a bloody fool to try and fight against this. She looked directly at him, and it was like she was seeing the very soul of him– everything that made him Lichio. He shook his head and turned back to Kare, his fear easing a little as he did.

"General Phelps," said the Empress, and the man who had led her army stepped forward and kneeled. "You have brought me my prize, as you said you would. I congratulate you."

The man visibly swelled with pride. "My Empress, I thank you."

The Empress turned back to where her prisoners were waiting.

"Kare Varnon," the Empress said. "Son of the famous rebel Ealyn."

"Empress," he acknowledged, his voice low and hoarse. Sweat ran down his forehead, into his eyes, and he was trembling under her stare but he was still, somehow, facing her.

"We've managed to remove you from your pseudo-kingdom, I see. Without your famous psyche, too. I command your fealty and if it's given, and given honestly, I will grant clemency."

Kare took his time. His breathing was heavy and loud in the quiet room, but he glared at his mother.

"No," he said, his voice low, but steady. "I won't."

A sharp sound resonated through the room. Lichio closed his eyes, knowing what would– must– happen next.

"Omendegon," the Empress said, and Lichio opened his eyes to see her turn and leave. The word echoed in his head, circling.

Kare was trailed roughly to his feet, a scream hastily bitten off, and pulled to the doorway of the castle. If he tried to delay, it wasn't obvious; if he pulled back at all, it made no difference. Numbly, Lichio was lifted from his knees and pushed through the door, Silom behind him. He stumbled down the twisting corridor, the cold stonework surrounding him. As the light from the entrance hall faded, Lichio le Payne struggled to remember any of the ancients' prayers.

CHAPTER THIRTY-SIX

Kare was pushed through the arch, his head buzzing from his mother's invasion. She'd tried to take the information she needed, right there and then. The base, the spies, everything, but when she'd touched the block, her invasion had stopped, no matter how she'd tried to force it. Without it, he'd have no defence against her. With it... he hardly dared to face what that meant.

He stumbled, his hands behind him, not able to save himself, and yelled out, sure he was going to fall. Somehow, he got his right foot down and managed to stay upright, but his cramped muscles twisted. A huge hand caught his shoulder– familiar already– and Beck spun him against the wall. His cheek banged off the rock. There was the sound of a lash and he screamed at a new pain– fresh, different– across his shoulders. Another crack and a second blossom of agony pierced him as his skin parted.

"Not another sound."

He stayed where he was, his cheek against the hot rock, and tried to nod. He bit down, hard, holding back a moan as Beck pushed him down the corridor, its slight incline making him lose his footing. This time he was sure he would fall. He didn't, but he had to grind his teeth together to stay silent. *Sadist.* His blood ran cold.

Ahead, an iron door stood, and above it a sign, old and faded, but he didn't need to be able to read the ancient Abendauii to know where he was: Omendegon, the place of pain. He tried to slow down, but another hard shove kept him moving. *If anyone cares about me, please stop this happening.* The door opened and he was forced through.

It stank. The iron tang of blood, a dark undertone of filth. Cages lined each side of the corridor, but he was marched past them. Behind, he heard one open, and then another: Lichio and Silom were staying here, for now. Beck took his arm, yanking it back, and he didn't cry out.

"Scared yet?" Beck's voice was close to his ear, menacing. *Gods, yes.* He nodded, sure if he tried to answer he'd start begging to be taken somewhere else. Anywhere else. A second iron door stood at the end of the corridor, and it opened into a different section, this one modern, with silvered doors lining each side, stretching to a distant, red stone wall.

Beck opened one of the doors and pushed Kare in. Inside there was a small desk with a chair either side. Sitting at the desk was an old man, his shoulders rounded as if permanently hunched, his skin sun-darkened. His soft, brown eyes met Kare's, and swept over him, appraising him. Kare swallowed, but said nothing.

The old man nodded to Beck. "Release his arms."

Beck undid the shackles holding Kare's arms. As his stretched muscles moved, he screamed, long, wrenched from him. Cramps ran across his back and shoulders.

"Sit down."

Kare did, forcing himself to concentrate on the old man. He looked kind: like someone you'd tell anything to.

"You're wondering who I am?"

Kare nodded.

"In here, I'm the Great Master. That's my only name to you. There are other masters here, but it's to me you'll tell your secrets. Now, let's get an idea of how cooperative you'll be. What's your name?"

There would be time later to hold back, but they knew who he was. "Kare Varnon."

"Good. You're a member of the Banned?"

"Yes."

"Rank?"

Kare opened his mouth, but when he tried to say his rank, nothing came out.

"Rank?" the man said again.

"I can't tell you," Kare said. "I have a block–"

The old man held his hand up. "I am aware of your block. We'll see what we can do to get round it." He nodded to Beck. "Room one."

Beck pulled Kare to his feet and led him back down the corridor to another of the doors. He opened it, and Kare walked in. The room was clinical, the only furniture a metal table with a single chair next to it. It wasn't unlike where he'd had his implant removed, back on the base.

"Strip." Beck waited, his expression bland. Kare didn't move. "Strip or I'll lash them off you."

He would; the stinging heat across his shoulders confirmed it. Kare unbuttoned his shirt and pulled off his boots and trousers until he stood, just his shorts left. It was horribly exposed. Fear gripped him, holding him, and there was no way out. The block was in place just as he'd planned, no way around it, no chink in it. He met Beck's eyes, saw the satisfaction within them.

"I said strip, Dog."

Kare swallowed, and pulled off his shorts, straightening and fighting the urge to hide. Beck openly assessed him, the disparity between owned and owner pronounced. He circled Kare, making him aware of his bare skin, how easily it had parted under the whip. Kare looked at the table, refusing to watch Beck, and another surge of fear coursed through him, stronger than before. He had to know what lay ahead; knowing had to be easier than this blind fear. "What does it do?"

"Lie on it."

Kare stood his ground, not moving. He couldn't keep obeying, or there'd be no end to the bastard's demands. Beck laughed and cuffed him lightly on the ear.

"What does it do?" asked Kare again. He took in a lever beside the table, straps on each corner, and his blood ran to ice.

"What does it do, *Master*." Beck reached out, his hands covering Kare's shoulders, and slammed him back against the table, jarring his spine so that he had to bite down against a yell. "You will learn."

He pushed Kare onto the table, holding him easily as he tried to twist. Each wrist was forced into a strap, followed by his ankles, stretching him, leaving him open and vulnerable. A wave of panic rose and he tried to count his breaths– in and out, in and out, steady and slow. At the sound of the door he opened his eyes and found himself looking at the kind face of the Great Master. Now the man was closer to him– so close he could smell his sour breath– there was something in his eyes, a sense of enjoyment, that wiped away any trace of kindness. Kare licked his dry lips.

"It does no good." The Great Master checked the straps. "Deep breathing. Meditation. Nothing you can do will stop the pain, unless you tell me what I need to know."

Kare swallowed, hard. Had his dad lain here, looking into those eyes? A click from where the old man sat took his attention, and then another. He tensed in anticipation. With the next soft click, his ankles and wrists pulled against their straps. His eyes met the old man's in horrified realisation.

"Tell me your rank, and I'll let you off," the Great Master said. "That's all I want to know today."

Kare opened his mouth. *Say it: you're a colonel.* His subconscious held stubbornly to the knowledge, refusing to let it out. He couldn't even feel the block, let alone find any way of opening it, without his psyche. And with Stitt dead, even with his powers he could do nothing.

211

"I can't." He put everything he had into the words; he needed these men to believe him. "I really can't."

"A pity," said the old man, and there was another click. Kare steeled himself as his body stretched, his already tender muscles aching. The skin where Beck had lashed him parted, cold metal burning the wound. He bit down.

Dimly, he heard the Great Master's voice. "You see how even the smallest stretch hurts; you did your job on the ship well, Beck."

Another click, and this time pain ripped through Kare, down his arms and legs, through his torso. A scream tore from his throat. His rib cage barely tolerated the shuddering gulp of air he took as it faded to a moan. The block was the only thing stopping him screaming the answer to their question; he'd been right to do it, to save his people from this. He had to hang on to that.

"Already," the Great Master continued, "he's wondering how far I'll go, how long it will go on for. Come, leave him to think."

His tormentors left and the pain wracked through him. He had no idea how long he lay there, time measured only by agonised breaths, but when he heard the sound of the door he let out a sob of fear. There was an injection, and then the old man moved back to where he could see him.

"It's difficult," he confided. "My Empress has made it clear she wants you to show remorse. She tells me not to allow you the release of oblivion. You understand?"

Kare didn't answer- there was no answer- and the Great Master pursed his lips in disappointment.

"Confirm your rank to me, Colonel Varnon," he said. "See, I already know it, all you have to do is nod, and I stop now."

Kare attempted to nod, but couldn't. He tried to think of anything to appease this man, something which might stop him, and finally thought of a word.

"Please," he whispered. The face of the Great Master was coming and going, blurred through the pain. He had a sense of something being shown to him, shining and long, but couldn't tell what it was.

"Where should I put it?" asked the Great Master. Kare shook his head, but something cold and metallic touched his chest. He tensed, causing needles of sharp agony. They faded and he stared at the Great Master, waiting, trying not to remember his father crying for the release of death, and yet he could think of nothing else.

A shock of pain seared into his chest muscles. He thrashed against it, pulling on his bonds. He was sure he'd be ripped apart, he

212

fought so much. His tormentor waited until his screams faded to gulping sobs.

"I'm a patient man," he whispered, his mouth close to Kare's ear, like a lover. "I can wait for you to tell me your secrets. While I wait, this body of yours..."

Kare moaned as the metal point ran down his body, knowing where it was meant for. He began to shake.

"No," he pleaded, his voice hitching. When the probe touched his balls there was a hot spurt of piss. Beck laughed, loud and mocking. Kare waited, knowing what must come, his breaths shallow against the pain, his eyes closed, mouthing the same words over and over again. "Please, no."

At last it came, the pain enveloping him, spreading through every nerve he had. His scream was the howl of an animal. It stopped, refusing him the oblivion of passing out, and then the probe moved. The old man waited so he knew what was to come, enjoying his torment, and when the next shock came, Kare sank into the pain.

CHAPTER THIRTY-SEVEN

am sat in the quiet church, looking, as intently as it was possible to, at the statue of his lady. He liked this particular chapel, cut from the red stone of the Belaudii desert: it reminded him of the churches of his childhood on Ligne. There, they worshipped a different God– only his Lady was allowed on Belaudii– but the sense of place was the same. He closed his eyes and prayed to his own God to give him the strength he needed.

The sound of a lash, Beck's grunt as he put all his weight into it. It was as vivid as when he'd been in the cell, watching. He could smell piss and old shit, see the healer being called forward from the shadows, the miracle of skin healing.

He drew in a breath and tried to clear his mind, focusing on the statue of the Empress. It wore a soft smile, not at all the hard one when she'd invaded the prisoner's mind, ignoring his last words of defiance, the look of undiluted hatred he'd fixed on her. His eyes– that brilliant green, impossible to ignore– had cast around the room, finding Sam, for a moment, counting the doctor as one of them. Another shock had torn his face skywards, brought a shriek that filled the room, even as his block had held. Sam's palms were sweating. He needed to stop this memory, to forget about what had happened, but still it ran on: the fury of the Empress as the prisoner had held against her; his pleas as she invaded him again; the final round of shocks that had left Varnon hanging, unmoving, his secrets screamed through the room, the block collapsed under her power.

Sam gasped and opened his eyes, refocusing on the statue. He'd worked in Omendegon for the last year: he'd known what the masters did. *Known*, yes, but he'd never *seen* it. He cursed softly and looked around, guilty, but there was no one near.

It had to come, sometime, he'd known that. With his last promotion, it had been made clear to him that he would be expected to cover the cells and not just the wards. He'd accepted it, not able to remember the last time a doctor had been called to attend the cells. Survival wasn't usually a criterion in Omendegon.

It was different with Varnon: he wasn't to die, not yet. And Sam had been the unlucky bastard on call when Beck had fucked up

214

and taken him too near the edge. That made Sam, according to Beck, the one. He hadn't even known what that meant. Now, he did: the one responsible for Varnon's health, for treating him, for deciding if a healer was needed, or if he could go on, while Beck broke him for the Empress. Not just broke him- made an example no one would forget. No one would oppose the Empress after what she planned to have done to her son. *Her son*. He took another deep breath- to do that to someone you'd borne...

He shook his head and focused on the statue. His psyche test was in half an hour and if he failed that.... The soft grey eyes watched him. She hadn't been soft in the chamber. *Stop!*

He squeezed his eyes shut, so tightly that blurred lines shifted inside his lids, and congratulated himself when his thoughts cleared. He relaxed, and a different memory assailed him. A man, stood against the bars of his cell: blond hair, lank and dirty; keen blue eyes filled with tears which spilled over and rolled, unchecked, down his cheeks; damaged hands held to his chest, cradled.

"Will he die?" le Payne had asked, his eyes flicking to Sam and then back to Varnon, lying still in his cell.

Sam had looked down at the thin body beside him, taking in the broken skin and shallow breaths. *Yes, sometime.* He didn't meet le Payne's eyes. "Hard to say."

"What they did...." Le Payne's voice cracked. "It was brutal."

Yes, it was. But it was repayment for the worst kind of treachery- against the Empress, from her own flesh. "I've seen worse."

Le Payne had looked between his friend- his leader- and Sam. "You call yourself a doctor, yet stand over it? You're a monster. As bad as any of them." He'd leaned forwards, loathing in his eyes, the snarl of his mouth unforgettable. "Worse, you bastard."

A shard of fear, that le Payne was right, that he knew the soul of Sam, shot through him. No human would stand over what had been done. The thought had held him there for long moments, staring at le Payne. Behind his youth and angelic face, he was a murderer. He had no right to judge Sam. The blue eyes had returned his gaze until Sam had turned away to focus on his patient. He'd lifted Varnon's wrist and checked his pulse. Thin, thready. When he looked up, le Payne was still watching him, accusing him.

"I do my job because I'm loyal to my Empress," he'd replied, drawing out every word. It was true, and the reason he hadn't protested about being brought to Abendau and the palace after his college scores had topped the league on Ligne, but celebrated instead. "You and your friend stood against her; it's her right to punish you."

It was, and Varnon- who'd stood against her openly- deserved to be where he was. He clenched his fists, convincing himself. He had to be convinced. There was no room for doubts. Not today.

He lifted his chin and concentrated on his Lady's peaceful eyes, how her hair pulled around her face and softened the high, sharp cheekbones. He let thoughts of her- and nothing but her, he had to be sure of that- dominate until his only focus was the need to please her. No doubts about the torture chambers or the broken body that lay in Beck's cell, eyes dulled with pain, twisted, broken, hands stretching, pleading, for release.

He took another moment, keeping his eyes on the statue, breathing deeply. Fifteen minutes. He got up and left, walking through the streets of Abendau, up the wide boulevard lined with rich embassies, to where the palace stood, white and glittering in the centre of this city of red stone. He reached the gate, showed his ID, and went into the gardens. The air- dusty and dry until now- filled with the scent of flowers and rich soil. He crossed a footbridge over the irrigation moat and entered the inner gardens with their clipped hedges and maze. At the entrance to the palace he waited while fuller ID checks were made- a pinprick of blood confirming his DNA- and passed into the main hall, through the archway to Omendegon. His heart started to beat loudly as he made his way along the sloping corridor, but he brought to mind the soft eyes of the statue. *For his Lady.*

The guard at the gate nodded. "Doc."

Nodding back, he walked to his office. At the desk sat the psycher- blonde hair, about forty, her hazel eyes polite, not friendly. She'd done his last test but one, too. His hands broke into a sweat as he sat opposite.

"Doctor Prentice?"

He licked his lips. "Yes, that's me. Again."

Her eyes stayed blank. She'd looked into his mind, seen every thought he had, and didn't remember him. It seemed unbelievable. He looked closer: her eyes looked bored. How could she get bored doing what she did?

"I'll start," she said.

He clenched his fists and nodded, breathing deeply. He brought to mind the Empress and the feeling infused from the church, and her presence around him, as it always was in the palace, gave him the strength to face the test. He felt the first touch of the psycher's mind in

216

his and even though he knew it was better not to fight he wanted to push her out. He breathed in again, a deep breath. *A couple of minutes, that's all.* A familiar fear leapt in him. What if there *were* doubts-doubts he didn't even know he had? He shuddered.

"Steady, doctor, we're almost there. A few moments."

He waited as she explored his thoughts and feelings. Did it make her feel dirty? The invasion started to ease, but stopped and strengthened again with a new focus. He swallowed, waiting until she finished and pulled out of his mind. He reached out, taking a sip from a glass of water- he felt sick, he always did- and set it back with shaking hands. He watched the psycher fill in a form. She passed it across the table to him.

"Sign."

He blinked. Was he signing to affirm his loyalty, or had he been found lacking?

"Did I pass?" His voice was a whisper.

There was a pause. "Yes, you passed."

A wave of relief as he signed. The psycher put the document in her bag.

"If I were you, I'd think about a transfer, though," she said, giving him a long look. His blood ran cold. She *had* seen something. She shrugged. "It's just- the images in your mind- I don't know how you do it."

She left and he thought about her words. *Transfer?* He felt like laughing, but if he did it would come out like something else. A howl, maybe. There was no transfer, not once you'd seen the inside of Omendegon, the dark heart of Abendau. He dropped his head into his hands, clutching his hair and pulling it. He had done nothing wrong. *Nothing.* But still, her long look. He got up; it was over for another six months.

"Doc!" shouted someone, one of the orderlies, presumably.

He stuck his head out into the corridor. "Yes?"

"Two prisoners need checked before they get sent to the quarries. Dr. Soong's taken one."

He crossed to the small room opposite and glanced at the notes on the door: they were going to Clenadii quarry, named, like half the planet, for one of the Empress' victories in the uprising reclaiming Belaudii for her. Only high security prisoners were sent there. He read the name on the card and his blood ran cold. Lichio le Payne.

He paused with his hand on the door. Had le Payne heard Varnon's shrieks at the end? Did he know his leader had broken? Of

217

course he did: Omendegon was designed so you didn't just face your own pain, but others' as well.

Sam took a deep breath and stepped into the room. Le Payne sat on the edge of a small bed, showered and deloused, wearing a pair of ragged prison trousers. The prisoner lifted his head, and their eyes met; there was no doubt he remembered Sam. Sam walked over, taking a scanner from the port on the wall. As he started his checks, le Payne's hand reached out. "Is he dead?"

Sam ignored him and concentrated on the scanner.

"*Please*. Is he?"

Sam looked at him, at the lash marks on his shoulders, the nail beds still trailing blood. Normally, a prisoner coming out of Omendegon was walled into their own torment, passively waiting for it to be over. Instead, le Payne met his eyes, waiting, until Sam said, "No."

Le Payne took a deep breath in, shuddering, and Sam completed the scan. He frowned; the prisoner had a temperature. "Lift your arms."

Arms, legs, the things that carried strength. They were important to the masters. The searing pain in the man's eyes wasn't.

"He has a wife, you know," said le Payne, his voice soft. He raised his two arms, pulling in a hiss of pain.

Sam ran the scanner along le Payne's right arm. He stopped, palpitated the deltoid muscle, and the other man flinched.

"We'll get that treated."

Le Payne put his arms down and there was silence. Outside, a door opened: Dester was clear, presumably. Any second now, the guards would come in and ask about le Payne. He would be sent to the quarry and Sam would never have to face these knowing eyes again.

Except he had a temperature, and the one thing– the *only* thing– that wasn't allowed was fever. Sam checked the lash wounds were clean and put a gel bandage on le Payne's upper arm as the other man said, "My sister should know if he dies."

Tears had formed in le Payne's eyes, but he blinked and focused on Sam. "Please, he means so much to her." The tears spilled over and down his cheeks. This wasn't a cold man, like Sam had been led to believe. He leaned forward, reached out, palm open, pleading. "She's lost their baby; she needs to know about Kare."

Sam didn't reply. He'd been here before: prisoners begging him to save them, or tell their family where they were, and the best answer– the only answer– was silence.

Le Payne glanced at the door. "The personal ads," he said. His words were quick and hoarse, whispered and urgent. "In the news reels- we monitor those. Please. He deserves to be remembered."

"Guards!" shouted Sam.

The door opened. "Finished?" asked the guard.

Sam stepped back. "Yes, but he'll have to stay under observation- he's threatening a fever. Get him deloused again, too: he's still crawling."

The guard took le Payne's arm and led him out. He made no effort to fight but, as he passed Sam, sent one final look. His lip curled. He'd called Sam a monster, had accused him of being worse than any of the torturers. Worse even than Beck.

Sam looked at the door for a long moment, and then turned and put the scanner back. There was nothing else to do, after all, but move on to the next prisoner, and then the next, and forget Lichio le Payne's hard words and soft, knowing eyes.

***

Fresh baked bread... Kare tried to curl up against the pain in his stomach but couldn't move his arms and legs.

"Say it." Beck's voice grated. He pulled Kare's head up, so he could see the bread as it was crumbled, smell its scent. He shook his head and Beck took the bread away. Kare drifted away, only half aware of where he was...

His head was yanked back, another smell. Meat juices dripped onto his lips, clenching his stomach.

"Say it." Beck drizzled more and this time they were salty, mixed with tears.

He needed it. "Master."

The chicken vanished. He needed it. Gods, he needed it. The chains opened and his hands fell before him and he looked at them, not knowing what to do. A hunk of bread and a bowl were set on the floor, and he remembered. He broke the hard bread, used the gruel to soften it, and ate, scooping the dregs, spilling them from his hands, they were shaking so much. He licked the bowl, needing what it had, and when Beck laughed, he didn't care. He needed it.

The bowl was taken away and Beck leaned close. "Who am I?"

There was no option, nowhere to go but that moment, that need. "My master," he whispered.

The chains went back on his wrists, pulling him against the wall. He shivered at the cold. The hood was put on; he fought against it, but it was pulled down and there was only darkness. There was always only darkness and the knowledge that he would come again, and that everywhere hurt.

219

CHAPTER THIRTY-EIGHT

Sam stood in the shower, scrubbing himself. *A collar.* Like a dog's, so tight the prisoner's rasping breath filled the room. What next? He looked up at the showerhead and the water ran onto his face.

He turned the shower off and stepped out. Varnon had been a week in the torture chambers and another week in solitary. Sam had asked Beck how long it would take, and he'd shrugged. Until Varnon didn't know who he was, he'd said.

What did that mean... would Sam have to keep going down there, every day? It seemed likely. He got dressed and walked down to the main clinic. Two guards stood outside a room, but stepped aside for him.

He looked at the chart and nodded. Le Payne's fever had broken. He could be moved down to the cells until the requisite forty-eight hours had passed. And then, the quarry, where it mightn't be quick, but it would be better than Omendegon.

He went in and found le Payne sitting up in the middle of the bed, his wrists and ankles chained to the bedstead. He swept his clear blue eyes over Sam, making Sam wonder what he could see on his face: revulsion, perhaps. He lifted the scanner from the wall.

"Have you seen him?"

Sam ignored the quiet voice and started the scan. "How do you feel?"

Le Payne shrugged. "Better, for what it's worth. The guards have told me I'm facing a lifetime of hard labour." He looked up at the ceiling and seemed very young, his throat bobbing as he swallowed. A moment later he turned back to Sam and gave a half smile, closer to a grimace. "They don't think it'll be a long sentence."

Sam stayed silent. It was better to tell the poor sod nothing- the truth would only torment him further.

"Gem 1- that was his call sign. I'm Cat 2. I was his second, you see." Le Payne's voice cracked, just a little. "He always got top billing." He paused, breathing in. "Is that what being Beck's plaything is? Top billing? The guards think so- they also seem to think someone with a fever can't hear."

Sam stepped back. The image of Kare Varnon, chained, hooded, shivering in a darkened cell, flashed in front of him. "You've said enough."

"Why- am I making you feel bad?" asked le Payne. "You

should, you bastard. You sat with him, held his hand, told him he couldn't die, and said nothing when they took him back." He sneered. "Did you enjoy it? Get secret kicks from it?"

No. Nightmares, unclean images he'd pay to get rid of. "*Enough!*" Sam turned away, his fists clenched.

Le Payne rattled his chains. "I think you'll win."

Sam dropped his fists. "Anything else, and I'll see you're sent back to Omendegon." His words were as weak as he was. He glanced at the door. "Guards!"

Le Payne gave a soft laugh. "Let them, I'm fucked anyway." He paused, and when he resumed it was in a quieter voice. "Do you think you're safe? The guards seemed relieved they hadn't seen him, seemed to think anyone who had might be... superfluous. That's what I took from it, anyway."

Sam drew in a deep breath, remembering Beck's flat eyes, the way they looked at him when he was there, like he was a tool, nothing more. The door opened.

"Well, Doc?" asked the guard.

Sam jerked his head back. "He can go to the quarry," he said. He glanced back at Le Payne's watching eyes.

The prisoner gave a nod, so small it was almost invisible, and Sam turned away.

***

Cold, so cold. Dark. A breath of air crossed Kare's naked body. Beck was coming. He pulled against his chains but they dug in, immovable. Something touched his thigh.

He went somewhere buried inside him, where Beck couldn't reach. Sometimes, there were others: Karia, or his father. Sonly. He burrowed into that place to see who was waiting for him. There was no one.

His hood was torn off. Beck's words came from miles away, his face blurred... "pit."

The world swirled as Kare was unchained and dragged to his feet. He couldn't walk, his leg wouldn't work. He couldn't retreat. He tried to hold Sonly before him, but didn't know what she looked like anymore and he didn't care, he just wanted it to end.

***

Sam stumbled to the door of Nina's apartment and paused, leaning against the door in a brief moment of lucidity. He shouldn't be here. He looked over his shoulder, checking behind him, before leaning on the bell, keeping it pressed down. He had nowhere else to go.

"Yes?" Nina asked, her voice cautious; no one who worked close to

221

the heart of Abendau palace, regardless of their job, was anything but.

"It's me," Sam said. She opened the door.

"I didn't expect you tonight," she said.

"Come out," he said to her. "Please, come out with me."

"Are you drunk?"

He leaned against the doorjamb for support. "A bit. Come on: we'll go somewhere. I need some fresh air."

"Let me get my coat."

He pulled the bottle out of his pocket. *Where's the rest of it?* Then he remembered, and smiled sheepishly. When she came back they walked out of the staff quarters to the palace gardens. He led her to the back of the kitchens, between two generators. Floodlights over the small yard illuminated anyone who might come near them.

"Why are we here?" asked Nina. She crossed her arms and hunched into her coat, and he wondered how much she'd already guessed. She was smart, Nina, good at reading between the lines.

"I've something I want to tell you," Sam said, leaning in so she could hear him. "A secret." He took a moment, hoping to get the words right. "You need to get away from Abendau: go home to Chen."

He took a swig and the palm spirit burned his throat, making him gag.

"Then I'd have to leave you," she said. It was casual, as if she was humouring him, but her eyes were sharp. She looked behind her, poised as if ready to run, and he didn't blame her; midnight conversations in a service yard weren't encouraged in the palace. But her rooms would be recorded, as would his– it was this or nothing. And nothing was driving him insane.

"Doesn't matter," he said. "I'm being transferred."

Her face showed the shock he'd felt before he'd killed it with drink. "Where to?"

He passed her the bottle. Maybe it'd help, but she refused it. The air, the clear, sweet air of the desert, was clearing his mind and he remembered, when he'd been a child, that his church had priests you could tell any secret to. They'd listen, and you'd be forgiven. He wished he could do the same here– tell them what he'd witnessed, tell them that no matter what anyone had done…. He grabbed her hands; that was why he'd decided to come to her. "Nina…"

He stopped. He couldn't. Bad enough that he knew too much, but to risk her, too….

"Are you okay?" she asked.

No. How could he be? He looked down at their entwined hands and pulled his away. *Dirty*. They hadn't been clean for months, not since he'd realised what it took for a man to forget his very self. He let out a soft moan and Nina snatched his hand back.

"Sam?"

He shook his head. He couldn't tell her. He couldn't tell anyone.

"What is it?" she asked. "Tell me."

He had to tell someone; he couldn't hold it in any longer. Not and turn up and do his job tomorrow without cracking, and if he cracked, she'd be pulled in. Pulled in and questioned about what she knew of him in Omendegon. Better he gave her the chance to get away.

"You know I haven't been allowed to leave the palace for the last five months?" He grabbed her hands; if anyone came, let them look like two lovers hiding in the shadows. "I told you I was on call."

"Yes."

"You asked me if I'd ever met them- the Banned prisoners."

She nodded, her eyes wary. He moved closer, whispering in her ear. "I met the three ringleaders in Omendegon. Since then I've been treating Varnon: they assigned me to him."

"Why you?" she asked, doubt in her voice, and he understood; he wouldn't have believed it six months ago, either: that you could be loyal to the Empress, do her bidding, and end up in the mess he was in.

"Bad luck," he said. "I've spent the last months watching a person be destroyed, bit by bit, inch by inch. In the most sadistic way you could imagine. Do you want to hear how? I've had his guard giving me a discourse for months."

"No."

"Okay, I won't."

"Sam, you shouldn't have told me this much."

I know; forgive me. But he had to- if she didn't know, she mightn't go. Once it was in her mind, she'd have to leave or wait to get found out at her next psyche test.

"I got a promotion," he said.

"Great."

Her eyes met his and he shook his head, just a tiny shake. "I'm being sent to the quarries with Varnon."

The quarries, where he'd be just as invisible as Varnon. He reached for her as hot tears rolled down his cheeks. Above him, the stars wheeled against the clear Belaudian sky, spinning their eternal watch. When she sank beside him he knew she understood, and, for the first time in weeks, he felt able to breathe; one of them, at least, would get away. Let it be enough.

CHAPTER THIRTY-NINE

Sonly stepped off the transport toward the ambassador. "Margueritte," she said. As always- more than ever- she felt grubby before the Tortdeniel. The new base didn't have access to wardrobes of clothes for meetings- there was the choice of new army fatigues, old fatigues, or nothing. At least the pair she'd found both fit and were clean. It didn't seem to bother Margueritte, though- she smiled and took Sonly's hand, clasping it warmly.

"I'm so sorry for your troubles."

Sonly pasted a smile on her face. "Thank you, it means a lot- your support."

The ambassador squeezed her arm.

"This way," she said, and led Sonly to a meeting room, leather footstools around the floor to sit on, low tables beside them.

"Thank you," said Sonly, sinking onto one and taking the small glass of scented tea offered her. She didn't drink it, instead inhaling its aroma. She wished Michael was here, but since the death of his granddaughter he had aged, leaving her to take on a more active role. The ambassador sat opposite her, her silken dress spilling across the floor in rich pinks and golds.

"You asked to meet," said the ambassador.

Sonly put on her warmest smile. "We're seeking support for the Banned, funding mainly..."

Her voice tailed off at the resigned look on the ambassador's face. This was Sonly's third meeting in a week and each one had been a polite, often regretful, but firm no. She gritted her teeth- Tortdeniel were very nearly her last chance.

"Sonly, you must know our support was based on your holding the outer rim *and* having a viable successor in place."

Sonly's eyes filled. A successor, that's what he was. Not a husband, or father, or...

"There is no evidence to say Kare is dead," she said. "Or that he doesn't support the Banned."

The other woman's eyes filled with sympathy, and Sonly steeled herself.

"I'm so sorry," said the ambassador. "The head of my house is in Abendau today, to see Kare give fealty to his mother. Several of the houses have already done so this week."

Sonly set the glass down as a roaring sound came into her ears, drowning out any other thought, and her vision darkened. *Don't faint.* She waited, the room unsteady, the footstool flimsy beneath her, and dug her nails into her palm. Only then did she realise she was shaking her head.

The ambassador moved across to her, taking her hand. "Shall I get a doctor?"

Sonly held her other hand up, waiting for the roaring to die down, and gulped in a breath. She looked at the ambassador and said, her voice shaking, "Then it's even more important we continue to fight against her. She can't be allowed to do this, to force her will like this. If Kare is giving his fealty, it's forced, you *know* that."

The ambassador gave a small nod. "What are you seeking?"

Sonly took a moment, deciding her tactics. "A thousand credits a week, to be repaid when we can. It will buy food for the children we're safeguarding." She held her breath; with Tortdeniel's reputation for philanthropy, starving children was a motivator.

"I have your word that it's for the children."

Sonly met her eyes. Weaponry money would have to come from somewhere else. She nodded. "You have my word."

The ambassador took a moment. "We will agree eight hundred a week, delivered anonymously." She paused. "You must know we agree this for the regard we hold you in and held your father in. For the faith you showed in us, and the work you allowed us to do in the outer rim."

Sonly inclined her head. "I am grateful for your trust." She met the ambassador's eyes. "You know, we will rebuild. It mightn't seem like it, but we will."

Margueritte stood, graceful, and waited while Sonly did the same. The ambassador leaned forward and gave Sonly a formal kiss on each cheek.

"You are your father's daughter," she said, and Sonly's tears spilled over and fell onto the other woman's gown. The ambassador hugged her tighter and whispered, "You have many troubles, Sonly le Payne. May our god, the Divine one, watch over you."

Sonly nodded, pulled away and composed herself, bowing a slight formal bow. "And may She grant you a blessing for your munificence. I won't forget it."

***

Later, Sonly sat in the central part of the old, previously disused, civic building that now served as the Banned base. The light in the room was dim, and when a ship came into port the extra power needed often meant it faded to nothing.

The building housed the remaining Banned group: six hundred support personnel from the old base, and an army of two thousand. It was formed around the building she was in and consisted of temporary accommodation, not fit for the winter ahead. The Banned held no planets now. She'd had to recall the army, and their ships had been chased and harried by the Empress' fleet. Few made it, and even when they did, she feared they would lead the Empress' forces to them, and had ordered differing positions for leaving hyperspace, ensuring there was little chance of traffic being matched and the link made. Besides, Kare had known where it was and she had no idea how long he could hold out, block or not.

So she'd moved to this one, buried in the Candelan system on a planet so remote it didn't have a name. Their sponsors had deserted her in droves, and– tears pricked her eyes, and she wiped them– Kare was gone, and Lichio, and Rjala, and everyone she needed.

And her baby. She tried to push the thought away, not able to think of Kerra, but it haunted her. She'd so nearly got her away; Silom had almost reached the transport when the soldiers broke through to him and he'd had to run. Her fists clenched: hours, that was all she'd been allowed with her. If she could, she'd go to Abendau and bring down the bitch herself.

She picked up one of the messages in front of her with a shaking hand. She read it and set it down again, not knowing what to do. They'd been picked up by a sympathiser on Chen from the news-dump personals, and had been waiting for her on her return.

'Care needs pain,' had been the first. The second, slightly different, but consistent: 'Pain applied only with care.' The third had followed the same pattern: 'Only to pain can I show care.'

The final one, posted today, had a contact-ref and just the word 'Gem 1'. Sonly picked them up, shuffled them into a pile, and spread them out in front of her again.

"What do you think?" she asked Michael. He pushed his glasses up to rub his eyes and looked as tired as she felt.

"I think if we don't make contact the Empress' army will," he said, his words slow, lacking their usual incisiveness. "Chen is in the Liternova system and controlled by the Hiactols– they will move robustly against it. It could be nothing. It could be someone who gets their kicks through bondage, for all I know. Or it could be someone luring us in. The reference is consistent, though: care and pain, Kare and you." He touched the last one. "This one, though – there's no doubt. Someone took a big chance posting this."

Sonly pushed the messages together and tried to find the words to refuse them. The ambassador's words came to her, about Kare giving his fealty. He wouldn't have done that, not the Kare she knew. She took a deep breath and said, "I have to know. If there's information on Kare, I have to know."

Michael nodded, reached for the final piece of paper, and typed something into the computer in front of him.

"We soon will," he told her.

***

"Doc!" Sam turned to see one of the guards gesturing to him. "Housekeeping called. Your room's being cleared, so they've allocated you one near the port."

Sam took the key from him. When he reached the room, he threw his bag on the bed before turning the light on and looking around. Pretty spartan, but serviceable. He lifted his bag and saw the message pod underneath. For just a moment, he wanted to deny its existence and not take the next step. He thought of the risks Nina must have taken, and thumbed the message request.

'In the gardens, by the maze.'

He looked at it for a moment longer before he ripped the filche from it and flushed it down the toilet. He picked up his coat, and headed out into the early evening dusk, under the aerial walkway to the port, and through the gardens. It seemed like he had a bubble around him, making the world distant and out of focus.

He reached the edge of the maze and shrank into the shadow of a nearby copse. He turned his head at a small noise and nearly shouted out when he saw a woman opposite. Middle aged, a little heavy around the middle, her dark skin and hair helped her blend into the shadows.

"Your friend sends her love; says she misses Oscar's in the Old Quarter," she said.

Sam relaxed at the agreed statement from Nina. "Are you from the B-" he started, but she held her hand up to stop him.

"Yes. No names, please."

"I'm a doctor," he told her. "I've been treating Ka... I work in Omendegon."

"Your friend gave us a good update on the circumstances, Doctor."

"Can you help him?"

"Doctor, our group has been decimated; there is no way we could assault Abendau, not for the few that are still here. Not even for him."

"I understand." Sam went to leave, but stopped at her voice.

"We can get you out, Doctor. You'd have to come with me, tonight, and you'll be fugitive, but we could get you somewhere safe."

Sam paused for a long moment, not sure if it was her voice or words that were seductive. His hands dampened with sweat, and there was a bitter taste in his mouth.

"I thought I'd say yes if you offered," he said. "But I can't."

"Why not, Doctor? You must know that if what your friend has told us– if you've seen and heard what she says you have– they won't let you live. We could use your expertise."

Her words cut through him, and he wanted to tell her that he would never be able to face Varnon's wife. Not after listening to him beg for her. Not after her brother's words to him, the accusation he'd never be able to fully shake. The spy's patient eyes watched him, until he croaked out, "I can't."

"Can't what, Doctor?"

The soft voice seemed to reach to him in the darkness. If he couldn't tell her the first reason, could he give his wife something back? He swallowed. "He's..." How did he describe it: the stoicism, the determination not to cede? "He..."

"Yes, he is. He knew what Omendegon would mean for him, you know. His father told him long ago, when he was a child."

"Yet he still opposed the Empress? Why?"

"He believed there must be a better way to rule, a fairer way. So do I; that's why he put me here, and worked with me so I stayed hidden," she said.

Sam took a moment, making sure he'd heard her right. "He put you here?"

"Yes."

He cast his mind back to the awful day with the Empress, the day she had broken the block. The Great Master had asked Kare question after question about the spies, and he'd mumbled that he didn't know, they were under Sonly's remit. For hours....

"He didn't give you up," he said. "They tortured him, and he said he didn't know.... I believed him, we all did. The Empress checked his mind. Even the Great Master believed him."

"We know."

Sam shook his head. "You weren't there– you don't know...."

No one knew what happened in Omendegon. It was how the place worked, in secret, never recognised for what it was. Torture could be tolerated, it seemed, if it happened in the shadows. "How did he put you in here?"

"The same way he put the block in himself."

"He could do that- get you past the mind sweeps?"

"There's very little he couldn't do, Doctor. With his powers, she'd never have taken him. She tried often enough. I assume the Empress took sperm from him? That's what she wanted him for: the bloodline."

"Of course she did," he told her. "And she's used it."

"Doctor, I can be reached through this," she said, and handed him a tiny comms unit. "We can't get to you- not in the quarry- but perhaps, when he dies, you'll tell us."

Sam turned it over and over before he put it in his pocket. "If I do, will you tell Nina? She'll know what it means for me."

"Of course."

"I'll keep you informed," he promised, not voicing his fear that he'd be dead first and none of them would ever know.

***

"Would Kare surrender?" Sonly asked. Even to her own ears, her voice was shocked.

Michael had refused to show her Simone's report but he'd told her what it contained. He'd made her sit down and had held her hand while he described what they'd done to Kare. He'd had to stop several times, his hands shaking, but he'd kept going. She'd listened, knowing he wasn't telling her everything, that he considered some things too much for her to know. What more could they have done?

A memory flashed in front of her of Kare, the day he'd been promoted to colonel, when she'd teased him into bed with her. After, as he'd got dressed- running late for his meeting- she'd watched him pull his clothes on. He'd been perfect, tall and strong. Now, according to the doctor, Kare had more scars than he had clear skin. He was like an old man, the report said, just about alive. Tears stung her eyes and she willed herself not to cry again. *Months. They've had him for months, and all this time, they've been torturing him.* Tears welled over her eyelashes and down her cheeks. She didn't try to wipe them away- why shouldn't she cry?

"I think so," Michael said. His skin was drawn and lined, his eyes rheumy. "I'm sorry, Sonly, about Kare."

229

"It's not just Kare," she said. "I miss them all." She wished Lichio was here, to wrap his arms around her. Or Silom. The doctor had said they were in one of the quarries. The idea of Lichio, her laughing little brother, being worked to death sickened her. And Silom. She hoped they, at least, were together and able to support each other. Would they be with each other when they died? At that, fresh tears started. She had to stop crying, somehow.

She went to the computer and read the message she'd composed, moving her hand over the "send" command. She waited a moment before she pressed it with a sharp stab of her finger. It was gone: moving across the star systems; bouncing from ship to planetary booster, into deep space to Belaudii.

"So that's it, then," she said. "I'm going to my bunk, Michael; if there's any response, let me know."

As she walked to the women's barracks, she wondered if Kare would have done things differently. She wished she had. She lifted her chin, determined to do what had to be done; she owed him that, at least.

CHAPTER FORTY

am followed Beck as he led the heavily shackled Kare to the small transport. They passed the port staff, who jeered and spat at Kare, but he kept his head down, docile.

"How long to the quarry?" Sam asked.

Beck turned his head to answer and Sam shivered, not for the first time, at the flat look in his eyes.

"Not far; twenty minutes."

Sam dug a bottle of water out of his bag and took a sip. He handed it to Beck, who took a swig and offered it back. Sam looked at the bottle. He couldn't bring himself to drink after him. "Keep it. I have another one."

They flew out of the port and over the palace gardens, a green oasis in the midst of the stone city spreading into the desert. As the city faded into the distance, they passed over one of the quarries and then soared high over the desert, the Abendauii winds pulling at the transport. They sat in silence, the only noise Kare's breathing, rasping against the constriction of his collar.

"Shut up," growled Beck.

"Yes, Master," whispered Kare.

He put his head back as far as the collar would let him, and his breathing quietened. As Sam drank his water, Kare licked his broken lips before he glanced at Beck and closed his mouth. Sam set his bottle down, not able to swallow any more of it. Whatever else le Payne was right about, he didn't enjoy seeing pain.

The ship swooped down to a smaller quarry beneath. Beck drank the last of his water before he checked the prisoner's chains, smiling as his rough tug forced a hiss of pain. Sam watched him, silently, sure this bastard would be his murderer as well as Varnon's.

They landed, and Sam left the transport. He waited while Beck and Kare got out. They entered a huge cargo lift and as it descended, the air become moist and warmer. A combined smell of diesel and sweat grew. When the lift stopped, he opened the doors and the quarry's intense heat enveloped him. Fine dust made him cough slightly. Almost immediately he heard the unmistakable sound of a lash.

"I'm going to take this dog to his cell, Doc; you're to report to the clinic," said Beck.

Sam nodded and stepped carefully across the quarry, past slaves who continued their work as he passed through a huge entranceway, hewn out of the red rock, on the other side of the cavern. He looked back at the quarry; it was similar to how he'd imagined hell.

***

Lichio tossed a rock into the cart alongside him, lifted his blunted pick, and leaned over to break the next. Months ago, the pick had seemed too heavy to lift, the giant Belaudii's gravity higher than that of Holbec's. They'd beaten that out of him; now he lifted and smashed all day, barely conscious of the weight. Sweat poured down his back and exhaustion ran through him like a wire joining each part of his body. He wanted to sit down and refuse to get back up again, but knew he'd be forced to go on.

He leant forwards, coughed, and pain ripped across his chest and back, worse today than previously. He heard the lift descend but concentrated on his work, careful to turn his head away as he cracked the rock. His arms and legs were toughened to the sharp shards, but he had a fear of them near his face and eyes.

At a soft hiss, he glanced at Silom on the tier above. He was thinner now, but still one of the strongest Banned prisoners.

"The lift." Silom brought his pick down, heavily.

Lichio looked down at the main section of the quarry and saw Beck, and the loss of Kare hit him harder than ever. As the most senior officer left, a le Payne to boot, he did his best but he was no Kare Varnon, and he missed him, every day.

Silom stopped work. He stood upright and stared at Beck, a look of hatred on his face.

"Stop it," Lichio said. "They'll see you."

Silom put his pick down and straightened his back. "Oh, sweet lord," he said, his face paling.

Lichio followed his gaze. He, too, stopped and stared. His mind tried to reject what his eyes were telling him. "That's not him."

"I'd know Kare anywhere, and that's him."

Lichio looked at the prisoner standing beside Beck. Silom was right, there was no one else it could be. He took in Kare's hair– pure white now, not black– and thin frame, so thin he looked barely able to stand. His eyes were cast down, no brilliant green defiance in place any longer, his neck encased by a–

232

Lichio spun to stop Silom, but he was already striding down the quarry path, his eyes fixed on Beck.

"Silom, no!" shouted Lichio, following. He caught up and put his hand out to stop Silom, but the bigger man shrugged him off and advanced on Beck, who waited with a sneer on his face. Two guards grabbed Silom and held him back.

"Kare!" called Silom, but Kare didn't lift his head. Lichio stood in silence, too stunned for thought. Beck walked over, and Lichio moved to stand beside Silom. He was dwarfed by the other men, but defiantly held his ground.

"I'll explain it once," said Beck. "Your friend took a long time to submit. He can't take any more pain; his mind will do what it must to limit it. The best thing you can do, if you really are his friends, is ignore him, let him go."

Lichio looked at Kare's scars, recognising what had caused some of them. He wanted to shake him for not submitting earlier but he guessed even if he did, Kare wouldn't know him. The idea of Kare not knowing him, not knowing Silom, seemed unreal– what did you have to do to someone to get him to that point? His fists clenched in helpless anger.

"You sick bastard," snarled Silom. "How much did you enjoy hurting him? Torturing him until you ruined him?"

Silom threw off his guards and punched Beck, solidly. Beck reeled backwards, but as Silom moved forward, more guards arrived and pulled him back.

Lichio yelled as a whip came down on his shoulders and its initial flare of agony started to grow and blossom. The guards pulled him to a whipping stand, Silom to another. As each lash fell, wrenching his skin apart in hot spears, his screams mingled with Silom's. Through it all, the vision of Kare remained, reminding him there were worse things to face than a lashing.

***

Sam walked into the small room at the medical centre, and put a jug of water on the cabinet beside a bed. He wrinkled his nose at the stench in the room and looked at Beck, who was lying on the bed, groaning.

"Your stomach?" Sam asked.

Beck nodded, and Sam rifled in his medicine bag before he took out a needle, carefully filling it with some clear fluid. He pulled Beck's sleeve back and injected him.

"That will help with the pain. I can't do anything else until I

233

know what's causing it. Did you eat anything?"

Beck shook his head and groaned.

"We'll have to quarantine you," said Sam. "What will I do about Varnon? Send him to the quarry?" Another shake. "Keep him in lockdown?" This time Beck nodded. "Right, I'll arrange it. Where are his meds?"

Beck pointed to a small cabinet beside him. Sam opened it and pulled out a small package.

"I'll arrange a guard," he told Beck, "and give them these. In the meantime, let me give you a drink."

The big guard rolled over and Sam looked at his pale, sweating face. He noticed the bruise on his jaw, and decided when he met Silom Dester he must shake the man's hand. The story had gone round the quarry, the resident guards proud that one of their resident tough-nuts had shown Beck it paid to be careful around the inmates of Clenadii Quarry.

Sam offered Beck a straw and he took a sip.

"Keep drinking– lots," Sam said. "I'll get a nurse down to you and they can clean you up. In the meantime, I'll order some tests."

At the sound of more filth voiding the torturer's body, Sam left, stopping briefly at the toilet before walking to the guardroom.

"Who do I talk to about getting a replacement? Beck: he's sick."

The captain of the guards turned to him. "We don't have guards to replace him. Tell Beck we'll keep a close eye on his prisoner, but he won't have a personal guard."

"He's supposed to have continual supervision. Plus, he has medication he has to take. Unless you want to face a very pissed-off psycher."

The guard laughed. "I don't think Varnon's going to keep us awake at night. He'll be dead in a week down here. But we'll keep an eye on him and you can give him his jabs."

Sam nodded. "Fine." He tossed the small box of medication from hand to hand, and opened the door that led back to the quarry.

CHAPTER FORTY-ONE

he little light pulsed in front of him– tiny, but real and important. He tried to hook it, but it danced out of his grasp. It took some time before he managed to grab it and pull it towards him.

Once pulled, it unravelled and spilt into every corner of his mind. It seemed like it would never stop, that he couldn't accommodate it, but it sank into strangely familiar places in his mind.

With the light came memories: a blonde woman, so close he tried to touch her. She faded away, replaced by a boy, red haired and earnest, who promised to protect him. One by one the visions came, confusing and elating in equal measure: an angelic youth; a harsh older woman; a cold, dark man; and then a girl, a child, with vivid green eyes. Karia, who looked exactly as she had when he'd said goodbye. He'd promised her it would be all right.

"Kare," she said. She rubbed his cheek, and he felt healed, stronger.

"I'm Kare," he replied, astonished. "I'd forgotten."

"You were alone; you shouldn't have been."

"I'm not alone now."

Karia shook her head and she seemed further away, as if she had faded a little.

"I can't stay," she said, "but there are others; you must go to them."

"I can't, I daren't; he'll hurt me."

"If you don't go now, you never will. They'll take you back, soon."

He tried to reach her, to join her where she was. "Take me with you," he pleaded, "don't leave me alone."

"Please Kare, go on. Sonly will be there for you; your friends are waiting. Please, be brave; do it for me."

"I'm so glad it wasn't you," he said, and when there was no response he realised she had gone. He remembered he couldn't say no to her, that he'd never been able to say no to her. He struggled to swim out of his dream, move up to the real world. He stopped several times, overwhelmed with effort, but finally managed to open his eyes.

***

Kare tried to turn his head, but it throbbed when he did. He looked at the ceiling instead, and tried to work out where he was. There was a knocking noise, metal on stone, but it wasn't familiar. Someone moved inside his cell, and he stiffened in fear. *Beck.* He forced himself to turn his head– *it's only pain*– and saw it wasn't Beck, but the doctor.

Kare moaned: whatever Beck inflicted, the doctor fixed, and the fixing often hurt at least as much. He kept looking at the doctor, not able to face moving again, and reached out with his psyche. *It worked.* It should have been amazing, like a miracle, but he could feel nothing: he was dead inside, hollowed out, a shell who'd forgotten what it was to feel. Tears sprang up as a sense of what he'd lost, how far he'd been taken, grew, a deep dragging loss that filled him, held him down, was too heavy to remove.

He tried to sense the doctor's feelings, but his head filled with the sensation of all the people around him and he couldn't concentrate or think. He stopped trying to do anything, and let his mind take over and sort through the information. Only after it had finished was he able to focus on the doctor.

Kare opened his mouth to ask why, but it was dry and his lips were cracked. The doctor lifted a bottle of water and poured some into Kare's mouth. Mostly, it went down his face and neck, but what little he did swallow soothed him. Kare licked his lips and winced at the sharp pain as they split.

"You brought it back," he croaked.

Sam shook his head. "I stopped the medicine. You did the rest."

"Why?" This was a game, a new way to hurt him. They'd let him believe it was back, that he had a chance, and then they'd take it again. The thought of being returned made his bladder loosen. *I can't, I daren't.* The need went away.

"Self-preservation," said the doctor.

Kare tried to respond, but it hurt too much. He imagined his lips healed: smooth, not cracked and sore, and his mind started to work at it. His whole mouth was sore, ulcers all through it, and he healed those, too. It was a drop in the ocean of pain that ran through him.

He swallowed and winced at the pain in his throat. Any minute now, Beck was going to walk in the door and laugh at him. Kare wondered if it would be possible to stop his own heart, and decided if Beck walked in, he'd try.

"I'm sorry. I shouldn't have stood back for so long," said the doctor.

This time, Kare felt the truth of the doctor's words. Again, he wanted to ask about Beck but didn't dare; it was as if saying his name might bring him here.

236

"I've missed it," Kare said, the words inadequate. Already his mouth was better, the forming of words uncomfortable instead of agonising.

"They couldn't have done what they did if you'd had your powers, could they?"

Kare tried to nod his head. He couldn't. "What's on my neck?"

"Your collar," said the doctor. "Leave it, it can't be removed."

Kare cast his mind back, and remembered Beck putting it on him and telling him he was his dog now. Beck had tightened it until he had choked, and then tightened it some more. He wondered why it seemed tighter in his memory than it did now, and realised they'd practically starved him. Again, he noticed how badly he needed a piss but when he tried, nothing happened. He looked at the ceiling, his eyes welling at the realisation he needed Beck to tell him to go.

"Bastards," he said, and knew it wasn't even close to what he meant, that there were no words to say what had been done to him. He snapped the collar off his neck, flexing his mind in the old way, and took a first single, deep breath; it was like honey.

"How did you do that?" asked the doctor, his eyes round.

"I did it with the part of my mind that opens things." He'd thought he would never say those words again.

"How much is back?"

"All of it," Kare said. "Every bit of it. I just have to remember how to control it; I'd forgotten what a monster it is."

"What will you do?"

Kare tried to sit up, but couldn't. He wondered how the hell he'd been able to walk for Beck, and then remembered: his master had ordered him, so he had.

"My best," he said.

"You need to put the collar back on. They'll know if it's off."

"Right," Kare said. He snapped it in place, looser so he could breathe easily. *Ask; you need to know.* "Where's Beck?"

"He's got a stomach bug," said the doctor, grinning.

"Good," said Kare, but his mind was racing. How long would a stomach upset hold Beck back? Panic made his throat constrict and it was a moment before he could speak again. "I assume you have something in mind?"

The doctor came closer. His voice was low, a whisper. "The Empress is due to leave Abendau tonight. She's on the way to meet your wife to arrange the formal surrender of the Banned."

Kare tried to sit up again, and this time realised why he

couldn't; his wrists were shackled to the wall. *Of course; I'm so dangerous, I have to be shackled all the time.* He almost released his wrists and then decided there was no point; he'd only have to put them back on again.

"You're lying," he said, sure this *was* a game. "She would die first, let everyone die, before she did that."

"She says if you can get to Abendau city, the spies will try to get you out."

The doctor's eyes met his, and Kare watched him, sure it was a trap. The doctor held his eyes, not looking away. *I have to know.* He reached out, touching the edge of the doctor's mind as the man tensed, ready to fight. He was no stranger to a psyche probe, evidently.

"Let me," said Kare.

The doctor took a deep breath, his chest rising. He looked away and then back, nodding. "Do it."

Kare sank into his mind, feeling his way through, touching sensations of guilt and fear. He felt the doctor's hatred of the invasion, but the memory of what had been done to him– what this man had watched being done– came back to him, and he sank further in, drilling into his mind, not caring if it hurt.

"Stop," whispered the doctor, his voice low and harsh, but still Kare drilled, searching for any sign that this was a trick, that he was going to be returned. There was nothing. He pulled out, slowly, still searching, and the sound of the other man's breathing started to dominate the cell.

Kare met the doctor's eyes, knowing his shame, feeling his need for absolution. He took a deep breath. "Thank you."

The doctor inclined his head. "Don't. You must have seen enough to know I shouldn't be thanked."

"I saw enough." Kare paused, glancing at the barred gate. How long did they have? He coughed a little and said, "My wife must think I'm a miracle worker. Did you mention my condition– the guards?"

"She seemed confident if you got your psyche back, you'd come up with something."

She would. "How many of my men are here?"

"I don't know," admitted the doctor. "Silom and Lichio are; you saw them when you got here."

"That was Silom and Lichio?" He stopped, thinking back. Of course it was, but they'd been so thin. "Do you know the symbol for the Banned?"

The doctor shook his head, and Kare took his index fingers and thumbs. He managed to stretch them enough to make two entwined circles. He pulled them so they locked, like a chain.

238

"Let them know you're on side. And then go check on Beck: keep him sealed down. I need to decide how to do things."

Sam left, and Kare closed his eyes, glad to be alone. He needed the toilet, so much so his stomach was aching. He tried to let go, but nothing happened. How painful would it be if his bladder burst? It would kill him, he guessed. He watched the door, ready for Beck to walk in, knowing he'd do nothing if he did– the very thought of turning on his master chilled him.

He shifted and pain shot from his bladder, making him gasp. He closed his eyes and *willed* himself to let go, but still nothing happened. He looked at the ceiling, breathed deeply and tried not to think. A first trickle came, and he bit down against the sharp agony and tasted blood. He clenched his fists until it flooded out and pooled under him. He panted, waiting for it to be over. Sharp tears flooded into his eyes: at least he was enough of a man to do that. But could he do any more?

He took the part of his mind that healed things, thinking at least he could try. It had to be better than waiting for Beck to come and finish him.

***

Lichio stood at the bars of his cell. His lash wounds were open and weeping, and the pain had wakened him. He'd have to try to sleep again soon, he knew. It took strength to get through a day in the quarry. He looked down the corridor to the quiet cell at the end, pretty sure that was where Kare had been taken. *What did they do to him?* Even thinking about it made Lichio sick.

The gate to Kare's cell opened and a figure came out. As he approached, Lichio recognised him as the doctor from Omendegon, one of a long list of people he would gladly murder. Lichio glared at the doctor, willing him to look and know Lichio le Payne hated him. The doctor nodded, as if to himself, linked his fingers together and walked on. Lichio cocked his head; he'd thought, the last time they'd met, that the doctor had been scared, and had hoped he might be frightened enough to do something. Hoped, but never believed.

"Silom," Lichio said.

Silom got up from the back of the cell, the speed of his response telling Lichio he wasn't the only one who couldn't sleep.

"The doc from Omendegon?" Lichio made the same symbol, carefully.

239

"You're joking."

"Would I?"

"Interesting," said Silom. "Earlier, I overheard a couple of the guards."

"Go on." Lichio kept his face casual and voice very, very low.

"Apparently Beck's got the worst case of the shits you've ever seen- completely incapacitated, keeps getting worse. They're talking about shipping him back to Abendau in case it's infectious."

"Couldn't have happened to a more deserving bloke."

Silom smiled grimly and glanced at Kare's cell. "Do you think?"

"No hope. You don't get over whatever happened there."

"I don't know, he always surprised us."

Lichio decided to humour the big man. "Absolutely; you never know."

They walked back to their blankets. The other slaves made way for them to pass, the odd glare from Silom reminding them who was in charge in this particular cell. It was, Lichio thought, very useful to be Silom's friend. He lay down and tried to sleep, but it wouldn't come, not with him jumping at every sound, prepared to take whatever chance presented itself.

**

"Is everything ready?" asked Sonly. She pulled at the lapel of her flight jacket, and understood why Kare had always complained about the Banned uniforms. She wished he was here, moaning about it now.

"They're ready," said Michael. "Are you sure you're up to this?"

"I'm up to it. Kare promised he'd try to make it back, but I think that goes both ways."

"If he doesn't manage to get out?"

His words cut through Sonly. The doctor was adamant that Kare was so badly hurt, his mind lost, that even with his psyche he could do nothing. And, Sonly admitted to herself, there was no way he could get them as far as the city. The best she could hope was that he was strong enough to fight back and get himself killed- quickly and free. *You never know*, said one stubborn part of her. The rest of her, the pragmatic Sonly, stamped down on her hope.

"Then I'll turn tail and come back before I meet the Empress. It won't do the Banned any good if I end up taking Kare's place in Omendegon," she said, trying to sound brave. Michael nodded but didn't voice the fact this was the last chance for the Banned- after, they were out of options.

CHAPTER FORTY-TWO

Kare lay in his cell, thinking, planning. He had little option– the manacles on his wrists gave him barely any room to move. He'd spent the night going over the plans he and Rjala had made for attacking Abendau. If he got to the port, they could reach the city and the spy network.

His breath hitched at the thought of returning to Abendau. His mother's presence ran through the city, binding it to her. A small moan of fear escaped. He remembered how she'd been in his mind, searching every corner, hurting him to his very core. Images of being Beck's dog– of the total dominance he'd been under– haunted him.

Stop. He had to focus: he was the one who'd studied Abendau; no one else could get them to safety. He stared at the ceiling, his thoughts whirling round and round. When the other slaves moved out to their work, he was still looking at the ceiling and thinking.

It was after the rest of slaves had come back that he heard footsteps stop outside his cell. He clenched and unclenched his hands, noticing his missing finger as he did; they'd done what he'd feared and taken him a piece at a time. The sound of the gate left him drenched in clammy sweat. He took a deep breath and tried to calm himself; it worked as well as it ever had.

Footsteps, loud on the hard cell floor. They stopped in front of him, and he opened his eyes. The doctor's feet, he recognised those, had stared at them often enough. Beside him, a second pair of booted feet. A pinprick of injection, like the insect sting he'd thought the first one was. *Oh, gods, don't take me back.*

"You coming, Doc?" asked the guard. His voice had a slight dialect Kare wasn't familiar with. His breathing steadied: it wasn't Beck.

"I'm going to check him over," Sam said. "Plus, I need to give him some water."

"Food?" asked the guard. Kare's mouth moistened and his stomach gripped in pain: now that he'd healed everywhere else, the hunger was vivid and agonising.

Sam laughed. "He's not hungry enough yet."

Kare bit his lip so the sob of need wouldn't escape. The guard walked out and locked the cell. "I'm at the end of the corridor. Shout when you're done with this dog."

His footsteps faded, and Kare lifted his head. The room swam around him.

"You look better," said the doctor. He crouched down and reached out, pushing Kare's hair back. His eyes looked like they had yesterday: direct and honest.

"I've healed what I can." Kare's voice was a whisper. He unlocked his shackles and rubbed his wrists together. He sat up, carefully, and glanced at the doctor, thinking of how he must look: starving; his skin crawling with lice, covered in bites; stinking of old piss. He ducked his head– the doctor knew what he'd done to please Beck and survive. He didn't know what to say, but when he looked down and saw the stain across the front of his ragged trousers, it seemed as good a place as any to start. "I stink. I'm sorry."

The doctor shrugged. "You should be with Beck just now; he's worse." He reached into his bag and handed Kare an energy bar. "I lied; you need to eat. That'll help for now."

Kare tried to pull the packet open, but his hands were shaking too much. The doctor took it from him and ripped it, handing it back. Kare took the proffered bar, his stomach contracting, making him gasp. He ripped a piece off: it was tasteless and bland, designed to give energy, not pleasure, but he chewed it as best he could, working around the gaps where he'd once had teeth. Tears pricked him as he did, but he blinked them away. He had to keep a grip on things. The doctor handed him a small bottle, and he drank it, a shot of energy flooding through him.

Kare looked at him. "You know what we're going to do tonight?"

The doctor looked shaky. "You'll kill the guards."

"Every one," confirmed Kare. "One by one, and I won't regret any of them."

"That makes you as bad as them." The doctor glanced away, his eyes focused on the gate. "I didn't do this for more to die."

"I'm a soldier. So are my men. Even our angelic Lichio can be a bad bastard. The worst, actually. How did you think I'd get us out of here? Ask?" Something clicked back into place in his mind. He *was* a soldier– or had been one– and he had to reach into the past and let that Kare, the Kare who'd been about to attack Abendau, who been prepared to face his mother, come to the fore.

The doctor swallowed. "No, I don't suppose I expected you to ask. Is there *any* other way?"

Kare shook his head. "I don't take pleasure from killing, doctor. I never have. If there was any other way for me to get us out of here- alive- I'd take it." He reached out his hand, but the doctor didn't take it. "I promise it will be quick, that none of them will suffer needlessly. That's all I can do."

The doctor nodded, but he still looked uncomfortable. "What do you need me to do?" He looked faintly embarrassed. "I can't kill someone."

"You don't have to. Stay close, but out of the way. Do Silom and Lichio know?"

"Lichio saw me do the sign."

"Well, hopefully they haven't removed his brains." Kare stood, and waited until the room had stopped spinning. He moved to the gate of the cell. "I'm going to get them and then we'll capture the quarry."

"Can you do it with only three?"

"I could probably do it on my own, but why take the chance? I want Silom because he's an excellent soldier, and I work well with Lichio."

"And then we get out of here?"

"Hell, no," Kare said, his decision made. If he ran, he'd always be running, knowing what she could do. He had to finish this, while she was away, and give himself a chance of peace. He straightened, and the collar rubbed his neck. Impatiently, he clicked it off, his skin pulling as he did. "Then, I do what my father wanted me to do- what he gave his life for me to do- I move on Abendau, and bring my mother's empire down."

"I thought we were getting out."

Kare opened the gate. "Next time you release the genie, doctor, you might want to check what it'll do, first. We're getting ahead of ourselves. Tonight, my job is to secure the quarry; then we'll decide what happens next."

He moved out of the cell, his eyes alert and powers cast out. The only guards he could sense were at the end of the corridor, at either side of the entranceway; they evidently didn't consider the slaves, once locked down, a big threat. Gently, Kare took their minds and set their focus on the corridor of cells opposite this one. He moved to the cell the doctor had indicated.

As he got there, two prisoners got up and moved forward. He snicked the gate and let it open enough for them to slip out, then pointed to his own cell. He could feel, now, some of the other slaves rousing, and he cast out. Their minds settled and moved down to sleep. *It's still working.*

He followed Silom and Lichio back to his cell where they stared at him as if he was a ghost. Both looked exhausted, their faces covered with a fine dust. Older, too.

243

"I'm real," Kare said. "Battered, but real." Let them not know how he really was, how close he was to giving up, to lying on his bed and letting Beck have his way with him.

"You're more than battered." Silom looked Kare up and down, his concern clear, and to see Silom, even this changed Silom, and know he was there– Kare felt safer already.

He hesitated, not sure what to say; how to start to tell them what had happened, to face it himself. He swallowed and tried to smile. Someday he'd go there. But not tonight. "I'm alive; that'll do for now. What about you two?"

Another hesitation and then Lichio answered. "Alive is as accurate as anything. What are you planning? I assume this isn't a quick catch up?"

"We need to take the quarry," Kare said.

"Are you in any shape to do that?" challenged Lichio.

Kare lifted his chin. Tonight wasn't the time for an analysis of what had happened– what they'd witnessed in the cells. Not ever, if he was honest.

"Sir," he said. His voice sounded more commanding, and he remembered he used to do this all time: give orders, lead.

"What?" Lichio said.

"You forgot the sir. Unless anyone demoted me in my absence, that is. Captain." He clenched his fists. "If we don't take the quarry, we don't get to Abendau. It's that simple." He held Lichio's eyes, daring him to oppose him.

"How do you plan to do that, sir?" Lichio asked, and coughed slightly.

"Most of the guards are asleep. Once we secure this section and clear the dorms, we can use the prison transports to get to Abendau city."

"Then home?" asked Lichio, and Kare knew his number two had read him as well as he'd always been able to.

"We'll see." He ignored Lichio's pained expression and soft curse.

"Any idea how many guards, sir?" Silom asked. He had barely taken his eyes off Kare, and now he moved closer to him. Kare swayed, not for the first time, and Silom's arm shot out, taking his elbow.

"I'm okay," said Kare, taking his arm away. "Two outside the entrance to the cell blocks. Two more at the other side."

He glanced at the doctor, and raised an eyebrow in question.

"There's about fifty in total, most of them in the dorms. There's a guard room between here and the dorms, and they have a comms link from there to the palace."

"Thank you," Kare said. "We'll take out the first ones, then see what faces us in the guard room."

"How will you know?" asked Sam.

Silom and Lichio exchanged a glance and a smirk. Kare glared at them both.

"I haven't time to explain how I do things, so take it on trust—if I say I can, I can," Kare said.

"The two at the other side are a problem, sir," Lichio said. "No way to sneak up on them."

Kare thought for a moment, making sure he'd placed the guards correctly.

"You take the one on the left of the doorway," he told Silom. "Lichio, the one on the right. I'll deal with the other two. Once they're out of the way, we can secure the main cell block."

They moved quietly down the corridor, Kare in the lead, scanning as he went. *Keep busy; don't think. One step at a time.* As he reached the end, Lichio and Silom moved forward while he sent his psyche out to the guards opposite. It took a moment to remember how he needed it to work, and then he twisted the bones in their neck until they snapped. It took all his strength to focus on them both, and his knees started to buckle. He leaned against the wall, concentrating until he was sure they were dead. He let them fall and heard a guttural noise from the guard on the right. Stepping forward, he broke the neck of the man Lichio had tried to throttle. Silom's, he noted, had been a clean kill.

"Neater next time," Kare told Lichio, who nodded. He looked exhausted, his blond hair lank against his face. Silom lifted a weapon and moved to watch for any relief guards. Kare nodded to him, glad of his solid reliability.

"How many Banned men are here?" asked Kare.

"Twenty three, plus us," Lichio said, pulling himself a little straighter.

"I hoped there'd be more," Kare admitted. "Where are the others?"

"There are some in the less secure slave pits, but most of them...." Lichio paused. "The quarry's harsh, sir." He cleared his throat. "Deadly. Few survived the first weeks. Those that did aren't in good shape."

Everywhere's harsh. "Then we can get a little vengeance for them, too, Captain." *And my family; Rjala; my soldiers on the base.* "Take one of the guards' security passes and get the others. Only the Banned soldiers."

Ten minutes later, Kare had a force of twenty-six soldiers and one fairly timid medic. His eyes scanned over them: no weapons; exhausted soldiers; a leader who was just about standing up. This was what was left of his army?

245

He turned to Lichio. "Split the group into pairs: experienced with less experienced. Keep the doc with you, and leave me on my own. I want this place secured, Captain, quietly and quickly."

He moved away from the prison cells and corridors. Ahead, he could see a light from under a heavy door, and when he reached in could sense at least ten guards.

He went back to the group. "I'm going to secure the exit door and take out the one operating the comms. Who has weapons?" Four of the soldiers, including Silom, stepped forward. "When I open the door, standard Banned room clearance drill; they should have nowhere to go."

"Yes, sir," came the responses, and it made Kare feel more like he remembered how to do this sort of thing. He waited until they were in place, his hands slippery but the nerves felt good, somehow; like he was doing something. He put his hands on the door, taking a deep breath, and pushed hard on it.

"Hey!" One of the guards was already on his feet, reaching for his blaster. "It's a break!" he yelled. "Send the code!"

Hell, if the operator got word out, this would be the shortest prison break in history. Kare stepped back, ignoring the guards; let Silom deal with them. He zoned out the yells, the sounds of returning fire, and focused on the guard on the comms unit. Already he was tapping in the number. Kare slammed his fingers, heard the snapping of bones. The tapping stopped.

"Take him out!" yelled Silom.

Kare focused on the comms operator. Nothing fancy, just like the guards at the cells. He twisted, met the man's eyes briefly as they rolled back, and the bones in his neck snapped. The eyes were still; the body sat for a moment, and then fell to the floor.

"Secured!" The Banned soldier to Kare's right yelled back at the waiting team. "We have the guard room."

Silom stepped forward, dispassionately shot one, and checked the next. Behind Lichio, the doctor winced but didn't look away. He was holding up, at least.

"Good job, well done," Kare said. "Make sure the weapons are distributed amongst the squad." He turned to Sam. "How many in each dorm?"

"Four at the most."

"How many dorms?"

"Ten. I checked, this afternoon."

Kare nodded his thanks and turned to his army. "Each pair take a dorm. No petty revenge; I just want them dead. Report to me

246

when you're sure each room is clear. Captain, you allocate the dorms." Lichio nodded, but looked so tired Kare wondered if he *could* be put in charge. He glanced at Silom, who was leaning against the wall but seemed much more alert. "Sergeant?" Silom nodded. "You're in charge of the attack- liaise with the captain on the ground. I'll do one last recce, check we have everyone."

Half an hour later, with no alarm raised to the outside, the quarry was secured and all the guards were dead.

"Where's Beck being held?" Kare asked Sam. He needed to end this, now- the walls had been shifting around him for the last half hour at least, and twice he had threatened to black out. Sam had been beside him the last time and had given him another of his drinks. Kare didn't know what it was, but he was feeling sharper since.

"In the medical wing. He's a bit better today; I ran out of supplies."

"Take me to him." Bile rose in him, sickening him. To face Beck again, to see his face, hear his voice.

"I'd like to come too, sir," Silom said.

Should he refuse? But the thought of facing Beck on his own was too much. "All right; but be careful. He's dangerous." His throat closed, made it hard to breathe. "Merciless."

"I know." Silom met Kare's eyes, his chin raised. He'd seen everything, no doubt- the scars, the broken bones. His mouth tightened, his chest puffed out. "I've seen what I need to. Sir."

They followed Sam through the complex, into a short corridor. He stopped outside one of the doors, and pointed to it. Kare walked up to the door. *Can I stand and face him like the man I was?* He took a deep breath, steadying himself. "Silom," he said, and waited until his cousin was beside him. He had to do this himself; he had to know he could. "He's mine." He opened the door and stepped inside.

"Hi, Beck," he said. "Miss me?"

Beck got to his feet, his hand over his stomach. Kare moved forward, the hatred surging though him giving him strength. He was more than ready to kill this bastard.

"You can't hurt me," Beck said. "I forbid it."

Kare stopped and held a hand out in front of him, focusing on the slender bones in Beck's neck. One snap, and it would be over. A wave of dizziness passed over him, and he couldn't find anything to pull on. He'd never been so drained before, that was all. Once more he flexed his mind, the action familiar. He'd done this so many times, it was like eating and breathing. Again, nothing happened. Kare stepped back: he couldn't do it. After everything Beck had done to him, he still couldn't do it. Beck started to laugh, reminding Kare he knew him better than anyone.

"Taken a piss yet, Dog?" asked Beck.

Yes, he had. It didn't change anything. Beck cuffed Kare lightly on the ear. Kare didn't try to stop him; he wouldn't know how to. He opened his mouth to call for Silom, but couldn't do that, either. Instead, he stood, paralysed, as the guard reached his hand out.

"Give me your weapon, and I'll kill you quickly. If you don't, I'll take you back." He leaned close, his breath sour. "I'll take you, and I'll finish you. You'll beg to die."

He had, many times. Kare closed his eyes, trying to force the images of his cell away, but it made no difference. He lifted his rifle, hating himself for his weakness.

"Open your eyes, Dog, or I'll have them stitched open. No hiding place, you know that."

Kare's eyes snapped open. Beck took the other end of his rifle and Kare started to release his hand. He met Beck's dark eyes, wanting to resist, wanting to find a way to repay the bastard. But another part of him, deep, deep inside felt only relief that it might finally be over and he wouldn't be hurt anymore. He remembered his father, how he'd retreated from reality, and wished he, too, could close the door and not have to deal with anything. He opened his hand...

Someone pushed him to the side. "What the *fuck* are you doing?" Silom, eyes staring, face puce. Kare tightened the grip on his rifle and wrenched it from Beck's hand.

"I can't do it. He's my master."

Silom's eyes hardened, and he brought his own rifle up. Beck backed away, his hands out.

"I can," Silom said.

Beck pointed at Kare, making his stomach turn to water. "Stop him, Dog."

"Give the order, *Kare*, and he's dead," said Silom. Please, his eyes said, let me. "Give the order, and you'll have killed him yourself."

Kare closed his eyes, telling himself not to look at Beck. He gasped in a breath of air.

"Silom," he said, the word trailed through gritted teeth. "Kill the bastard."

He turned and walked out, forcing himself to put one foot in front of the other and not look back. In the corridor Sam was waiting and he stood beside him. He wiped his mouth, feeling sick.

"You're lucky he's in charge," he heard Silom say,

conversationally. "If it'd been up to me, I'd have hung you up and ripped your guts out. Slowly. I've been looking forward to it since we met." There was a gunshot, and a scream. "Shit, my aim's gone to hell," said Silom. "I'll aim higher, this time."

"*Kill* him," whispered Kare. "Do it."

The doctor looked sick. There was another shot and scream. Kare closed his eyes, needing this to be done.

"Kill him!" he shouted. Sam put a hand on his shoulder, and it calmed him a little. "Now, Silom!"

There was another shot, and then silence. He leaned against the wall. He'd won; Beck was dead.

Silom came out of the room. "I wanted him to beg." He ran a hand through his hair. "I wanted him to know what it was like, to be scared enough to beg." He breathed out, a whoosh of air. "I wanted him to *know*."

"I just wanted him dead." Kare's voice came out as a croak.

Silom clapped a hand on his shoulder. "Well, he is. You did it. You gave the order. He's not your master anymore."

"It's good," said Sam, still a little pale. "Someone like that- he'd have kept on hurting."

Silom walked away, Sam beside him, but Kare paused. Beck wasn't his master any more, Silom had said. He looked back at the swinging door. *Wasn't he?*

* * *

"What now, sir?" asked Lichio. They sat at the main desk of the guards' recreation room with Silom and the doctor. Lichio coughed, and Kare noticed the doctor frown a little.

"We wait," Kare said. "If I push the squad tonight, they've had no sleep, bugger all food and we're rushing." Besides which, he needed to recharge. They all did. "Silom, sort the slaves out. Keep them in the main quarry, and allow them open access to the cells but not to here."

"Should we put guards on?"

"Any troublemakers?"

"A few, a couple of grievances."

"Keep the ones you're worried about in the cells for now," Kare said. "We don't have enough people to guard them." He saw Lichio yawn. "Then get some sleep. Once we leave here, we won't get another chance. Four hours, then I want you both back in here." As they went to leave he called Lichio back. "Take your shirt off and sit down."

"What?" Lichio said.

"Now, Captain."

Lichio did as he'd been ordered.

"This will hurt," warned Kare, as he put his hands on Lichio's chest.

He could feel the damage in Lichio's lungs and the fine dust that clogged them. *Can I do it?* Kare tried not to think about what he was doing, but let his mind do what it was used to. A few moments later there was a surprised yell from Lichio. "Shit, Kare, that hurts!"

Kare kept going for a few more minutes, until he was satisfied. "Better?" he asked.

Lichio took a deep breath and smiled. "Better, sir."

"Good. I don't do it very often, so don't advertise it; I'm not fixing everyone's cuts and bruises. Now go, get some rest."

So, he could heal Lichio, he could kill guards- why the hell wouldn't it work with Beck? Because he didn't believe he could kill him? His dad had always said there was no room for doubt if you were a psycher. It was understandable his confidence had failed with Beck: it was a one-off. He pushed it from his thoughts, but not before he had a single, shocking new thought. *What happens when I meet the Empress?*

A noise in the room made him look up, and he saw Sam was still there.

"How are you doing?" asked the doctor, his voice kind.

He drew in a breath, his shoulders shuddering. "Okay." He supposed.

"You know, everything that happened in Omendegon...?" Sam said. Kare stiffened, his hands clenching into fists, pain shooting through his fingers. "I'm finding this hard," continued Sam. "I'm finding it hard to face you- I let it happen."

His voice caught a little, making Kare look up at him. "That's two of us. You saw the things I did...."

Sam shook his head. "I saw what you were forced to do. Maybe we can try to- look, it was an impossible place..."

"An impossible place," said Kare, echoing the weak words. "Try again. Hell? A sadist's playground?" He looked down at his hands, misshapen from the breaks. If so, he'd been his toy.

"Yes." Sam looked down at the table. "I should have done more." His hand clenched. "I should have done something." He raised his head- his eyes were screwed half-closed, his mouth drawn into a harsh line.

Kare paused, wanting to say he was right, that he should have done something. The doctor would haunt his dreams for years: a shadowy figure who'd facilitated.

Who'd risked everything to help him. "You don't need to say

anything else about it."

"When are you going to rest?" asked the doctor. "You must be exhausted."

The thought of stopping, of lying down for any time, sent a cold spike through Kare. If he stopped, would he ever manage to start again? He shook his head. "I'm fine. My psyche will keep me going."

"You'd be better if you rest. I'll wake you in a while."

The doctor was right, he was dead on his feet. Still, he hesitated, checked round the room and, once satisfied only Sam remained, walked to the sofa and stretched out, a guard's blaster held against his chest. He might have showered and changed earlier, and it was good to be clean and unshackled, but he wanted something solid in his hands. Clutching it, he fell asleep in moments.

***

Sam wasn't surprised when Kare woke up; he'd listened to him pleading with someone for the last ten minutes and guessed the nightmare had finally come to a climax.

"Tea?" asked Sam. He handed Kare a cup and another of the energy bars, assessing him. He'd have to move to something more substantial soon, but Beck's standard fare of thin gruel every couple of days, and scraps- fed as a master feeds his pet- needed to be built on carefully.

Kare took a drink. "The nightmares?" he began.

"Be astonishing if you didn't have them." And much, much worse. Kare nodded and opened his mouth to say something else, and Sam held his hand up. The man was barely holding himself together. "No one needs to know. I'm a doctor; we're very discreet."

"Thank you. I don't want Silom and Lichio clucking over me." He glanced at the doctor over his cup. "What's your first name?"

"Sam."

"Did you have a family before you came to work for her, Sam?" asked Kare, his eyes softer than during the previous night.

"I had a family: a mum and some sisters."

"You know, you don't have to stay with us; you've more than repaid your debt. Not that I think you had anything to repay. You didn't do it to me, you didn't order it done, you just got caught up in some sadistic bastard's dream. He knew you hated it, and Beck knew how to hit everyone where it hurt most."

"Thank you," Sam said. He wasn't entirely sure how much of that was true, but he accepted the lifeline offered. He took another sip, watching the other man. He seemed ageless, like a magical creature. His men accepted

251

his sudden resurgence as the ancients accepted the phoenix, the miracle of rain after a drought. It seemed they viewed it as the resurrection they had never doubted would come. Kare looked up at him over his cup, and Sam saw his hands were shaking, his eyes flitting, not settling anywhere. A resurrection that was costing this man more than anyone knew.

"How old are you?" Sam asked.

"How long have I been here?"

"Six months. Give or take a few weeks."

Kare blinked. "That's all?" He paused, seeming to work something out. "I must still be twenty-five, then."

Twenty-five? He looked sixty. Sam swallowed– to be facing this at twenty-five, to have those sort of nightmares– and tried to smile. "You seem so much older."

"You saw what they did to me," he said, his voice breaking a little. "I can't tell you how old I feel."

"I don't know how you're coping."

Kare smiled, but there was no real warmth in it. "Physically, I've taken care of things. But I don't know who I am or what I'm doing here. Am I Ealyn because I'm sure he's been here, in this moment, living it as me? Or am I Kare, and if so am I the same, or an entirely new Kare? Or is a bit of me Karia, who made me change my future and gave me the skills I use today? I don't know, when this is over, how to find my way back. Or even if there is a way back. If there is, it feels very distant."

Sam waited for him to continue but he didn't. "Sonly?" Sam finally asked.

Kare nodded, and looked down at his cup. "Amongst other things, but yes, Sonly, and what they did to me– I don't know how to get past it, and back to her." The door opened and Kare shook himself. It was like a different man had taken his place, this one harder, more focused. "For now, though, I have a rebellion to lead. The offer stands, Sam– if you want to go, you can. You've done your part; you owe me nothing more."

Sam stood and as he stretched he felt the tiredness in his back and shoulders and heard the clicks and bangs of stress. He wondered how it would feel to go back to his home, to his family, maybe to Nina. Then he looked at Kare again and realised he had never met anyone who moved him, affected him, the way he did.

"Colonel, I'm yours to command, if you'll have me."

"I'd be proud to." Kare turned to Silom and Lichio, as they reached him. "Sam's just become the Banned's newest recruit and the first member of this little force's medical corps. Lieutenant. Effective immediately."

CHAPTER FORTY-THREE

ichio leaned back in his seat. "I don't suppose there's any chance you'll take the transports and get us off Belaudii and back to the Banned?" "You're home and dry; all you have to do is go, sir."

"Where's your sense of adventure?" Silom's tone was joking, but his eyes never strayed far from Kare. "People join the army to have adventures, not ass around with computer systems."

"I'm going to try for the palace," Kare told them. "I don't have enough to take the city, but we have a chance at the palace. Sam tells me Sonly's on the way with aerial support and ground troops."

"Will she back you? I thought she's coming to get us off Belaudii, not an assault," Lichio said.

Kare looked at him steadily. "Rjala's dead, your hateful shit of a brother's dead; that means I'm head of the military. She'll come, and she'll back me."

"You're still planning to take the port with a handful of soldiers and some spies."

"And me," Kare said. "I do turn the scales a little."

"You're great for reconnaissance," Lichio told him, "but you're not an army, Kare."

He didn't have time for this. What little strength he had wasn't going to last. He needed Lichio and Silom on board, now.

"Don't push me, Captain. This is my decision," he said, his voice hard. "I value your input but I expect your full support. And it's sir." He stared at Lichio and knew he wasn't going to back down, not this time.

"Colonel," Lichio said, his voice less challenging, "are you really telling me you're in any state to take command of an attack force? To lead them? I know what they did to you, sir." He drummed the table. "You've been tortured for months." He looked at Silom, perhaps seeking support. "We can talk around it, we can try to pretend it's something else, or we can face the truth." He spread his hands, palm up. "Sir, if I didn't care, I wouldn't speak up. Please, get away. Give yourself time and space. Don't feel you have to keep going, pretend nothing happened."

It would be so easy. Walk away and never look back. But it wouldn't stop the nightmares, not as long as his mother was alive, seeking revenge. He drew in a deep breath, and focused on Silom. "And you, Sergeant? Do you doubt me, too?"

Silom hesitated and Kare waited, his breath held: this was Silom's chance to tell Lichio what had happened with Beck. Once that was known, what little belief Lichio still had in him would be gone.

"I think you've been hurt enough. We all have. I'm with the captain; we should go."

"And if I decide not to?"

There was the faintest of pauses. "Then I'll stand with you. You know that."

Kare moved his gaze to Lichio, who waited a moment longer before throwing his hands up. "You know I will. If you go for it, I'll be with you. But ask yourself, and be honest; can you? Can you hold together long enough? Because, sir, you're not fooling me and you're not fooling Silom."

"I don't need to fool you, but I need the soldiers to believe in me. If you support me, they will. General Rjala and I planned an attack on the port before the raid. I know its layout, I know its weaknesses and I can assure you both, if we get inside, this attack is viable. Otherwise, I wouldn't consider it. With Sonly's force, I'll have more than Rjala and I planned. Plus, the Empress will be off-planet; that's a big advantage."

"So, how?" asked Silom.

"There are four docking bays and two access points: one at the back, one in the control room. The control room links directly to the palace. The back access door is hard to reach quickly; we have about fifteen minutes from the alarm being raised."

"The docking bays have cargo doors," Lichio said. "That's how they took us across to the palace."

"It'll be near dark, in Abendau; nothing that isn't essential flies at night. The port will be in lock down and the cargo doors closed. So, three squads: first one is a twelve-man squad, two pairs take each of three bays. Silom leads that one. You, Lichio, have an eight-man squad. Secure the docking bay, one pair keep it locked down, the other three secure the access door. Last six are with me at the control room, which gives access to the port's defence systems. Once we have that, they won't be able to retake it."

Lichio looked at Silom and then back at Kare.

"Well?" Kare asked. One part of him wanted them to say no, and force him to give this up. Another wanted to take Abendau and finish it forever. *Forever?* His mother was still to be faced. He drew himself up a little straighter and reminded himself he was here, still alive and fighting. Just about.

"Sounds achievable," Silom said, and Lichio nodded.

"It is," Kare said. "Silom, get the men equipped. The one thing we don't have is communication sets; otherwise the arsenal is well stocked. That means you two need to communicate directly to me. Just voice it, I'll pick it up."

Silom nodded and left, and Kare turned to Lichio. "I need a pilot and co-pilot. At four forty-five I want the men here. I'll inform the port there's been an accident and we'll go in as guards and prisoners."

"They use voice recognition," Lichio said. "They'll never open up for us, sir."

Kare raised an eyebrow. "That bastard le Payne has no confidence in anything I say." The voice, the cadence, the timing were all unmistakable: Captain Beck had just spoken.

"I'd forgotten you could do that," admitted Lichio. "But, sir, this isn't impression night at the barracks."

Returning to his own voice, Kare assured Lichio, "It's identical. It will pass any voice recognition check. It's not just an impression, it never was. It's about the only fun quirk my parents landed me with."

"I still think you're mad," Lichio said, quietly, to him. "You should run for it. But, if you're determined to do it, I'm with you. Apart from anything else, my big sister will kill me if I abandon you. And that's much more frightening than anything I might face in Abendau."

Kare smiled and beckoned to Sam. He'd been lucky to have Sam come across to them, luckier than he deserved to be. He made a mental note to keep the doctor close during the attack, make sure he made it through.

"Right," he said. "Who's your contact, and how do I reach them?"

"I don't know her name," Sam said. "Tall lady, middle aged. Seductive voice, beautiful eyes."

"She's still there," said Kare. He'd put her into the palace, had spent hours getting her story in place, making her believe she wasn't Cadence from the Banned anymore, but Simone, looking for a job as a housekeeper.

Sam handed over the comms unit and Kare waited for a moment before it was answered.

"Simone?"

"Yes, who is this?" came the reply, calm and unruffled as ever. He smiled at the familiar voice. He hadn't given the spies up, but he'd come so, so, close, his mother's mind worming into his. That

255

day- the lashings, the shocks; oh *gods*, the shocks- had faded into a red circle of horror but he still remembered how he'd been on the verge of saying their names and only their faces- faces he'd chosen, trained and placed- had stopped him.

"Is the line secure?"

"Yes."

"It's Colonel Varnon," he told her.

"You're alive, then," she said. "That's good, we were worried. I was worried, sir."

Kare smiled at her lack of emotion, knowing the small statement said more than any inflection might have done. "Alive, and not too bad, all things considered. Do you recognise my authority?"

"Sonly has sent a very clear message, sir. Yours is the commanding authority in Abendau."

"How many agents do you have available?" Kare asked, and hoped his relief didn't show in his voice. Up until now he hadn't been sure, not completely, that Sonly *would* back him.

"I have twenty in the palace, ten in the city and five of those are military," he said.

"Good. Can you report back that I aim to take the port this evening?"

"Yes, sir."

"Once I secure the port, Sonly can bring her assault force in. I land at five-thirty this evening; the port will be expecting a prison convoy. Have your people at the back door to the port, waiting."

"Do you need anything further from us, sir?"

"No," Kare said. "I'll make contact once we're in."

As he put the comms unit down, Sam placed a bowl in front of him. He frowned. "*More* food?"

Sam shrugged. "It's nothing much. Porridge."

Kare lifted the spoon and then set it down again. "I've eaten breakfast and lunch, Sam. I don't want to get carried away with dinner as well."

Sam crossed his arms. "Eat. I'm the doctor, and I say you need it. Now eat."

***

Later, Kare looked at the drawings of the port and palace in front of him. They were drawn from memory, but he was pleased by how much he recalled. The two seats opposite were pulled out from the table and he looked up to see Lichio and Silom.

"Well?" Kare asked.

"I managed to find one pilot," Lichio said. "The only other with *any* flying experience is you; you'll have to co-pilot."

Kare winced at the thought of flying a heavy desert transporter to Abendau. "That sounds fine. Silom, show Sam how to use his gun, make sure he knows how not to shoot himself, at least. Or me," he added, remembering his decision to keep the doctor close. "Lichio, your big sis is bringing the cavalry, so we will have an assault force."

Kare walked into the main room of the barracks and waited as the soldiers pulled themselves to attention. He knew them all, some better than others. One looked to be about eighteen, young but hardened after Omendegon and the quarry. Kare took a deep breath; he had to convince them to give him their respect and loyalty. *I didn't run or betray them. I've been through worse than them, and I'm still here, standing with them; let that be enough.* He stepped forwards.

"Six months ago, I commanded a force of thousands. They died at the Empress' hands. The base was destroyed. Children slaughtered." He pointed at one of the soldiers in the back row, one of the base security team. "Tomas, your partner." And another. "Your mother, Amir."

He lifted his chin. His child, his family. "Tonight, we avenge them. We show our enemies we are still here and fighting. That they *cannot* take our will." His voice had grown stronger, but he lowered it, letting the words hold the essence of a betrayal that would never be forgiven.

"I will not betray you as Eevan did. I will fight beside you until my last breath. I will hold the memories of those I fight for, and they will give me strength." He saw the belief in their faces– they would follow him. He lifted his right hand, fist clenched. "Together we take the fight to the Empress. We will destroy all she has built. Teach her the rebellion does not end. That no matter how she crushes our spirit, we come back." He took a breath and cast his eyes around the room. *Please, let him come back.* "All of us."

CHAPTER FORTY-FOUR

Kare opened the comms link to the Palace. "This is Clenadii Quarry." He waited, breath held, as they checked his voice patterns. It should work, he and Rjala had tested it, but even so....

The comms unit crackled to life. "Go ahead, Boyce."

He breathed out. "Sir, we have a problem here; the plant's overheating. We have to evacuate."

"When do you plan to evacuate, Boyce? Can it wait until morning?"

"We're in the process now, sir. The first ship will be with you in forty-five minutes. It'll be a small transport; we're bringing the high-security prisoners in first."

"Do you need additional support?"

"No, sir," Kare said smoothly. "It's better if you leave it to us; we're used to handling them."

"See you when you get here then, Boyce."

Kare reached for the collar he'd worn until the previous evening, and panic rose in him. He gulped. "You're sure I have to wear it?"

Sam nodded. "Everyone knows what they did to you; without the collar, they'll know something's not right. And you can't go in as a guard- neither can Silom or Lichio- you're far too well known."

Kare snapped the collar loosely into place, and fought to keep his voice steady. "All right, but next time it comes off, it's staying off. Let's go."

Sam climbed onboard and headed to the prisoner hold of the transport. Kare joined the pilot. As the heavy transport lifted off, the winds of the desert plains pulled at it, threatening to take it off course.

"There's no way we can use the automatic settings to fly. The winds are too unpredictable," said the pilot. "It's no wonder they use Controllers."

"I'd prefer if we had a bit more experience, Jin," admitted Kare as he scanned the charts. But few pilots had been taken from the Banned; most had been killed in the battle for the base. He saw the perspiration on the other pilot's brow. "Actually, I'd prefer it if you were my dad."

"Makes two of us," said Jin.

They sat in silence, Jin concentrating on the controls, and Kare on the charts. The ship dipped, threatening to crash into the mountains. Sweat broke as the control panel screamed at them to bank. He reached forward and silenced the alarms. Thank the gods for his father; flying with Ealyn had given him good nerves, at least. Even so, he almost let out a yell when the ship dropped too close to the ground.

"Abendau," said Jin, his voice terse. "Just ahead, sir."

Kare saw the lights of the city emerge against the encroaching darkness. It was the first time he'd had a chance to take in the full extent of the city, and how it spread into the desert, a massive oasis carved out of the land. The palace and port were near the centre, standing tall over the rest of the city.

"Well done," he said, biting back his nerves. The port were taking too long to make contact. He glanced at Jin, who looked sick. The comms unit burst into life.

"Permission to land granted; docking bay three."

Kare sucked in a breath and Jin gave a thumbs-up. He moved to the main prisoner hold where Lichio held a pair of cuffs out to him.

"You'll have to do it; he never cuffed me in front." He put his hands behind his back. The eyes of his men were on him as Lichio took his wrist and encircled it with the cold metal. Kare struggled not to tremble but Lichio must have felt it, because he gave the other wrist a gentle squeeze as he clicked the cuff on. Kare tested the bonds, straining a little.

"Thanks," he croaked.

"No problem." Lichio settled his own hands into cuffs, taking care not to lock them, and walked over to join his squad.

"Are those cuffs locked? They look locked," Sam said.

"It doesn't matter if they are or not, Sam."

"You know none of what you're doing is possible? You shouldn't even be having this conversation; you were practically catatonic."

"It's a bit late to bring it up," Kare said.

"I asked what would happen if you got your powers back, and only Sonly believed you could do something. I went for it because I didn't see any other option."

"I know it seems impossible, but so is seeing the future, and taking peoples' minds– but Ealyn could, and Averrine does. Who knows why or how it works? They think it's to do with the processing centre of the brain– that it's enhanced. All I know is its real, and it does. It's sir, by the way, Lieutenant."

"Do you get tired? I mean, does there come a point where you need to charge up again? Sir."

"Do you get tired if you read too much?" Sam nodded. "It's the same. Mostly, I know what I want to do, and my mind does it. To be fair, it took years of practice but now it's easy. But if I push it, I drain myself."

The transport doors opened and Kare let himself be forced out. *Head down. Passive.* He felt for the port security, sensing where they were.

The prisoner behind, dressed as a guard, pushed him forward, not gently. Port security gathered in the bay, ready to see him reduced and beaten. Kare smiled inwardly; let them look, it made his job easier.

"Where's Beck?" asked one of the port guards, and Kare held his breath, hoping the Banned corporal remembered his role.

"He has the shits," the corporal said. "He's following with the med staff."

He pushed Kare again and Kare deliberately stumbled, snicking his cuffs not off, but free, as he did. He allowed himself to be spun into the access corridor opposite. Silom was led to the edge of the port, ready to move out of the bay, and Lichio hung back. Kare brought his head up and nodded, first to Lichio, then Silom. He straightened fully, the bulk of the guards trapped between the three Banned squads. As he brought his hands forward, free, he took the weapon Sam proffered, and turned with his men.

"Now," Kare ordered, and Lichio's squad opened fire, the port guards trapped and cut down easily and quickly. Kare waited, the cold floor beneath him, and almost smiled; he'd never reckoned on leading an uprising shirtless and barefoot.

Silom's squad moved out of the main hangar, and Kare led his into the access corridor which ran to the main control room. Behind him the firing stopped as Lichio's team secured the hangar.

"Like the quarry," Kare said to the soldiers around him. "We'll storm it. I'll place the grenade. Two, three and four position in the room; follow room clearance drill. Give me a grenade."

He held out his hand and someone handed him a grenade. Opening the door, he rolled it in. He shut the door, heard shouts on the other side and felt frantic attempts to open either door. He held firm until there was a muffled bang and some screams. Waves of pain and fear coming from the room hit his mind and he turned his head away, reminding himself there was no choice. It had been almost a decade since he'd done something similar on Dignad– it hadn't got any easier.

"Take it," Kare told his squad. He waited during the short

skirmish and then went in, Sam following, looking a bit green. He glanced round at the array of computers and security equipment.

"No access codes, sir, plus there's some damage," said his second. "And we're coming under some heavy fire from the palace walkway."

Kare walked over to one of the computers and then grinned. Finally, something he was confident he could do.

"You've no access, why are you smiling, sir?" challenged Sam.

Kare, seated already at the computer desk, brought up a screen. "The other thing I'm really, really good at?"

"Computers, sir?" Sam said, a resigned look on his face. "As well as the psyche?"

"I've always been a high achiever. It's best to have more than one skill, don't you think? I could do with Lichio here, though."

He started to work with the system, quickly moving through its security. He nodded to his second. "Sergeant, go and relieve Captain le Payne; I need him here." He brought the screen up to view the walkway and the soldiers on it. He scrolled through his options, selected one and was rewarded by the pulse of a laser. A line of soldiers went down. He started to bring up the other screens, and saw the defence troops were launching a concerted counter-attack. Armoured vehicles moved out from the palace to the port, their blast cannons pounding the cargo doors. The port shook with each hit. Just like the attack on the base, thought Kare, and he worked through the system quicker.

He got to the second from last connection and realised the damage from his attack had caused it to fail. He climbed under the desk to look at the connections and see what he could do.

"Wow, like a toy shop, sir," a familiar voice said.

Kare rolled his eyes. "It's good you're pleased, but I need you to work the defences, not rub your hands in delight."

"You're feeling more like yourself, I see," said Lichio.

Kare ignored him. "There should be a shield for the port if I get through the last security level. Once that's up, they'll not be able to take it." He saw where the damaged connection was and reconnected it. When he emerged, Lichio, for all his talk, was working the system, firing at the Empress' troops.

"Are the spies in?" Kare asked.

"Yes, sir."

"I'll have to hunt out Simone later and thank her. Assuming we survive long enough," Kare said, and grinned at Lichio's look of concern. Kare zoned the sounds of the attack out, calmly working

261

his way through the last few screens. "You have laser cannons mounted on each entranceway, Lich; use those, too. If I open the bombard cannons it'll slow the shield."

"Okay, but we need that shield up," Lichio said. "Bay three's cargo door is nearly compromised."

"A couple of minutes."

There was another assault on the door, the armoured vehicles unaffected by the port's lasers. Their mounted cannons continued to send out targeted blasts, one after another. Kare cleared the last security level and waited for the system to confirm. On the screen, the cargo door buckled further. Silom's squad had gathered inside.

"Colonel," warned Lichio. "We need it now."

"Listen," Kare said. The noise from the explosions became muffled.

"It's up?"

"It's up, and they'll know it. They'll pull back. Have a good look at the defences when you get the chance. This place is pretty close to impenetrable."

"They've pulled away from the back door, sir."

"Good. I think we can say we've secured the port, then."

He opened the comms link and typed in a familiar configuration, one he had never expected to use again. "Banned fleet," he said, "this is Colonel Varnon. The port is ours. I say again; the port is ours. Bring your ships in."

He spun his seat to face Lichio. "Any happier?"

Lichio looked at him, and Kare could see the respect back in his eyes.

"Yes. How do you plan to run it, sir?"

"As soon as the Banned forces are in, start an aerial assault. Keep Abendau locked down. They'll try to use whatever fighters they have at the port in Bendau. Make sure we have coverage over the desert, take down anything that comes across. Use any Controllers Sonly brings for that- that's where they'll use theirs. Hold the ground forces back; we have to reduce their defences first."

"If I may, sir?" Kare nodded his assent. "I think we would be better assaulting tonight, before they can get the defences in place. If we wait, they could fortify the palace more, bring in troops from the city."

Kare hesitated while he considered Lichio's words, then shook his head. "No, we do it my way. If we hit them hard enough we should be in position for a ground assault tomorrow, or the next day, and have a better chance to win."

Lichio looked like he wanted to argue further, but after a moment he nodded. "Yes, sir."

262

"Thank you, Lichio. You take it for now; I want to meet the ships as they come in, see what we have."

"I'll liaise with them. With all this to play with, I could stay here all day."

"That's good," Kare said. "I have a shortage of techies, so you probably will." He turned to go.

"Kare," Lichio said softly, and Kare turned back at the use of his first name. "Take the collar off, and put on a shirt. You don't want to frighten her."

Kare paused. "What the hell am I going to say to her, Lich?"

Lichio looked at him with sympathy. "I'm planning to start with hello. Do you want me to tell her? You know, about the- "

"No, I will," Kare interrupted, his voice harsh. "Sometime. Somehow. But, thank you."

He snapped the collar off, and held it in his hands for a moment before he set it down. He took a jacket from the back of one of the seats and started to walk to the port, buttoning it up as he did. Sonly was here and he could hardly remember what she looked like. His hands dampened and he wiped them on his jacket, and realised he was as scared now as he had been when he'd faced Beck. He belonged to her, as she did him, and he wanted back to that. But he was afraid he might still be Beck's, and wasn't sure he could be both. He paused for a moment, trying to tell himself it was Sonly, not a stranger. He started walking again, still worried that too much had happened to go back.

CHAPTER FORTY-FIVE

he ship swooped over the great city of Abendau, diving when the palace guns fired on it. Below, armoured vehicles were in defensive lines at each of the access points to the city and palace. There were no enemy ships in the air.

"No aerial defences at all?" Sonly checked.

"No. It looks like the colonel has the port defences operational, too."

She moved to the exit hatch before the ship landed, clenching and unclenching her hands. She was actually going to see him. Her stomach churned, part excitement, part fear. Margueritte Tortdeniel's words came back, her description of a Kare who had capitulated. The details of the reports received from Sam's partner. However Kare was, he'd be changed.

As soon as the hatch opened she stepped out and looked round the port, but Kare wasn't in sight. She climbed down, planning to find the control room, and stopped at the sound of his voice. Her heart started to beat faster, and as she walked down the gangway, the floor swam in front of her.

She got to the bottom and looked around. Someone was watching her from about fifteen feet away, and at first she wondered if it was the doctor she'd heard about. Then she looked past the white hair and lined face to the unmistakable green eyes, and stood for a moment, shock running through her, so sharp it was a physical pain. This couldn't be him: Kare was in his twenties, not this old man. Her breath was coming too quickly, making her dizzy and sick; what had they done to change him so much?

His eyes were fixed on her and she knew he could tell what she was thinking- even without his powers, he would have known. She told herself it didn't matter, that nothing mattered except he was back. That got her moving. She ran past a cargo truck and through a squad of soldiers, until she got to about three feet from him. She stopped- he hadn't moved. He swallowed, as if he was nervous, and she noticed for the first time the scar on his neck, the one Michael had warned her about. It was red and vivid against his pale skin.

"Kare?" she asked. He nodded but didn't seem to know what to say. The silence stretched, and she thought he mightn't find any words, that she'd have to speak again.

"Hello, Sonly," he said at last, his voice choked and husky. "I made it back to you. Well, most of me did."

Sonly closed the final few feet and threw her arms around him. He was thinner than she'd ever known, and tense, so tense it felt like he could break. He stood, not embracing her back, and she didn't know if she should hold him closer or give him space. Her throat closed at a rush of tears. She'd always known what to do for him. She'd held him through nightmare after nightmare, reaching for him in the darkness of their room, and he'd taken her comfort, had used it to find strength, as she'd used his. Now he was stiff and still, a stranger, and she'd never felt so useless and lost.

"I missed you," she said, into his chest, and felt him nod. She looked up and saw his eyes were filled with tears, but when he blinked, they cleared, as if she'd imagined it. He pushed her away, not roughly, but firmly.

"Kare...." She had to say something. The missing months, what had happened to him, hung heavy between them. "What can I do? What will help?"

"I- I...." He looked away, and then glanced back, not quite meeting her eyes. He was shaking. "Please- don't push. I can't take it." He swallowed, his adam's apple prominent in his thin throat. "I'm just about coping as it is."

He turned to leave and she caught his arm to stop him, the bones of his wrists hard. "It will be okay." He didn't move, didn't show any life in him or any sign of hope. "Won't it, Kare?"

His eyes held hers for just a moment too long. "I don't know." He pulled his hand away. "I don't know anything. Not anymore."

He'd always had the answers; he was smart, he knew what he wanted. He wasn't this shadow, this shaking person whose eyes shifted around the room, watching, whose arms had crossed in front of him, as if holding the world at a distance.

"I can help," she said, but didn't know if she could. She could barely find the words to say to him, or know how to comfort him- how was she ever going to help him through this? She wanted to wrap him in her arms and never let go, keep him where no one could hurt him again. She took a step forward, but he leaned back, rejecting her, and the words she should say- that she loved him, that they'd find a way past this- died.

"You will," he said. His voice was soft. "But there's too much going on right now. I need to finish the attack, take Abendau. Make us safe. Then I can think about things. Not before." His eyes were pleading. "Please. Give me that time."

He was right. With the chance of his mother returning he needed safety, not a bare port in a war zone.

265

"What can I do?" she asked. "I didn't come to watch."

"Heaven forbid," he said, and she could tell how hard it had been for him to make the small joke. "I need you to add to the pressure. Politically. I plan to take Abendau, and you need to find out what position that will put us in. In the meantime, I have to get the ships in and find somewhere to put your troops; there are no beds here. I'll also have to figure out how the hell to feed them."

Now he was talking about the campaign, he seemed more confident. It appeared he was right and it *was* all he could cope with– after they won, they could talk.

"We've brought supplies: ship's rations, uniforms, whatever weaponry we had. There are transports following, too– that should help with the accommodation," she said, and he nodded his thanks.

"Sir, the clinic? Where do you want it?" asked a sandy-haired man.

Sonly turned at the interruption, then looked at Kare quizzically.

"One of the transports? One that's not being used for sleeping." Kare turned to Sonly. "This is Sam Prentice, the doctor; he holds the rank of lieutenant with us. Sam, this is Sonly, my wife."

"Colonel!" shouted Silom from the other side of the hangar.

"There's a command meeting in fifteen minutes. I'd like you both there," Kare said, and walked across to Silom.

"It's nice to finally meet you," Sam said, a little awkwardly. "He talks a lot about you."

Sonly pulled her eyes away from Kare and realised Sam's eyes were full of sympathy.

"He's different," she said. "From before."

"Very different. He probably doesn't know this, but if he's going to recover, he needs you. He might push you away– if he does, try and stick with him."

"Can you tell me what they did? I know some of it, but not all."

Sam shook his head, and he looked guilty as hell. "It's his to tell and he will, when he can. Come on, I'll walk over with you."

They walked to the control room, where Lichio was sitting in one of the swivel chairs. He, too, looked older and thinner but it wasn't as dramatic as with Kare. He stood, a smile on his face which was, at least, welcoming.

"Lichio," she gasped. She threw her arms around him. "I was scared you were dead."

He took her arms down, and hugged her lightly instead. "Me too. We didn't know if anyone survived."

Again she put her arms around him, and this time he hissed with pain.

266

"What is it?" she asked.

Lichio removed her arms. "The remnants of the last whipping the bastards are going to give me." His voice and eyes were hard, harder than she'd ever imagined him to be.

"They *whipped* you?" she said. She'd known they had, of course. In fact, she knew they'd done worse to him, but hadn't expected to be confronted by it so vividly.

"Yes, they whipped me. How the hell else do you think they got me to work in a quarry?"

She couldn't decide if it was a joke or not, until she saw the glint of mischief in his eyes. She started to smile. Behind her, a familiar, deep voice made her jump.

"Kare should have thought of it years ago; it was an excellent motivator for your lazy brother."

She spun, saw Silom and reached out to hug him. He caught her arms. "I'm with Lich, though. No hugs. Not for a couple of days."

They both stared at each other, Sonly remembering how he'd been cornered, her baby pulled from his arms. She'd heard Kerra cry and then the shot, and had tried to jump from the transport, but the hatch had started to come up and she couldn't. She'd screamed Silom's name, hoping he'd fight them off and reach her. He'd tried, had got past two of them, but there'd been too many.

"I'm sorry," he said.

"It wasn't your fault. You tried to get her away."

He nodded, and there was something about him: his height, his reliability, maybe, that made her feel things might be all right for the first time since the alarms had ripped through the base.

"Glad everyone's caught up. Now, let's get down to work," said Kare, behind her.

She sat in one of the chairs, watching him check the screens and talk to Silom about troops. He was managing, but she could tell he was struggling: his movements were a little too quick; his eyes were flitting as if he was ready to run; his hand never strayed far from his blaster. Behind him, she noticed an iron ring, and she looked from it to Kare's scar and it made her nauseous. He turned and leaned against one of the desks, his arms folded.

"We've done well for the first day," he said, "but it will take time before we're in the position for a ground assault. I want to get the attack plans finalised, and the soldiers prepared. Lichio, transfer to ops-command; the men are used to you as my second. Silom, I need you to run the ground troops; Lyle, you stay with the air units. I have a good idea what defences they have, but I don't know what ships we've got here, our troop capacity."

267

Lyle nodded, "I have an inventory of the ships underway."

"I'll compile a list of ranks and specialities," Silom said, and Kare nodded his thanks.

"Do that; we'll meet again first thing. You can go now."

Kare waited for them to leave, checked the screens in front of him and leaned back in his chair. Sonly sat beside him.

"You're doing fine," she said. He nodded. "Can you take the palace?" He didn't answer. "Kare, this is like pulling teeth. Can you take the palace?"

"Yes," Kare said quietly. "I think I can. If I do, where does it put us?"

"When I left, Michael was in liaison with much of the outer rim, and I think they'll support us. I spoke to the Peiret family. They have been wavering for months, you know that. They'll back us, if you take Abendau, and I'm sure Tortdeniel will, too. If Balandt come onboard, with their wealth, we can force it through. I'm sure of it."

"So, that's the outer rim and three of the families, assuming Abendau is forced to surrender. Not bad for a slave revolt," he said.

"They had a good leader." He didn't respond, and she tried a different tack. "Don't you need to sleep? You must be tired."

"I'm not. Sonly, I can do things I never imagined; I feel almost like I'm some sort of superhuman. I don't know if it's because I haven't used my psyche for so long, or just I'm not used to it, but I feel like there is nothing I can't do with my powers."

A chill ran through Sonly. "Don't get ridiculous notions. Your mother thinks she's a god; it's not a nice family trait."

He smiled a little at that. "Anyway, what are my options?"

"You're planning to depose the Empress?" He had to, surely. There was no other option. This was their one chance at Abendau– the Banned didn't have the army to fight on. But she couldn't tell him that this was the make-or-break moment, the point where history pivoted. He didn't need any more pressure.

"I think if I take the palace, her symbolic home, then yes– I'll be in that position. Especially if you can deliver what you just said."

"If you depose her, the families will recognise you, and the middle sector will follow. Inter-planetary trading, apart from anything else, is too linked not to. You'll have your republic." No matter what Michael said, or the great families. If Kare wanted his mother's empire razed to the ground, she'd support him in it. She'd support him in anything that would give him peace, and space, and the chance to recover.

"I don't think it'll work, not anymore. I've seen how the palace works and been with her people. They're brainwashed. They need someone to take her place and that someone needs to be strong enough to hold them. Bind them to the leader."

Her mouth fell open, and she stood for a moment, taking in his hard eyes, how they swept dispassionately across the screens instead of meeting hers.

"You're thinking of taking her place," she said. "You're thinking of taking her empire."

The strangeness of this Kare washed over her. If she'd suggested this to Kare a year ago, he'd have refused it and asked if she wasn't listening. Now, not only was he considering it, it was likely he could be Emperor.

"Why not?" he asked.

"Because you've never wanted it."

"I do now. Think about it- if I take the empire, we can bring about all the changes we dreamed of."

"You don't bring about change by shifting personnel; you have to change beliefs and cultures. You give power back to the people, not take it for yourself." She paused. "That's what you've been telling me for years."

"And if they don't want that? If they actually want a leader, what then?"

"Then, it might be a possibility," she conceded. "But you need to ask first; you can't assume." She reached out, but he avoided her touch. "Kare, you're in no shape to make that sort of decision. You need to give yourself some time. Some space from- " She should say it, say the name Omendegon, face it. She'd always been brave. "From what's happened to you."

He started to pace. If he'd heard what she'd said, he didn't show it. "I think it's the only way I can oust her," he said. "I'll use the role to bring about change and give the power back, once I'm sure it's safe."

"You know who you sound like, don't you?"

Kare turned his face away, and Sonly reached out. She touched his chin, bringing his face round to face her.

He pulled away. "Don't."

"You sound like your mother." Maybe he could be shocked into the truth. Maybe then he'd listen, and she could tell him to stop, just stop. That he'd done enough. "I don't think you'd give it back. I think you'd take what's left of Ealyn's son and replace it with your mother's heir."

"That's not true."

"Then look at me when you say that." He didn't. "Kare, your mother thinks power is there to be taken, that she's more important than anyone else." She could see that her words had awakened something in him. She pushed further. "Kare, what are you afraid of?"

He looked at her and the pain in his eyes made her step back,

269

shocked. He looked like he'd seen every hell there was.

"You have no idea what I'm afraid of, Sonly. Everything. Going back. What can be done to a person. What has been done to me. I have to put myself in the place where she can't hurt me again. Which means I either hide in a hole or I make myself so powerful, she daren't."

For a moment, she didn't know what to say. She wanted to reach out to him, hug him and tell him it would be all right, that she would keep him safe. "It's the wrong reason," she said, instead.

"Will you stay with me?" He looked at her, his eyes desperate. "If I did, would you stand with me and be my Empress?"

"If you were asking me because it's the right thing to do, I'd say of course." If she thought it would make things better for him, she'd seize it with both hands. "But I remember how passionate you were about tearing down her empire, overthrowing it, not taking it for yourself."

"So, that's a no then." He turned away, and she moved forward and put her arms around him. He tensed.

"I want to be with you. I want to support your republic, to stand by your side when you rip down what your mother built," she said. She'd never imagined not being. Her ears were roaring, she couldn't think straight, she just knew that somehow she had to reach him. "But it needs to be the right future; I can't support you if I think it'll hurt you." She swallowed. "I *won't* support you if it'll hurt you. I never will." Finally, he was looking at her, and she grabbed his hand. "You are everything to me, and I will never do anything to hurt you. And this is wrong. I can't say yes." She reached up and stroked his cheek, his skin harsh under her fingers. She saw him wince and didn't know if she'd hurt him, or if her words were too much, but she didn't care. He needed to know.

"I love you," she said, and then again, "I love you."

She didn't move away, and after a moment he took a breath, but it was shuddering. He took her hand and squeezed it gently, before lifting it away. His voice, when he spoke, sounded hoarse and she realised he was barely holding himself together.

"I want our future too, but I don't know what mine is anymore."

She left him and walked to the transports. When she remembered how excited she had been to hear he'd escaped and was okay, she cursed herself. Whoever he was now, he wasn't her Kare, and it was him she wanted, not this shadow. She bit back the tears: she was lucky he was here at all. Still, she couldn't shake the memory of his eyes watching her, hard and remote and scared.

CHAPTER FORTY-SIX

Silom watched his army forming up in the hangar, pleased at the number of troops. Commander Lyle turned to him. "We have a chance?"

Silom nodded. "A good chance. Taking the Skywalk is key; then we link the palace and port for personnel."

He turned away, his shoulders still aching, and wished he could take his uniform off to let air at the gashes. He half-smiled– what sort of leader was he, moaning about a couple of lash marks? He cast his eyes over the soldiers, and a corporal came up to him, saluting. "Sir, another personnel list."

Silom took it, and walked away to read it. He needed to concentrate and couldn't do it with Lyle beside him. *Liar.* He nodded, half to himself– yes, and a bloody awful one. He turned to the W's, and saw there were about five. He swallowed, forcing himself to scan down them, as he had every other list that day: Wagh, Wells, Welsh, Wlowski, Woods. He put his hand out, supporting himself against the side of a transport. *Woods, Kymberly.* He looked up, his eyes smarting, and called the corporal over to him. "I want you to bring Sergeant Woods to me." The corporal left and Silom sat on a set of wheeled stairs leading to the transport's rear hatch. *She was alive.* He set the document down, his hands shaking. There were footsteps and, like a miracle, she was there, still the same Kym, a rifle slung across her chest, her hair mussed, a helmet held in her other hand. He stood up, blinked, and realised he didn't have a clue what to say.

"Silom?" she said.

He climbed down the steps. "I didn't know..." he started, but stopped. He didn't know if he'd lost her, too. He didn't know if an attack seeking Kare– Kare, who he'd supported, who he was still supporting– had taken another he loved. She came to him and he found her in his arms, hugging him, causing his lash wounds to flare up, but he didn't care. He lifted her off her feet and kissed her, deep and slow, and it tasted of toffee, familiar and tantalising. There was a cheer behind him and he half-smiled, before kissing her even deeper and raising a single finger behind her back. The cheers increased and he started to hope Charl had survived too– he was a lucky enough bastard.

He put her down and they stood back from each other. Her eyes were shining with tears, and he touched the edge of them. "Don't cry. You never cry."

She gave a smile instead. "I was sure you were dead."

Silom shrugged. "I'm too bloody minded to kill." He brought her round so they were out of sight of the rest of the soldiers, and pushed her against the transport. She shifted against him, the way she knew turned him on, and he pushed her hair back from her forehead and kissed her again. When he pulled away, he said, "You know, we had things we talked about doing."

She nodded.

"When we're finished here," he said. "I'd like them, too. If you'll have me."

"Of course I'll have you." She glanced down, grinning, and then up. Her eyes were crinkled, full of the mischief he remembered. "Looks like you'll have me, too."

***

"That's the last ship in, sir," said Commander Lyle.

"Thank you. Go and see to your men, Tom." Kare rubbed his eyes. Lack of sleep was irritating them more than any other part of him. The screens of the floodlit exterior of the port showed no movement by the defence troops.

"Are your men prepared?" he asked Silom.

"They're bored. We've been here for two days; there's only so much preparation they can do. We've carried out the attack drills, the equipment is ready– now the nerves are starting."

"I know they are," Kare said. "What do you want me to do– send them over the walkway and let them get slaughtered for entertainment?"

"Of course not: I'm just saying they're bored, since you asked. Maybe we should have attacked sooner."

"We couldn't have; I hadn't enough troops here to begin with."

They all wanted miracles. Did they think he could take the palace by clicking his fingers? He clenched his hands around each other, relishing the pain in his misshapen fingers; it distracted him from his worries.

"Are you all right? You seem annoyed," said Silom.

"I'm fine, and I would be a lot better if everyone would stop asking me if I'm all right, or okay, or coping, or every other way you have found to ask it."

"Right," Silom said, and his voice, finally, sounded a little offended.

After a moment's silence, Silom stood up. "I'm going. But, you know, the only reason we ask is we're worried."

"I know," Kare said, but he couldn't bring himself to say sorry.

Silom's footsteps faded away, replaced a few minutes later by a familiar tread. Kare tensed: he could deal with Silom and Lichio by focusing on work; Sam's persistence was wearisome, but he was able to avoid him a lot of the time; there was nothing he could do to stop Sonly worming her way past all his defences, the way she always had done. The room spun, and his throat tightened. He saw Lichio beside Sonly, his face serious.

"Kare," Sonly said, her voice nonconfrontational, as if she was managing him.

"Yes?" he asked.

"Lichio says he'll run things for a while. Will you come with me? I need to talk to you."

"What about?" he asked, and knew he was being impossible. He wondered if this was what one of those hamsters on their little wheels felt like.

"An update; we always get interrupted here."

It was hard to tell if she was lying, without looking into her thoughts. She'd never know if he did. He forced the idea away. He had promised never to: at least let him keep that promise.

"Okay," he said, and pushed his chair back. "The next offensive is planned at oh-two-forty-five, Lichio. I'll be back for it."

He followed Sonly to the transport Sam had taken for his clinic. It was quiet and comfortable, with blankets for bedding. As they went in he saw Sam, but the doctor backed away and left them. Kare sat on one of the blankets, making room for Sonly beside him.

"Kare," she said, her voice quiet and calm. "I know you think you're fine, but I'm sure if Rjala were here, she'd pull you off the attack." He couldn't see her face clearly in the dark transport. "You've managed to piss off most of your officers, and the campaign isn't going anywhere. I asked Lichio and he reckons it could be weeks before you take the palace."

"So pull me off it," he told her.

"I can't. You know that; I don't have anyone else who can lead it."

"Then what do you suggest, Sonly? We spend the next year in the port? Or run home, and wait to be drummed out of existence?"

"I think you need to tell me what happened. I think you're so stressed you can't possibly do what you need to. You're pushing away everyone who would support you, you're not taking advice, and you *know* you can't lead a campaign like that."

"Sonly," Kare said. He clenched his fists and tried to push the panic back. *Breathe; that's all, keep breathing.* "I can't tell you. I don't have the words."

Sam stepped into sight. "Then tell me, Kare. I already know. Tell me, and Sonly will listen because she's right, you need to tell her."

Kare dropped his head. Could he tell Sam? Sam, who was almost as ashamed as he was. Sam, who'd been there and still helped, who hadn't been disgusted by him. He couldn't hold out much longer, not against their combined barrage.

"All of it?" he asked. He was exhausted, totally drained, but one part of him was relieved that this moment had arrived. At least it'd be over, and he'd know what she thought of him.

"All of it," Sam said. "Just focus on me."

Kare looked at Sam, and ignored Sonly. He told them about the attack on the base, about Phelps handing him to Beck, how he'd known he was in his dad's vision. He talked about the flight, how he'd pissed himself and thought it was such a big thing. He even managed to tell them about being taken to Omendegon, the place he'd dreaded all his life, and the first day with the Great Master, how the pain had started to blur into a single entity, even then.

"It wasn't the pain that was the worst," he told them. "It was what came after– " He stopped, his mouth closing against his next words, and shook his head. "I can't..."

"You're doing well," said Sam. "This was all before I met you, isn't that right?"

"Yes." He breathed in, as deeply as he could. "They warned me in Omendegon if I didn't let go of the block, they'd show me I had no control over anything." The memories were rushing back, and it was like he was in the torture room, being dragged from it, unable to speak through the pain and fear. "I was so tired and sore, I didn't care what they'd planned. They took me back to the cell and chained me down."

In the darkness of the quiet transport he turned to Sam, but Sonly reached out and held his hand. He wondered if she could feel the scars that ran across his palms, and the badly knitted bones.

"That's one of the things I do remember; that he chained me down, as if I had any chance against them. Anyway, that night, a group of them, they.... " He stopped, looked up at the ceiling of the transport, and tried to force the lump in his throat away. "They–

274

they r..." He looked at Sam, desperate for help. "I can't..."

"You're doing well," said Sam. "Can you say what they did?"

Can I? Kare closed his eyes– *he said he'd stitch them open if I tried to hide*– and willed himself not to throw up. It was only one thing in a long list of horrors, but this one, telling Sonly... it was the hardest to voice. He opened them and looked at Sam, who nodded, encouraging him.

"They raped me," Kare said, and it was out. He didn't look at Sonly, couldn't look at Sonly, but she squeezed his hand, and he could feel waves of worry and horror coming off her. "More than once. Very roughly, very painfully. Each time one left me, I thought it was over, and they came again. Silom and Lichio were there– they could hear it all. After, they brought Sam in, and then a healer, and when he put his hands on me I felt like I was a kid, with Karia."

Kare looked at Sam desperately. *Help me.* His throat closed with remembered fear, and he heard his breath rasping, the way it used to when he'd worn his collar.

"They healed you and took you back to the torture rooms. They kept that up for most of the day," Sam said. "Healing you, hurting you; trying to get past the block."

Sonly's fingers tightened in his, and Kare glanced at her. She gave him a small, brave smile of support, but he could see the tears in her eyes and wished he could hold her, or let her hold him.

"I'm not trying to be evasive," Kare said, "but I was... I...I can't remember the details. My mother kept coming into my mind, invading it, and I had nowhere to hide. She knew everything about me."

"You called her a twisted bitch," Sam said.

"Did I?" Kare thought for a moment. "Well, that was stupid of me." Once reminded, he vaguely remembered the unceasing pain, and the Empress revelling in it, enjoying her power over him. He'd shouted something at her with the very last of his strength.

"She broke the block," he whispered. "And I told her everything..."

"Nearly everything," said Sam. "You knew the Banned was ruined– you said so– but you didn't give up the spies."

"No, I held onto that, just. Should I go on?" Kare asked, and Sonly nodded.

"Now you've started, you should finish, I think. If you can." Her voice trembled and he glanced at her, hoping that she'd hold herself together, knowing if she didn't he couldn't go on.

"I thought I'd survived Omendegon; what more could they do?" he said, speaking now to Sonly and not Sam. "I honestly believed the worst might be behind me. And then, the day I was released from the hospital block, he brought in the collar and told me he'd make me his dog." He swallowed at the memory of the collar going on and choking him. "I didn't believe him, not then. But he was utterly relentless– he never stopped, ever– until I got to the point where I'd do anything to please him, and stop him hurting me." *I did.* "Pretty much anything you can think of to demean a person, he had me do. Sam knows, he watched."

"Sonly knows some of it; I reported back."

Sam looked away and Kare knew he wasn't the only person reliving it here in this dark, quiet transport. He looked at Sonly, swallowing so that it was painful. "It's so hard, telling you."

She nodded, tears falling down her face, but she hadn't turned away. Not yet. Gently, he reached out and wiped her cheek, and she didn't flinch from him.

"I talked to myself," he told her, his eyes focused on her. "I sang to myself. I talked to you and told myself at some point they'd fuck up the medicine, or I'd grow used to it, and my powers would come back. And every day I clung on and on, for as long as I could."

"I know you did," Sonly said. "You were so brave."

"The last thing was the pit," he said, and his own tears came now, hot against his cheek, surprising him. "I had to submit; he was never going to stop until I did. I've been dreaming about it for years but when I was there, it was so much worse. When they released me from it, I let them do anything they liked with me. They paraded me to the planetary leaders, the dignitaries. I went on my knees before the Empress and gave her my fealty many times. I thought, as much as I thought anything, that it would be good to die: the sooner the better." He paused. "I still do."

Sonly pulled him against her. He stopped talking and let the tears flow, finding it hard to believe the hitching sobs were coming from him. Now they'd started, he was frightened they wouldn't stop and he'd been right not to want to do this: that he would be sitting in this transport forever, trapped by his own fear.

"You mustn't feel like that," she said to him, speaking to him like he was a child. "It's going to be hard, love. You need time."

"I'm so angry," Kare said, through the tears. "I'm angry about everything: that the others didn't face as much; that they heard it and don't know what to say; that you didn't come when I begged you to; that Sam didn't help sooner. I'm angry at my mother, too, but at least I'm doing something about her." Sonly nodded at that. "Mostly, though, I'm angry at myself for letting it happen. For being so sure I could survive anything they threw at me."

Kare looked up and realised Sam had left, and he was glad. He stayed against her, he didn't know for how long, until the tears eased, and he sat up and tried to compose himself. Her face was white, shocked, but she didn't look away.

"So now you know why I can't let anyone come close. I can't let anyone touch me: I'm so angry, and ashamed, and scared."

"It wasn't your fault, Kare."

But he'd known what opposing his mother could bring on him. He'd known that and still stood for the Banned.

"I know. Logically I know. Maybe I should lock myself away for six months, and then come back out." *I just made a joke.* He smiled a little at that.

"The only thing I want is for you to be at peace," Sonly said. "If you want to walk away, I'll support you. If you want to keep going, I'll back you, but you have to do it properly: with breaks, with support. If you don't, I'll end the campaign, because I want what's best for you. I love you."

"That's the one thing I do know, Sonly. I love you, as well. As much as ever. And, Sonly, something I haven't said to you, and should have done. I'm so, so sorry about Kerra. It must have been hard for you, losing everyone at once. I'm only starting to be able to think about her now; you've had to live with it for months."

"I miss her," she admitted. "We had her for such a short time. There are so few memories to carry of her."

"I do, too. You know, that makes my mind up. She's another one to repay the Empress for. We can't pull out, not when we're so close."

"Okay. We'll do it, for Kerra."

"For all of them," he told her. "If I'm going to do this I need, amongst other things, to sleep- but every time I stop, I panic. So then I start up again, and now I'm exhausted."

"Sleep here," she said. "I won't disturb you."

"I have nightmares," he warned her. "Worse than ever. I had them in my cell. Beck used to kick me awake and boot me around the place to shut me up. Somehow, that didn't cure me."

He paused, remembering the cycle of nightmares, the screams trailed from him in his sleep, the horror of knowing he'd brought another beating on himself.

The cell door opened and his collar, tethered to the wall rings, stopped him seeing who was there.

"Nightmare again? I'll give you something to have nightmares about." *Beck laughed and drew back his boot, or lifted his whip, and Kare knew the trap had sprung again, the cyclical nightmare he had no way of breaking.*

Kare pulled himself out of the flashback, focused again on Sonly.

"The few times I have slept, they've been awful. Worse than Dad's," he admitted.

"Then have them. It won't be the first time. I promise not to kick you, no matter how much noise you make." She reached her hand up, and stroked his cheek, so gently it was as if he was a child, and it gave comfort with no demand. He found himself taking a deep breath, and then another. "Kare, I had no idea. Or, I did, but it's worse, so much worse than I ever imagined. I don't know how you survived, how you managed to come back."

"I know. I never imagined they'd do what they did." Even through his father's visions, his own dreams over the years, he'd had no idea. He'd been a fool. He stretched out on the blanket and found himself slipping into sleep. He heard, at one point, the sound of ships coming and going and thought distantly he should go and help Lichio, but sank further into sleep. As the battle waged, Kare slept, a healing sleep. He had no nightmares that night, curled up against Sonly, her hand on his forehead, comforting him, keeping him safe.

CHAPTER FORTY-SEVEN

Kare sat up and looked around, trying to place where he was. It wasn't until he saw Sonly that he remembered and almost groaned at how he'd broken down. She was still here, though; he took that as a good sign. He got up, as quietly as he could, but when he opened the door of the transport it disturbed her.

"Where are you going?" she asked.

"I told Lichio I'd be back hours ago."

Sonly sat up, her short hair tousled, and Kare noticed for the first time that she, too, was thinner, her face older. *It wasn't just me.* He stopped for a moment as he took that in; it was, he suspected, the first thing that had come through the wall of shock he'd been operating in. It wasn't just him. It was her; and Silom, cast into a nightmare he'd no right to face, forced to watch Kare- who he'd promised to protect long, long ago- destroyed; and Lichio, who'd joined the army before he'd been old enough to know if he wanted to be a soldier, faced with something that had lurked in his nightmares, too. Enough stories about Omendegon circled the Banned, after all; he had to know what lay ahead for him if he was taken.

"It's okay," said Sonly. "I checked while you were sleeping. Lichio said he was fine."

Kare stood in the door of the transport for a moment, enjoying the weak morning light flooding in from the hangar doors. His clothes were crumpled and he was grubby and hungry. To notice all this seemed a miracle to him; like he'd reconnected with reality for the first time in months. As he left the transport, Sam walked over.

"You okay?" asked the doctor.

"I'm fine. Thank you."

"You're not angry?" Typical Sam, always checking on others, keeping things running, the troops fed, the soldiers in one piece. "I pushed you into talking."

"I'm not. I feel like I can breathe again, think clearer."

"You know, it'll take time. A lot of time," warned Sam.

Kare almost said that he knew more than anyone how long this was going to take. He felt better today, that was true, but still a million miles from the man who'd been taken to Abendau.

"The voice of experience?" he said, instead.

"Well, it wasn't an uncommon thing to happen in Omendegon." Sam paused. "And you faced more of it– everything– than anyone."

"I'm not making light of it. But it has helped, getting it out into the open: Sonly knowing. Sleeping. You were right, I was exhausted."

"Baby steps. Don't rush it."

"I'll take it as slowly as I can. For now, I'm going to get something to eat and a shower, if Lichio's okay to sit on for another half hour."

Sam reeled back in mock horror. "You go get a shower and I'll find something to eat, sir. I'll send a runner to Lichio."

Later, Kare pushed his plate away. "Actually, for reconstituted stuff, that's not bad. Maybe it was Dad's cooking, or perhaps the food has improved."

"Maybe you've got less picky. Anything has to be better than Beck's offerings."

"That, too." Kare stood. "I've got to go. I do have a campaign to run."

On his way to the control room he stopped to speak to a couple of soldiers, letting them show him the preparations they'd made. They seemed glad of his attention, and lifted by it. He looked around the hangar, at the ships coming in from the battle, and a wave of sick fear crossed him. Had he made a hash of the campaign, and blown his one chance at taking Abendau? He pushed the doubts away, but could feel them lurking for the next chink to attack through.

"We had a good raid last night, sir," Lichio said as Kare entered the control room. "They launched an offensive early this morning, and I let them expose their lines a little before I responded. We've done a lot of damage and I've been keeping the pressure on. I think you might want to consider bringing the ground attack forward, sir."

Kare read through the detail, taking his time. "You did well, Lichio, thank you. Take a break; you have four hours, and then I need you back here. On your way through, send Silom and Lyle in to me."

He continued to read through Lichio's data until they filed in.

"You look better, sir," Silom said, and Kare smiled.

"Much better." He pulled Silom to him, and embraced him the way he had done in the past: as his brother.

"I'm sorry," whispered Silom, and he sounded half the man he was. "I should have stopped them. I should have done something."

"It wasn't your fault," Kare said. "If it's anyone's fault, it's mine. Move on, Silom. I'm going to try to."

He stepped back as Silom wordlessly nodded, and it felt as if things were going back to where they should be, as if something that had shifted was mending.

"To work," Kare said. "Time to end your men's boredom, Sergeant. Have them ready and convened in hangar one for two-fifteen. First five platoons go in at two-thirty. Once they've secured the walkway, the others follow to take the palace."

He turned to Commander Lyle, who looked at him, then Silom, and seemed relieved at the improved atmosphere.

"Keep a continuous assault on the palace. I want your strafe fighters out at two o'clock. Focus on the walkway and its defences; clear it for the ground troops. Use lasers to take out the soldiers, plasma bombs for the fortifications. Hit them hard. But keep the skywalk intact; we need it."

***

Kare swept his gaze across the force in front of him; they were as ready now as they could be. He caught Silom's eye and Silom nodded to him, confirming everything was in order, and joined the waiting Lichio.

"I never fell for it, Lich," Kare said, conversationally, as they walked to the control room.

"Fell for what?"

"The very able number two act. I told Sonly, early on, that when you decided to get your act together, you'd be the best of the lot." Kare stopped and looked with pride at the younger man. "You seem to have got it together. The first thing I'm going to do when this is over is promote you. You broke through last night and you've been running half this campaign while I wallowed in my misery."

"You had a fair bit to wallow through, sir."

"Still some more to get through. Anyway, your skills are right up there with your brother's. I know Eevan was a treacherous shit, but he was a fantastic strategist; you're easily his equal now."

"Thank you, Colonel."

"It's deserved," Kare said. "One other thing: you're running things today, not me."

Lichio looked at him in surprise. "Where will you be, sir?"

"I'm going in with the troops. There're too many things still fluid down there; I'll liaise with you from the ground. Plus, there're no psychers there; we might need one."

"Have you told Sonly?"

Kare laughed. "Lichio, do you think I'm totally mad? Of course I'm not telling Sonly. She's on the comms unit, wheeling and

281

dealing, but she'll be down at some point- you can let her know then. I'll be in the thick of it."

"Thanks," Lichio said. "You fucking better promote me after this."

"'Fucking better promote me, sir'; I haven't done it yet, Captain," pointed out Kare, with a grin. He pulled an armoured jacket over his combat clothes.

Lichio looked at him, eyes narrowed. He crossed his arms. "Don't you think you should put some boots on?"

Kare shook his head. "I'll be better barefoot, more surefooted." He left Lichio and joined Silom, who nodded his acknowledgement.

"Stay back, sir; I don't want you disrupting platoon formations," he said, and Kare reminded himself to tell Silom at some stage that he, too, had done a fantastic job. The difference was that neither had expected anything less.

He listened to the air attack outside, waiting for the crack of light to appear as the doors opened. He checked the charge on his weapon and gulped some air in. Fear ran through him, heightening his senses, but it wasn't the sick dread of Omendegon, but the honest fear of facing battle and he welcomed and embraced it. As the gate opened he saw, with surprise, the young soldier from the quarry beside him.

"Sarge says I'm to come back here with you, sir. He says he doesn't want you to get killed on his watch."

"What's your name?"

"Private Perrault, sir."

A *private.* A *survivor.* "I'm going to have to promote the lot of you," Kare muttered. "Sonly won't be happy; it'll cost her a fortune in uniforms."

Kare heard Silom's order to advance and looked across the skywalk to the palace. The closed gate waited at the other end, and heavy fortifications were in place where the walkway widened. There were bodies and rubble from the air strikes. The first of his soldiers moved to a defensive position, firing across, whilst the next squad moved past them. The Empress' soldiers, with their stronger fortifications, returned fire. He saw his first soldier fall, then another, and reminded himself he had to attack some time, and he couldn't do it without losses.

A shot hit close to Kare and he brought a shield up. He moved forward, standing up, not seeking to turn from the shots aimed at him, and the lasers and bullets bounced off while he cast out and looked behind the gate. The entrance hall was full of soldiers, many more on the stairs. His men would be slaughtered when- if- they reached it. Kare ignored the gunfire and concentrated on the scene inside. He felt the dimensions of the room and extended his psyche towards it. A shot hit his shield and it gave a little and then reformed, as it always did.

282

You know what you're doing is impossible. He looked around, sure Sam must be standing behind him, his voice was so clear. Seeing no one but Perrault, Kare shook his head. He snaked his power to where he needed it, and flexed in the familiar fashion.

Nothing happened. Kare stood, shocked. His power had failed. Pain seared across his thigh, a burning agony familiar from Omendegon. He fell to the ground and rolled away from another beam. Frantically, he tried to bring up a shield, but nothing happened. Arms grabbed him and pulled him behind some rubble. His leg was a searing mass of pain. He realised it was Private Perrault who had saved him and was now crouched beside him, firing.

"They've reached the gate, sir," Perrault told him. "The sergeant, he's like a lion."

"We have to stop him," Kare said. Another shot clipped his shoulder and he gasped. "There're thousands waiting in there."

The private stood, but Kare pulled him down, knowing he would draw their fire. The soldier fell on him with a cry of pain, a huge wound on his chest where the laser had burnt through his armour. Kare looked to see where the shots were coming from and saw a squad of the Empress' soldiers opposite them. He brought his gun round to fire but his shoulder was slow and sluggish and he felt tired, so tired. A shot hit his side, and he cried out at the godawful pain and realised this one wasn't caused by a laser, but a bullet, ripping through his skin. Warm, sticky blood flowed from it.

Perrault tried to shield him. He wasn't worthy of such loyalty; squads of the Empress' army were coming, encircling him and his men. He'd given them days to get into position. Another shot came at the young private, this one aimed at his head, deadly, and something moved within Kare: a reflex to protect his own. The shot touched the hastily built shield, and bounced off.

I brought them this far. We should all be dead already, but we're not; we're here.

Slowly, through waves of hideous pain, he pulled himself to his knees, ignoring the shots, and looked at where Silom's soldiers were. Without thinking what he was doing- or how, or why- Kare reached out and *pulled* at the ceiling of the hall. This time there was a muffled thump and screams. He pushed the squads on the walkway to the edge and over into the gardens below, clearing the way across.

"Can you walk?"

Perrault shook his head. Kare pulled up from his knees, the pain almost crippling him, and held his arm out, hauling the private up.

283

They moved across the walkway, Perrault's arm draped over Kare's shoulder. Kare half-pulled, half-carried Perrault, limping badly, his teeth gritted against the pain, head swimming as Perrault's pain hit him, and the private's sure knowledge that he was dying. Twice his vision blurred so badly he had to stop, but at last he made it to Silom's platoon. Silom moved out from the shadow of a ruined parapet as they approached, looked at their wounds and swore softly.

"It's looks worse than it is," lied Kare, and Silom didn't argue. He took Perrault and propped him against the wall. Kare shifted onto his good leg and it felt stiff. He touched his trousers and they were wet with blood. Whether it was his, or Perrault's, or both, he couldn't tell. Another wave of dizziness hit him.

"There's more behind the gate," Silom said. "I think we should pull back; we're taking too many losses, sir."

"Behind the gate's taken care of," Kare said, his words slow.

Silom glanced at his cousin. "Are you able to do something with the ones in front?"

He reached his arm out and snaked it under Kare's shoulders. Kare looked at the metal barricades, but they kept moving as his vision blurred. The pain sent sick spasms through him. He tried to flex his psyche, but nothing happened. He reminded himself they were here because he'd done the impossible, and something clicked in his mind. He focused on the barriers, pushed out as hard as he could, but was too weak. As he crumpled, Silom lowered him to the ground and propped him beside Perrault.

Kare moved his good arm, clenched his hand on Silom's, and gave a tired nod.

Silom nodded back. "We'll do it the hard way then," he said. He pulled his hand away.

"Engage," Silom ordered. His soldiers formed back into their platoons and began firing on the enemy in front of the gates to Abendau palace. Kare sat, Perrault leaning against him. In a moment he'd have to heal himself. For now, though, it was peaceful just to sit and watch the battle. The port guns and cannons razed the palace walls and Silom's troops were shooting at the fortifications. He'd done enough; they were breaking through. Kare's eyes closed as his blood dripped onto the ground, spreading out amongst the corpses.

***

Later, much later, the call came through to tell Lichio the palace had been taken and the last defenders were being routed. That it came from Silom and not Kare compounded his worry at the lack of communication during the battle. Beside him, Sonly listened, her face strained.

"He'll be all right," said Lichio, knowing he was lying. If it was all right, Silom would have told him, or Kare would have been on the comms unit, laying out an insanely long set of commands for him.

Sonly's face was strained: not fooled. "Ask him," she said. "Now the battle's over. Ask. Is Kare alive?"

Lichio nodded. "Sergeant," he said.

"Go ahead," said Silom.

"What about the colonel?" Lichio couldn't bring himself to say his name.

There was a pause, and Sonly trembled against him. He moved his hand and put it over hers, squeezing slightly.

"He's hurt." Silom's voice echoed in the small control room.

"Is he dead?" asked Sonly, and Lichio shushed her.

"Sergeant, how badly?"

"He was bad. You can send the medics in now. The palace is secure."

Lichio nodded behind him to Sam, who was already on his feet and heading out the door. "They're on the way. Will he live, Silom?"

"I don't know. He'd lost a lot of blood."

"Can you see him?" Sonly asked, leaning forward to the comms unit.

There was a harsh sound at the other end. "I'm in the palace, overseeing his attack. He's on the parapet. All I know is when I left him, he was alive." His voice took on a softer tone. "When you hear from Sam, tell me."

Lichio ended the comms and glanced at Sonly.

"He'll be all right," he said. "He's as tough as nails, Kare is. After what he's survived, this will be a walk in the park."

Sonly's lower lip trembled, but she lifted her chin and met his eyes. "A walk in the park, that's right, Lich."

He pulled her to him, and hugged her tighter when her shoulders started to shake. There was silence from Sam and it stretched on and on, telling Lichio what he needed to know. The comms unit buzzed and he reached for it.

"It's me," said Sam.

"Lieutenant Prentice," Lichio said. At some stage he'd have to explain to Sam how an army communicated. "How is he?"

"He's alive," said Sam. "He's not in good shape, but he is alive. I'm taking him to the clinic now."

Lichio nodded to Sonly, who got up, wiping her eyes. "Sonly will meet you there." He put the comms unit down and grinned at his sister. "See, I told you. A walk in the park." A park in hell.

CHAPTER FORTY-EIGHT

Sam straightened. "You'll live," he said. "I've seen you much worse than this."

"You're the expert." Kare winced as he tried to sit up.

From the side of the bed, Sonly glared at him. "You left a captain in charge while you played at being a soldier. I feel like killing you myself."

"If I hadn't gone, we would never have got through; there were thousands waiting once they forced the gate. Besides, I thought it needed either me or Lichio there."

There was silence for a moment, and then she crossed her arms, not mollified. "We nearly lost the commander of this army; how would that have helped matters?"

"I'm alive," Kare said. "It's more than many of my men. How's Perrault?"

"Not as well as you, but he'll live," Sam said. "Whatever you did saved him."

"I don't remember. When I passed out, we were sitting against each other; I guess I healed both of us."

The door burst open and Silom came in, his uniform bloody, his hair sticking to his scalp, a field bandage on one of his forearms. He sat on the end of the bed, his glare daring the doctor to tell him to move; it seemed Sam had more sense. Kare looked at Silom, questioningly.

"It's over," Silom said. "We've captured the commander of the garrison; he wants to surrender. It's Phelps, by the way."

"I'll see him," Sonly said, but Kare shook his head.

"Give me a couple of hours. I'm not as bad as I look. Wheel me down to an office and I'll gladly accept his surrender. It might speed my recovery."

It took more than a couple of hours for Sam to agree Kare was strong enough, but later that afternoon he found himself sitting in a chair in one of the Empress' antechambers. "How do I look?" he asked Sonly.

"Pale," she said. "Too thin. But alert, focused."

That would have to do. The door to the outer room opened, and he straightened in his chair. General Phelps came in, somewhat older, but still with the same air of smug confidence about him. Kare remembered being dragged in front of him and handed over to Beck in the control room of the Banned; it felt like it had happened years ago. *I look older than him, now.* The thought served as a stark reminder what this man had delivered him to.

"Phelps."

"Colonel," Phelps replied, the word obviously distasteful to him. "I'm here to surrender the garrison of the palace to you."

"You can't surrender the garrison; I've already taken it. Arrange the surrender of the planet and I'll accept it. Otherwise, I'll raze Abendau City to the ground if I have to."

"I have my own terms."

"We have nothing further to discuss until you agree to my terms. Belaudii, Phelps. All of it." Kare nodded to the soldiers to take Phelps away.

"I don't know how you did this– you were a beaten man when I last saw you– but I knew once you took the port, the palace would fall. I put a little bit of insurance in place," said Phelps.

The first low worm of worry started. Phelps was clever, and ruthless. "What insurance?"

"Look into my mind, Varnon. See what I know, see who I know about."

Kare let his psyche sink into the other man, who put up no resistance.

"Your Empress has you well-housebroken," Kare said, and then stopped. He pulled out of Phelps' mind and glared at him; Phelps lifted his chin and met Kare's eyes.

"You bastard," Kare said, and he forgot himself enough to try to stand, pain shooting through his side in response to his move. He sank back into the seat. "It wasn't enough to screw me; you had to take it further."

"Maybe. But if you want her, you need to negotiate," said Phelps.

"I know where she is. It's in your mind."

"She's guarded by a full platoon of soldiers, Varnon, with one order; if you attack, she dies."

"Who dies?" asked Sonly, but the general didn't answer, just rocked smugly back on his heels. "Who dies, Kare?" she asked, but he could see she already knew; her blue eyes full of combined fear and hope.

"Kerra. No wonder I was so fucking expendable. Not only had they taken what they needed for a spare, they already had their heir."

"You can't let her die," Sonly said. "Not again."

If only it was that easy, but the decision he should take as a

287

colonel was different from that of a father. He saw Lichio's shocked face and understood that this time the decision was his alone. His anger rose, but he bit down on it; it wouldn't help.

"Your terms?" Kare's voice was clipped and cold.

"I get off the planet– you get the girl."

"And your assurance?"

"Check my mind and you'll see the orders I've given. They're clear; once I'm off the planet, I'll order the release of the child. You take her from the messenger, and that's it. You need to decide. If they haven't heard from me in another couple of hours, they'll kill her."

"What about the Empress?" Kare asked. "Won't your mistress be displeased?"

Phelps looked uncomfortable for the first time. "I don't intend to go anywhere near the Empress," he said, his voice tight.

"I doubt that; she has a hold on you like I've rarely seen."

"Your decision?"

"Get him out of my sight," Kare said, coldly. He watched as the door closed and then looked at Sonly, Lichio's arms around her, and said, "What do you want me to do, Sonly? He's not bluffing; he has her."

"Could you get her?"

"Maybe, but I'd have to go myself– they couldn't do it without a psycher." He hesitated. "Even if I was up to it– and I'm not, I can barely move– my powers have failed twice now: a psycher who can't be relied on is worse than not having one."

"What do you mean, failed?" asked Sonly.

"What does fail ever mean? It didn't work. I couldn't kill Beck with it– Silom had to do it– and I couldn't take down the ceiling. Not the first time, anyway."

"Fuck. That's all we need," said Lichio. "Is there any chance he'll double-cross you?"

"No. He knows I'd have seen it. The deal on the table, that's genuine."

"Then deal," Sonly said. "Or I will." She looked at him directly. She would, too. She'd do whatever it took to get Kerra back. For a moment, he was tempted to let her, tired of everything coming down to him, but he thought of Phelps, the kind of man he was. The only thing he'd respond to was power of the sort he wielded, strength of arm and will and, for Phelps, it was Kare who represented that.

"You can't; it's a military decision. He knows, just like you know, what I should say. He's the one who did it, Sonly: the base, all those people. Out there, in Abendau, the children and babies there, what about them? If I let him go, I can't get a surrender, and I'll have to attack the city to take it."

"You told me last night what happened to you," Sonly said, after a moment. "What about me? Silom reached Kerra up to me, and my hand touched her as the soldiers came and he had to run with her. My milk came in while I sat in the transport and I had no baby for it. My womb contracted, and with every pain my whole being longed for her. It still does."

"Sonly, I know. I want her back too."

"You don't know," she said, "or we wouldn't even be talking about it. You said there was a black hole when you lost your psyche. Well, my black hole's still there and I *need* her back, Kare. We can work through everything else: what happened to you, what happens next; but I need her back."

Lichio let her bury her head against him and looked, with sympathy, at Kare.

Kare lifted his comms unit. He held Lichio's eyes. "Prepare a ship: a small one." He turned back to Sonly. "I'll deal, but we need to secure the city through this. I won't have the deaths of the innocents on our hands."

"I agree." She smiled. "I can do better than that."

"How?"

Sonly shrugged. "I'm assuming he won't want to read a forty page document before he signs. Especially if you threaten to change your mind a few times."

Kare started to smile. "I suspect not."

She broke away from Lichio. "I want the bastard sunk. He stole my daughter. I'll make sure we take everything we can from him."

Kare turned to the soldiers at the door. "Bring the general back in."

***

Later, as the ship lifted into the sky, Kare nudged Lichio. "Can we track it?"

"We didn't have time."

"It's definitely Kerra?"

"Yes. She has the most lovely pair of green eyes," Lichio said.

Kare smiled. "You owe Silom, then." The ship was quickly fading in the sky. "It feels wrong, letting him go."

"Absolutely not," Lichio said. "You were right. We have the city with no bloodshed- your Barefoot Revolution will be remembered for not hurting the little people."

"Barefoot Revolution?"

289

"It's what the soldiers are calling it," Lichio told him, an apologetic smile on his face.

"I've heard worse. I gambled, Lichio, on my daughter's life."

"You did well. I didn't think you'd get a surrender."

Neither had he. But Sonly had been sure. "All he wanted was to save his skin. God help him," Kare said as the ship vanished from the sky.

"What do you mean?"

"He either has to face the Empress, or learn to live without her. She has such a hold on him, he'll be destroyed either way. Keeping him here, killing him, that would have been the merciful thing to do."

"So, it worked out well. Smile, Kare."

Kare looked at Lichio, no smile on his face. "Smile? He read me, Lichio; he knew I couldn't take any more. He knew we- both me and Sonly- have had enough. And he might be right- how much more can we take? It worries me."

"Why?"

"If he knows it, so does the Empress. There's been nothing from her and it's concerning me, that's all."

"She'll have to contact you. You have the baby and the palace, all the bloodline. And, presumably, if there are others carrying your child, they're in Abendau, which you hold, and she can't take," Lichio said, firmly. "She has to deal, and she knows it."

"She'll contact us because she thinks if she takes out Kare, the figurehead, we'll fall," said new voice behind them. Kare turned to see Sonly, the baby in her arms, and he wasn't surprised she'd worked it out. "She'll come," she said, her eyes meeting his, "and she'll finish you if she can."

Kare walked to her, still stiff, and held out his arms, his eyebrow raised. She handed him the baby and he held Kerra close, as astonished now as he had been on the day of her birth. She was sitting up in his arms, not lying down, looking around. She was heavier than he remembered, her skin softer than any he'd felt, and he tightened his hold on her, not believing she was here, real and alive. She appeared well cared for, but they'd lost so much time with her- all her babyhood. He glanced at Sonly and saw a wistful look on her face.

"You said, if she can," he said. "I'll stop her if I can. At some point, it'll come down to who's stronger. I always knew it would. Why do you think I worked so hard to get my psyche as honed, as varied, as I can? She didn't want to face me with it. Now she has to."

"Can you face her?" said Sonly.

"I'll have to, and the longer we leave it, the better for us."

"Why?" asked Lichio.

"Psyching," explained Kare, "is partly about confidence, and how much you believe you can do it." The baby reached for a button on his jacket, attracted by its shininess. He put his hand on hers, holding it between his thumb and forefinger, and she tightened her grip on his thumb. This was who he was fighting for, a child as easy to hurt- to kill- as those on Corun, another pawn in his mother's war. He smiled down at her and she seemed to smile back. She could sense him. He dropped her hand. He needed to be strong enough to finish this job- then he'd get to know her, when it was safe. "Anyone else, yes, my skills are enough to get me through. But, both of you know how I've been. How I still am. Do you want to bet on me at the moment?" He saw their faces, and nodded. "Me, neither. Which is why I think you're right, Lichio- she'll contact us, and she'll do it soon."

He stroked the baby's soft hair, blonde, not dark. "First Varnon blonde. I like blondes."

"I'm glad we dealt," Sonly said as he gave the baby back to her.

"So am I. I wouldn't have risked her, you know. It might have looked like it, but I was careful."

"I know you wouldn't, Kare; that's why I let you go as far as you did." She looked different, holding Kerra. Softer, somehow.

"We've done well, so far."

He left Sonly and Lichio and walked up the great staircase and along to the office he'd taken. The palace was obscenely opulent on a planet full of beggars and desert tribes, little more than nomads. His feet sank into the thick carpet and, when he touched the wall, the wallpaper, a rich gold and red brocade, was thick enough to trace its design. He pushed through the gilded doors at the end of the corridor and found himself in an anteroom with three rooms off. His mother's private chambers.

The sense of her remained in them, the touch of her mind, the lack of warmth, and he focused on her. He'd never understand her: how she could do what she'd done; how this palace, with all its riches, couldn't be enough. He thought back to holding Kerra. He'd do anything to keep her safe. Yet his mother had destroyed him, despite being inside his head and touching him as he'd touched Kerra. Despite having carried him and Karia. He could never understand her. All he could do was rid himself of her.

He went into her office and sat at the desk, reading through the reports of the attack on the palace. It was at least an hour later when there was a quiet knock on the door, and Sonly came in.

"Could you have advertised your intentions a little clearer?" she asked him, her eyes wide. "I presume these are your mother's chambers."

He looked around the opulent room, with its huge desk and comfortable seats. "I suppose it is a little obvious."

She pointed to his comms unit. "In about half a minute, you'll be getting a call."

"The Empress?"

"The Empress." Sonly closed the door and came over to the desk. "Remember, you're her equal." She gave a soft smile. "More than her equal. She'll never come close to you."

And yet he could feel the steel will in this room, the cold determination that ran through everything his mother did. He pushed the doubts away and lifted the comms unit, his hands shaking. He perched at the end of the desk, swinging his leg. Sonly looked at him and gave a small, tight smile, and he knew he wasn't fooling her. The unit flashed and he took a deep breath before he flicked it so Sonly could hear it too. He put a finger to his lips and she nodded.

"Kare," his mother said, her voice grating through the room. He should have put a visual unit in, let her see where he was; it would do no harm for her to be shaken a little, too.

"This is Colonel Varnon."

Sonly gave him the thumbs-up and he turned away with a smile so she couldn't distract him.

"You'll be a general next, no doubt," she replied. "Or perhaps you wish to be Emperor."

"You contacted me; I assume it wasn't to discuss my rank. Not again."

"I recognise your authority in the city, Colonel," she told him. "But I hold the rest of the empire. I'd like to meet with you."

His heart thumped at her words. "How many men are on your ship?"

"A platoon."

"I'll let you land," he said. He reached for the glass on his desk- her glass- and took a sip of water. "But your troops remain on your ship."

"And your assurance?"

He glanced at Sonly, who nodded, firmly. "You have my assurance; if you show no hostility, nor will we." He switched the comms unit off. "Well, that's it. Are you sure?"

"I'm sure. We have nothing to lose."

"We might have to let her go."

"We might," she said, "but if she leaves you in Abendau she's ceded, and we'll announce it as such."

"You're putting a lot of faith in me, Sonly." *Too much.*

"That's because I think you can do it." She put her arms around him, pulling him close, and he hoped she didn't feel how much he tensed, how being touched made him want to run. She smiled up at him, and it was sad enough to know that she had. "In fact, I know you can. You can do anything."

Gods, he hoped she was right; he needed her to be right.

***

It took an hour for the Empress' ship to appear on the screen. It must have already been nearing orbit; she must have known he'd let her land. It flew down to the planet, taking its time, and he wished he'd been able to delay this meeting. Forever, preferably.

"I'll meet her at the port." Kare pulled at his uncomfortable uniform, still surprised Sonly had brought it with her. If there was anything he'd hoped would never reappear, it was the Banned formal uniforms.

"I'll come too, sir," Lichio said, equally smartly dressed.

Kare shook his head. "Silom can come."

"There should be a le Payne there."

"Today I'll be taking Kare's name, Lichio," Sonly said. "The Empress has to see he holds an equally strong claim to the Banned as he does to her empire."

Kare looked around them: Silom, Lichio, Sonly and Sam, his team.

"Do you remember the time we were taken, Lichio? When she came to the hall and spoke to me?"

"I remember," Lichio said, and his face looked worried, scared even. "How you managed to face her, I still don't know."

That's two of us. "Silom?" he said.

"I didn't feel her," Silom said.

"What?" asked Lichio, and Sam echoed it.

"I looked around the hall, and there was a girl there, one of the staff and she had some figure..." Silom started to describe the figure with his hands.

"Quite," interrupted Kare, trying not to smile. He should have known. "Silom learned, long ago, how to keep me out; he fills his head with that sort of crap instead. How long did it take you to learn it?"

"A couple of years," Silom said.

"And Sonly has been able to do it for years now." He pointed to

293

Lichio. "You're not as good at it. And, Sam, you've never learned how to. More than that, you've been taught to open your mind to it."

"Are you saying you could have Influenced me?" asked Lichio.

Kare smiled. "You're a pushover, Lich, if I wanted to. Which I don't; I like you far too much the way you are. You put so much energy into outsmarting people, too much belief in the value of logic, a good brain, instead of instinct. You couldn't withstand a mind sweep- you saw that when you met the Empress. Not unlike our friend Phelps, actually."

Lichio went a little pale at that. "So, should I stay out of her way?"

"And lose that excellent brain from my team?" asked Kare. "No, focus on me. Don't look at her, watch me. Actually, all of you, no matter how strong you are, do that. She's very different from me- she does it more, she's very adept."

"What does her psyche feel like?" asked Sonly.

"Sam, you tell her. You've been around it most."

"She comes into your mind," Sam said. "It's not like a thought, exactly, more like a presence."

"Kare does the same, when he wants to," Sonly said.

Sam shook his head, firmly. "It's not the same. You always know when Kare's there, yes, and if he wants to, he can turn it on. But, with the Empress, it's fear you feel and it's hard to resist. Very hard. When I turned against her, it had been months since I'd seen her in person, and I had to do it to save my life, but it was still incredibly hard."

"You were lucky," Kare said, and then he amended it. "We were lucky. What you watched went against the beliefs you were brought up with; that makes it harder to hold you. Your religion probably saved us, Sam."

Kare looked, not at the screen this time, but out of the window and he could see the ship now, a white dot against the blue sky.

"We should go," he said.

"I'm not going down to greet her," Sonly said. She had changed, too, out of the military-style fatigues she'd been wearing earlier, into a crisp, white, one-piece suit, tightly tailored. Her hair was up, almost severely so, and what make-up she had on was muted. It sent as strong a message as his uniform did- that she didn't need any trappings of power, or a mask, to hide behind. She was Sonly le Payne, leader of the Banned, daughter of Darwin. She needed nothing more.

"Why not?"

She smiled. "My dear colonel, I'm the one she'll have to deal with. Your revolution was carried out on my behalf. I gave the Banned forces the authority to recognise your command; otherwise you would merely have been the leader of a gang of slaves."

"It was my revolution," Kare said, "and she's asked to meet me, not you, Sonly. I don't want you putting yourself in the firing line for me."

"Unless you're planning to usurp me as well, I have the authority, not you. This is constitutional now."

A smile spread slowly over Kare's face, at the thought of what Sonly might do to his mother, and then he sobered. He pulled away from the rest and beckoned her to him.

"What is it?" she asked.

"The night we talked about taking the palace?" She nodded. "I said some things I didn't mean. The Emperorship, I can't take it. Whatever we decide- and you're a good enough politician to force something through- it can't be that. I can't be her heir, take her name, not after what she's done to me."

"It'll be hard- we don't hold planets like we did- we don't have our own army," she said. "We're reliant on the great families, and they'll want a clear handover. But, I think we can force it- if you're prepared to be president."

"Yes, I'll take that. Anything but the empire." He glanced at the others and back to her. "Promise me you'll find another way."

She nodded, but bit her lip. "Okay, we'll force through the presidency. I promise."

"Thank you." He turned to Silom. "Ready?"

"I'll be waiting," said Sonly. "I have a few concerns about some of the things your mother authorised. Most of all, the way she treated my colonel when she had him in her power."

Sonly reached out and straightened his uniform, and then looked him critically up and down.

"You look good," she said. "The hair makes you seem older, adds gravitas. And you can't see the scar; she'll hate that, it's her symbol of mastery over you. Remember, Kare, confidence all the way; you deserve to be here. You won the planet, you're married to the opposition's dynasty, the future is yours."

"Right," he said, and turned to go.

"Kare," she said.

He looked back.

"Shoes. I insist."

A short time later, Kare watched his mother's ship swoop down to Abendau.

"Can we impound the ship?" he murmured. "It's beautiful."

"I don't think so," Silom said. "Not while she's our guest."

"Damn," Kare said, and Silom smiled.

"It's good, you know? You. Like this. You'll be doing impersonations next."

"I'm bluffing." It was the understatement of the decade. He was terrified, utterly terrified. Already his shirt was drenched with sweat, and his hair was sticking to his scalp.

As the ship opened, his mouth went dry. The Empress stood, framed in the doorway, her red dress in stark contrast to his dark uniform, her psyche casting through the people waiting and binding her escort close. He enhanced his own psyche, very slightly, and when she felt it she turned her focus on him.

"Mother," he greeted her, and heard a small intake of surprise from one of her advisors.

"I didn't expect you to take the time to greet me in person, Kare," she said, her voice dripping with scorn.

"I'm here on behalf of my commander-in-chief, Sonly Varnon. She invites you to come and meet with her."

"My invitation was for you to meet with me."

"You can see if our commander will change her requirements, but I normally find my wife isn't inclined to do so," he said, and felt her pique rise as he reminded her again of Sonly's claim on him. "This way, if you will."

CHAPTER FORTY-NINE

Sonly only looked at Lichio and then Sam. "Remind me what they did to him," she said.

Sam looked at Lichio, questioningly, and Lichio shrugged.

"Which bit?" asked Sam.

She drew her shoulders back. It had to be faced. "The worst you can remember."

Sam relived for her, again, the last day in Omendegon, and as he did Sonly spared herself nothing in her imagining, seeing how Kare's arms must have been pulling out of their sockets, the flesh sloughed, the flow of water over him as he jerked from shock after shock. She imagined Lichio and Silom, both terribly wounded, huddling in their cells listening to it, and the Empress in her full regalia watching Kare, adding to his torture by doing the one thing a psycher can't abide: taking his mind and invading it, touching all the hidden corners and tormenting it. *I will do whatever it takes to make her pay for what she did to him.*

At the sound of the door opening Sonly looked at the Empress, straight in her eyes. *You will not take me.* The Empress' focus turned to her and Sonly was, briefly, affected by it, before she pulled herself straighter. She'd lived with a psycher long enough to know how to stand against it. *Bring it on, you bitch.*

"I never bought into that with your son; I'm not going to start with you," Sonly said. The Empress' presence drew back from her, and she smiled– no one was about to hold sway over *her* mind.

Sonly moved on to the matters at hand. Kare took up a position by the door, his stance confident, gaze steady. He was carrying out his role to perfection. He'd be fine, he just needed to calm down a little, let it happen. She turned to the Empress. "Sit down."

"Empress," Averrine reminded her. "I have a title."

"For now. I'm not going to waste time; I want you to abdicate. If you do, we'll let you set up wherever you choose and you'll be allowed to keep recognition of your former position."

"I'm not here to surrender," the Empress said coldly. "You may have Abendau: I have the army, and the families. Once I unleash my forces, I will destroy you."

"And your city," Sonly said.

"Which can be rebuilt. I have the steel to do so, which is more than you or your pet psycher does. Tell me, how long do you think, really, he can keep it up against me? My psyche has been engulfing his since I arrived, and he seems to be weakening."

Sonly looked at Kare, who showed no reaction to the Empress' words.

"Did you think putting him in a fancy suit means he's my equal again? You have no understanding of what it takes to wield the sort of power I have, and he had. No, Sonly, this isn't a case of you putting your weakened husband on my throne. If you want my empire, you'll have to fight for it, planet by planet, city by city, homestead by homestead, and you don't have an army to do that," said the Empress, calmly. "Nor the will."

If not having the will to murder millions for the sake of an empire was a bad thing, she could live with the criticism. She handed the Empress a message filche. "This went out to the planets as your ship docked. It's an agreement, by the general of your forces, to surrender."

"This is a surrender of Belaudii."

"And a direct order to surrender in any territory which becomes partnered with the Banned," Sonly said. "Clause 4.b sub note 3; I don't think Phelps read the sub note."

"You have no governments, and no army to surrender to."

"Lichio?" asked Sonly, glad to see his focus firmly on Kare and not the Empress. She glanced at Kare, worried, and saw he'd slipped off his shoes and now balanced on the edge of a desk, his uniform swamping his thin frame, his head down, taking no part in the proceedings.

"Of the outer rim, thirty planets have so far agreed to our terms and their garrisons have surrendered. It's speeding up, though."

Sonly saw, for the first time, a look of doubt cross the Empress' face, quickly smothered.

"I hold the combined planets," said Averrine. "Dignatis, Clorinda, Peiret, the rest. Holding the outer rim means you still have no power base, and no army."

"Except Belaudii's," Sonly said. But she needed the Hiactol family on board. They were the key military family– to fully hold the army, their support was vital. And so far there had been nothing from them.

"And Peiret," added Lichio. "They've confirmed their support, and so have Tortdeniel and Balandt. Clorinda has also opened negotiations with us."

That helped. Balandt held the financial balance of power. Clorinda, along with Peiret, were the two closest planets to Belaudii and the two largest families. If they were all onboard, even Hiactol couldn't stand alone. She nodded, satisfied, and, when the Empress went to speak, held up her hand.

298

"I'm in command," Sonly said. "I've given you your chance to accept our terms– now I'm imposing them. I have your palace, I hold at least half the planets, and your army are in the process of surrendering. They follow their general's instructions in the absence of any other."

She hesitated at a feeling of oppression in the room, and she looked around to see what had unsettled her. Frightened her, actually. Lichio turned his gaze to the Empress and Sam dropped to his knees. Lichio knelt, too. Now, the imperious gaze moved from them to Sonly and the compelling need to please the Empress ran through her.

She looked at the still passive Kare. *Help me.* He lifted his head and met her eyes, but didn't move. *Kare, help.* The Empress pulled at her and Sonly was forced to turn, fighting all the way, and focus on the Empress. Peace, overwhelming peace swept over her– it was right for her to give herself to the Empress. Maybe Kare, too, could cede, and they would be blessed by the Empress' benevolence. He'd been taught how wrong he was to stand against her; perhaps he could be forgiven. How wrong *we* were, she amended, and was rewarded by a crescendo of pleasure, warming her, making her crave more.

Sonly sank fully to her knees. Kare, she thought, and tried to look at him, but couldn't turn away from the Empress, who smiled in triumph.

"I want your fealty," the Empress told them, and Sonly knew it was the right thing to do. She heard Sam offer his, saw Lichio bow and confirm his and then the gaze was on her, the soft grey eyes demanding absolute loyalty, and Sonly sank under it. She forgot about Kare, forgot about anything other than her mistress in front of her.

Dimly, she noticed movement and realised it was Silom, striding forward to join his cousin. She forced herself to look at him as he took his place beside Kare. She caught Kare's eyes, so different from the Empress', their green colour harder, more demanding, yet kinder, and her fear receded a little.

Kare raised his eyebrow, questioning her, inviting her in his familiar way. His stance was relaxed and welcoming. She pulled herself to her feet, painfully slowly, and although the fear grew, she focused on Kare's eyes. She thought of his laugh, of him asking her to marry him because it would piss Eevan off. She remembered him touching her and loving her. The Empress' mind focused on her again, and she staggered, stumbling forwards. He smiled at her, encouraging her, and she took the last four steps to him. As she fell into his embrace, the fear disappeared.

"Well done," he whispered into her hair. She looked round to Sam and Lichio. Lichio looked at Kare, and she willed him to pull away from the Empress. He tried to stand, but failed. Instead, he crawled to them, clumsily, not at all like Lichio. He looked back not once, but twice, each time hesitating before he continued. Kare held his hand out to Lichio- his long, slender fingers clawed- and Lichio grabbed him as if it was the key to life. Kare pulled him the rest of the way, until Lichio knelt at his colonel's feet. Slowly, he stood, still using Kare's hand to give him the strength he needed.

As Lichio joined them, the presence in the room lessened, and now she focused on Sam, who'd once been the Empress' man, but had fought back. Sonly called his name and he turned to her, before he looked again at his Empress and then he, too, crawled, each tiny movement seeming to cost him more and more. He got halfway and, like a drowning man, held his hand out to Kare, who didn't take it.

"A little more, Sam," Kare said. "Just a little more."

To Sonly's amazement Sam crawled another couple of feet and then Silom reached for him and pulled him to his feet so the five of them were gathered together, in a tight circle around Kare. *You clever bastard*, thought Sonly.

Kare pulled himself from the centre of the circle and said, very quietly, "Thank you."

Then he pushed them behind him and walked across to his mother and Sonly could feel a new presence growing and growing and growing, this one familiar and strong. Stronger than she'd ever imagined it could be. And crueller, driven by a hate she'd never known in him before. If she'd been facing it, she'd have backed away.

His mother didn't. She met his eyes, glaring back, hers as hate-filled as his.

"It's about confidence," Kare said, conversationally. "That's why you're here now; you know if you leave it any longer I'll have bags of it. You knew I always did, that's why you stole my powers from me. That's why you stole everything you could from me."

As suddenly as the Empress' presence in the room had appeared, it vanished, and when Sonly heard a gasp she realised the Empress had taken all her power, every bit of it, and focused it purely on Kare. Sonly saw him sway slightly and, briefly, close his eyes against the power. As he dropped his head, Sonly was sure he would cave in at any moment. She could hear his breathing, watched as his knees started to buckle, and he sank onto one of them in front of his mother.

"Yield," she told him.

He moaned, a long moan, and nodded his head, very slightly. He couldn't do it. Tears pricked Sonly's eyes– he might have been able to once, but he'd been too harmed, too damaged, to do it now.

"Fight, Kare," she said, not realising until the words had left her that she'd said them aloud. The Empress turned her attention to Sonly for one moment, and Sonly quailed under her glare.

She looked again at Kare and saw he had opened his eyes and was watching her. Slowly, he got off his knee and straightened, his eyes moving from Sonly back to his mother.

"So, why would I have no confidence? I've taken your city," Kare told the Empress. Sonly could see the tightness in his jaw and knew every word was being forced out of him. "I've survived what my father told me would either kill me or make me."

Now he took a step forward and Averrine moved back, very slightly. Silom grinned with pride, a look in his eyes which said he'd told everyone so, continually, over the years.

"I wielded no power, yet they came to me. Some were too strong for you, some had to crawl as you clung to them, some just had love to guide them, but they came to me. Who's going to come to you just for the love of it?"

His mouth tightened into a thin line and he stepped towards her. His eyes focused on her, and Sonly could feel the power coming from him, sharp and precise. His mother gasped, her eyes becoming uncertain, and he stepped forward again. Sam closed his eyes beside her, his breath coming in gasps. She touched his arm and he opened his eyes.

"Can't you *feel* it?" he asked. "Maybe... he's done it to me once, maybe that's why, but it's *so* strong."

He put his hands up to the side of his head just as the Empress shrieked, high and pain-filled, and now Sonly *could* feel it, like a buzz in the air, not aimed at her, but too strong to miss. She glanced at Lichio, saw he was pale, his hands trembling, and at Silom. Even he was breathing heavily.

"Stop!" yelled the Empress. Sonly whipped her head round and saw her clutching her hair, pulling it.

"Yield," Kare said, his voice hard and implacable. His mother shook her head, drew herself straighter, and for a moment the two psychers stood, neither willing to back down.

Kare stepped forward once more, and this time the Empress stepped back, putting her hands out, as if to hold him back.

"My empire," he told his mother. "My people. My city. Accept

301

it or I destroy you; and I will. My terms- a place in the outer rim, with no one to manipulate. A room: luxurious, fitting for your stature, where there is no outlet for your power. You'll be like Ealyn; the power turning inward until it destroys you."

"You can't do that," the Empress said. "You know what it would do."

"Trust me, Mother. After what you did to me, to Ealyn, and especially to Karia, I can and will do it if you oppose me further." He turned to Sonly. "Draw up a document, an official abdication; she'll sign."

The Empress looked at him and opened her mouth. He cut her off.

"If you don't, I will incarcerate you. You can't take me, you can't take them, and you certainly aren't retaking your empire. Not after what it cost me to get it."

***

Kare sat in the room with his mother, only Silom with him as he waited for Sonly to complete the document. He didn't talk to her, didn't talk to Silom, but at no point did he let his psyche fall back or give her a chance to establish hers. Tiredness lay as a tight band around his head, and he was relieved when the door opened and Sonly and Lichio entered.

Sonly set the filche in front of the Empress, who read it. She looked at Kare, as if calculating what to do, and he flared his psyche a little more, leaving her in no doubt that if he had to, he could hold her even more firmly. He wished he had some supply of whatever concoction she'd been giving him but they hadn't, so far, found it.

Slowly, Averrine picked up the filche and prepared to put her mark on it. Once again, she looked around the small room and Kare, alert-ready for her- felt her reach out and saw Silom move towards him.

Kare looked at Silom, but her focus wasn't on his cousin. Too late, he turned and saw Lichio, blaster raised, his hand shaking.

Kare saw the bolt coming for him, but had no time to stop it. He tried to shield himself, but he was shaking with exhaustion now, the effort of holding his mother back tiring him. He dived to the side, but knew he was too slow. Something blurred in front of him. He saw a gush of blood and a falling body, and then Silom fell to the floor, a great wound in his stomach, red spreading from it.

"Sam!" shouted Kare as he turned back to his mother. He had to close her down, stop her using her power to hurt others, to hurt him anymore. He remembered the block he'd placed in his own mind, how it had stood against all the Great Master's knowledge.

He took his psyche and pushed against his mother, fury giving him a strength he didn't know he had. His powers formed a wall in front of hers, holding it in place, holding it so she could not get around it. He realised to hold her forever, he would have to leave his own psyche inside her, blocking her. *Can I do it: become powerless again?* This was the glory Ealyn had foreseen. Not the pain but this, the surrendering of his powers to finish Averrine's reign. Resolved, Kare pushed his mind in front of hers, and slammed it in place.

"What have you done?" she hissed, as she felt his wall. "Where are my powers?" She put her hands up to either side of her head. "You bast- "

"Take her away. I'll deal with her later." He dropped to his knees beside Silom. Sam was already there, trying to stem the flow of blood from a stomach wound gaping through Silom's ripped uniform, a wound too wide to staunch. Sonly was holding Silom's hand, telling him to wait for Kare.

"We were at the end," Kare whispered. He grabbed Silom's other hand; it was warm, life still in it. There was hope- if they could get a medicine team quickly enough, if they had the right equipment, if he could find a way to do something. Distantly, he was aware of Lichio's blaster clattering to the ground, of him joining the group, but it didn't matter, nothing but Silom did.

Silom's hand tightened on Kare's and Kare leaned down to him. He made out the whisper of a name and nodded to one of the soldiers. "Get Sergeant Woods. Quickly." His voice tailed off and there was only silence and Silom's breathing, thick and wet.

A clatter of footsteps, and Sonly was pushed aside. *Kym.* She fell to her knees, taking Silom's hand from Kare, cupping it like it was something precious.

"Don't you *dare,*" she said. Silom's hand tightened on hers, and Kare drew in a breath. *Fight.* She pushed Silom's hair back, ran a hand down his cheek. "I mean it. We've got things to do. A baby. Marriage. Coming off the front line." Her voice cracked; she swallowed, throat rippling. "You promised."

Silom should get his chance; it would never be right if he didn't. Kare reached inside himself, found the place his psyche should be, the power that could bring Silom back, that would stop this and give him- them- the future they deserved. Silom had pulled Lichio through the quarries, he'd taken the palace for Kare, there had to be something left for him. Had to be. He put his hands to his head, tugged at his hair, seeking any last remnant that could make a difference: there was nothing.

"*Please*, Silom." Kym's voice, infinitely gentle. "The medics will be here soon. You said you were too tough to kill– prove it."

His mouth moved, the words a low whisper, drawn out and pained. "Love you." His breath stopped; his chest stilled.

Kare ripped at Silom's jacket. He put one hand over the other, ready to press on his heart, keep it beating, not give in. Sam touched his arm, gave a soft shake of his head; there was nothing that could be done. The knowledge tore through him, sucking the breath from him.

Sonly had taken Kym in her arms, holding her as her shoulders shook, murmuring distant, useless words of comfort.

"No." Kym lifted her head and glared at Kare, eyes swimming with tears. She pushed to her feet, and he didn't look away, meeting her gaze, embracing the hatred in her eyes.

"This is your fault." Her voice was cold, brittle. "You made him follow you, took him to the edge."

"Kym..." He looked at Silom again, and then up to see the others watching him. He could see no way past where he was now. He'd won, he tried to tell himself: if he had, the price was too high.

"I won't forget," she said. "Everyone else might buy into you. I don't."

Kare got to his feet. Silom's chest was still, his big body unmoving. He had always been the strongest, the one able to go on, to survive another day in the quarry, to lead soldiers into battle through exhaustion and pain. Someone covered his face; Sam said quiet words over his body, a blessing or a prayer. Kare stumbled back, let two soldiers lift the body. The floor was red underneath, the deep carpet stained. Kym followed, soldiers from her squad joining her at the door, encircling her, giving the comfort she needed, the rigour of the army.

Two more soldiers entered the room– his mother's escort, he recognised.

"Is she in the cells?" His words came from a distance, from someone else, someone who knew what he was supposed to do. "Guarded?"

"Yes, sir. With no one to enter the cells, except on your orders."

His orders. Hell, he didn't know how to think, let alone command. Distantly, he heard Lichio on the comms unit, ordering a squad to the room, presumably a clean-up. Sonly was beside him, face pale, eyes flitting from Lichio to Kare, as if unsure who needed her more. The normality of it all, the crystal nature of everyone's actions, was at odds with the fracturing inside him. Silom was dead and things were going on the way they always had.

He sucked in a breath. The day Karia had died, he'd felt like this. He'd walked in a daze, barely knowing what steps he'd taken, relying on the direction-finder to take him to Shug. There was no direction-finder this time. Nothing to tell him what should be. His legs buckled; his vision darkened.

"Kare!" Sonly called. He felt hands on him, but pushed them away. *Breathe.* He grew steadier, but his mind was frozen. He managed to start walking, steps slow, and left the room. No one stopped him; in the corridor people moved away, making space for him to leave. Silom wasn't amongst them. He was gone, like his father, Karia, Marine. Dead because of him. He couldn't breathe, and he unbuttoned the top button of his jacket. He stopped and this time his legs didn't hold him; he sank to the floor and wondered how he'd ever get up again.

Arms under his shoulders pulled him to his feet. His name was called, but it was faint and far away. Slowly, he looked and saw Sam on one side of him, Lichio on the other, his face streaked with tears. Sonly stood in front of him.

"Kare, come on, love," Sonly said. She sounded like she was coaxing a child, and that was okay because he felt like when he was a child, shocked and out of place, and glad for someone to take over.

"Where to?" asked Lichio.

"Somewhere quiet," Sam said.

Kare closed his eyes and saw Silom's eyes staring at him, dead and accusing. He stopped, leaning forward, hands on his knees, head against the cold wall. Someone rubbed his back, and he tried to straighten up. *He's dead, fucking dead, and it's my fault.*

"Get him into one of the anterooms," said Lichio.

A small crowd had gathered, watching him. His soldiers. He let Lichio take him to an antechamber, and sank into a seat. They moved around him, Sonly, Sam and Lichio, all that was left, and he knew they were talking about him, but didn't care. He wanted a bubble around him, one he'd never come out of again. He looked down at his hands and realised they were shaking. Sam came forward, holding a syringe, and Kare didn't ask what it was, or try to stop him. A pinprick and the room slowly faded, blurring as it did, and he was glad. He couldn't do any more. All he wanted was to let everything go, to stop being the one who mattered, who brought hurt to everyone he cared about. Slowly, the world faded into the distance, and he let it.

EPILOGUE

Sonly held the paper in front of her. Her hand shook slightly, no matter how hard she tried to stop it. "This is a declaration of a new empire."

Tom Peiret, dressed in his usual trademark grey, and Maxin Clorinda, in a slightly battered pilot's jacket, nodded. She wasn't fooled by their lack of formality. In fact, the very fact they'd elected to come here in casual dress told her more than any uniform could have done: they thought this was a done deal, that she had ran out of negotiation space. They might even be right.

Still, she had to try. She shook her head. "I can't sign this- only Kare Varnon could agree to the terms, and he won't. He's made it very clear he intends to dissolve the empire."

"The document is a declaration for your daughter," said Maxin Clorinda. His grey eyes were like stones, challenging her to refuse it.

"For Kerra?" Lichio's voice, beside her, was smooth and she was grateful for him.

The two men exchanged glances and Tom leaned forward. He was the softer of the two, as ever. Playing each other off.

"Sonly, we'll be honest with you, no games. Your husband has failed to convince anyone of his plans. If no one takes action, there will be war in the central zone- millions will die."

Sonly closed her eyes, briefly. Until a week ago, her husband was just about getting up each morning, and mostly because Sam was forcing him to. That this had come now, when he was showing some signs of coming back to himself, when he'd actually started to engage and ask sensible questions about what was happening and what sort of mess his revolution had left behind, was an irony she didn't miss. All she'd needed was another few weeks, a month at most, and she'd have been able to get him involved. Or at least put on a decent pretense that he was a functional leader.

"In fact," said Maxin, "in the four months since the abdication, we've dealt with you and your brother." Damn, they were turning the screw. The families knew they had to act before Kare came back. He'd been open about his views all the time he was at the Banned- they knew an empire wouldn't be what he sought. And he'd had a

306

chance, in those first weeks when the families were in disarray and ready to agree anything that might get rid of the vacuum the Empress' removal had left. But that impetus had gone, and the families had regrouped. "An absentee leader is not what we need."

"He's working through us," she said, her words calm despite the quick panic that had leaped in her. She reached and took a sip of water, proud to see her hands were steady. Beside her, Lichio glanced at her and then back to the two men.

"There's a lot to put in place," he said smoothly. "But Kare is very aware of the plans outlined and will not support an empire. He has been clear on the matter."

Maxin Clorinda's mouth tightened. "No more games. Kare Varnon has been playing no part in any plans. Now, we appreciate, after such an... ordeal– "

"Torture is the word we're using," said Lichio. "We'll be open– he was badly hurt; he no longer has the powers that sustained him. On medical grounds, he has to be cautious until he fully recovers. But he is directing us in every matter."

Sonly saw Tom shake his head and knew they'd found out– however they'd done it– that Kare was... what? Destroyed by what had happened– breaking down. No amount of arguing that he was improving would change their views. It would only make her seem weak.

She read it again and set it down. "I can't allow it."

Maxin slammed his hand on the table. "He won't sign to be Emperor, he won't meet any of us, and the empire is teetering."

"Fighting for Abendau again won't stop that." She put steel in her voice, determined to hold firm for Kare, as she had all along.

Tom Peiret held his hand up, his family's signet ring, with its huge amber stone, glistening. It was a sign that he spoke for all of Peiret, that this *was* a formal meeting.

"Sonly, this is what's on the table. If you can get Kare to take the Emperorship, we will accept that outcome. But he must take it formally– a coronation, a true commitment. Otherwise, your daughter succeeds. We will not support a presidency– and we, the great families, hold the army."

Hiactol were still holding out, damn them. They'd never given their support to Kare's faction. That Phelps was part of their family, that he'd returned to them from Belaudii, had only strengthened their resolve. And Peiret was right– without Hiactol, the army would never be held.

Sonly glanced at Lichio and saw his knuckles had whitened as he'd clenched his hands. Kare– a coronation? But Kerra... she couldn't give her up to the families and their scheming. She'd be a target everywhere she went, even more than now. She looked down at the document again and it was swimming under her eyes. She picked it up and scrunched it.

"This is Kare's empire," she said. "No one else's."

Lichio turned to her, his mouth open, but she shook her head. If she didn't do this, Kare would lose everything he'd fought for. If she didn't do this, Kerra would be forced to it, and she *knew* Kare wouldn't want that. Not if he was thinking straight. *Please let him forgive me.* "I'll see that he takes the Emperorship. You'll have your coronation. I promise."

She got up and left, turning in to the corridor that led to the personal suite she'd taken with Kerra. Halfway down, she had to stop and lean against the wall. She'd done what she'd promised she'd never do, and forced Kare into the position of Emperor. She hadn't been strong enough to fight for him, she'd put their daughter first. She stood, head swimming, and knew he'd never forgive her. That this would stand between them, a betrayal of all they'd been to each other, and she hated herself for it.

THE END

Lightning Source UK Ltd.
Milton Keynes UK
UKOW04f0205130715

255010UK00001B/6/P